# Sir Tom by Margaret Oliphant

Margaret Oliphant Wilson was born on April 4th, 1828 to Francis W. Wilson, a clerk, and Margaret Oliphant, at Wallyford, near Musselburgh, East Lothian.

Her youth was spent in establishing a writing style and by 1849 she had her first novel published: Passages in the Life of Mrs. Margaret Maitland.

Two years later, in 1851 Caleb Field was published and also an invitation to contribute to Blackwood's Magazine; the beginning of a life time business relationship.

In May 1852, Margaret married her cousin, Frank Wilson Oliphant. Their marriage produced six children but, tragically, three died in infancy. When her husband developed signs of the dreaded consumption (tuberculosis) they moved to Florence, and then to Rome where, sadly, he died.

Margaret was naturally devastated but was also now left without support and only her income from writing to support the family. She returned to England and took up the burden of supporting her three remaining children by her literary activity.

Her incredible and prolific work rate increased both her commercial reputation and the size of her reading audience. Tragedy struck again in January 1864 when her only remaining daughter Maggie died.

In 1866 she settled at Windsor to be closer to her sons, who were being educated at near-by Eton School.

For more than thirty years she pursued a varied literary career but family life continued to bring problems. Cyril Francis, her eldest son, died in 1890. The younger son, Francis, who she nicknamed 'Cecco', died in 1894.

With the last of her children now lost to her, she had little further interest in life. Her health steadily and inexorably declined.

Margaret Oliphant Wilson Oliphant died at the age of 69 in Wimbledon on 20th June 1897. She is buried in Eton beside her sons.

## Index of Contents

# CHAPTER I

## HOW SIR TOM BECAME A GREAT PERSONAGE

Sir Thomas Randolph had lived a somewhat stormy life during the earliest half of his career. He had gone through what the French called a jeunesse orageuse; nothing very bad had ever been laid to his charge; but he had been adventurous, unsettled, a roamer about the world even after the period at which youthful extravagances cease. Nobody ever knew when or where he might appear. He set off to the farthest parts of the earth at a day's notice, sometimes on pretext of sport, sometimes on no pretext at all, and re-appeared again as unexpectedly as he had gone away. He had run out his fortune by these and other extravagances, and was at forty in one of the most uncomfortable positions in which a man can find himself, with the external appearance of large estates and an established and important position, but in reality with scarcely any income at all, just enough to satisfy the mortgagees, and leave himself a pittance not much more than the wages of a gamekeeper. If his aunt, Lady Randolph, had not been so good to him it was uncertain whether he could have existed at all, and when the heiress, whom an eccentric will had consigned to her charge, fell in his way, all her friends concluded as a matter of certainty that Sir Tom would jump at this extraordinary windfall, this gift of a too kind Providence, which sometimes will care for a prodigal in a way which he is quite unworthy of, while leaving the righteous man to struggle on unaided. But for some time it appeared as if society for once was out in its reckoning. Sir Tom did not pounce upon the heiress. He was a person of very independent mind, and there were some who thought he was happier in his untrammelled poverty, doing what he pleased, than he ever had been as a great proprietor. Even when it became apparent to the wise and far-seeing that little Miss Trevor was only waiting till his handkerchief was thrown at her to become the happiest of women, still he did nothing. He exasperated his kind aunt, he made all his friends indignant, and what was more, he exposed the young heiress hourly to many attempts on the part of the inferior class, from which as a matter of fact she herself sprang; and it was not until she was driven nearly desperate by those attempts that Sir Tom suddenly appeared upon the scene, and moved, it was thought, more by a half-fatherly kindness and sympathy for her, than either by love or desire of wealth, took her to himself, and made her his wife, to the great and grateful satisfaction of the girl herself, whose strange upbringing and brief introduction into a higher sphere had spoiled her for that homely country-town existence in which every woman flattered and every man made love to her.

Whether Lucy Trevor was in love with him was as uncertain as whether he was in love with her. So far as any one knew neither one nor the other had asked themselves this question. She had, as it were, thrown herself into his arms in sudden delight and relief of mind when he appeared and saved her from her suitors; while he had received her tenderly when she did this, out of kindness and pleasure in her genuine, half-childish appreciation of him. There were, of course, people who said that Lucy had been violently in love with Sir Tom, and that he had made up his mind to marry her money from the first moment he saw her; but neither of these things was true. They married with a great deal more pleasure and ease of mind than many people do who are very much in love, for they had mutual faith in each other, and felt a mutual repose and satisfaction in their union. Each supplied something the other wanted. Lucy obtained a secure and settled home, a protector and ever kind and genial guardian, while Sir Tom got not only a good and dutiful and pleasant companion, with a great deal of sense, and good-nature and good looks,—all of which gifts he prized highly,—but at the same time the control of a great fortune, and money enough at once to clear his estates and restore him to his position as a great landowner.

There were very peculiar conditions attached to the great fortune, but to these for the moment he paid very little heed, considering them as fantastic follies not worth thinking about, which were never likely to become difficulties in his way. The advantage he derived from the marriage was enormous. All at once, at a bound, it restored him to what he had lost, to the possession of his own property, which had been not more than nominally his for so many years, and to the position of a man of weight and importance, whose opinion told with all his neighbours and the county generally, as did those of few others in the district.

Sir Tom, the wanderer, had not been thought very highly of in his younger days. He had been called wild. He had been thought untrustworthy, a fellow here to-day and gone to-morrow, who had no solidity in him. But when the mortgages were all paid off, and the old hall restored, and Sir Thomas Randolph came to settle down at home, with his pretty little wife, and an establishment quite worthy of his name, the county discovered in a day, almost in a moment, that he was very much improved. He had always been clever enough, they said, for anything, and now that he had sown his wild oats and learned how to conduct himself, and attained an age when follies are naturally over, there was no reason why he should not be received with open arms. Such a man had a great many more experiences, the county thought with a certain pride, than other men who had sown no wild oats, and had never gone farther afield than the recognised round of European cities. Sir Tom had been in all the four quarters of the globe; he had travelled in America long before it became fashionable to do so, and even had been in Africa while it was as yet untrod by any white foot but that of a missionary. And it was whispered that in the days when he was "wild" he had penetrated into regions nearer at hand, but more obscure and mysterious even than Africa. All this made the county think more of him now when he appeared staid yet genial, in the fulness of manhood, with a crisp brown beard and a few gray hairs about his temples mingled with his abundant locks, and that capability of paying his way which is dear to every well-regulated community. But for this last particular the county would not have been so tolerant, nay almost pleased, with the fact that he had been "wild." They saw all his qualities in the halo that surrounded the newly-decorated hall, the liberated farms, the lands upon which no creditor had now any claim. He was the most popular man in the district when Parliament was dissolved, and he was elected for the county almost without opposition, he, at whom all the sober people had shaken their heads only a few years before. The very name of "Sir Tom," which had been given rather contemptuously to denote a somewhat careless fellow, who minded nothing, became all at once the sign of popular amity and kindness. And if it had been necessary to gain votes for him by any canvassing tricks, this name of his would have carried away all objections. "Sir Tom!" it established a sort of affectionate relationship at once between him and his constituency. The people felt that they had known him all his life, and had always called him by his Christian name.

Lady Randolph was much excited and delighted with her husband's success. She canvassed for him in a modest way, making herself pleasant to the wives of his supporters in a unique manner of her own which was not perhaps quite dignified considering her position, but yet was found very captivating by those good women. She did not condescend to them as other titled ladies do, but she took their advice about her baby, and how he was to be managed, with a pretty humility which made her irresistible. They all felt an individual interest thenceforward in the heir of the Randolphs, as if they had some personal concern in him; and Lady Randolph's gentle accost, and the pretty blush upon her cheeks, and her way of speaking to them all, "as if they were just as good as she was," had a wonderful effect. When she received him in the hotel which was the headquarters of his party, as soon as the result of the election was known, Sir Tom, coming in flushed with applauses and victory, took his wife into his arms and kissed her. "I owe this to you, as well as so much else, Lucy," he said.

"Oh, don't say that! when you know I don't understand much, and never can do anything; but I am so glad, nobody could be more glad," said Lucy. Little Tom had been brought in, too, in his nurse's arms, and crowed and clapped his fat little baby hands for his father; and when his mother took him and stepped out upon the balcony, from which her husband was speaking an impromptu address to his new constituents, with the child in her arms, not suspecting that she would be seen, the cheers and outcries ran into an uproar of applause. "Three cheers for my lady and the baby," the crowd shouted at the top of its many voices; and Lucy, blushing and smiling and crying with pleasure, instead of shrinking away as everybody feared she would do, stood up in her modest, pretty youthfulness, shy, but full of sense and courage, and held up the child, who stared at them all solemnly with big blue eyes, and, after a moment's consideration, again patted his fat little hands together, an action which put the multitude beside itself with delight. Sir Tom's speech did not make nearly so much impression as the baby's "patti-cake." Every man in the crowd, not to say every woman, and with still more reason every child, clapped his or her hands too, and shouted and laughed and hurrahed.

The incident of the baby's appearance before the public, and the early success he had gained—the earliest on record, the newspapers said—made quite a sensation throughout the county, and made Farafield famous for a week. It was mentioned in a leading article in the first newspaper in the world. It appeared in large headlines in the placards under such titles as "Baby in Politics," "The Nursery and the Hustings," and such like. As for the little hero of the moment, he was handed down to his anxious nurse just as symptoms of a whimper of fear at the alarming tumult outside began to appear about the corners of his mouth. "For heaven's sake take him away; he mustn't cry, or he will spoil all," said the chairman of Sir Tom's committee. And the young mother, disappearing too into the room behind, sat down in a great chair behind their backs, and cried to relieve her feelings. Never had there been such a day. If Sir Tom had not been the thoroughly good-humoured man he was, it is possible that he might have objected to the interruption thus made in his speech, which was altogether lost in the tumult of delight which followed his son's appearance. But as a matter of fact he was as much delighted as any one, and proud as man could be of his pretty little wife and his splendid boy. He took "the little beggar," as he called him, in his arms, and kissed the mother again, soothing and laughing at her in the tender, kindly, fatherly way which had won Lucy.

"It is you who have got the seat," he said; "I vote that you go and sit in it, Lady Randolph. You are a born legislator, and your son is a favourite of the public, whereas I am only an old fogey."

"Oh, Tom!" Lucy said, lifting her simple eyes to his with a mist of happiness in them. She was accustomed to his nonsense. She never said anything more than "Oh, Tom!" and indeed it was not very long since she had given up the title and ceased to say "Oh, Sir Tom!" which seemed somehow to come more natural. It was what she had said when he came suddenly to see her in the midst of her early embarrassments and troubles; when the cry of relief and delight with which she turned to him, uttering in her surprise that title of familiarity, "Oh, Sir Tom!" had signified first to her middle-aged hero, with the most flattering simplicity and completeness, that he had won the girl's pure and inexperienced heart.

There was no happier evening in their lives than this, when, after all the commotion, threatenings of the ecstatic crowd to take the horses from their carriage, and other follies, they got off at last together and drove home through roads that wound among the autumn fields, on some of which the golden sheaves were still standing in the sunshine. Sir Tom held Lucy's hand in his own. He had told her a dozen times over that he owed it all to her.

"You have made me rich, and you have made me happy," he said, "though I am old enough to be your father, and you are only a little girl. If there is any good to come out of me, it will all be to your credit, Lucy. They say in story books that a man should be ashamed to own so much to his wife, but I am not the least ashamed."

"Oh, Tom!" she said, "how can you talk so much nonsense," with a laugh, and the tears in her eyes.

"I always did talk nonsense," he said; "that was why you got to like me. But this is excellent sense and quite true. And that little beggar; I am owing you for him, too. There is no end to my indebtedness. When they put the return in the papers it should be Sir Thomas Randolph, etc., returned as representative of his wife, Lucy, a little woman worth as much as any county in England."

"O, Sir Tom," Lucy cried.

"Well, so you are, my dear," he said, composedly. "That is a mere matter of fact, you know, and there can be no question about it at all."

For the truth was that she was so rich as to have been called the greatest heiress in England in her day.


CHAPTER II

HIS WIFE

Young Lady Randolph had herself been much changed by the progress of these years. Marriage is always the great touchstone of character at least with women; but in her case the change from a troubled and premature independence, full of responsibilities and an extremely difficult and arduous duty, to the protection and calm of early married life, in which everything was done for her, and all her burdens taken from her shoulders, rather arrested than aided in the development of her character. She had lived six months with the Dowager Lady Randolph after her father's death; but those six months had been all she knew of the larger existence of the wealthy and great. All she knew—and even in that short period she had learned less than she might have been expected to learn; for Lucy had not been introduced into society, partly on account of her very youthful age, and partly because she was still in mourning, so that her acquaintance with life on the higher line consisted merely in a knowledge of certain simple luxuries, of larger rooms and prettier furniture, and more careful service than in her natural condition. And by birth she belonged to the class of small townsfolk who are nobody, and whose gentility is more appalling than their homeliness. So that when she came to be Sir Thomas Randolph's wife and a great lady, not merely the ward of an important personage, but herself occupying that position, the change was so wonderful that it required all Lucy's mental resources to encounter and accustom herself to it.

Sir Tom was the kindest of middle-aged husbands. If he did not adore his young wife with the fervour of passion, he had a sincere affection for her, and the warmest desire to make her happy. She had done a great deal for him, she had changed his position unspeakably, and he was fully determined that no lady in England should have more observance, more honour and luxury, and what was better, more happiness, than the little girl who had made a man of him. There had always been a sweet and serious simplicity about her, an air of good sense and reasonableness, which had attracted everybody whose opinion was worth having to Lucy; but she was neither beautiful nor clever. She had been so brought up that, though she was not badly educated, she had no accomplishments, and not more knowledge than falls to the lot of an ordinary schoolgirl. The farthest extent of her mild experiences was Sloane Street and Cadogan Place: and there were people who thought it impossible that Sir Tom, who had been everywhere, and run through the entire gamut of pleasures and adventures, should find anything interesting in this bread-and-butter girl, whom, of course, it was his duty to marry, and having married to be kind to. But when he found himself set down in an English country house with this little piece of simplicity opposite to him, what would he do, the sympathising spectators said? Even his kind aunt, who felt that she had brought about the marriage, and who, as a matter of fact, had fully intended it from the first, though she herself liked Lucy, had a little terror in her soul as she asked herself the same question. He would fill the house with company and get over it in that way, was what the most kind and moderate people thought. But Sir Tom laughed at all their prognostications. He said afterwards that he had never known before how pretty it was to know nothing, and to have seen nothing, when these defects were conjoined with intelligence and delightful curiosity and never-failing interest. He declared that he had never truly enjoyed his own adventures and experiences as he did when he told them over to his young wife. You may be sure there were some of them which were not adapted for Lucy's ears: but these Sir Tom left religiously away in the background. He had been a careless liver no doubt, like so many men, but he would rather have cut off his right hand, as the Scripture bids, than have soiled Lucy's white soul with an idea, or an image, that was unworthy of her. She knew him under all sorts of aspects, but not one that was evil. Their solitary evenings together were to her more delightful than any play, and to him nearly as delightful. When the dinner was over and the cold shut out, she would wait his appearance in the inner drawing-room, which she had chosen for her special abode, with some of the homely cares that had been natural to her former condition, drawing her chair to the fire, taking pride in making his coffee for him, and a hundred little attentions. "Now begin," she would say, recalling with a child's eager interest and earnest recollection the point at which he had left off. This was the greater part of Lucy's education. She travelled with him through very distant regions, and went through all kinds of adventure.

And in the season they went to London, where she made her appearance in society, not perhaps with éclat, but with a modest composure which delighted him. She understood then, for the first time, what it was to be rich, and was amused and pleased—amused above all by the position which she occupied with the utmost simplicity. People said it would turn the little creature's head, but it never even disturbed her imagination. She took it with a calm that was extraordinary. Thus her education progressed, and Lucy was so fully occupied with it, with learning her husband and her life and the world, that she had no time to think of the responsibilities which once had weighed so heavily upon her. When now and then they occurred to her and she made some passing reference to them, there were so many other things to do that she forgot again—forgot everything except to be happy and learn and see, as she had now so many ways of doing. She forgot herself altogether, and everything that had been hers, not in excitement, but in the soft absorbing influence of her new life, which drew her away into endless novelties and occupations, such as were, indeed, duties and necessities of her altered sphere.

If this was the case in the first three or four years of her marriage, when she had only Sir Tom to think of, you may suppose what it was when the baby came, to add a hundredfold to the interests of her existence. Everything else in life, it may be believed, dwindled into nothing in comparison with this boy of boys—this wonderful infant. There had never been one in the world like him it is unnecessary to say: and everything was so novel to her, and she felt the importance of being little Tom's mother so deeply, that her mind was quite carried away from all other thoughts. She grew almost beautiful in the light of this new addition to her happiness. And how happy she was! The child grew and throve. He was a splendid boy. His mother did not sing litanies in his praise in public, for her good sense never forsook her: but his little being seemed to fill up her life like a new stream flowing into it, and she expanded in life, in thought, and in understanding. She began to see a reason for her own position, and to believe in it, and take it seriously. She was a great lady, the first in the neighbourhood, and she felt that, as little Tom's mother, it was natural and befitting that she should be so. She began to be sensible of ambition within herself, as well as something that felt like pride. It was so little like ordinary pride, however, that Lucy was sorry for everybody who had not all the noble surroundings which she began to enjoy. She would have liked that every child should have a nursery like little Tom's, and every mother the same prospects for her infant, and was charitable and tender beyond measure to all the mothers and children within reach on little Tom's account, which was an extravagance which her husband did not grudge, but liked and encouraged, knowing the sentiment from which it sprang. It was with no view to popularity that the pair thus endeavoured to diffuse happiness about them, being so happy themselves; but it answered the same purpose, and their popularity was great.

When the county conferred the highest honour in its power upon Sir Tom, his immediate neighbours in the villages about took the honour as their own, and rejoiced as, even at a majority or a marriage, they had never rejoiced before, for so kind a landlord, so universal a friend, had never been.

The villages were model villages on the Randolph lands. Sir Tom and his young wife had gone into every detail about the labourers' cottages with as much interest as if they had themselves meant to live in one of them. There were no such trim gardens or bright flower-beds to be seen anywhere, and it was well for the people that the Rector of the parish was judicious, and kept Lady Randolph's charities within bounds. There had been no small amount of poverty and distress among these rustics when the Squire was poor and absent, when they lived in tumbledown old houses, which nobody took any interest in, and where neither decency nor comfort was considered; but now little industries sprang up and prospered, and the whole landscape smiled. A wise landlord with unlimited sway over his neighbourhood and no rivals in the field can do so much to increase the comfort of everybody about him; and such a small matter can make a poor household comfortable. Political economists, no doubt, say it is demoralising: but when it made Lucy happy and the poor women happy, how could Sir Tom step in and arrest the genial bounty? He gave the Rector a hint to see that she did not go too far, and walked about with his hands in his pockets and looked on. All this amused him greatly; even the little ingratitudes she met with, which went to Lucy's heart, made her husband laugh. It pleased his satirical vein to see how human nature displayed itself, and the black sheep appeared among the white even in a model village. But as for Lucy, though she would sometimes cry over these spots upon the general goodness, it satisfied every wish of her heart to be able to do so much for the cottagers. They did not, perhaps, stand so much in awe of her as they ought to have done, but they brought all their troubles to her with the most perfect and undoubting confidence.

All this time, however, Lucy, following the dictates of her own heart, and using what after all was only a little running over of her great wealth to secure the comfort of the people round, was neglecting what she had once thought the great duty of her life as entirely as if she had been the most selfish of worldly women. Her life had been so entirely changed—swung, as one might say, out of one orbit into another—that the burdens of the former existence seemed to have been taken from her shoulders along with its habits and external circumstances. Her husband thought of these as little as herself; yet even he was somewhat surprised to find that he had no trouble in weaning Lucy from the extravagances of her earlier independence. He had not expected much trouble, but still it had seemed likely enough that she would at least propose things that his stronger sense condemned, and would have to be convinced and persuaded that they were impracticable; but nothing of the kind occurred, and when he thought of it Sir Tom himself was surprised, as also were various other people who knew what Lucy's obstinacy on the subject before her marriage had been, and especially the Dowager Lady Randolph, who paid her nephew a yearly visit, and never failed to question him on the subject.

"And Lucy?" she would say. "Lucy never makes any allusion? She has dismissed everything from her mind? I really think you must be a magician, Tom. I could not have believed it, after all the trouble she gave us, and all the money she threw away. Those Russells, you know, that she was so ridiculously liberal to, they are as bad as ever. That sort of extravagant giving of money is never successful. But I never thought you would have got it out of her mind."

"Don't flatter me," he said; "it is not I that have got it out of her mind. It is life and all the novelties in it—and small Tom, who is more of a magician than I am—"

"Oh, the baby!" said the dowager, with the indifference of a woman who has never had a child, and cannot conceive why a little sprawling tadpole in long clothes should make such a difference. "Yes, I suppose that's a novelty," she said, "to be mother of a bit of a thing like that naturally turns a girl's head. It is inconceivable the airs they give themselves, as if there was nothing so wonderful in creation. And so far as I can see you are just as bad, though you ought to know better, Tom."

"Oh, just as bad," he said, with his large laugh. "I never had a share in anything so wonderful. If you only could see the superiority of this bit of a thing to all other things about him—"

"Oh! spare me," cried Lady Randolph the elder, holding up her hands. "Of course I don't undervalue the importance of an heir to the property," she said in a different tone. "I have heard enough about it to be pretty sensible of that."

This the Dowager said with a slight tone of bitterness, which indeed was comprehensible enough: for she had suffered much in her day from the fact that no such production had been possible to her. Had it been so, her nephew who stood by her would not (she could scarcely help reflecting with some grudge against Providence) have been the great man he now was, and no child of his would have mattered to the family. Lady Randolph was a very sensible woman, and had long been reconciled to the state of affairs, and liked her nephew, whom she had been the means of providing for so nobly; and she was glad there was a baby; still, for the sake of her own who had never existed, she resented the self-exaltation of father and mother over this very common and in no way extraordinary phenomenon of a child.

Sir Tom laughed again with a sense of superiority, which was in itself somewhat ludicrous; but as nobody is clear-sighted in their own concerns, he was quite unconscious of this. His laugh nettled Lady Randolph still more. She said, with a certain disdain in her tone,—

"And so you think you have sailed triumphantly over all that difficulty—thanks to your charms and the baby's, and are going to hear nothing of it any more?"

Sir Tom felt that he was suddenly pulled up, and was a little resentful in return.

"I hope," he said, "that is, I do more than hope, I feel convinced, that my wife, who has great sense, has outgrown that nonsense, and that she has sufficient confidence in me to leave her business matters in my hands."

Lady Randolph shook her head.

"Outgrown nonsense—at three and twenty?" she said. "Don't you think that's premature? and, my dear boy, take my word for it, a woman when she has the power, likes to keep the control of her own business just as well as a man does. I advise you not to holloa till you are out of the wood."

"I don't expect to have any occasion to holloa; there is no wood for that matter; Lucy, though perhaps you may not think it, is one of the most reasonable of creatures."

"She is everything that is nice and good," said the Dowager, "but how about the will? Lucy may be reasonable, but that is not. And she cannot forget it always."

"Pshaw! The will is a piece of folly," cried Sir Tom. He grew red at the very thought with irritation and opposition. "I believe the old man was mad. Nothing else could excuse such imbecility. Happily there is no question of the will."

"But there must be, some time or other."

"I see no occasion for it," said Sir Tom coldly; and as his aunt was a reasonable woman, she did not push the matter any farther. But if the truth must be told this sensible old lady contemplated the great happiness of these young people with a sort of interested and alarmed spectatorship (for she wished them nothing but good), watching and wondering when the explosion would come which might in all probability shatter it to ruins. For she felt thoroughly convinced in her own mind that Lucy would not always forget the conditions by which she held her fortune, and that all the reason and good sense in the world would not convince her that it was right to ignore and baulk her father's intentions, as conveyed with great solemnity in his will. And when the question should come to be raised, Lady Randolph felt that it would be no trifling one. Lucy was very simple and sweet, but when her conscience spoke even the influence of Sir Tom would not suffice to silence it. She was a girl who would stand to what she felt to be right if all the world and even her husband were against her—and the Dowager, who wished them no harm, felt a little alarmed as to the issue. Sir Tom was not a man easy to manage, and the reddening of his usually smiling countenance at the mere suggestion of the subject was very ominous. It would be better, far better, for Lucy if she would yield at once and say nothing about it. But that was not what it was natural for her to do. She would stand by her duty to her father, just as, were it assailed, she would stand by her duty to her husband; but she would never be got to understand that the second cancelled the first. The Dowager Lady Randolph watched the young household with something of the interest with which a playgoer watches the stage. She felt sure that the explosion would come, and that a breath, a touch, might bring it on at any moment; and then what was to be the issue? Would Lucy yield? would Lucy conquer? or would the easy temper with which everybody credited Sir Tom support this trial? The old lady, who knew him so well, believed that there was a certain fiery element below, and she trembled for the peace of the household which was so happy and triumphant, and had no fear whatever for itself. She thought of "the torrent's smoothness ere it dash below," of the calm that precedes a storm, and many other such images, and so frightened did she become at the dangers she had conjured up that she put the will hurriedly out of her thoughts, as Sir Tom had done, and would think no more of it. "Sufficient," she said to herself, "is the evil to the day."

In the meantime, the married pair smiled serenely at any doubts of their perfect union, and Lucy felt a great satisfaction in showing her husband's aunt (who had not thought her good enough for Sir Tom, notwithstanding that she so warmly promoted the match) how satisfied he was with his home, and how exultant in his heir.

In the following chapters the reader will discover what was the cause which made the Dowager shake her head when she got into the carriage to drive to the railway at the termination of her visit. It was all very pretty and very delightful, and thoroughly satisfactory; but still Lady Randolph, the elder, shook her experienced head.

## CHAPTER III

## OLD MR. TREVOR'S WILL

Lucy Trevor, when she married Sir Thomas Randolph, was the heiress of so great a fortune that no one ventured to state it in words or figures. She was not old enough, indeed, to have the entire control of it in her hands, but she had unlimited control over a portion of it in a certain sense, not for her own advantage, but for the aggrandisement of others. Her father, who was eccentric and full of notions, had so settled it that a large portion of the money should eventually return, as he phrased it, to the people from whom it had come, and this not in the way of public charities and institutions, as is the common idea in such cases, but by private and individual aid to struggling persons and families. Lucy, who was then all conscience and devotion to the difficult yet exciting duty which her father had left to her to do, had made a beginning of this extraordinary work before her marriage, resisting all the arguments that were brought to bear upon her as to the folly of the will, and the impossibility of carrying it out. It is likely, indeed, that the trustees and guardians would have taken steps at once to have old Trevor's will set aside but for the fact that Lucy had a brother, who in that case would divide the inheritance with her, but who was specially excluded by the will, as being a son of Mr. Trevor's second wife, and entirely unconnected with the source from which the fortune came. It was Lucy's mother who had brought it into the family, although she was not herself aware of its magnitude, and did not live long enough to have any enjoyment of it. Neither did old Trevor himself have any enjoyment of it, save in the making of the will by which he laid down exactly his regulations for its final disposal. In any case Lucy was to retain the half, which was of itself a great sum; but the condition of her inheritance, and indeed the occupation of her life, according to her father's intention, was that she should select suitable persons to whom to distribute the other half of her fortune. It is needless to say that this commission had seriously occupied the thoughts of the serious girl who, without any sense of personal importance, found herself thus placed in the position of an official bestower of fortune, having it in her power to confer comfort, independence, and even wealth; for she was left almost entirely unrestricted as to her disposition of the money, and might at her pleasure confer a very large sum upon a favourite. Everybody who had ever heard of old Trevor's will considered it the very maddest upon record, and there were many who congratulated themselves that Lucy's husband, if she was so lucky as to marry a man of sense, would certainly put a stop to it—or even that Lucy herself, when she came to years of serious judgment, would see the folly; for there was no stipulation as to the time at which the distributions should be made, these, as well as the selection of the objects of her bounty, being left to herself. She had been very full of this strange duty before her marriage, and had selected several persons who, as it turned out, did but little credit to her choice, almost forcing her will upon the reluctant trustees, who had no power to hinder her from carrying it out, and whose efforts at reasoning with her had been totally unsuccessful. In these early proceedings Sir Tom, who was intensely amused by the oddity of the business altogether, and who had then formed no idea of appropriating her and her money to himself, gave her a delighted support.

He had never in his life encountered anything which amused him so much, and his only regret was that he had not known the absurd but high-minded old English Quixote who, wiser in his generation than that noble knight, left it to his heir to redress the wrongs of the world, while he himself had the pleasure of the anticipation only, not perhaps unmixed with a malicious sense of all the confusions and exhibitions of the weakness of humanity it would produce. Sir Tom himself had humour enough to appreciate the philosophy of the old humorist, and the droll spectator position which he had evidently chosen for himself, as though he could somehow see and enjoy all the struggles of self-interest raised by his will, with one of those curious self-delusions which so often seem to actuate the dying. Sir Tom, however, had thought it little more than a folly even at the moment when it had amused him the most. He had thought that in time Lucy would come to see how ridiculous it was, and would tacitly, without saying anything, give it up, so sensible a girl being sure in the long run to see how entirely unsuited to modern times and habits such a disposition was. And had she done so, there was nobody who was likely to awaken her to a sense of her duty. Her trustees, who considered old Trevor mad, and Lucy a fool to humour him, would certainly make no objection; and little Jock, the little brother to whom Lucy was everything in the world, was still less likely to interfere. When it came about that Lucy herself, and her fortune, and all her right, were in Sir Tom's own hands, he was naturally more and more sure that this foolish will (after giving him a great deal of amusement, and perhaps producing a supernatural chuckle, if such an expression of feeling is possible in the spiritual region where old Trevor might be supposed to be) would be henceforward like a testament in black letter, voided by good sense and better knowledge and time, the most certain agency of all. And his conviction had been more than carried out in the first years of his married life. Lucy forgot what was required of her. She thought no more of her father's will. It glided away into the unseen along with so many other things, extravagances, or if not extravagances, still phantasies of youth. She found enough in her new life—in her husband, her baby, and the humble community which looked up to her and claimed everything from her—to occupy both her mind and her hands. Life seemed to be so full that there was no time for more.

It had been no doing of Sir Tom's that little Jock, the brother who had been Lucy's child, her Mentor, her counsellor and guide, had been separated from her for so long. Jock had been sent to school with his own entire concurrence and control. He was a little philosopher with a mind beyond his years, and he had seemed to understand fully, without any childish objection, the reason why he should be separated from her, and even why it was necessary to give up the hope of visiting his sister. The first year it was because she was absent on her prolonged wedding tour: the next because Jock was himself away on a long and delightful expedition with a tutor, who had taken a special fancy to him. Afterwards the baby was expected, and all exciting visits and visitors were given up. They had met in the interval. Lucy had visited Jock at his school, and he had been with them in London on several occasions. But there had been little possibility of anything like their old intercourse. Perhaps they could never again be to each other what they had been when these two young creatures, strangely separated from all about them, had been alone in the world, having entire and perfect confidence in each other. They both looked back upon these bygone times with a sort of regretful consciousness of the difference; but Lucy was very happy in her new life, and Jock was a perfectly natural boy, given to no sentimentalities, not jealous, and enjoying his existence too completely to sigh for the time when he was a quaint old-fashioned child, and knew no life apart from his sister.

Their intercourse then had been so pretty, so tender and touching; the child being at once his sister's charge and her superior in his old-fashioned reflectiveness, her pupil and her teacher, the little judge of whose opinions she stood in awe, while at the same time quite subject and submissive to her—that it was a pity it should ever come to an end; but it is a pity, too, when children grow up, when they grow out of all the softness and keen impressions of youth into the harder stuff of man and woman. To their parents it is a change which has often little to recommend it—but it is inevitable, as we all know; and so it was a pity that Lucy and Jock were no longer all in all to each other; but the change was in their case, too, inevitable, and accepted by both. When, however, the time came that Jock was to arrive really on his first long visit at the Hall, Lucy prepared for this event with a little excitement, with a lighting up of her eyes and countenance, and a pleasant warmth of anticipation in which even little Tom was for the moment set aside. She asked her husband a dozen times in the previous day if he thought the boy would be altered. "I know he must be taller and all that," Lucy said. "I do not mean the outside of him. But do you think he will be changed?"

"It is to be hoped so," said Sir Tom, serenely. "He is sixteen. I trust he is not what he was at ten. That would be a sad business, indeed—"

"Oh, Tom, you know that's not what I mean!—of course he has grown older; but he always was very old for his age. He has become a real boy now. Perhaps in some things he will seem younger too."

"I always said you were very reasonable," said her husband, admiringly. "That is just what I wanted you to be prepared for—not a wise little old man as he was when he had the charge of your soul, Lucy."

She smiled at him, shaking her head. "What ridiculous things you say. But Jock was always the wise one. He knew much better than I did. He did take care of me whatever you may think, though he was such a child."

"Perhaps it was as well that he did not continue to take care of you. On the whole, though I have no such lofty views, I am a better guide."

Lucy looked at him once more without replying for a moment. Was her mind ever crossed by the idea that there were perhaps certain particulars in which little Jock was the best guide? If so the blasphemy was involuntary. She shook it off with a little movement of her head, and met his glance with her usual serene confidence. "You ought to be," she said, "Tom; but you liked him always. Didn't you like him? I always thought so; and you will like him now?"

"I hope so," said Sir Tom.

Then a slight gleam of anxiety came into Lucy's eyes. This seemed the only shape in which evil could come to her, and with one of those forewarnings of Nature always prone to alarm, which come when we are most happy, she looked wistfully at her husband, saying nothing, but with an anxious question and prayer combined in her look. He smiled at her, laying his hand upon her head, which was one of his caressing ways, for Lucy, not an imposing person in any particular, was short, and Sir Tom was tall.

"Does that frighten you, Lucy? I shall like him for your sake, if not for his own, never fear."

"That is kind," she said, "but I want you to like him for his own sake. Indeed, I should like you if you would, Tom," she added almost timidly, "to like him for your own. Perhaps you think that is presuming, as if he, a little boy, could be anything to you; but I almost think that is the only real way—if you know what I mean."

"Now this is humbling," said Sir Tom, "that one's wife should consider one too dull to know what she means. You are quite right, and a complete philosopher, Lucy. I will like the boy for my own sake. I always did like him, as you say. He was the quaintest little beggar, an old man and a child in one. But it would have been bad for him had you kept on cultivating him in that sort of hot-house atmosphere. It was well for Jock, whatever it might be for you, that I arrived in time."

Lucy pondered for a little without answering; and then she said, "Why should it be considered so necessary for a boy to be sent away from home?"

"Why!" cried Sir Tom, in astonishment; and then he added, laughingly, "It shows your ignorance, Lucy, to ask such a question. He must be sent to school, and there is an end of it. There are some things that are like axioms in Euclid, though you don't know very much about that—they are made to be acted upon, not to be discussed. A boy must go to school."

"But why?" said Lucy undaunted. "That is no answer." She was untrammelled by any respect for Euclid, and would have freely questioned the infallibility of an axiom, with a courage such as only ignorance possesses. She was thinking not only of Jock, but had an eye to distant contingencies, when there might be question of a still more precious boy. "God," she said, reverentially, "must have meant surely that the father and mother should have something to do in bringing them up."

"In the holidays, my dear," said Sir Tom; "that is what we are made for. Have you never found that out?"

Lucy never felt perfectly sure whether he was in jest or earnest. She looked at him again to see what he meant—which was not very easy, for Sir Tom meant two things directly opposed to each other. He meant what he said, and yet said what he knew was nonsense, and laughed at himself inwardly with a keen recognition of this fact. Notwithstanding, he was as much determined to act upon it as if it had been the most certain truth, and in a way pinned his faith to it as such.

"I suppose you are laughing," said Lucy, "and I wish you would not, because it is so important. I am sure we are not meant only for the holidays, and you don't really think so, Tom; and to take a child away from his natural teachers, and those that love him best in the world, to throw him among strangers! Oh, I cannot think that is the best way, whatever Euclid may make you think."

At this Sir Tom laughed, as he generally did, though never disrespectfully, at Lucy's decisions. He said, "That is a very just expression, my dear, though Euclid never made us think so much as he ought to have done. You are thinking of that little beggar. Wait till he is out of long clothes."

"Which shows all you know about it. He was shortcoated at the proper time, I hope," said Lucy, with some indignation, "do you call these long clothes?"

These were garments which showed when he sprawled, as he always did, a great deal of little Tom's person, and as his mother was at that time holding him by them, while he "felt his feet," upon the carpet, the spectacle of two little dimpled knees without any covering at all triumphantly proved her right. Sir Tom threw himself upon the carpet to kiss those sturdy, yet wavering little limbs, which were not quite under the guidance of Tommy's will as yet, and taking the child from his mother, propped it up against his own person. "For the present, I allow that fathers and mothers are the best," he said.

Lucy stood and gazed at them in that ecstasy of love and pleasure with which a young mother beholds her husband's adoration for their child. Though she feels it to be the highest pride and crown of their joint existence, yet there is always in her mind a sense of admiration and gratitude for his devotion. She looked down upon them at her feet, with eyes running over with happiness. It is to be feared that at such a moment Lucy forgot even Jock, the little brother who had been as a child to her in her earlier days; and yet there was no want of love for Jock in her warm and constant heart.

## CHAPTER IV

### YOUNG MR. TREVOR

John Trevor, otherwise Jock, arrived at the Hall in a state of considerable though suppressed excitement. It was not in his nature to show the feelings which were most profound and strongest in his nature, even if the religion of an English public school boy had not forbidden demonstration. But he had very strong feelings underneath his calm exterior, and the approach to Lucy's home gave him many thoughts. The sense of separation which had once affected him with a deep though unspoken sentiment had passed away long ago into a faint grudge, a feeling of something lost—but between ten and sixteen one does not brood upon a grievance, especially when one is surrounded by everything that can make one happy; and there was a certain innate philosophy in the mind of Jock which enabled him to see the justice and necessity of the separation. He it was who in very early day, had ordained his own going to school with a realisation of the need of it which is not usually given to his age—and he had understood without any explanation and without any complaint that Lucy must live her own life, and that their constant brother and sister fellowship became impossible when she married. The curious little solemn boy, who had made so many shrewd guesses at the ways of life while he was still only a child, accepted this without a word, working it out in his own silent soul; but nevertheless it had affected him deeply. And when the time came at last for a real meeting, not a week's visit in town where she was fully occupied, and he did not well know what to do with himself—or a hurried rapid meeting at school, where Jock's pride in introducing his tutor to his sister was a somewhat imperfect set-off to the loss of personal advantage to himself in thus seeing Lucy always in the company of other people—his being was greatly moved with diverse thoughts. Lucy was all he had in the world to represent the homes, the fathers and mothers and sisters and brothers of his companions. The old time when they had been all in all to each other had a more delicate beauty than the ordinary glow of childhood. He thought there was nobody like her, with that mingled adoration and affectionate contempt which make up a boy's love for the women belonging to him. She was not clever: but he regarded the simplicity of her mind with pride. This seemed to give her her crowning charm. "Any fellow can be clever," Jock said to himself. It was part of Lucy's superiority that she was not so. He arrived at the railway station at Farafield with much excitement in his mind, though his looks were quiet enough. The place, though it was the first he had ever known, did not attract a thought from the other and more important meeting. It was a wet day in August, and the coachman who had been sent for him gave him a note to say that Lucy would have come to meet him but for the rain. He was rather glad of the rain, this being the case. He did not want to meet her on a railway platform—he even regretted the long stretches of the stubble fields as he whirled past, and wished that the way had been longer, though he was so anxious to see her. And when he jumped down at the great door of the hall and found himself in the embrace of his sister, the youth was thrilling with excitement, hope, and pleasure. Lucy had changed much less than he had. Jock, who had been the smallest of pale-faced boys, was now long and weedy, with limbs and fingers of portentous length. His hair was light and limp; his large eyes, well set in his head, had a vague and often dreamy look. It was impossible to call him a handsome boy. There was an entire want of colour about him, as there had been about Lucy in her first youth, and his gray morning clothes, like the little gray dress she had worn as a young girl were not very becoming to him. They had been so long apart that he met her very shyly, with an awkwardness that almost looked like reluctance, and for the first hour scarcely knew what to say to her, so full was he of the wonder and pleasure of being by her, and the impossibility of expressing this. She asked him about his journey, and he made the usual replies, scarcely knowing what he said, but looking at her with a suppressed beatitude which made Jock dull in the very intensity of his feeling. The rain came steadily down outside, shutting them in as with veils of falling water. Sir Tom, in order to leave them entirely free to have their first meeting over, had taken himself off for the day. Lucy took her young brother into the inner drawing-room, the centre of her own life. She made him sit down in a luxurious chair, and stood over him gazing at the boy, who was abashed and did not know what to say. "You are different, Jock. It is not that you are taller and bigger altogether, but you are different. I suppose so am I."

"Not much," he said, looking shyly at her. "You couldn't change."

"How so?" she asked with a laugh. "I am such a great deal older I ought to look wiser. Let me see what it is. Your eyes have grown darker, I think, and your face is longer, Jock; and what is that? a little down, actually, upon your upper lip. Jock, not a moustache!"

Jock blushed with pleasure and embarrassment, and put up his hand fondly to feel those few soft hairs. "There isn't very much of it," he said.

"Oh, there is enough to swear by; and you like school as well as ever? and MTutor, how is he? Are you as fond of him as you used to be, Jock?"

"You don't say you're fond of him," said Jock, "but he's just as jolly as ever, if that is what you mean."

"That is what I mean, I suppose. You must tell me when I say anything wrong," said Lucy. She took his head between her hands and gave him a kiss upon his forehead. "I am so glad to see you here at last," she said.

And then there was a pause. Her first little overflow of questions had come to an end, and she did not exactly know what to say, while Jock sat silent, staring at her with an earnest gaze. It was all so strange, the scene and surroundings, and Lucy in the midst, who was a great lady, instead of being merely his sister—all these confused the boy's faculties. He wanted time to realise it all. But Lucy, for her part, felt the faintest little touch of disappointment. It seemed to her as if they ought to have had so much to say to each other, such a rush of questions and answers, and full-hearted confidence. Jock's heart would be at his lips, she thought, ready to rush forth—and her own also, with all the many things of which she had said to herself: "I must tell that to Jock." But as a matter of fact, many of these things had been told by letter, and the rest would have been quite out of place in the moment of reunion, in which indeed it seemed inappropriate to introduce any subject other than their pleasure in seeing each other again, and those personal inquiries which we all so long to make face to face when we are separated from those near to us, yet which are so little capable of filling all the needs of the situation when that moment comes. Jock was indeed showing his happiness much more by his expressive silence and shy eager gaze at her than if he had plunged into immediate talk; but Lucy felt a little disappointed, and as if the meeting had not come up to her hopes. She said, after a pause which was almost awkward, "You would like to see baby, Jock? How strange that you should not know baby! I wonder what you will think of him." She rose and rang the bell while she was speaking in a pleasant stir of fresh expectation. No doubt it would stir Jock to the depths of his heart, and bring out all his latent feeling, when he saw Lucy's boy. Little Tom was brought in state to see "his uncle," a title of dignity which the nurse felt indignantly disappointed to have bestowed upon the lanky, colourless boy who got up with great embarrassment and came forward reluctantly to see the creature quite unknown and unrealised, of whom Lucy spoke with so much exultation. Jock was not jealous, but he thought it rather odd that "a little thing like that" should excite so much attention. It seemed to him that it was a thing all legs and arms, sprawling in every direction, and when it seized Lucy by the hair, pulling it about her face with the most riotous freedom, Jock felt deeply disposed to box its ears. But Lucy was delighted. "Oh, naughty baby!" she said, with a voice of such admiration and ecstasy as the finest poetry, Jock reflected, would never have awoke in her; and when the thing "loved" her, at its nurse's bidding, clasping its fat arms round her neck, and applying a wide-open wet mouth to her cheek, the tears were in her eyes for very pleasure. "Baby, darling, that is your uncle; won't you go to your uncle? Take him, Jock. If he is a little shy at first he will soon get used to you," Lucy cried. To see Jock holding back on one side, and the baby on the other, which strenuously refused to go to its uncle, was as good as a play.

"I'm afraid I should let it fall," said Jock, "I don't know anything about babies."

"Then sit down, dear, and I will put him upon your lap," said the young mother. There never was a more complete picture of wretchedness than poor Jock, as he placed himself unwillingly on the sofa with his knees put firmly together and his feet slanting outwards to support them. "I sha'n't know what to do with it," he said. It is to be feared that he resented its existence altogether. It was to him a quite unnecessary addition. Was he never to see Lucy any more without that thing clinging to her? Little Tom, for his part, was equally decided in his sentiments. He put his little fists, which were by no means without force, against his uncle's face, and pushed him away, with squalls that would have exasperated Job; and then, instead of consoling Jock, Lucy took the little demon to her arms and soothed him. "Did they want it to make friends against its will," Lucy was so ridiculous as to say, like one of the women in Punch, petting and smoothing down that odious little creature. Both she and the nurse seemed to think that it was the baby who wanted consoling for the appearance of Jock, and not Jock who had been insulted; for one does not like even a baby to consider one as repulsive and disagreeable. The incident was scarcely at an end when Sir Tom came in, fresh, smiling, and damp from the farm, where he had been inspecting the cattle and enjoying himself. Mature age and settled life and a sense of property had converted Sir Tom to the pleasure of farming. He shook Jock heartily by the hand, and clapped him on the back, and bade him welcome with great kindness. Then he took "the little beggar" on his shoulder and carried him, shrieking with delight, about the room. It seemed a very strange thing to Jock to see how entirely these two full-grown people gave themselves up to the deification of this child. It was not bringing themselves to his level, it was looking up to him as their superior. If he had been a king his careless favours could not have been more keenly contended for. Jock, who was fond of poetry and philosophy and many other fine things, looked on at this new mystery with wondering and indignant contempt. After dinner there was the baby again. It was allowed to stay out of bed longer than usual in honour of its uncle, and dinner was hurried over, Jock thought, in order that it might be produced, decked out in a sash almost as broad as its person. When it appeared rational conversation was at an end, Sir Tom, whom Jock had always respected highly, stopped the inquiries he was making, with all the knowledge and pleasure, of an old schoolboy, into school life, comparing his own experiences with those of the present generation—to play bo-peep behind Lucy's shoulder with the baby. Bo-peep! a Member of Parliament, a fellow who had been at the University, who had travelled, who had seen America and gone through the Desert! There was consternation in the astonishment with which Jock looked on at this unlooked-for, almost incredible, exhibition. It was ridiculous in Lucy, but in Sir Tom!

"I suppose we were all like that one time?" he said, trying to be philosophical, as little Tom at last, half smothered with kisses, was carried away.

"Like that—do you mean like baby? You were a little darling, dear, and I was always very, very fond of you," said Lucy, giving him the kindest look of her soft eyes. "But you were not a beauty, like my boy."

Sir Tom had laughed, with something of the same sentiment very evident in his mirth, when Lucy spoke. He put out his hand and patted his young brother-in-law on the shoulder. "It is absurd," he said, "to put that little beggar in the foreground when we have somebody here who is in Sixth form at sixteen, and is captain of his house, and has got a school prize already. If Lucy does not appreciate all that, I do, Jock, and the best I can wish for Tommy is that he should have done as much at your age."

"Oh, I was not thinking of that," said Jock with a violent blush.

"Of course he was not," said Lucy calmly, "for he always had the kindest heart though he was so clever. If you think I don't appreciate it as you say, Tom, it is only because I knew it all the time. Do you think I am surprised that Jock has beaten everybody? He was like that when he was six, before he had any education. And he will be just as proud of baby as we are when he knows him. He is a little strange at first," said Lucy, beaming upon her brother; "but as soon as he is used to you, he will go to you just as he does to me."

To this Jock could not reply by betraying the shiver that went over him at the thought, but it gave great occupation to his mind to make out how a little thing like that could attain, as it had done, such empire over the minds of two sensible people. He consulted MTutor on the subject by letter, who was his great referee on difficult subjects, and he could not help betraying his wonder to the household as he grew more familiar and the days went on. "He can't do anything for you," Jock said. "He can't talk; he doesn't know anything about—well, about books: I know that's more my line than yours, Lucy—but about anything. Oh! you needn't flare up. When he dabs his mouth at you all wet—"

"Oh! you little wretch, you infidel, you savage," Lucy cried; "his sweet mouth! and a dear big wet kiss that lets you know he means it."

Jock looked at her as he had done often in the old days, with mingled admiration and contempt. It was like Lucy, and yet how odd it was. "I suppose, then," he said, "I was rather worse than that when you took me up and were good to me. What for, I wonder? and you were fond of me, too, although you are fonder of it—"

"If you talk of It again I will never speak to you more," Lucy said, "as if my beautiful boy was a thing and not a person. He is not It: he is Tom, he is Mr. Randolph: that is what Williams calls him." Williams was the butler who had been all over the world with Sir Tom, and who was respectful of the heir, but a little impatient and surprised, as Jock was, of the fuss that was made about Tommy for his own small sake.

By this time, however, Jock had recovered from his shyness—his difficulty in talking, all the little mist that absence had made—and roamed about after Lucy, hanging upon her, putting his arm through hers, though he was much the taller, wherever she went. He held her back a little now as they walked through the park in a sort of procession, Mrs. Richens, the nurse, going first with the boy. "When I was a little slobbering beast, like—" he stopped himself in time, "like the t'other kind of baby, and nobody wanted me, you were the only one that took any trouble."

"How do you know?" said Lucy; "you don't remember and I don't remember."

"Ah! but I remember the time in the Terrace, when I lay on the rug, and heard papa making his will over my head. I was listening for you all the time. I was thinking of nothing but your step coming to take me out."

"Nonsense!" said Lucy, "you were deep in your books, and thinking of them only; of that—gentleman with the windmills—or Shakspeare, or some other nonsense. Oh, I don't mean Shakspeare is nonsense. I mean you were thinking of nothing but your books, and nobody would believe you understood all that at your age."

"I did not understand," said Jock with a blush. "I was a little prig. Lucy, how strange it all is, like a picture one has seen somewhere, or a scene in a play or a dream! Sometimes I can remember little bits of it, just as he used to read it out to old Ford. Bits of it are all in and out of As You Like It, as if Touchstone had said them, or Jaques. Poor old papa! how particular he was about it all. Are you doing everything he told you, Lucy, in the will?"

He did not in the least mean it as an alarming question, as he stooped over, in his awkward way holding her arm, and looked into her face.


CHAPTER V

CONSULTATIONS

Lucy was much startled by her brother's demand. It struck, however, not her conscience so much as her recollection, bringing back that past which was still so near, yet which seemed a world away, in which she had made so many anxious efforts to carry out her father's will and considered it the main object of her life. A young wife who is happy, and upon whom life smiles, can scarcely help looking back upon the time when she was a girl with a sense of superiority, an amused and affectionate contempt for herself. "How could I be so silly?" she will say, and laugh, not without a passing blush. This was not exactly Lucy's feeling; but in three years she had, even in her sheltered and happy position, attained a certain acquaintance with life, and she saw difficulties which in those former days had not been apparent to her. When Jock began to recall these reminiscences it seemed to her as if she saw once more the white commonplace walls of her father's sitting-room rising about her, and heard him laying down the law which she had accepted with such calm. She had seen no difficulty then. She had not even been surprised by the burden laid upon her. It had appeared as natural to obey him in matters which concerned large external interests, and the well-being of strangers, as it was to fill him out a cup of tea. But the interval of time, and the change of position, had made a great difference; and when Jock asked, "Are you doing all he told you?" the question brought a sudden surging of the blood to her head, which made a singing in her ears and a giddiness in her brain. It seemed to place her in front of something which must interrupt all her life and put a stop to the even flow of her existence. She caught her breath. "Doing all he told me!"

Jock, though he did not mean it, though he was no longer her self-appointed guardian and guide, became to Lucy a monitor, recalling her as to another world.

But the effect though startling was not permanent. They began to talk it all over, and by dint of familiarity the impression wore away. The impression, but not the talk. It gave the brother and sister just what they wanted to bring back all the habits of their old affectionate confidential intercourse, a subject upon which they could carry on endless discussions and consultations, which was all their own, like one of those innocent secrets which children delight in, and which, with arms entwined and heads close together, they can carry on endlessly for days together. They ceased the discussion when Sir Tom appeared, not with any fear of him as a disturbing influence, but with a tacit understanding that this subject was for themselves alone. It involved everything; the past with all those scenes of their strange childhood, the homely living, the fantastic possibilities always in the air, the old dear tender relationship between the two young creatures who alone belonged to each other. Lucy almost forgot her present self as she talked, and they moved about together, the tall boy clinging to her arm as the little urchin had done, altogether dependent, yet always with a curious leadership, suggesting a thousand things that would not have occurred to her.

Lucy had no occasion now for the advice which Jock at eight years old had so freely given her. She had her husband to lead and advise her. But in this one matter Sir Tom was put tacitly out of court, and Jock had his old place. "It does not matter at all that you have not done anything lately," Jock said; "there is plenty of time—and now that I am to spend all my holidays here, it will be far easier. It was better not to do things so hastily as you began."

"But, Jock," said Lucy, "We must not deceive ourselves; it will be very hard. People who are very nice do not like to take the money; and those who are willing to take it—"

"Does the will say the people are to be nice?" asked Jock. "Then what does that matter? The will is all against reason, Lucy. It is wrong, you know. Fellows who know political economy would think we are all mad; for it just goes against it, straight."

"That is strange, Jock; for papa was very economical. He never could bear waste: he used to say—"

"Yes, yes; but political economy means something different. It is a science. It means that you should sell everything as dear as you can, and buy it as cheap as you can—and never give anything away—"

"That is dreadful, Jock," said Lucy. "It is all very well to be a science, but nobody like ourselves could be expected to act upon it—private people, you know."

"There is something in that," Jock allowed; "there are always exceptions. I only want to show you that the will being all against rule, it must be hard to carry it out. Don't you do anything by yourself, Lucy. When you come across any case that is promising, just you wait till I come, and we'll talk it all over. I don't quite understand about nice people not taking it. Fellows I know are always pleased with presents—or a tip, nobody refuses a tip. And that is just the same sort of thing, you know."

"Not just the same," said Lucy, "for a tip—that means a sovereign, doesn't it?"

"It sometimes means—paper," said Jock, with some solemnity. "Last time you came to see me at school Sir Tom gave me a fiver—"

"A what?"

"Oh, a five-pound note," said Jock, with momentary impatience; "the other's shorter to say and less fuss. MTutor thought he had better not; but I didn't mind. I don't see why anybody should mind. There's a fellow I know—his father is a curate, and there are no end of them, and they've no money. Fellow himself is on the foundation, so he doesn't cost much. Why they shouldn't take a big tip from you, who have too much, I'm sure I can't tell; and I don't believe they would mind," Jock added, after a pause.

This, which would have inspired Lucy in the days of her dauntless maidenhood to calculate at once how much it would take to make this family happy, gave her a little shudder now.

"I don't feel as if I could do it," she said. "I wish papa had found an easier way. People don't like you afterwards when you do that for them. They are angry—they think, why should I have all that to give away, a little thing like me?"

"The easiest way would be an exam.," said Jock. "Everybody now goes in for exams.; and if they passed, they would think they had won the money all right."

"Perhaps there is something in that, Jock; but then it is not for young men. It is for ladies, perhaps, or old people, or—"

"You might let them choose their own subjects," said the boy. "A lady might do a good paper about—servants, or sewing, or that sort of thing; or housekeeping—that would be all right. MTutor might look over the papers—"

"Does he know about housekeeping?"

"He knows about most things," cried Jock, "I should like to see the thing he didn't know. He is the best scholar we have got; and he's what you call an all-round man besides," the boy said with pride.

"What is an all-round man?" Lucy asked, diffidently. "He is tall and slight, so it cannot mean his appearance."

"Oh, what a muff you are, Lucy; you're awfully nice, but you are a muff. It means a man who knows a little of everything. MTutor is more than that, he knows a great deal of everything; indeed, as I was saying," Jock added defiantly, "I should just like to see the thing he didn't know."

"And yet he is so nice," said Lucy, with a gentle air of astonishment.

MTutor was a subject which was endless with Jock, so that the original topic here glided out of sight as the exalted gifts of that model of all the virtues became the theme. This conversation, however, was but one of many. It was their meeting ground, the matter upon which they found each other as of old, two beings separated from the world, which wondered at and did not understand them. What a curious office it was for them, two favourites of fortune as they seemed, to disperse and give away the foundation of their own importance! for Jock owed everything to Lucy, and Lucy, when she had accomplished this object of her existence, and carried out her father's will, would no doubt still be a wealthy woman, but not in any respect the great personage she was now. This was a view of the matter which never crossed the minds of these two. Their strange training had made Lucy less conscious of the immense personal advantage which her money was to her than any other could have done. She knew, indeed, that there was a great difference between her early home in Farafield and the house in London where she had lived with Lady Randolph, and still more, the Hall which was her home—but she had been not less but more courted and worshipped in her lowly estate than in her high one, and her father's curious philosophy had affected her mind and coloured her perceptions. She had learned, indeed, to know that there are difficulties in attempting to enact the part of Providence, and taking upon herself the task of providing for her fellow-creatures; but these difficulties had nothing to do with the fact that she would herself suffer by such a dispersion. Perhaps her imagination was not lively enough to realise this part of the situation. Jock and she ignored it altogether. As for Jock, the delight of giving away was strong in him, and the position was so strange that it fascinated his boyish imagination. To act such a part as that of Haroun-al-Raschid in real life, and change the whole life of whatsoever poor cobbler or fruit-seller attracted him, was a vision of fairyland such as Jock had not yet outgrown. But the chief thing that he impressed on his sister was the necessity of doing nothing by herself. "Just wait till we can talk it over," he said, "two are always better than one: and a fellow learns a lot at school. You wouldn't think it, perhaps, but there's all sorts there, and you learn a lot when you have your eyes well open. We can talk it all over and settle if it's good enough; but don't go and be rash, Lucy, and do anything by yourself."

"I sha'n't, dear; I should be too frightened," Lucy said.

This was on one of his last days, when they were walking together through the shrubbery. It was September by this time, and he might have been shooting partridges with Sir Tom, but Jock was not so much an out-door boy as he ought to have been, and he preferred walking with his sister, his arm thrust through hers, his head stooping over her. It was perhaps the last opportunity they would have of discussing their family secrets, a matter (they thought) which really concerned nobody else, which no one else would care to be troubled with. Perhaps in Lucy's mind there was a sense of unreality in the whole matter; but Jock was entirely in earnest, and quite convinced that in such an important business he was his sister's natural adviser, and might be of a great deal of use. It was towards evening when they went out, and a red autumnal sunset was accomplishing itself in the west, throwing a gleam as of the brilliant tints which were yet to come, on the still green and luxuriant foliage. The light was low, and came into Lucy's eyes, who shaded them with her hand. And the paths had a touch of autumnal damp, and a certain mistiness, mellow and golden by reason of the sunshine, was rising among the trees.

"We will not be hasty," said Jock; "we will take everything into consideration: and I don't think you will find so much difficulty, Lucy, when you have me."

"I hope not, dear," Lucy said; and she began to talk to him about his flannels and other precautions he was to take; for Jock was supposed not to be very strong. He had grown fast, and he was rather weedy and long, without strength to support it. "We have been so happy together," she said. "We always were happy together, Jock. Remember, dear, no wet feet, and as little football as you can help, for my sake."

"Oh, yes," he said, with a wave of his hand; "all right, Lucy. There is no fear about that. The first thing to think of is poor old father's will, and what you are going to do about it. I mean to think out all that about the examinations, and I suppose I may speak to MTutor—"

"It is too private, don't you think, Jock? Nobody knows about it. It is better to keep it between you and me."

"I can put it as a supposed case," said Jock, "and ask what he would advise; for you see, Lucy, you and even I are not very experienced, and MTutor, he knows such a lot. It would always be a good thing to have his advice, you know; he—"

There was no telling how long Jock might have gone on on this subject. But just at this moment a quick step came round the corner of a clump of wood, and a hand was laid on the shoulder of each. "What are you plotting about?" asked the voice of Sir Tom in their ears. It was a curious sign of her mental condition which Lucy remembered with shame afterwards, without being very well able to account for it, that she suddenly dropped Jock's arm and turned round upon her husband with a quick blush and access of breathing, as if somehow—she could not tell how—she had been found out. It had never occurred to her before, through all those long drawn out consultations, that she was concealing anything from Sir Tom. She dropped Jock's arm as if it hurt her, and turned to her husband in the twinkling of an eye.

"Jock," she said quickly, "and I—were talking about MTutor, Tom."

"Ah! once landed on that subject, and there is no telling when we may come to an end," Sir Tom said, with a laugh, "but never mind, I like you all the better for it, my boy."

Jock gave an astonished look at Lucy, a half-defiant one at her husband.

"That was only by the way," he said, lifting up his shoulders with a little air of offence. He did not condescend to any further explanation, but walked along by their side with a lofty abstraction, looking at them now and then from the corner of his eye. Lucy had taken Sir Tom's arm, and was hanging upon her tall husband, looking up in his face. The little blush of surprise—or was it of guilt?—with which she had received him was still upon her cheek. She was far more animated than usual, almost a little agitated. She asked about the shooting, about the bag, and how many brace was to Sir Tom's own gun, with that conciliating interest which is one of the signs of a conscious fault; while Sir Tom, on his side bending down to his little wife, received all her flatteries with so complacent a smile, and such a beatific belief in her perfect sincerity and devotion, that Jock, looking on from his superiority of passionless youth, regarded them both with a wondering disdain. Why did she "make up" in that way to her husband, dropping her brother as if she had been plotting harm? Jock was amazed, he could not understand it. Perhaps it was only because he thus fell in a moment from being the chief object of interest to the position of nobody at all.

CHAPTER VI

A SHADOW OF COMING EVENTS

Lucy's mind had sustained a certain shock when her husband appeared. During her short married life there had not been a cloud, or a shadow of a cloud, between them. But then there had been no question between them, nothing to cause any question, no difference of opinion. Sir Tom had taken all her business naturally into his hands. Whatever she wished she had got—nay, before she expressed a wish it had been satisfied. He had talked to her about everything, and she had listened with docile attention, but without concealing the fact that she neither understood nor wished to understand; and he had not only never chided her, but had accepted her indifference with a smile of pleasure as the most natural thing in the world. He had encouraged her in all her liberal charities, shaking his head and declaring with a radiant face that she would ruin herself, and that not even her fortune would stand it. But the one matter which had given Lucy so much trouble before her marriage, and which Jock had now brought back to her mind, was one that had never been mentioned between them. He had known all about it, and her eccentric proceedings and conflict with her guardians, backing her up, indeed, with much laughter, and showing every symptom of amiable amusement; but he had never given any opinion on the subject, nor made the slightest allusion since to this grand condition of her father's will. In the sunny years that were past Lucy had taken no notice of this omission. She had not thought much on the subject herself. She had withdrawn from it tacitly, as one is apt to do from a matter which has been productive of pain and disappointment, and had been content to ignore that portion of her responsibilities. Even when Jock forcibly revived the subject it continued without any practical importance, and its existence was a question between themselves to afford material for endless conversation which had been pleasant and harmless. But when Sir Tom's hand was laid on her shoulder, and his cheerful voice sounded in her ear, a sudden shock was given to Lucy's being. It flashed upon her in a moment that this question which she had been discussing with Jock had never been mentioned between her and her husband, and with a sudden instinctive perception she became aware that Sir Tom would look upon it with very different eyes from theirs. She felt that she had been disloyal to him in having a secret subject of consultation even with her brother. If he heard he would be displeased, he would be taken by surprise, perhaps wounded, perhaps made angry. In any wise it would introduce a new element into their life. Lucy saw, with a sudden sensation of fright and pain, an unknown crowd of possibilities which might pour down upon her, were it to be communicated to Sir Tom that his wife and her brother were debating as to a course of action on her part, unknown to him. All this occurred in a moment, and it was not any lucid and real perception of difficulties, but only a sudden alarmed compunctious consciousness that filled her mind. She fled, as it were, from the circumstances which made these horrors possible, hurrying back into her former attitude with a penitential urgency. Jock, indeed, was very dear to her, but he was no more than second, nay he was but third, in Lady Randolph's heart. Her husband's supremacy he could not touch, and though he had been almost her child in the old days, yet he was not, nor ever would be, her child in the same ineffable sense as little Tom was, who was her very own, the centre of her life. So she ran away (so to speak) from Jock with a real panic, and clung to her husband, conciliating, nay almost wheedling him, if we may use the word, with a curious feminine instinct, to make up to him for the momentary wrong she had done, and which he was not aware of. Sir Tom himself was a little surprised by the warmth of the reception she gave him. Her interest in his shooting was usually very mild, for she had never been able to get over a little horror she had, due, perhaps, to her bourgeois training, of the slaughter of the birds. He glanced at the pair with an unusual perception that there was something here more than met the eye. "You have been egging her up to some rebellion," he said; "Jock, you villain; you have been hatching treason behind my back!" He said this with one of those cordial laughs which nobody could refrain from joining—full of good humour and fun, and a pleased consciousness that to teach Lucy to rebel would be beyond any one's power. At any other moment she would have taken the accusation with the tranquil smile which was Lucy's usual reply to her husband's pleasantries; but this time her laugh was a little strained, and the warmth of her denial, "No, no! there has been no treason," gave the slightest jar of surprise to Sir Tom. It sounded like a false note in the air; he did not understand what it could mean.

Jock went away the next day. He went with a basket of game for MTutor and many nice things for himself, and all the attention and care which might have been his had he been the heir instead of only the young brother and dependent. Lucy herself drove in with him to Farafield to see him off, and Sir Tom, who had business in the little town and meant to drive back with his wife, appeared on the railway platform just in time to say good-bye. "Now, Lucy, you will not forget," were Jock's last words as he looked out of the window when the train was already in motion. Lucy nodded and smiled, and waved her hand, but she did not make any other reply. Sir Tom said nothing until they were driving along the stubble fields in the afternoon sunshine. Lucy lay back in her corner with that mingled sense of regret and relief with which, when we are very happy at home, we see a guest go away—a gentle sorrow to part, a soft pleasure in being once more restored to the more intimate circle. She had not shaken off that impression of guiltiness, but now it was over, and nothing further could be said on the subject for a long time to come.

"What is it, Lucy, that you are not to forget?"

She roused herself up, and a warm flush of colour came to her face. "Oh, nothing, Tom, a little thing we were consulting about. It was Jock that brought it to my mind."

"I think it must be more than just a little thing. Mayn't I hear what this secret is?"

"Oh, it is nothing, Tom," Lady Randolph repeated; and then she sat up erect and said, "I must not deceive you. It is not merely a small matter. Still it is just between Jock and me. It was about—papa's will, Tom."

"Ah! that is a large matter. I don't quite see how that can be between you and Jock, Lucy. Jock has very little to do with it. I don't want to find fault, my dear, but I think as an adviser you will find me better than Jock."

"I know you are far better, Tom. You know more than both of us put together."

"That would not be very difficult," he said, with a smile.

Perhaps this calm acceptance of the fact nettled Lucy. At least she said, with a little touch of spirit, "And yet I know something about our kind of people better than you will ever do, Tom."

"Lucy, this is a wonderful new tone. Perhaps you may know better, but I am doubtful if you understand the relation of things as well. What is it, my dear?—that is to say, if you like to tell me, for I am not going to force your confidence."

"Tom—oh dear Tom! It is not that. It is rather that it was something to talk to Jock about. He remembers everything. When papa was making that will—" here Lucy stopped and sighed. It had not been doing her a good service to make her recollect that will, which had enough in it to make her life wretched, though that as yet nobody knew. "He recollects it all," she said. "He used to hear it read out. He remembers everything."

"I suppose, then," said Sir Tom, with a peculiar smile, "there is something in particular which he thought you were likely to forget?"

Here Lucy sighed again. "I am afraid I had forgotten it. No, not forgotten, but—I never knew very well what to do. Perhaps you don't remember either. It is about giving the money away."

Sir Tom was a far more considerable person in every way than the little girl who was his wife, and who was not clever nor of any great account apart from her wealth; and she was devoted to him, so that he could have very little fear how any conflict should end when he was on one side, if all the world were on the other. But perhaps he had been spoiled by Lucy's entire agreement and consent to whatever he pleased to wish, so that his tone was a little sharp, not so good-humoured as usual, but with almost a sneer in it when he replied quickly, not leaving her a moment to get her breath, "I see; Jock having inspiration from the fountain head, was to be your guide in that."

She looked at him alarmed and penitent, but reproachful. "I would have done nothing, I could have done nothing, oh Tom! without you."

"It is very obliging of you Lucy to say so; nevertheless, Jock thought himself entitled to remind you of what you had forgotten, and to offer himself as your adviser. Perhaps MTutor was to come in, too," he said, with a laugh.

Sir Tom was not immaculate in point of temper any more than other men, but Lucy had never suffered from it before. She was frightened, but she did not give way. The colour went out of her cheeks, but there was more in her than mere insipid submission. She looked at her husband with a certain courage, though she was so pale, and felt so profoundly the displeasure which she had never encountered before.

"I don't think you should speak like that, Tom. I have done nothing wrong. I have only been talking to my brother of—of—a thing that nobody cares about but him and me in all the world."

"And that is—"

"Doing what papa wished," Lucy said in a low voice. A little moisture stole into her eyes. Whether it came because of her father, or because her husband spoke sharply to her, it perhaps would have been difficult to say.

This made Sir Tom ashamed of his ill-humour. It was cruel to be unkind to a creature so gentle, who was not used to be found fault with; and yet he felt that for Lucy to set up an independence of any kind was a thing to be crushed in the bud. A man may have the most liberal principles about women, and yet feel a natural indignation when his own wife shows signs of desiring to act for herself; and besides, it was not to be endured that a boy and girl conspiracy should be hatched under his very nose to take the disposal of an important sum of money out of his hands. Such an idea was not only ridiculous in itself, but apt to make him ridiculous, a man who ought to be strong enough to keep the young ones in order. "My dear," he said, "I have no wish to speak in any way that vexes you; but I see no reason you can have—at least I hope there has been nothing in my conduct to give you any reason—to withdraw your confidence from me and give it to Jock."

Lucy did not make him any reply. She looked at him pathetically through the water in her eyes. If she had spoken she would have cried, and this in an open carriage, with a village close at hand, and people coming and going upon the road, was not to be thought of. By the time she had mastered herself Sir Tom had cooled down, and he was ashamed of having made Lucy's lips to quiver and taken away her voice.

"That was a very nasty thing to say," he said, "wasn't it, Lucy? I ought to be ashamed of myself. Still, my little woman must remember that I am too fond of her to let her have secrets with anybody but me."

And with this he took the hand that was nearest to him into both of his and held it close, and throwing a temptation in her way which she could not resist, led her to talk of the baby and forget everything else except that precious little morsel of humanity. He was far cleverer than Lucy; he could make her do whatever he pleased. No fear of any opposition, any setting up of her own will against his. When they got home he gave her a kiss, and then the momentary trouble was all over. So he thought at least. Lucy was so little and gentle and fair, that she appeared to her husband even younger than she was; and she was a great deal younger than himself. He thought her a sort of child-wife, whom a little scolding or a kiss would altogether sway. The kiss had been quite enough hitherto. Perhaps, since Jock had come upon the scene, a few words of admonition might prove now and then necessary, but it would be cruel to be hard upon her, or do more than let her see what his pleasure was.

But Lucy was not what Sir Tom thought. She could not endure that there should be any shadow between her husband and herself, but her mind was not satisfied with this way of settling an important question. She took his kiss and his apology gratefully, but if anything had been wanted to impress more deeply upon her mind the sense of a duty before her, of which her husband did not approve, and in doing which she could not have his help, it would have been this little episode altogether. Even little Tom did not efface the impression from her mind. At dinner she met her husband with her usual smile, and even assented when he remarked upon the pleasantness of finding themselves again alone together. There had been other guests besides Jock, so that the remark did not offend her; but yet Lucy was not quite like herself. She felt it vaguely, and he felt it vaguely, and neither was entirely aware what it was.

In the morning, at breakfast, Sir Tom received a foreign letter, which made him start a little. He started and cried, "Hollo!" then, opening it, and finding two or three closely-scribbled sheets, gave way to a laugh. "Here's literature!" he said. Lucy, who had no jealousy of his correspondents, read her own calm little letters, and poured out the tea, with no particular notice of her husband's interjections. It did not even move her curiosity that the letter was in a feminine hand, and gave forth a faint perfume. She reminded him that his tea was getting cold, but otherwise took no notice. One of her own letters was from the Dowager Lady Randolph, full of advice about the baby. "Mrs. Russell tells me that Katie's children are the most lovely babies that ever were seen; but she is very fantastic about them; will not let them wear shoes to spoil their feet, and other vagaries of that kind. I hope, my dear Lucy, that you are not fanciful about little Tom," Lady Randolph wrote. Lucy read this very composedly, and smiled at the suggestion. Fanciful! Oh, no, she was not fanciful about him—she was not even silly, Lucy thought. She was capable of allowing that other babies might be lovely, though why the feet of Katie's children should be of so much importance she allowed to herself she could not see. She was roused from these tranquil thoughts by a little commotion on the other side of the table, where Sir Tom had just thrown down his letter. He was laughing and talking to himself. "Why shouldn't she come if she likes it?" he was saying. "Lucy, look here, since you have set up a confidant, I shall have one too," and with that Sir Tom went off into an immoderate fit of laughing. The letter scattered upon the table all opened out, two large foreign sheets, looked endless. Nobody had ever written so much to Lucy in all her life. She could see it was largely underlined and full of notes of admiration and interrogation, altogether an out-of-the-way epistle. Was it possible that Sir Tom was a little excited as well as amused? He put his roll upon a hot plate, and began to cut it with his knife and fork in an absence of mind, which was not usual with him, and at intervals of a minute or two would burst out with his long "Ha, ha," again. "That will serve you out, Lucy," he said, with a shout, "if I set up a confidant too."

# CHAPTER VII

## A WARNING

"I wonder if I shall like her," Lucy said to herself.

She had been hearing from her husband about the Contessa di Forno-Populo, who had promised to pay them a visit at Christmas. He had laughed a great deal while he described this lady. "What she will do here in a country-house in the depth of winter, I cannot tell," he said, "but if she wants to come why shouldn't she? She and I are old friends. One time and another we have seen a great deal of each other. She will not understand me in the character of a Benedick, but that will be all the greater fun," he said with a laugh. Lucy looked at him with a little surprise. She could not quite make him out.

"If she is a friend she will not mind the country and the winter," said Lucy; "it will be you she will want to see—"

"That is all very well, my dear," said Sir Tom, "but she wants something more than me. She wants a little amusement. We must have a party to meet her, Lucy. We have never yet had the house full for Christmas. Don't you think it will be better to furnish the Contessa with other objects instead of letting her loose upon your husband. You don't know what it is you are treating so lightly."

"I—treat any one lightly that you care for, Tom! Oh, no; I was only thinking. I thought she would come to see you, not a number of strange people—"

"And you would not mind, Lucy?"

"Mind?" Lucy lifted her innocent eyes upon him with the greatest surprise. "To be sure it is most nice of all when there is nobody with us," she said—as if that had been what he meant. Enlightenment on this subject had not entered her mind. She did not understand him; nor did he understand her. He gave her a sort of friendly hug as he passed, still with that laugh in which there was no doubt a great perception of something comic, yet—an enlightened observer might have thought—a little uneasiness, a tremor which was almost agitation too. Lucy too had a perception of something a little out of the way which she did not understand, but she offered to herself no explanation of it. She said to herself, when he was gone, "I wonder if I shall like her?" and she did not make herself any reply. She had been in society, and held her little place with a simple composure which was natural to her, whoever might come in her way. If she was indeed a little frightened of the great ladies, that was only at the first moment before she became used to them; and afterwards all had gone well—but there was something in the suggestion of a foreign great lady, who perhaps might not speak English, and who would be used to very different "ways," which alarmed her a little; and then it occurred to her with some disappointment that this would be the time of Jock's holidays, and that it would disappoint him sadly to find her in the midst of a crowd of visitors. She said to herself, however, quickly, that it was not to be expected that everything should always go exactly as one wished it, and that no doubt the Countess of — what was it she was the Countess of?—would be very nice, and everything go well; and so Lady Randolph went away to her baby and her household business, and put it aside for the moment. She found other things far more important to occupy her, however, before Christmas came.

For that winter was very severe and cold, and there was a great deal of sickness in the neighbourhood. Measles and colds and feverish attacks were prevalent in the village, and there were heartrending "cases," in which young Lady Randolph at the Hall took so close an interest that her whole life was disturbed by them. One of the babies, who was little Tom's age, died. When it became evident that there was danger in this case it is impossible to describe the sensations with which Lucy's brain was filled. She could not keep away from the house in which the child was. She sent to Farafield for the best doctor there, and everything that money could procure was got for the suffering infant, whose belongings looked on with wonder and even dismay, with a secret question like that of him who was a thief and kept the bag—to what purpose was this waste? for they were all persuaded that the baby was going to die.

"And the best thing for him, my lady," the grandmother said. "He'll be better done by where he's agoing than he ever could have been here."

"Oh, don't say so," said Lucy. The young mother, who was as young as herself, cried; yet if Lucy had been absent would have been consoled by that terrible philosophy of poverty that it was "for the best." But Lady Randolph, in such a tumult of all her being as she had never known before, with unspeakable yearning over the dying baby, and a panic beyond all reckoning for her own, would not listen to any such easy consolation. She shut her ears to it with a gleam of anger such as had never been seen in her gentle face before, and would have sat up all night with the poor little thing in her lap if death had not ended its little plaints and suffering. Sir Tom, in this moment of trial, came out in all his true goodness and kindness. He went with her himself to the cottage, and when the vigil was over appeared again to take her home. It was a wintry night, frosty and clear, the stars all twinkling with that mysterious life and motion which makes them appear to so many wistful eyes like persons rather than worlds, and as if there was knowledge and sympathy in those far-shining lights of heaven. Sir Thomas was alarmed by Lucy's colourless face, and the dumb passion of misery and awe that was about her. He was very tender-hearted himself at sight of the dead baby which was the same age as his lovely boy. He clasped the trembling hand with which his wife held his arm, and tried to comfort her. "Look at the stars, my darling," he said, "the angels must have carried the poor little soul that way." He was not ashamed to let fall a tear for the little dead child. But Lucy could neither weep nor think of the angels. She hurried him on through the long avenue, clinging to his arm but not leaning upon it, hastening home. Now and then a sob escaped her, but no tears. She flew upstairs to her own boy's nursery, and fell down on her knees by the side of his little crib. He was lying in rosy sleep, his little dimpled arms thrown up over his head, a model of baby beauty. But even that sight did not restore her. She buried her wan face in her hands and so gasped for breath that Sir Tom, who had followed her, took her in his arms and carrying her to her own room laid her down on the sofa by the fire and did all that man could to soothe her.

"Lucy, Lucy! we must thank God that all is well with our own," he said, half terrified by the gasping and the paleness; and then she burst forth:

"Oh, why should it be well with him, and little Willie gone? Why should we be happy and the others miserable? My baby safe and warm in my arms, and poor Ellen's—poor Ellen's—"

This name, and the recollection of the poor young mother, whom she had left in her desolation, made Lucy's tears pour forth like a summer storm. She flung her arms round her husband's neck, and called out to him in an agony of anxiety and excitement:

"Oh, what shall we do to save him? Oh, Tom, pray, pray! Little Willie was well on Saturday—and now—How can we tell what a day may bring forth?" Lucy cried, wildly pushing him away from her, and rising from the sofa.

Then she began to pace about the room as we all do in trouble, clasping her hands in a wild and inarticulate appeal to heaven. Death had never come across her path before save in the case of her father, an old man whose course was run, and his end a thing necessary and to be looked for. She could not get out of her eyes the vision of that little solemn figure, so motionless, so marble white. The thought would not leave her. To see the calm Lucy pacing up and down in this passion of terror and agony made Sir Tom almost as miserable as herself. He tried to take her into his arms, to draw her back to the sofa.

"My darling, you are over-excited. It has been too much for you," he said.

"Oh, what does it matter about me?" cried Lucy; "think—oh, God! oh, God I—if we should have that to bear."

"My dear love—my Lucy, you that have always been so reasonable—the child is quite well; come and see him again and satisfy yourself."

"Little Willie was quite well on Saturday," she cried again. "Oh, I cannot bear it, I cannot bear it! and why should it be poor Ellen and not me?"

When a person of composed mind and quiet disposition is thus carried beyond all the bounds of reason and self-restraint, it is natural that everybody round her should be doubly alarmed. Lucy's maid hung about the door, and the nurse, wrapped in a shawl, stole out of little Tom's room. They thought their mistress had the hysterics, and almost forced their way into the room to help her. It did Sir Tom good to send these busybodies away. But he was more anxious himself than words could say. He drew her arms within his, and walked up and down with her. "You know, my darling, what the Bible says, 'that one shall be taken and another left; and that the wind bloweth where it listeth,'" he said, with a pardonable mingling of texts. "We must just take care of him, dear, and hope the best."

Here Lucy stopped, and looked him in the face with an air of solemnity that startled him.

"I have been thinking," she said; "God has tried us with happiness first. That is how He always does—and if we abuse that then there comes—the other. We have been so happy. Oh, so happy!" Her face, which had been stilled by this profounder wave of feeling, began to quiver again. "I did not think any one could be so happy," she said.

"Well, my darling! and you have been very thankful and good—"

"Oh, no, no, no," she cried. "I have forgotten my trust. I have let the poor suffer, and put aside what was laid upon me—and now, now—" Lucy caught her husband's arm with both her hands, and drew him close to her. "Tom, God has sent his angel to warn us," she said, in a broken voice.

"Lucy, Lucy, this is not like you. Do you think that poor little woman has lost her baby for our sake? Are we of so much more importance than she is, in the sight of God, do you think? Come, come, that is not like you."

Lucy gazed at him for a moment with a sudden opening of her eyes, which were contracted with misery. She was subdued by the words, though she only partially comprehended them.

"Don't you think," he said, "that to deprive another woman of her child in order to warn you, would be unjust, Lucy? Come and sit down and warm your poor little hands, and take back your reason, and do not accuse God of wrong, for that is not possible. Poor Ellen I don't doubt is composed and submissive, while you, who have so little cause—"

She gave him a wild look. "With her it is over, it is over!" she cried, "but with us—"

Lucy had never been fanciful, but love quickens the imagination and gives it tenfold power; and no poet could have felt with such a breathless and agonised realisation the difference between the accomplished and the possible, the past which nothing can alter, and the pain and sickening terror with which we anticipate what may come. Ellen had entered into the calm of the one. She herself stood facing wildly the unspeakable terror of the other. "Oh, Tom, I could not bear it, I could not bear it!" she cried.

It was almost morning before he had succeeded in soothing her, in making her lie down and compose herself. But by that time nature had begun to take the task in hand, wrapping her in the calm of exhaustion. Sir Tom had the kindest heart, though he had not been without reproach in his life. He sat by her till she had fallen into a deep and quiet sleep, and then he stole into the nursery and cast a glance at little Tom by the dim light of the night lamp. His heart leaped to see the child with its fair locks all tumbled upon the pillow, a dimpled hand laid under a dimpled cheek, ease and comfort and well-being in every lovely curve; and then there came a momentary spasm across his face, and he murmured "Poor little beggar!" under his breath. He was not panic-stricken like Lucy. He was a man made robust by much experience of the world, and a child more or less was not a thing to affect him as it would a young mother; but the pathos of the contrast touched him with a keen momentary pang. He stole away again quite subdued, and went to bed thankfully, saying an uncustomary prayer in the emotion that possessed him: Good God, to think of it; if that poor little beggar had been little Tom!

Lucy woke to the sound of her boy's little babbling of happiness in the morning, and found him blooming on her bed, brought there by his father, that she might see him and how well he was, even before she was awake. It was thus not till the first minute of delight was over that her recollections came back to her and she remembered the anguish of the previous night; and then with a softened pang, as was natural, and warm flood of thankfulness, which carried away harsher thoughts. But her mind was in a highly susceptible and tender state, open to every impression. And when she knelt down to make her morning supplications, Lucy made a dedication of herself and solemn vow. She said, like the little princess when she first knew that she was to be made queen, "I will be good." She put forth this promise trembling, not with any sense that she was making a bargain with God, as more rigid minds might suppose, but with all the remorseful loving consciousness of a child which feels that it has not made the return it ought for the good things showered upon it, and confronts for the first time the awful possibility that these tender privileges might be taken away. There was a trembling all over her, body and soul. She was shaken by the ordeal through which she had come—the ordeal which was not hers but another's: and with the artlessness of the child was mingled that supreme human instinct which struggles to disarm Fate by immediate prostration and submission. She laid herself down at the feet of the Sovereign greatness which could mar all her happiness in a moment, with a feeling that was not much more than half Christian. Lucy tried to remind herself that He to whom she knelt was love as well as power. But nature, which still "trembles like a guilty thing surprised" in that great Presence, made her heart beat once more with passion and sickening terror. God knew, if no one else did, that she had abandoned her father's trust and neglected her duty. "Sell all thou hast and give to the poor." Lucy rose from her knees with anxious haste, feeling as if she must do this, come what might and whoever should oppose; or at least since it was not needful for her to sell all she had, that she must hurry forth, and forestall any further discipline by beginning at once to fulfil the duty she had neglected. She could not yet divest herself of the thought that the baby who was dead was a little warning messenger to recall her to a sense of the punishments that might be hanging over her. A messenger to her of mercy, for what, oh! what would she have done if the blow had fallen upon little Tom?

CHAPTER VIII

THE SHADOW OF DEATH

After this it may perhaps be surprising to hear that Lucy did nothing to carry out that great trust with which she had been charged. She had felt, and did feel at intervals, for a long time afterwards, as if God Himself had warned her what might come upon her if she neglected her duty. But if you will reflect how very difficult that duty was, and how far she was from any opportunity of being able to discharge it! In early days, when she was fresh from her father's teaching, and deeply impressed with the instant necessity of carrying it out, Providence itself had sent the Russell family, poor and helpless people, who had not the faculty of getting on by themselves, into her way, and Lucy had promptly, or at least as promptly as indignant guardians would permit, provided for them in the modest way which was all her ideas reached to at the time. But around the Hall there was nobody to whom the same summary process could be applied. The people about were either working people, whom it is always easy to help, or well-off people, who had no wants which Lucy could supply. And this continued to be so even after her fright and determination to return to the work that had been allotted to her. No doubt, could she have come down to the hearts and lives of the neighbours who visited Lady Randolph on the externally equal footing which society pretends to allot to all gentlefolks, she would have found several of them who would have been glad to free her from her money; but then she could not see into their hearts. She did not know what a difficult thing it was for Mr. Routledge of Newby to pay the debts of his son when he had left college, or how hardly hit was young Archer of Fordham in the matter of the last joint-stock bank that stopped payment. If they had not all been so determined to hold up their heads with the best, and keep up appearances, Lucy might have managed somehow to transfer to them a little of the money which she wanted to get rid of, and of which they stood so much in need. But this was not to be thought of; and when she cast her eyes around her it was with a certain despair that Lucy saw no outlet whatever for those bounties which it had seemed to her heaven itself was concerned about, and had warned her not to neglect. Many an anxious thought occupied her mind on this subject. She thought of calling her cousin Philip Rainy, who was established and thriving at Farafield, and whose fortune had been founded upon her liberality, to her counsels. But if Sir Tom had disliked the confidences between her and her brother, what would he think of Philip Rainy as her adviser? Then Lucy in her perplexity turned again to the thought of Jock. Jock had a great deal more sense in him than anybody knew. He had been the wisest child, respected by everybody; and now he was almost a man, and had learned, as he said, a great deal at school. She thought wistfully of the poor curate of whom Jock had told her. Very likely that poor clergyman would do very well for what Lucy wanted. Surely there could be no better use for money than to endow such a man, with a whole family growing up, all the better for it, and a son on the foundation! And then she remembered that Jock had entreated her to do nothing till he came. Thus the time went on, and her passionate resolution, her sense that heaven itself was calling upon her, menacing her with judgment even, seemed to come to nothing—not out of forgetfulness or sloth, or want of will—but because she saw no way open before her, and could not tell what to do. And after that miserable night when Ellen Bailey's baby died, and death seemed to enter in, as novel and terrible as if he had never been known before, for the first time into Lucy's Paradise, she had never said anything to Sir Tom. Day after day she had meant to do it, to throw herself upon his guidance, to appeal to him to help her; but day after day she had put it off, shrinking from the possible contest of which some instinct warned her. She knew, without knowing how, that in this he would not stand by her. Impossible to have been kinder in that crisis, more tender, more indulgent, even more understanding than her husband was; but she felt instinctively the limits of his sympathy. He would not go that length. When she got to that point he would change. But she could not have him change; she could not anticipate the idea of a cloud upon his face, or any shadow between them. And then Lucy made up her mind that she would wait for Jock, and that he and she together, when there were two to talk it over, would make out a way.

All was going on well again, the grass above little Willie's grave was green, his mother consoled and smiling as before, and at the Hall the idea of the Christmas party had been resumed, and the invitations, indeed, were sent off, when one morning the visitor whom Lucy had anticipated with such dread came out of the village, where infantile diseases always lingered, and entered the carefully-kept nursery. Little Tom awoke crying and fretful, hot with fever, his poor little eyes heavy with acrid tears. His mother had not been among the huts where poor men lie for nought, and she saw at a glance what it was. Well! not anything so very dreadful—measles, which almost all children have. There was no reason in the world why she should be alarmed. She acknowledged as much, with a tremor that went to her heart. There were no bad symptoms. The baby was no more ill than it was necessary he should be. "He was having them beautiful," the nurse said, and Lucy scarcely allowed even her husband to see the deep, harrowing dread that was in her. By and by, however, this dread was justified; she had been very anxious about all the little patients in the village that they should not catch cold, which in the careless ignorance of their attendants, and in the limited accommodation of the cottages, was so usual, so likely, almost inevitable. A door would be left open, a sudden blast of cold would come upon the little sufferer; how could any one help it? Lucy had given the poor women no peace on this subject. She had "worrited them out o' their lives." And now, wonder above all finding out, it was in little Tom's luxurious nursery, where everything was arranged for his safety, where one careful nurse succeeded another by night and by day, and Lady Randolph herself was never absent for an hour, where the ventilation was anxiously watched and regulated, and no incautious intruder ever entered—it was there that the evil came. When the child had shaken off his little complaint and all was going well, he took cold, and in a few hours more his little lungs were labouring heavily, and the fever of inflammation consuming his strength. Little Tom, the heir, the only child! A cloud fell over the house; from Sir Tom himself to the lowest servant, all became partakers, unawares, of Lucy's dumb terror. It was because the little life was so important, because so much hung upon it, that everybody jumped to the conclusion that the worst issue might be looked for. Humanity has an instinctive, heathenish feeling that God will take advantage of all the special circumstances that aggravate a blow.

Lucy, for her part, received the stroke into her very soul. She was outwardly more calm than when her heart had first been roused to terror by the death of the little child in the village. That which she had dreaded was come, and all her powers were collected to support her. The moment had arrived—the time of trial—and she would not fail. Her hand was steady and her head clear, as is the case with finer natures when confronted with deadly danger. This simple girl suddenly became like one of the women of tragedy, fighting, still and strong, with a desperation beyond all symbols—the fight with death. But Sir Tom took it differently. A woman can nurse her child, can do something for him; but a man is helpless.

At first he got rid of his anxieties by putting a cheerful face upon the matter, and denying the possibility of danger. "The measles! every child had the measles. If no fuss was made the little chap," he declared, "would soon be all right. It was always a mistake to exaggerate." But when there could no longer be any doubt on the subject, a curious struggle took place in Sir Tom's mind. That baby—die? That crowing, babbling creature pass away into the solemnity of death! It had not seemed possible, and when he tried to get it into his mind his brain whirled. Wonder for the moment seemed to silence even the possibility of grief. He had himself gone through labours and adventures that would have killed a dozen men, and had never been conscious even of alarm about himself; and the idea of a life quenched in its beginning by so accidental a matter as a draught in a nursery seemed to him something incomprehensible. When he had heard of a child's death he had been used to say that the mother would feel it, no doubt, poor thing; but it was a small event, that scarcely counted in human history to Sir Tom. When, however, his own boy was threatened, after the first incredulity, Sir Tom felt a pang of anger and wretchedness which he could not understand. It was not that the family misfortune of the loss of the heir overwhelmed him, for it was very improbable that poor little Tom would be his only child; it was a more intimate and personal sensation. A sort of terrified rage came over him which he dared not express; for if indeed his child was to be taken from him, who was it but God that would do this? and he did not venture to turn his rage to that quarter. And then a confusion of miserable feelings rose within him. One night he did not go to bed. It was impossible in the midst of the anxiety that filled the house, he said to himself. He spent the weary hours in going softly up and down stairs, now listening at the door of the nursery and waiting for his wife, who came out now and then to bring him a bulletin, now dozing drearily in his library downstairs. When the first gleams of the dawn stole in at the window he went out upon the terrace in the misty chill morning, all damp and miserable, with the trees standing about like ghosts. There was a dripping thaw after a frost, and the air was raw and the prospect dismal; but even that was less wretched than the glimmer of the shaded lights, the muffled whispering and stealthy footsteps indoors. He took a few turns up and down the terrace, trying to reason himself out of this misery. How was it, after all, that the little figure of this infant should overshadow earth and heaven to a man, a reasonable being, whose mind and life were full of interests far more important? Love, yes! but love must have some foundation. The feeling which clung so strongly to a child with no power of returning it, and no personal qualities to excite it, must be mere instinct not much above that of the animals. He would not say this before Lucy, but there could be no doubt it was the truth. He shook himself up mentally, and recalled himself to what he attempted to represent as the true aspect of affairs. He was a man who had obtained most things that this world can give. He had sounded life to its depths (as he thought), and tasted both the bitter and the sweet; and after having indulged in all these varied experiences it had been given to him, as it is not given to many men, to come back from all wanderings and secure the satisfactions of mature life, wealth, and social importance, and the power of acting in the largest imperial concerns. Round about him everything was his; the noble woods that swept away into the mist on every side; the fields and farms which began to appear in the misty paleness of the morning through the openings in the trees. And if he had not by his side such a companion as he had once dreamed of, the beautiful, high-minded ideal woman of romance, yet he had got one of the best of gentle souls to tread the path of life along with him, and sympathise even when she did not understand. For a man who had not perhaps deserved very much, how unusual was this happiness. And was it possible that all these things should be obscured, cast into the shade, by so small a matter as the sickness of a child? What had the baby ever done to make itself of so much importance? Nothing. It did not even understand the love it excited, and was incapable of making any response. Its very life was little more than a mechanical life. The woman who fed it was far more to it than its father, and there was nothing excellent or noble in the world to which it would not prefer a glittering tinsel or a hideous doll. If the little thing had grown up, indeed, if it had developed human tastes and sympathies, and become a companion, an intelligence, a creature with affections and thoughts,—but that the whole house should thus be overwhelmed with miserable anxiety and pain because of a being in the embryo state of existence, who could neither respond nor understand, what a strange thing it was! No doubt this instinct had been implanted in order to preserve the germ and keep the race going; but that it should thus develop into an absorbing passion and overshadow everything else in life was a proof how the natural gets exaggerated, and, if we do not take care, changes its character altogether, mastering us instead of being kept in its fit place, and in check, as it ought to be by sense and reason. From time to time, as Sir Tom made these reflections, there would flit across his mind, as across a mirror, something which was not thought, which was like a picture momentarily presented before him. One of the most persistent of these, which flashed out and in upon his senses like a view in a magic lantern, was of that moment in the midst of the flurry of the election when little Tom, held up in his mother's arms, had clapped his baby hands for his father. This for a second would confound all his thoughts, and give his heart a pang as if some one had seized and pressed it with an iron grasp; but the next moment he would pick up the thread of his reflections again, and go on with them. That, too, was merely mechanical, like all the little chap's existence up to this point. Poor little chap! here Sir Tom stopped in his course of thought, impeded by a weight at his heart which he could not shake off; nor could he see the blurred and vague landscape round him—something more blinding even than the fog had got into his eyes.

Then Sir Tom started and his heart sprang up to his throat beating loudly. It was not anything of much importance, it was only the opening of the window by which he himself had come out upon the terrace. He turned round quickly, too anxious even to ask a question. If it had been a king's messenger bringing him news that affected the whole kingdom, he would have turned away with an impatient "Pshaw!" or struck the intruder out of his way. But it was his wife, wrapped in a dressing-gown, pale with watching, her hair pushed back upon her forehead, her eyes unnaturally bright. "How is he?" cried Sir Tom, as if the question was one of life or death.

Lucy told him, catching at his arm to support herself, that she thought there was a little improvement. "I have been thinking so for the last hour, not daring to think it, and yet I felt sure; and now nurse says so too. His breathing is easier. I have been on thorns to come and tell you, but I would not till I was quite sure."

"Thank God! God be praised!" said Sir Tom. He did not pretend to be a religious man on ordinary occasions, but at the present moment he had no time to think, and spoke from the bottom of his heart. He supported his little wife tenderly on one arm, and put back the disordered hair on her forehead. "Now you will go and take a little rest, my darling," he said.

"Not yet, not till the doctor comes. But you want it as much as I."

"No; I had a long sleep on the sofa. We are all making fools of ourselves, Lucy. The poor little chap will be all right. We are queer creatures. To think that you and I should make ourselves so miserable over a little thing like that, that knows nothing about it, that has no feelings, that does not care a button for you and me."

"Tom, what are you talking of? Not of my boy, surely—not my boy!"

"Hush, my sweet. Well," said Sir Tom, with a tremulous laugh, "what is it but a little polypus after all? that can do nothing but eat and sleep, and crow perhaps—and clap its little fat hands," he said, with the tears somehow getting into his voice, and mingling with the laughter. "I allow that I am confusing my metaphors."

At this moment the window opening upon the terrace jarred again, and another figure in a dressing-gown, dark and ghost-like, appeared beckoning to Lucy, "My lady! my lady!"

Lucy let go her husband's arm, thrust him away from her with passion, gave him one wild look of reproach, and flew noiselessly like a spirit after the nurse to her child. Sir Tom, with his laugh still wavering about his mouth, half hysterically, though he was no weakling, tottered along the terrace to the open window, and stood there leaning against it, scarcely breathing, the light gone out of his eyes, his whole soul suspended, and every part of his strong body, waiting for what another moment might bring to pass.


CHAPTER IX

A CHRISTMAS VISIT

Little Tom did not die, but he became "delicate,"—and fathers and mothers know what that means. The entire household was possessed by one pervading terror lest he should catch cold, and Lucy's life became absorbed in this constant watchfulness. Naturally the Christmas guests were put off, and it was understood in respect to the Contessa di Forno-Populo, that she was to come at Easter. Sir Tom himself thought this a better arrangement. The Parliamentary recess was not a long one, and the Contessa would naturally prefer, after a short visit to her old friend, to go to town, where she would find so many people she knew.

"And even in the country the weather is more tolerable in April," said Sir Tom.

"Oh, yes, yes. The doctor says if we keep clear of the east winds that he may begin to go out again and get up his strength," said Lucy.

"My love, I am thinking of your visitors, and you are thinking of your baby," Sir Tom said.

"Oh, Tom, what do you suppose I could be thinking of?" his wife cried.

Sir Tom himself was very solicitous about the baby, but to hear of nothing else worried him. He was glad when old Lady Randolph, who was an invariable visitor, arrived.

"How is the baby?" was her first question when he met her at the train.

"The baby would be a great deal better if there was less fuss made about him," he said. "You must give Lucy a hint on that subject, aunt."

Lady Randolph was a good woman, and it was her conviction that she had made this match. But it is so pleasant to feel that you have been right, that she was half pleased, though very sorry, to think that Sir Tom (as she had always known) was getting a little tired of sweet simplicity. She met Lucy with an affectionate determination to be very plain with her, and warn her of the dangers in her path. Jock had arrived the day before. He rose up in all the lanky length of sixteen from the side of the fire in the little drawing-room when the Dowager came in. It was just the room into which one likes to come after a cold journey at Christmas; the fire shining brightly in the midst of the reflectors of burnished steel and brass, shining like gold and silver, of the most luxurious fireplace that skill could contrive (the day of tiled stoves was not as yet), and sending a delicious glow on the soft mossy carpets into which the foot sank; a table with tea, reflecting the firelight in all the polished surfaces of the china and silver, stood near; and chairs invitingly drawn towards the fire. The only drawback was that there was no one to welcome the visitor. On ordinary occasions Lucy was at the door, if not at the station, to receive the kind lady whom she loved. Lady Randolph was somewhat surprised at the difference, and when she saw the lengthy boy raising himself up from the fireside, turned round to her nephew and asked, "Do I know this young gentleman? There is not light enough to see him," with a voice in which Jock, shy and awkward, felt all the old objection to his presence as a burden upon Lucy, which in his precocious toleration he had accepted as reasonable, but did not like much the better for that. And then she sat down somewhat sullenly at the fire. The next minute Lucy came hastily in with many apologies: "I did not hear the carriage, aunt. I was in the nursery—"

"And how is the child?" Lady Randolph said.

"Oh, he is a great deal better—don't you think he is much better, Tom? Only a little delicate, and that, we hope, will pass away."

"Then, Lucy, my dear, though I don't want to blame you, I think you should have heard the carriage," said Aunt Randolph. "The tea-table does not look cheerful when the mistress of the house is away."

"Oh, but little Tom—" Lucy said, and then stopped herself, with a vague sense that there was not so much sympathy around her as usual. Her husband had gone out again, and Jock stood dumb, an awkward shadow against the mantelpiece.

"My dear, I only speak for your good," the elder lady said. "Big Tom wants a little attention too. I thought you were going to have quite a merry Christmas and a great many people here."

"But, Aunt Randolph, baby—"

"Oh, my dear, you must think of something else besides baby. Take my word for it, baby would be a great deal stronger if you left him a little to himself. You have your husband, you know, to think of, and what harm would it have done baby if there had been a little cheerful company for his father? But you will think I have come to scold, and I don't in the least mean that. Give me a cup of tea, Lucy. Tom tells me that this tall person is Jock."

"You would not have known him?" said Lucy, much subdued in tone.

She occupied herself with the tea, arranging the cups and saucers with hands that trembled a little at the unexpected and unaccustomed sensation of a repulse.

"Well, I cannot even see him. But he has certainly grown out of knowledge—I never thought he would have been so tall; he was quite a little pinched creature as a child. I daresay you took too much care of him, my dear. I remember I used to think so; and then when he was tossed into the world or sent to school—it comes to much the same thing, I suppose—he flourished and grew."

"I wonder," said Lucy, somewhat wistfully, "if that is really so? Certainly it is since he has been at school that he has grown so much." Jock all this time fidgeted about from one leg to another with unutterable darkness upon his brow, could any one have seen it. There are few things so irritating, especially at his age, as to be thus discussed over one's own head.

"My dear Lucy," said Lady Randolph, "don't you remember some one says—who was it, I wonder? it sounds like one of those dreadfully clever French sayings that are always so much to the point—about the advantages of a little wholesome neglect?"

"Can neglect ever be wholesome? Oh, I don't think so—I can't think so—at least with children."

"It is precisely children that are meant," said the elder Lady Randolph. But as she talked, sitting in the warm light of the fire, with her cup in her hand, feeling extremely comfortable, discoursing at her ease, and putting sharp arrows as if they had been pins into the heart of Lucy, Sir Tom's large footsteps became audible coming through the great drawing-room, which was dark. The very sound of him was cheerful as he came in, and he brought the scent of fresh night air, cold but delightful, with him. He passed by Lucy's chair and said, "How is the little 'un?" laying a kind hand upon her head.

"Oh, better. I am sure he is better. Aunt Randolph thinks—"

"I am giving Lucy a lecture," said Lady Randolph, "and telling her she must not shut herself up with that child. He'll get on all the better if he is not coddled too much."

Sir Tom made no reply, but came to the fire, and drew a chair into the cheerful glow. "You are all in the dark," he said, "but the fire is pleasant this cold night. Well, now that you are thawed, what news have you brought us out of the world? We are two hermits, Lucy and I. We forget what kind of language you speak. We have a little sort of talk of our own which answers common needs about babies and so forth, but we should like to hear what you are discoursing about, just for a change."

"There is no such thing as a world just now," said Lady Randolph, "there are nothing but country-houses. Society is all broken up into little bits, as you know as well as I do. One gleans a little here and a little there, and one carries it about like a basket of eggs."

"Jock has a world, and it is quite entire," said Sir Tom, with his cordial laugh. "No breaking up into little bits there. If you want a society that knows its own opinions, and will stick to them through thick and thin, I can tell you where to find it; and to see how it holds together and sits square whatever happens—"

Here there came a sort of falsetto growl from Jock's corner, where he was blushing in the firelight. "It's because you were once a fellow yourself, and know all about it."

"So it is, Jock; you are right, as usual," said Sir Tom; "I was once a fellow myself, and now I'm an old fellow, and growing duller. Turn out your basket of eggs, Aunt Randolph, and let us know what is going on. Where did you come from last—the Mulberrys? Come; there must have been some pretty pickings of gossip there."

"You shall have it all in good time. I am not going to run myself dry the first hour. I want to know about yourselves, and when you are going to give up this honeymooning. I expected to have met all sorts of people here."

"Yes," said Sir Tom, and then he burst forth in a laugh, "La Forno-Populo and a few others; but as little Tom is not quite up to visitors, we have put them off till Easter."

"La Forno-Populo!" said Lady Randolph, in a voice of dismay.

"Why not?" said Sir Tom. "She wrote and offered herself. I thought she might find it a doubtful pleasure, but if she likes it— However, you may make yourself easy, nobody is coming," he added, with a certain jar of impatience in his tone.

"Well, Tom, I must say I am very glad of that," Lady Randolph said gravely—and then there was a pause. "I doubt whether Lucy would have liked her," she added, after a moment. Then with another interval, "I think, Lucy, my love, after that nice cup of tea, and my first sight of you, that I will go to my own room. I like a little rest before dinner—you know my lazy way."

"And it's getting ridiculously dark in this room," Sir Tom said, kicking a footstool out of the way. This little impatient movement was like one of those expletives that seem to relieve a man's mind, and both the ladies understood it as such, and knew that he was angry. Lucy, as she rose from her tea-table to attend upon her visitor, herself in a confused and painful mood, and vexed with what had been said to her, thought her husband was irritated by his aunt, and felt much sympathy with him, and anxiety to conduct Lady Randolph to her room before it should go any farther. But the elder lady understood it very differently. She went away, followed by Lucy through the great drawing-room, where a solitary lamp had been placed on a table to show the way. It had been the Dowager's own house in her day, and she did not require any guidance to her room. Nor did she detain Lucy after the conventional visit to see that all was comfortable.

"That I haven't the least doubt of," Lady Randolph said, "and I am at home, you know, and will ask for anything I want; but I must have my nap before dinner; and do you go and talk to your husband."

Lucy could not resist one glance into the nursery, where little Tom, a little languid but so much better, was sitting on his nurse's knee before the fire, amused by those little fables about his fingers and toes which are the earliest of all dramatic performances. The sight of him thus content, and the sound of his laugh, was sweet to her in her anxiety. She ran downstairs again without disturbing him, closing so carefully the double doors that shut him out from all draughts, not without a wondering doubt as she did so, whether it was true, perhaps, that she was "coddling" him, and if there was such a thing as wholesome neglect. She went quickly through the dim drawing-room to the warm ruddy flush of firelight that shone between the curtains from the smaller room, thinking nothing less than to find her husband, who was fond of an hour's repose in that kindly light before dinner. She had got to her old place in front of the fire before she perceived that Sir Tom's tall shadow was no longer there. Lucy uttered a little exclamation of disappointment, and then she perceived remorsefully another shadow, not like Sir Tom's, the long weedy boyish figure of her brother against the warm light.

"But you are here, Jock," she said, advancing to him. Jock took hold of her arm, as he was so fond of doing.

"I shall never have you, now she has come," Jock said.

"Why not, dear? You were never fond of Lady Randolph—you don't know how good and kind she is. It is only when you like people that you know how nice they are," Lucy said, all unconscious that a deeper voice than hers had announced that truth.

"Then I shall never know, for I don't like her," said Jock uncompromising. "You'll have to sit and gossip with her when you're not in the nursery, and I shall have no time to tell you, for the holidays last only a month."

"But you can tell me everything in a month, you silly boy; and if we can't have our walks, Jock (for it's cold), there is one place where she will never come," said Lucy, upon which Jock turned away with an exclamation of impatience.

His sister put her hand on his shoulder and looked reproachfully in his face.

"You too! You used to like it. You used to come and toss him up and make him laugh—"

"Oh, don't, Lucy! can't you see? So I would again, if he were like that. How you can bear it!" said the boy, bursting away from her. And then Jock returned very much ashamed and horror-stricken, and took the hand that dropped by her side, and clumsily patted and kissed it, and held it between his own, looking penitently, wistfully, in her face all the while: but not knowing what to say.

Lucy stood looking down into the glowing fire, with her head drooping and an air of utter dejection in her little gentle figure. "Do you think he looks so bad as that?" she said, in a broken voice.

"Oh, no, no; that is not what I mean," the boy cried. "It's—the little chap is not so jolly; he's—a little cross; or else he's forgotten me. I suppose it's that. He wouldn't look at me when I ran up. He's so little one oughtn't to mind, but it made me—your baby, Lucy! and the little beggar cried and wouldn't look at me."

"Is that all?" said Lucy. She only half believed him, but she pretended to be deceived. She gave a little trembling laugh, and laid her head for a moment upon Jock's boyish breast, where his heart was beating high with a passion of sorrow and tender love. "Sometimes," she said, leaning against him, "sometimes I think I shall die. I can't live to see anything happen to him: and sometimes— But he is ever so much better; don't you think he looks almost himself?" she said, raising her head hurriedly, and interrogating the scarcely visible face with her eyes.

"Looks! I don't see much difference in his looks, if he wouldn't be so cross," said Jock, lying boldly, but with a tremor, for he was not used to it. And then he said hurriedly, "But there's that clergyman, the father of the fellow on the foundation. I've found out all about him. I must tell you, Lucy. He is the very man. There is no call to think about it or put off any longer. What a thing it would be if he could have it by Christmas! I have got all the particulars—they look as if they were just made for us," Jock cried.

CHAPTER X

Lady Randolph found her visit dull. It is true that there had been no guests to speak of on previous Christmases since Sir Tom's marriage; but the house had been more cheerful, and Lucy had been ready to drive, or walk, or call, or go out to the festivities around. But now she was absorbed by the nursing, and never liked to be an hour out of call. The Dowager put up with it as long as she was able. She did not say anything more on the subject for some days. It was not, indeed, until she had been a week at the Hall that, being disturbed by the appeals of Lucy as to whether she did not think baby was looking better than when she came, she burst forth at last. They were sitting by themselves in the hour after dinner when ladies have the drawing-room all to themselves. It is supposed by young persons in novels to be a very dreary interval, but to the great majority of women it is a pleasant moment. The two ladies sat before the pleasant fire; Lucy with some fleecy white wool in her lap with which she was knitting something for her child, Lady Randolph with a screen interposed between her and the fire, doing nothing, an operation which she always performed gracefully and comfortably. It could not be said that the gentlemen were lingering over their wine. Jock had retired to the library, where he was working through all the long-collected literary stores of the Randolph family, with an instinctive sense that his presence in the drawing-room was not desired. Sir Tom had business to do, or else he was tired of the domestic calm. The ladies had been sitting for some time in silence when Lady Randolph suddenly broke forth—

"You know what I said to you the first evening, Lucy? I have not said a word on the subject since—of course I didn't come down here to enjoy your hospitality and then to find fault."

"Oh, Aunt Randolph! don't speak of hospitality; it is your own house."

"My dear, it is very pretty of you to say so. I hope I am not the sort of person to take advantage of it. But I feel a sort of responsibility, seeing it was I that brought you together first. Lucy, I must tell you. You are not doing what you ought by Tom. Here he is, a middle-aged man, you know, and one of the first in the county. People look to him for a great many things: he is the member: he is a great landowner: he is (thanks to you) very well off. And here is Christmas, and not a visitor in the house but myself. Oh, there's Jock! a schoolboy home for his holidays—that does not count; not a single dinner that I can hear of—"

"Yes, aunt, on the 6th," said Lucy, with humility.

"On the 6th, and it is now the 27th! and no fuss at all made about Christmas. My dear, you needn't tell me it's a bore. I know it is a bore—everywhere wherever one goes; still, everybody does it. It is just a part of one's responsibilities. You don't go to balls in Lent, and you stand on your heads, so to speak, at Christmas. The country expects it of you; and it is always a mistake to take one's own way in such matters. You should have had, in the first place," said Lady Randolph, counting on her fingers, "your house full; in the second, a ball, to which everybody should have been asked. On these occasions no one that could possibly be imagined to be gentlefolk should be left out. I would even stretch a point— doctors and lawyers, and so forth, go without saying, and those big brewers, you know, I always took in; and some people go as far as the 'vet.,' as they call him. He was a very objectionable person in my day, and that was where I drew the line; then three or four dinners at the least."

"But, Aunt Randolph, how could we when baby is so poorly—"

"What has baby to do with it, Lucy? You don't have the child down to receive your guests. With the door of his nursery shut to keep out the noise (if you think it necessary: I shouldn't think it would matter) what harm would it do him? He would never be a bit the wiser, poor little dear. Yes, I dare say your heart would be with him many a time when you were elsewhere; but you must not think of yourself."

"I did not mean to do so, aunt. I thought little Tom was my first duty."

"Now, I should have thought, my dear," said the Dowager, smiling blandly, "that it would have been big Tom who answered to that description."

"But, Tom—" Lucy paused, not knowing in what shape to put so obvious a truth, "he is like me," she said. "He is far, far more anxious than he lets you see. It is his—duty too."

"A great many other things are his duty as well; besides, there is so much, especially in a social point of view, which the man never sees till his wife points it out. That's one of the uses of a woman. She must keep up her husband's popularity, don't you see? You must never let it be said: 'Oh, Sir Tom! he is all very well in Parliament, but he does nothing for the county.'"

"I never thought of that," said Lucy, with dismay.

"But you must learn to think of it, my love. Never mind, this is the first Christmas since the election. But one dinner, and nothing else done, not so much as a magic lantern in the village! I do assure you, my dearest girl, you are very much to blame."

"I am very sorry," said Lucy, with a startled look, "but, dear aunt, little Tom—"

"My dear Lucy! I am sure you don't wish everybody to get sick of that poor child's very name."

Lucy sprang up from her chair at this outrage; she could not bear any more. A flush of almost fury came upon her face. She went up to the mantelpiece, which was a very fine one of carved wood, and leant her head upon it. She did not trust herself to reply.

"Now, I know what you are thinking," said Lady Randolph blandly. "You are saying to yourself, that horrid old woman, who never had a child, how can she know?—and I don't suppose I do," said the clever Dowager pathetically. "All that sweetness has been denied to me. I have never had a little creature that was all mine. But when I was your age, Lucy, and far older than you, I would have given anything—almost my life—to have had a child."

Lucy melted in a moment, threw herself down upon the hearth-rug upon her knees, and took Lady Randolph's hands in her own and kissed them.

"Oh, dear aunt, dear aunt!" she cried, "to think I should have gone on so about little Tom and never remembered that you— But we are all your children," she said, in the innocence and fervour of her heart.

"Yes, my love." Lady Randolph freed one of her hands and put it up with her handkerchief to her cheek. As a matter of fact she did not regret it now, but felt that a woman when she is growing old is really much more able to look after her own comforts when she has no children; and yet, when she remembered how she had been bullied on the subject, and all the reproaches that had been addressed to her as if it were her fault, perhaps there was something like a tear. "That is why I venture to say many things to you that I would not otherwise. Tom, indeed, is too old to have been my son; but I have felt, Lucy, as if I had a daughter in you." Then shaking off this little bit of sentiment with a laugh, the Dowager raised Lucy and kissed her and put her into a chair by her own side.

"Since we are about it," she said, "there is one other thing I should like to talk to you about. Of course your husband knows a great deal more of the world than you do, Lucy; but it is perhaps better that he should not decide altogether who is to be asked. Men have such strange notions. If people are amusing it is all they think of. Well, now, there is that Contessa di Forno-Populo. I would not have her, Lucy, if I were you."

"But it was she who was the special person," said Lucy, in amaze. "The others were to come to meet her. She is an old friend."

"Oh, I know all about the old friendship," said Lady Randolph. "I think Tom should be ashamed of himself. He knows that in other houses where the mistress knows more about the world. Yes, yes, she is an old friend. All the more reason, my dear, why you should have as little to say to her as possible; they are never to be reckoned upon. Didn't you hear what he called her. La Forno-Populo? Englishmen never talk of a lady like that if they have any great respect for her; but it can't be denied that this lady has a great deal of charm. And I would just keep her at arm's length, Lucy, if I were you."

"Dear Aunt Randolph, why should I do that?" said Lucy, gravely. "If she is Tom's friend, she must always be welcome here. I do not know her, therefore I can only welcome her for my husband's sake; but that is reason enough. You must not ask me to do anything that is against Tom."

"Against Tom! I think you are a little goose, Lucy, though you are so sensible. Is it not all for his sake that I am talking? I want you to see more of the world, not to shut yourself up here in the nursery entirely on his account. If you don't understand that, then words have no meaning."

"I do understand it, aunt," said Lucy meekly. "Don't be angry; but why should I be disagreeable to Tom's friend? The only thing I am afraid of is, should she not speak English. My French is so bad—"

"Oh, your French will do very well; and you will take your own way, my dear," said the elder lady, getting up. "You all do, you young people. The opinion of others never does any good; and as Tom does not seem to be coming, I think I shall take my way to bed. Good-night, Lucy. Remember what I said, at all events, about the magic lantern. And if you are wise you will have as little to do as possible with La Forno-Populo as you can—and there you have my two pieces of advice."

Lucy was disturbed a little by her elder's counsel, both in respect to the foreign lady, whom, however, she simply supposed Lady Randolph did not like—and in regard to her own nursery tastes and avoidance of society;—could that be why Tom sat so much longer in the dining-room and did not come in to talk to his aunt? She began to think with a little ache in her heart, and to remember that in her great preoccupation with the child he had been left to spend many evenings alone, and that he no longer complained of this. She stood up in front of the fire and pressed her hot forehead to the mantel-shelf. How was a woman to know what to do? Was not he that was most helpless and had most need of her the one to devote her time to? There was not a thought in her that was disloyal to Sir Tom. But what if he were to form the habit of doing without her society? This was an idea that filled her with a vague dread. Some one came in through the great drawing-room as she stood thinking, and she turned round eagerly, supposing that it was her husband; but it was only Jock, who had been on the watch to hear Lady Randolph go upstairs.

"I never see you at all now, Lucy," cried Jock. "I never have a chance but in the holidays, and now they're half over, and we have not had one good talk. And what about poor Mr. Churchill, Lucy? I thought he was the very man for you. He has got about a dozen children and no money. Somebody else pays for Churchill, that's the fellow I told you of that's on the foundation. I shouldn't have found out all that, and gone and asked questions and got myself thought an inquisitive beggar, if it hadn't been for your sake."

"Oh, Jock, I'm sure I am much obliged to you," said Lucy, dolefully; "and I am so sorry for the poor gentleman. It must be dreadful to have so many children and not to be able to give them everything they require."

At this speech, which was uttered with something between impatience and despair, and which made no promise of any help or succour, her brother regarded her with a mixture of anger and disappointment.

"Is that all about it, Lucy?" he said.

"Oh, no, Jock! I am sure you are right, dear. I know I ought to bestir myself and do something, but only— How much do you think it would take to make them comfortable? Oh, Jock, I wish that papa had put it all into somebody's hands, to be done like business—somebody that had nothing else to think of!"

"What have you to think of, Lucy?" said the boy, seriously, in the superiority of his youth. "I suppose, you know, you are just too well off. You can't understand what it is to be like that. You get angry at people for not being happy, you don't want to be disturbed." He paused remorsefully, and cast a glance at her, melting in spite of himself, for Lucy did not look too well off. Her soft brow was contracted a little; there was a faint quiver upon her lip. "If you really want to know," Jock said, "people can live and get along when they have about five hundred a year. That is, as far as I can make out. If you gave them that, they would think it awful luck."

"I wish I could give them all of it, and be done with it!"

"I don't see much good that would do. It would be two rich people in place of one, and the two would not be so grand as you. That would not have done for father at all. He liked you to be a great heiress, and everybody to wonder at you, and then to give your money away like a queen. I like it too," said Jock, throwing up his head; "it satisfies the imagination: it is a kind of a fairy tale."

Lucy shook her head.

"He never thought how hard it would be upon me. A woman is never so well off as a man. Oh, if it had been you, Jock, and I only just your sister."

"Talking does not bring us any nearer a settlement," said Jock, with some impatience. "When will you do it, Lucy? Have you got to speak to old Rushton, or write to old Chervil, or what? or can't you just draw them a cheque? I suppose about ten thousand or so would be enough. And it is as easy to do it at one time as another. Why not to-morrow, Lucy? and then you would have it off your mind."

This proposal took away Lucy's breath. She thought with a gasp of Sir Tom and the look with which he would regard her—the laugh, the amused incredulity. He would not be unkind, and her right to do it was quite well established and certain. But she shrank within herself when she thought how he would look at her, and her heart jumped into her throat as she realised that perhaps he might not laugh only. How could she stand before him and carry her own war in opposition to his? Her whole being trembled even with the idea of conflict. "Oh, Jock, it is not just so easily managed as that," she said faltering; "there are several things to think of. I will have to let the trustees know, and it must all be calculated."

"There is not much need for calculation," said Jock, "that is just about it. Five per cent is what you get for money. You had better send the cheque for it, Lucy, and then let the old duffers know of it afterwards. One would think you were afraid!"

"Oh, no," said Lucy, with a slight shiver, "I am not afraid." And then she added, with growing hesitation, "I must—speak to— Oh! Is it you, Tom?" She made a sudden start from Jock's side, who was standing close by her, argumentative and eager, and whose bewildered spectatorship of her guilty surprise and embarrassment she was conscious of through all.

"Yes, it is I," said Sir Tom, putting his hand upon her shoulders; "you must have been up to some mischief, Jock and you, or you would not look so frightened. What is the secret?" he said, with his genial laugh. But when he looked from Jock, astonished but resentful and lowering, to Lucy, all trembling and pale with guilt, even Sir Tom, who was not suspicious, was startled. His little Lucy! What had she been plotting that made her look so scared at his appearance? Or was it something that had been told to her, some secret accusation against himself? This startled Sir Tom also a little, and it was with a sudden gravity, not unmingled with resentment, that he added, "Come! I mean to know what it is."


CHAPTER XI

AN INNOCENT CONSPIRACY

"It was only something that Jock was saying," said Lucy, "but, Tom, I will tell you another time. I wish you had come in before Lady Randolph went upstairs. I think she was a little disappointed to have only me."

"Did she share Jock's secret?" Sir Tom said with a keen look of inquiry. It is perhaps one advantage in the dim light which fashion delights in, that it is less easy to scrutinise the secrets of a face.

"We are all a little put wrong when you do not come in," said Lucy. The cunning which weakness finds refuge in when it has to defend itself came to her aid. "Jock is shy when you are not here. He thinks he bores Lady Randolph; and so we ladies are left to our own devices."

"Jock must not be so sensitive," Sir Tom said; but he was not satisfied. It occurred to him suddenly (for schoolboys are terrible gossips) that the boy might have heard something which he had been repeating to Lucy. Nothing could have been more unlikely, had he thought of it, than that Jock should carry tales on such a subject. But we do not stop to argue out matters when our own self-regard is in question. He looked at the two with a doubtful and suspicious eye.

"He will get over it as he grows older," said Lucy; but she gave her brother a look which to Sir Tom seemed one of warning, and he was irritated by it; he looked from one to another and he laughed; but not with the genial laugh which was his best known utterance.

"You are prodigiously on your guard," he said. "I suppose you have your reasons for it. Have you been confiding the Masons' secret or something of that awful character to her, Jock?"

"Why shouldn't I tell him?" cried Jock with great impatience. "What is the use of making all those signs? It's nothing of the sort. It's only I've heard of somebody that is poor—somebody she ought to know of—the sort of thing that is meant in father's will."

"Oh!" said Sir Tom. It was the simplest of exclamations, but it meant much. He was partially relieved that it was not gossip, but yet more gravely annoyed than if it had been.

Lucy made haste to interpose.

"I will tell you afterwards," she said. "If I made signs, as Jock said, it was only that I might tell it you, Tom, myself, when there was more time."

"I am at no loss for time," said Sir Tom, placing himself in the vacant chair. The others were both standing, as became this accidental moment before bed-time. And Lucy had been on thorns to get away, even before her husband appeared. She had wanted to escape from the discussion even with Jock. She had wanted to steal into the nursery, and see that her boy was asleep, to feel his little forehead with her soft hand, and make sure there was no fever. To be betrayed into a prolonged and agitating discussion now was very provoking, very undesirable; and Lucy had grown rather cowardly and anxious to push away from her, as far as she could, everything that did not belong to the moment.

"Tom," she said, a little tremulously, "I wish you would put it off till to-morrow. I am—rather sleepy; it is nearly eleven o'clock, and I always run in to see how little Tom is going on. Besides," she added, with a little anxiety which was quite fictitious, "it is keeping Fletcher up—"

"I am not afraid of Fletcher, Lucy."

"Oh! but I am," she said. "I will tell you about it to-morrow. There is nothing in the least settled, only Jock thought—"

"Settled!" Sir Tom said, with a curious look. "No, I hope not."

"Oh! nothing at all settled," said Lucy. She stood restlessly, now on one foot now on the other, eager for flight. She did not even observe the implied authority in this remark, at which Jock pricked up his ears with incipient offence. "And Jock ought to be in bed—oh, yes, Jock, you ought. I am sure you are not allowed to sit up so late at school. Come now, there's a good boy—and I will just run and see how baby is."

She put her hand on her brother's arm to take him away with her, but Jock hung back, and Sir Tom interposed, "Now that I have just settled myself for a chat, you had better leave Jock with me at least, Lucy. Run away to your baby, that is all right. Jock and I will entertain each other. I respect his youth, you see, and don't try to seduce him into a cigar—you should be thankful to me for that."

"If I was not in sixth form," said Jock sharply, nettled by this indignity, "I should smoke; but it is bad form when you are high up in school. In the holidays I don't mind," he added, with careless grandeur, upon which Sir Tom, mollified, laughed as Lucy felt like himself.

"Off duty, eh?" he said, "that's a very fine sentiment, Jock. You may be sure it's bad form to do anything you have promised not to do. You will say that sounds like a copy-book. Come now, Lucy, are not you going, little woman? Do you want to have your share in the moralities?"

For this sudden change had somehow quenched Lucy's desire both to inspect the baby and get to bed. But what could she do? She looked very earnestly at Jock as she bade him good-night, but neither could she shake his respect for her husband by giving him any warning, nor offend her husband by any appearance of secret intelligence with Jock. Poor little Lucy went away after this through the stately rooms and up the grand staircase with a great tremor in her heart. There could not be a life more guarded and happy than hers had been—full of wealth, full of love, not a crumpled rose-leaf to disturb her comfort. But as she stole along the dim corridor to the nursery her heart was beating full of all the terrors that make other hearts to ache. She was afraid for the child's life, which was the worst of all, and looked with a suppressed yet terrible panic into the dark future which contained she knew not what for him. And she was afraid of her husband, the kindest man in the world, not knowing how he might take the discovery he had just made, fearing to disclose her mind to him, finding herself guilty in the mere idea of hiding anything from him. And she was afraid of Jock, that he would irritate Sir Tom, or be irritated by him, or that some wretched breach or quarrel might arise between these two. Jock was not an ordinary boy; there was no telling how he might take any reproof that might be addressed to him— perhaps with the utmost reasonableness, perhaps with a rapid defiance. Lady Randolph thus, though no harm had befallen her, had come into the usual heritage of humanity, and was as anxious and troubled as most of us are; though she was so happy and well off. She was on thorns to know what was passing in the room she had just left.

This was all that passed. Jock, standing up against the mantelpiece, looked down somewhat lowering upon Sir Tom in the easy chair. He expected to be questioned, and had made up his mind, though with great indignation at the idea that any one should find fault with Lucy, to take the whole blame upon himself. That Lucy should not be free to carry out her duty as seemed to her best was to Jock intolerable. He had put his boyish faith in her all his life. Even since the time, a very early one, when Jock had felt himself much cleverer than Lucy; even when he had been obliged to make up his mind that Lucy was not clever at all—he had still believed in her. She had a mission in the world which separated her from other women. Nobody else had ever had the same thing to do. Many people had dispensed charities and founded hospitals, but Lucy's office in the world was of a different description—and Jock had faith in her power to do it. To see her wavering was trouble to him, and the discovery he had just made of something beneath the surface, a latent opposition in her husband which she plainly shrank from encountering, gave the boy a shock from which it was not easy to recover. He had always liked Sir Tom; but if— One thing, however, was apparent, if there was any blame, anything to find fault with, it was he, Jock, and not Lucy, that must bear that blame.

"So, Jock, Lucy thinks you should be in bed. When do they put out your lights at school? In my time we were up to all manner of tricks. I remember a certain dark lantern that was my joy; but that was in old Keate's time, you know, who never trusted the fellows. You are under a better rule now."

This took away Jock's breath, who had been prepared for a sterner interrogation. He answered with a sudden blush, but with the rallying of all his forces: "I light them again sometimes. It's hard on a fellow, don't you think, sir, when he's not sleepy and has a lot to do?"

"I never had much experience of that," said Sir Tom. "We were always sleepy, and never did anything in my time. It was for larking, I'm afraid, that we wanted light. And so it is seen on me, Jock. You will be a fellow of your college, whereas I—"

"I don't think so," said Jock generously. "That construe you gave me, don't you remember, last half? MTutor says it is capital. He says he couldn't have done it so well. Of course, that is his modest way," the boy added, "for everybody knows there isn't such another scholar! but that's what he says."

Sir Tom laughed, and a slight suffusion of colour appeared on his face. He was pleased with this unexpected applause. At five-and-forty, after knocking about the world for years, and "never opening a book," as people say, to have given a good "construe" is a feather in one's cap. "To be second to your tutor is all a man has to hope for," he said, with that mellow laugh which it was so pleasant to hear. "I hope I know my place, Jock. We had no such godlike beings in my time. Old Puck, as we used to call him, was my tutor. He had a red nose, which was the chief feature in his character. He looked upon us all as his natural enemies, and we paid him back with interest. Did I ever tell of that time when we were going to Ascot in a cab, four of us, and he caught sight of the turn-out?"

"I don't think so," said Jock, with a little hesitation. He remembered every detail of this story, which indeed Sir Tom had told him perhaps more than once; for in respect to such legends the best of us repeat ourselves. Many were the thoughts in the boy's mind as he stood against the mantelpiece and looked down upon the man before him, going over with much relish the tale of boyish mischief, the delight of the urchins and the pedagogue's discomfiture. Sir Tom threw himself back in his chair with a peal of joyous laughter.

"Jove! I think I can see him now with the corners of his mouth all dropped, and his nose like a beacon," he cried. Jock meanwhile looked down upon him very gravely, though he smiled in courtesy. He was a different manner of boy from anything Sir Tom could ever have been, and he wondered, as young creatures will, over the little world of mystery and knowledge which was shut up within the elder man. What things he had done in his life—what places he had seen! He had lived among savages, and fought his way, and seen death and life. Jock, only on the threshold, gazed at him with a curious mixture of awe and wonder and kind contempt. He would himself rather look down upon a fellow (he thought) who did that sort of practical joke now. MTutor would regard such an individual as a natural curiosity. And yet here was this man who had seen so much, and done so much, who ought to have profited by the long results of time, and grown to such superiority and mental elevation—here was he, turning back with delight to the schoolboy's trick. It filled Jock with a great and compassionate wonder. But he was a very civil boy. He was one who could not bear to hurt a fellow-creature's feelings, even those of an old duffer whose recollections were all of the bygone ages. So he did his best to laugh. And Sir Tom enjoyed his own joke so much that he did not know that it was from the lips only that his young companion's laugh came. He got up and patted Jock on the shoulders with the utmost benevolence when this pastime was done.

"They don't indulge in that sort of fooling nowadays," he said. "So much the better—though I don't know that it did us much harm. Now come along, let us go to bed, according to my lady's orders. We must all, you know, do what Lucy tells us in this house."

Jock obeyed, feeling somewhat "shut up," as he called it, in a sort of blank of confused discomfiture. Sir Tom had the best of it, by whatever means he attained that end. The boy had intended to offer himself a sacrifice, to brave anything that an angry man could say to him for Lucy's sake, and at the same time to die if necessary for Lucy's right to carry out her father's will, and accomplish her mission uninterrupted and untrammelled. When lo, Sir Tom had taken to telling him schoolboy stories, and sent him to bed with good-humoured kindness, without leaving him the slightest opening either to defend Lucy or take blame upon himself. He was half angry, and humbled in his own esteem, but there was nothing for it but to submit. Sir Tom for his part, did not go to bed. He went and smoked a lonely cigar, and his face lost its genial smile. The light of it, indeed, disappeared altogether under a cloud, as he sat gravely over his fire and puffed the smoke away. He had the air of a man who had a task to do which was not congenial to him. "Poor little soul," he said to himself. He could not bear to vex her. There was nothing in the world that he would have grudged to his wife. Any luxury, any adornment that he could have procured for her he would have jumped at. But it was his fate to be compelled to oppose and subdue her instead. The only thing was to do it quickly and decisively, since done it must be. If she had been a warrior worthy of his steel, a woman who would have defended herself and held her own, it would have been so much more easy; but it was not without a compunction that Sir Tom thought of the disproportion of their forces, of the soft and compliant creature who had never raised her will against his or done other than accept his suggestions and respond to his guidance. He remembered how Lucy had stuck to her colours before her marriage, and how she had vanquished the unwilling guardians who regarded what they thought the squandering of her money with a consternation and fury that were beyond bounds. He had thought it highly comic at the time, and even now there passed a gleam of humour over his face at the recollection. He could not deny himself a smile when he thought it all over. She had worsted her guardians, and thrown away her money triumphantly, and Sir Tom had regarded the whole as an excellent joke. But the recollection of this did not discourage him now. He had no thought that Lucy would stand out against him. It might vex her, however, dear little woman. No doubt she and Jock had been making up some fine Quixotic plans between them, and probably it would be a shock to her when her husband interfered. He had got to be so fond of his little wife, and his heart was so kind, that he could not bear the idea of vexing Lucy. But still it would have to be done. He rose up at last, and threw away the end of his cigar with a look of vexation and trouble. It was necessary, but it was a nuisance, however. "If it were done when 'tis done, then 'twere well it were done quickly," he said to himself; then laughed again, as he took his way upstairs, at the over-significance of the words. He was not going to murder anybody; only when the moment proved favourable, for once and only once, seeing it was inevitable, he had to bring under lawful authority—an easy task—the gentle little feminine creature who was his wife.

## CHAPTER XII

### THE FIRST STRUGGLE

Lucy knew nothing of this till the next forenoon after breakfast, and after the many morning occupations which a lady has in her own house. She looked wistfully at both her brother and her husband when they met at table, and it was a great consolation to her, and lightening of her heart, when she perceived that they were quite at ease with each other; but still she was burning with curiosity to know what had passed. Sir Tom had not said a word. He had been just as usual, not even looking a consciousness of the unexplained question between them. She was glad and yet half sorry that all was about to blow over, and to be as if it had not been. After going so far, perhaps it would have been better that it had gone farther and that the matter had been settled. This she said to herself in the security of a respite, believing that it had passed away from Sir Tom's mind. She wanted to know, and yet she was afraid to ask, for her heart revolted against asking questions of Jock which might betray to him the fear of a possible quarrel. After she had superintended little Tom's toilet, and watched him go out for his walk (for the weather was very mild for the time of the year), and seen Mrs. Freshwater, the housekeeper, and settled about the dinner, always with a little quiver of anxiety in her heart, she met Jock by a happy chance, just as she was about to join Lady Randolph in the drawing-room. She seized his arm with energy, and drew him within the door of the library; but after she had done this with an eagerness not to be disguised, Lucy suddenly remembered all that it was inexpedient for her to betray to Jock. Accordingly she stopped short, as it were, on the threshold, and instead of saying as she had intended, "What did he say to you?" dropped down into the routine question, "Where are you going—were you going out?"

"I shall some time, I suppose. What do you grip a fellow's arm for like that? and then when I thought you had something important to say to me, only asking am I going out?"

"Yes, clear," said Lucy, recovering herself with an effort. "You don't take enough exercise. I wish you would not be always among the books."

"Stuff, Lucy!" said Jock.

"I am sure Tom thinks the same. He was telling me—now didn't he say something to you about it last night?"

"That's all bosh," said the boy. "And if you want to know what he said to me last night, he just said nothing at all, but told me old stories of school that I've heard a hundred times. These old d— fellows," (Jock did not swear; he was going to say duffers, that was all) "always talk like that. One would think they had not had much fun in their life when they are always turning back upon school," Jock added, with fine sarcasm.

"Oh, only stories about school!" said Lucy with extreme relief. But the next moment she was not quite so sure that she was comfortable about this entire ignoring of a matter which Sir Tom had seemed to think so grave. "What sort of stories?" she said dreamily, pursuing her own thoughts without much attention to the answer.

"Oh, that old stuff about Ascot and about the old master that stopped them. It isn't much. I know it," said Jock, disrespectfully, "as well as I know my a, b, c."

"It is very rude of you to say so, Jock."

"Perhaps it is rude," the boy replied, with candour; but he did not further explain himself, and Lucy, to veil her mingled relief and disquietude, dismissed him with an exhortation to go out.

"You read and read," she cried, glad to throw off a little excitement in this manner, though she really felt very little anxiety on the subject, "till you will be all brains and nothing else. I wish you would use your legs a little too." And then, with a little affectionate push away from her, she left him in undisturbed possession of his books, and the morning, which, fine as it was, was not bright enough to tempt him away from them.

Then Lucy pursued her way to the drawing-room: but she had not gone many steps before she met her husband, who stopped and asked her a question or two. Had the boy gone out? It was so fine it would do him good, poor little beggar; and where was her ladyship going? When he heard she was going to join the Dowager, Sir Tom smilingly took her hand and drew it within his own. "Then come here with me for a minute first," he said. And strange to say, Lucy had no fear. She allowed him to have his way, thinking it was to show her something, perhaps to ask her advice on some small matter. He took her into a little room he had, full of trophies of his travels, a place more distinctively his own than any other in the house. When he had closed the door a faint little thrill of alarm came over her. She looked up at him wondering, inquiring. Sir Tom took her by her arms and drew her towards him in the full light of the window. "Come and let me look at you, Lucy," he said. "I want to see in your eyes what it is that makes you afraid of me."

She met his eyes with great bravery and self-command, but nothing could save her from the nervous quiver which he felt as he held her, or from the tell-tale ebb and flow of the blood from her face. "I—I am not afraid of you, Tom."

"Then have you ceased to trust me, Lucy? How is it that you discuss the most important matters with Jock, who is only a boy, and leave me out? You do not think that can be agreeable to me."

"Tom," she said; then stopped short, her voice being interrupted by the fluttering of her heart.

"I told you: you are afraid. What have I ever done to make my wife afraid of me?" he said.

"Oh, Tom, it is not that! it is only that I felt—there has never been anything said, and you have always done all, and more than all, that I wished; but I have felt that you were opposed to me in one thing. I may be wrong, perhaps," she added, looking up at him suddenly with a catching of her breath.

Sir Tom did not say she was wrong. He was very kind, but very grave. "In that case," he said, "Lucy, my love, don't you think it would have been better to speak to me about it, and ascertain what were my objections, and why I was opposed to you—rather than turn without a word to another instead of me?"

"Oh!" cried Lucy, "I could not. I was a coward. I could not bear to make sure. To stand against you, how could I do it? But if you will hear me out, Tom, I never, never turned to another. Oh! what strange words to say. It was not another. It was Jock, only Jock; but I did not turn even to him. It was he who brought it forward, and I— Now that we have begun to talk about it, and it cannot be escaped," cried Lucy, with sudden nervous boldness, freeing herself from his hold, "I will own everything to you, Tom. Yes, I was afraid. I would not, I could not do it, for I could feel that you were against it. You never said anything; is it necessary that you should speak for me to understand you? but I knew it all through. And to go against you and do something you did not like was more than I could face. I should have gone on for years, perhaps, and never had courage for it," she cried. She was tingling all over with excitement and desperate daring now.

"My darling," said Sir Tom, "it makes me happier to think that it was not me you were afraid of, but only of putting yourself in opposition to me; but still, Lucy, even that is not right, you know. Don't you think that it would be better that we should talk it over, and that I should show you my objections to this strange scheme you have in your head, and convince you—"

"Oh!" cried Lucy, stepping back a little and putting up her hands as if in self-defence, "that was what I was most frightened for."

"What, to be convinced?" he laughed: but his laugh jarred upon her in her excited state. "Well, that is not at all uncommon; but few people avow it so frankly," he said.

She looked up at him with appealing eyes. "Oh, Tom," she cried, "I fear you will not understand me now. I am not afraid to be convinced. I am afraid of what you will think when you know that I cannot be convinced. Now," she said, with a certain calm of despair, "I have said it all."

To her astonishment her husband replied by a sudden hug and a laugh. "Whether you are accessible to reason or not, you are always my dear little woman," he said. "I like best to have it out. Do you know, Lucy, that it is supposed your sex are all of that mind? You believe what you like, and the reason for your faith does not trouble you. You must not suppose that you are singular in that respect."

To this she listened without any response at all either in words or look, except, perhaps, a little lifting of her eyelids in faint surprise; for Lucy was not concerned about what was common to her sex. Nor did she take such questions at all into consideration. Therefore, this speech sounded to her irrelevant; and so quick was Sir Tom's intelligence that, though he made it as a sort of conventional necessity, he saw that it was irrelevant too. It might have been all very well to address a clever woman who could have given him back his reply in such words. But to Lucy's straightforward, simple, limited intellect such dialectics were altogether out of place. Her very want of capacity to understand them made them a disrespect to her which she had done nothing to deserve. He coloured in his quick sense of this, and sudden perception that his wife in the limitation of her intellect and fine perfection of her moral nature was such an antagonist as a man might well be alarmed to meet, more alarmed even than she generously was to displease him.

"I beg your pardon, Lucy," he said, "I was talking to you as if you were one of the ordinary people. All this must be treated between you and me on a different footing. I have a great deal more experience than you have, and I ought to know better. You must let me show you how it appears to me. You see I don't pretend not to know what the point was. I have felt for a long time that it was one that must be cleared up between you and me. I never thought of Jock coming in," he said with a laugh. "That is quite a new and unlooked-for feature; but begging his pardon, though he is a clever fellow, we will leave Jock out of the question. He can't be supposed to have much knowledge of the world."

"No," said Lucy, with a little suspicion. She did not quite see what this had to do with it, nor what course her husband was going to adopt, nor indeed at all what was to follow.

"Your father's will was a very absurd one," he said.

At this Lucy was slightly startled, but she said after a moment, "He did not think what hard things he was leaving me to do."

"He did not think at all, it seems to me," said Sir Tom; "so far as I can see he merely amused himself by arranging the world after his fashion, and trying how much confusion he could make. I don't mean to say anything unkind of him. I should like to have known him: he must have been a character. But he has left us a great deal of botheration. This particular thing, you know, that you are driving yourself crazy about is sheer absurdity, Lucy. Solomon himself could not do it,—and who are you, a little girl without any knowledge of the world, to see into people's hearts, and decide whom it is safe to trust?"

"You are putting more upon me than poor papa did, Tom," said Lucy, a little more cheerfully. "He never said, as we do in charities, that it was to go to deserving people. I was never intended to see into their hearts. So long as they required it and got the money, that was all he wanted."

"Well, then, my dear," said Sir Tom, "if your father in his great sense and judgment wanted nothing but to get rid of the money, I wonder he did not tell you to stand upon Beachy Head or Dover Cliff on a certain day in every year and throw so much of it into the sea—to be sure," he added with a laugh, "that would come to very much the same thing—for you can't annihilate money, you can only make it change hands—and the London roughs would soon have found out your days for this wise purpose and interrupted it somehow. But it would have been just as sensible. Poor little woman! Here I am beginning to argue, and abusing your poor father, whom, of course, you were fond of, and never so much as offering you a chair! There is something on every one of them, I believe. Here, my love, here is a seat for you," he said, displacing a box of curiosities and clearing a corner for her by the fire. But Lucy resisted quietly.

"Wouldn't it do another time, Tom?" she said with a little anxiety, "for Aunt Randolph is all by herself, and she will wonder what has become of me; and baby will be coming back from his walk." Then she made a little pause, and resumed again, folding her hands, and raising her mild eyes to his face. "I am very sorry to go against you, Tom. I think I would rather lose all the money altogether. But there is just one thing, and oh, do not be angry! I must carry out papa's will if I were to die!"

Her husband, who had begun to enter smilingly upon this discussion, with a certainty of having the best of it, and who had listened to her smilingly in her simple pleas for deferring the conversation, pleas which he was very willing to yield to, was so utterly taken by surprise at this sudden and most earnest statement, that he could do nothing but stare at her, with a loud alarmed exclamation, "Lucy!" and a look of utter bewilderment in his face. But she stood this without flinching, not nervous as many a woman might have been after delivering such a blow, but quite still, clasping her hands in each other, facing him with a desperate quietness. Lucy was not insensible to the tremendous nature of the utterance she had just made.

"This is surprising, indeed, Lucy," cried Sir Tom. He grew quite pale in that sensation of being disobeyed, which is one of the most disagreeable that human nature is subject to. He scarcely knew what to reply to a rebellion so complete and determined. To see her attitude, the look of her soft girlish face (for she looked still younger than her actual years), the firm pose of her little figure, was enough to show that it was no rash utterance, such as many a combatant makes, to withdraw from it one hour after. Sir Tom, in his amazement, felt his very words come back to him; he did not know what to say. "Do you mean to tell me," he said, almost stammering in his consternation, "that whatever I may think or advise, and however mad this proceeding may be, you have made up your mind to carry it out whether I will or not?"

"Tom! in every other thing I will do what you tell me. I have always done what you told me. You know a great deal better than I do, and never more will I go against you; but I knew papa before I knew you. He is dead; I cannot go to him to ask him to let me off, to tell him you don't like it, or to say it is more than I can do. If I could I would do that. But he is dead: all that he can have is just that I should be faithful to him. And it is not only that he put it in his will, but I gave him my promise that I would do it. How could I break my promise to one that is dead, that trusted in me? Oh, no, no! It will kill me if you are angry; but even then, even then, I must do what I promised to papa."

The tears had risen to her eyes as she spoke: they filled her eyelids full, till she saw her husband only through two blinding seas: then they fell slowly one after another upon her dress: her face was raised to him, her features all moving with the earnestness of her plea. The anguish of the struggle against her heart, and desire to please him, was such that Lucy felt what it was to be faithful till death. As for Sir Tom, it was impossible for such a man to remain unmoved by emotion so great. But it had never occurred to him as possible that Lucy could resist his will, or, indeed, stand for a moment against his injunction; he had believed that he had only to say to her, "You must not do it," and that she would have cried, but given way. He felt himself utterly defeated, silenced, put out of consideration. He did nothing but stare and gasp at her in his consternation; and, more still, he was betrayed. Her gentleness had deceived him and made him a fool; his pride was touched, he who was supposed to have no pride. He stood silent for a time, and then he burst out with a sort of roar of astonished and angry dismay.

"Lucy, do you mean to tell me that you will disobey me?" he cried.

## CHAPTER XIII

### AN IDLE MORNING

The Dowager Lady Randolph had never found the Hall so dull. There was nothing going on, nothing even to look forward to: one formal dinner-party was the only thing to represent that large and cordial hospitality which she was glad to think had in her own time characterised the period when the Hall was open. She had never pretended to be fond of the county society. In the late Sir Robert's time she had not concealed the fact that the less time she spent in it the better she was pleased. But when she was there, all the county had known it. She was a woman who loved to live a large and liberal life. It was not so much that she liked gaiety, or what is called pleasure, as that she loved to have people about her, to be the dispenser of enjoyment, to live a life in which there was always something going on. This is a temperament which meets much censure from the world, and is stigmatised as a love of excitement, and by many other unlovely names; but that is hard upon the people who are born with it, and who are in many cases benefactors to mankind. Lady Randolph's desire was that there should always be something doing—"a magic lantern at the least," she had said. Indeed, there can be no doubt that in managing that magic lantern she would have given as much satisfaction to everybody, and perhaps managed to enjoy herself as much, as if it had been the first entertainment in Mayfair. She could not stagnate comfortably, she said; and as so much of an ordinary woman's life must be stagnation more or less gracefully veiled, it may be supposed that Lady Randolph had learned the useful lesson of putting up with what she could get when what she liked was not procurable. And it was seldom that she had been set down to so languid a feast as the present. On former occasions a great deal more had been going on, except the last year, which was that of the baby's birth, on which occasion Lucy was, of course, out of the way of entertainment altogether. Lady Randolph had, indeed, found her visits to the Hall amusing, which was delightful, seeing they were duty visits as well. She had stayed only a day or two at that time—just long enough to kiss the baby and talk for half an hour at a time, on two or three distinct opportunities, to the young mother in very subdued and caressing tones. And she had been glad to get away again when she had performed this duty, but yet did not grudge in the least the sacrifice she had made for her family. The case, however, was quite different now: there was no reason in the world why they should be quiet. The baby was delicate!—could there be a more absurd reason for closing your house to your friends, putting off your Christmas visits, entertaining not at all, ignoring altogether the natural expectations of the county, which did not elect a man to be its member in order that he might shut himself up and superintend his nursery? It was ridiculous, his aunt felt; it went to her nerves, and made her quite uncomfortable, to see all the resources of the house, with which she was so well acquainted, wasted upon four people. It was preposterous—an excellent cook, the best cook almost she had ever come across, and only four to dine! People have different ideas of what waste is—there are some who consider all large expenditure, especially in the entertainment of guests, to be subject to this censure. But Lady Randolph took a completely different view. The wickedness of having such a cook and only a family party of four persons to dine was that which offended her. It was scandalous, it was wicked. If Lucy meant to live in this way let her return to her bourgeois existence, and the small vulgar life in Farafield. It was ridiculous living the life of a nobody here, and in Sir Tom's case was plainly suicidal. How was he to hold up his face at another election, with the consciousness that he had done nothing at all for his county, not even given them a ball, nor so much as a magic lantern, she repeated, bursting with a reprobation which could scarcely find words?

All this went through her mind with double force when she found herself left alone in Lucy's morning-room, which was a bright room opening out upon the flower garden, getting all the morning sun, and the full advantage of the flowers when there were any. There were none, it is true, at this moment, except a few snow-drops forcing their way through the smooth turf under a tree which stood at the corner of a little bit of lawn. Lady Randolph was not very fond of flowers, except in their proper place, which meant when employed in the decoration of rooms in the proper artistic way, and after the most approved fashion. Thus she liked sunflowers when they were approved by society, and modest violets and pansies in other developments of popular taste, but did not for her own individual part care much which she had, so long as they looked well in her vases, and "came well" against her draperies and furniture. She had come down on this bright morning with her work, as it is the proper thing for a lady to do, but she had no more idea of being left here calmly and undisturbed to do that work than she had of attempting a flight into the inviting and brilliant, if cold and frosty, skies. She sat down with it between the fire and the sunny window, enjoying both without being quite within the range of either. It was an ideal picture of a lady no longer young or capable of much out-door life, or personal emotion; a pretty room; a sunny, soft winter morning, almost as warm as summer, the sunshine pouring in, a cheerful fire in the background to make up what was lacking in respect of warmth; the softest of easiest chairs, yet not too low or demoralising; a subdued sound breaking in now and then from a distance, which pleasantly betrayed the existence of a household; and in the midst of all, in a velvet gown, which was very pretty to look at, and very comfortable to wear, and with a lace cap on her head that had the same characteristics, a lady of sixty, in perfect health, rich enough for all her requirements, without even the thought of a dentist to trouble her. She had a piece of very pretty work in her hand, the newspapers on the table, books within reach. And yet she was not content! What a delightful ideal sketch might not be made of such a moment! How she might have been thinking of her past, sweetly, with a sigh, yet with a thankful thought of all the good things that had been hers; of those whom she had loved, and who were gone from earth, as only awaiting her a little farther on, and of those about her, with such a tender commendation of them to God's blessing, and cordial desire for their happiness, as would have reached the height of a prayer. And she might have been feeling a tranquil pleasure in the material things about her: the stillness, the warmth, the dreamy quiet, even the pretty work, and the exemption from care which she had arrived at in the peaceful concluding chapter of existence. This is what we all like to think of as the condition of mind and circumstances in which age is best met. But we are grieved to say that this was not in the least Lady Randolph's pose. Anything more distasteful to her than this quiet could not be. It was her principle and philosophy to live in the present. She drew many experiences from the past, and a vast knowledge of the constitutions and changes of society; but personally it did not amuse her to think of it, and the future she declined to contemplate. It had disagreeable things in it, of that there could be no doubt; and why go out and meet the disagreeable? It was time enough when it arrived. There was probably illness, and certainly dying, in it; things which she was brave enough to face when they came, and no doubt would encounter in quite a collected and courageous way. But why anticipate them? She lived philosophically in the day as it came. After all whatever you do or think, you cannot do much more. Your one day, your hour, is your world. Acquit yourself fitly in that, and you will be able to encounter whatever occurs.

This was the conviction on which Lady Randolph acted. But her pursuit for the moment was not entertaining; she very quickly tired of her work. Work is, on the whole, tiresome when there is no particular use in it, when it is done solely for the sake of occupation, as ladies' work so often is. It wants a meaning and a necessity to give it interest, and Lady Randolph's had neither. She worked about ten minutes, and then she paused and wondered what could have become of Lucy. Lucy was not a very amusing companion, but she was somebody; and then Sir Tom would come in occasionally to consult her, to give her some little piece of information, and for a few minutes would talk and give his relative a real pleasure. But even Lucy did not come; and soon Lady Randolph became tired of looking out of the window and then walking to the fire, of taking up the newspaper and throwing it down again, of doing a few stitches, then letting the work fall on her lap; and above all, of thinking, as she was forced to do, from sheer want of occupation. She listened, and nobody came. Two or three times she thought she heard steps approaching, but nobody came. She had thought of perhaps going out since the morning was so fine, walking down to the village, which was quite within her powers, and of planning several calls which might be made in the afternoon to take advantage of the fine day. But she became really fretted and annoyed as the morning crept along. Lucy was losing even her politeness, the Dowager thought. This is what comes of what people call happiness! They get so absorbed in themselves, there is no possibility of paying ordinary attention to other people. At last, after completely tiring herself out, Lady Randolph got up and put down her work altogether, throwing it away with anger. She had not lived so long in its sole company for years, and there is no describing how tired she was of it. She got up and went out into the other rooms in search of something to amuse her. Little Tom had just come in, but she did not go to the nursery. She took care not to expose herself to that. She was willing to allow that she did not understand babies; and then to see such a pale little thing the heir of the Randolphs worried her. He ought to have been a little Hercules; it wounded her that he was so puny and pale. She went through the great drawing-room, and looked at all the additions to the furniture and decorations that Tom and Lucy had made. They had kept a number of the old things; but naturally they had added a good deal of bric-à-brac, of old things that here were new. Then Lady Randolph turned into the library. She had gone up to one of the bookcases, and was leisurely contemplating the books, with a keen eye, too, to the additions which had been made, when she heard a sound near her, the unmistakable sound of turning over the leaves of a book. Lady Randolph turned round with a start, and there was Jock, sunk into the depths of a large chair with a tall folio supported on the arms of it. She had not seen him when she came in, and, indeed, many people might have come and gone without perceiving him, buried in his corner. Lady Randolph was thankful for anybody to talk to, even a boy.

"Is it you?" she said. "I might have known it could be nobody but you. Do you never do anything but read?"

"Sometimes," said Jock, who had done nothing but watch her since she came into the room. She gave him a sort of half smile.

"It is more reasonable now than when you were a child," she said; "for I hear you are doing extremely well at school, and gaining golden opinions. That is quite as it should be. It is the only way you can repay Lucy for all she has done for you."

"I don't think," said Jock, looking at her over his book, "that Lucy wants to be repaid."

"Probably not," said Lady Randolph. Then she made a pause, and looked from him to the book he held, and then to him again. "Perhaps you don't think," she said, "there is anything to be repaid."

They were old antagonists; when he was a child and Lucy had insisted on carrying him with her wherever she went, Lady Randolph had made no objections, but she had not looked upon Jock with a friendly eye. And afterwards, when he had interposed with his precocious wisdom, and worsted her now and then, she had come to have a holy dread of him. But now things had righted themselves, and Jock had attained an age of which nobody could be afraid. The Dowager thought, as people are so apt to think, that Jock was not grateful enough. He was very fond of Lucy, but he took things as a matter of course, seldom or never remembering that whereas Lucy was rich, he was poor, and all his luxuries and well-being came from her. She was glad to take an opportunity of reminding him of it, all the more as she was of opinion that Sir Tom did not sufficiently impress this upon the boy, to whom she thought he was unnecessarily kind. "I suppose," she resumed, after a pause, "that you come here always in the holidays, and quite consider it as your home?"

Jock still sat and looked at her across his great folio. He made her no reply. He was not so ready in the small interchanges of talk as he had been at eight, and, besides, it was new to him to have the subject introduced in this way. It is not amusing to plant arrows of this sort in any one's flesh if they show no sign of any wound, and accordingly Lady Randolph grew angry as Jock made no reply. "Is it considered good manners," she said, "at school—when a lady speaks to you that you should make no answer?"

"I was thinking," Jock said. "A fellow, whether he is at school, or not, can't answer all that at once."

"I hope you do not mean to be impertinent. In that case I should be obliged to speak to my nephew," said Lady Randolph. She had not intended to quarrel with Jock. It was only the vacancy of the morning, and her desire for movement of some sort, that had brought her to this; and now she grew angry with Lucy as well as with Jock, having gone so much farther than she had intended to go. She turned from him to the books which she had been languidly examining, and began to take them out one after another, impatiently, as if searching for something. Jock sat and looked at her for some time, with the same sort of deliberate observation with which he used to regard her when he was a child, seeing (as she had always felt) through and through her. But presently another impulse swayed him. He got himself out behind his book, and suddenly appeared by her side, startling her nerves, which were usually so firm.

"If you will tell me what you want," he said, "I'll get it for you. I know where they all are. If it is French you want, they are up there. I like going up the ladder," he added, half to himself.

Perhaps it was this confession of childishness, perhaps the unlooked-for civility, that touched her. She turned round with a subdued half frightened air, feeling that there was no telling how to take this strange creature, and said, half apologetically, "I think I should like a French—novel. They are not—so—long, you know, as the English," and sat down in the chair he rolled towards her. Jock was at the top of the ladder in a moment. She watched him, making a little comment in her own mind about Tom's motive in placing books of this description in such a place—in order to keep them out of Lucy's way, she said to herself. Jock brought her down half a dozen to choose from, and even the eye of Jock, who doubtless knew nothing about them, made Lady Randolph a little more scrupulous than usual in choosing her book. She was one of those women who like the piquancy and freedom of French fiction. She would say to persons of like tastes that the English proprieties were tame beside the other, and she thought herself old enough to be altogether beyond any risk of harm. Perhaps this was why she divined Sir Tom's motive in placing them at the top of the shelves; divined and approved, for though she read all that came in her way, she would not have liked Lucy to share that privilege. She said to Jock as he brought them to her,

"They are shorter than the English. I can't carry three volumes about, you know; all these are in one; but I should not advise you to take to this sort of reading, Jock."

"I don't want to," said Jock, briefly; then he added more gravely, "I can't construe French like you. I suppose you just open it and go straight on?"

"I do," said Lady Randolph, with a smile.

She was mollified, for her French was excellent, and she liked a little compliment, of whatever kind.

"You should give your mind to it; it is the most useful of all languages," she said.

"And Lucy is not great at it either," said Jock.

"That is true, and it is a pity," said Lady Randolph, quite restored to good-humour. "I would take her in hand myself, but I have so many things to do. Do you know where she is, for I have not seen her all this morning?"

"No more have I," said Jock. "I think they have just gone off somewhere together. Lucy never minds. She ought to pay a little attention when there are people in the house."

"That is just what I have been thinking," Lady Randolph said. "I am at home, of course, here; it does not matter for me, and you are her brother—but she really ought; I think I must speak seriously to her."

"To whom are you going to speak seriously? I hope not to me, my dear aunt," said Sir Tom, coming in. He did not look quite his usual self. He was a little pale, and he had an air about him as of some disagreeable surprise. He had the post-bag in his hand—for there was a post twice a day—and opened it as he spoke. Lady Randolph, with her quick perception, saw at once that something had happened, and jumped at the idea of a first quarrel. It was generally the butler Williams who opened the letter-bag; but he was out of the way, and Sir Tom had taken the office on himself. He took out the contents with a little impatience, throwing across to her her share of the correspondence. "Hallo," he said. "Here is a letter for Lucy from your tutor, Jock. What have you been doing, my young man?"

"Oh, I know what it's about," Jock said in a tone of satisfaction. Sir Tom turned round and looked at him with the letter in his hand, as if he would have liked to throw it at his head.

## CHAPTER XIV

## AN UNWILLING MARTYR

Lucy came into the morning-room shortly after, a little paler than usual, but with none of the agitation about her which Lady Randolph expected from Sir Tom's aspect to see. Lucy was not one to bear any outward traces of emotion. When she wept her eyes recovered rapidly, and after half an hour were no longer red. She had a quiet respect for other people, and a determination not to betray anything which she could not explain, which had the effect of that "proper pride" which is inculcated upon every woman, and yet was something different. Lucy would have died rather than give Lady Randolph ground to suppose that she had quarrelled with her husband, and as she could not explain the matter to her, it was necessary to efface all signs of perturbation as far as that was possible. The elder lady was reading her letters when Lucy came in, but she raised her eyes at once with the keenest watchfulness. Young Lady Randolph was pale—but at no time had she much colour. She came in quite simply, without any explanation or giving of reasons, and sat down in her usual place near the window, from which the sunshine, as it was now afternoon, was beginning to die away. Then Lucy gave a slight start to see a letter placed for her on the little table beside her work. She had few correspondents at any time, and when Jock and Lady Randolph were both at the Hall received scarcely any letters. She took it up and looked at its outside with a little surprise.

"I forgot to tell you, Lucy," the Dowager said at this point, "that there was a letter for you. Tom placed it there. He said it was from Jock's tutor, and I hope sincerely, my dear, it does not mean that Jock has got into any scrape—"

"A scrape," said Lucy, "why should he have got into a scrape?" in unbounded surprise; for this was a thing that never had happened throughout Jock's career.

"Oh, boys are so often in trouble," Lady Randolph said, while Lucy opened her letter in some trepidation. But the first words of the letter disturbed her more than any story about Jock was likely to do. It brought the crisis nearer, and made immediate action almost indispensable. It ran as follows:—

"Dear Lady Randolph—In accordance with Jock's request, which he assured me was also yours, I have made all the inquiries you wished about the Churchill family. It was not very difficult to do, as there is but one voice in respect to them. Mr. Churchill himself is represented to me as a model of all that a clergyman ought to be. Whatever we may think of his functions, that he should have all the virtues supposed to be attached to them is desirable in every point of view; and he is a gentleman of good sense and intelligence besides, which is not always implied even in the character of a saint. It seems that the failure of an inheritance, which he had every reason to expect, was the cause of his first disadvantage in the world; and since then, in consonance with that curious natural law which seems so contrary to justice, yet constantly consonant with fact, this evil has been cumulative, and he has had nothing but disappointments ever since. He has a very small living now, and is never likely to get a better, for he is getting old, and patrons, I am told, scarcely venture to give a cure to a man of his age lest it should be said they were gratifying their personal likings at the expense of the people. This seems contrary to abstract justice in such a case; but it is a doctrine of our time to which we must all bow.

"The young people, so far as I know, are all promising and good. Young Churchill, whom Jock knows, is a boy for whom I have the greatest regard. He is one whom Goethe would have described as a beautiful soul. His sisters are engaged in educational work, and are, I am told, in their way equally high-minded and interesting; but naturally I know little of the female portion of the family.

"It is extremely kind of you and Sir Thomas to repeat your invitation. I hope, perhaps at Easter, if convenient, to be able to take advantage of it. I hear with the greatest pleasure from Jock how much he enjoys his renewed intercourse with his home circle. It will do him good, for his mind is full of the ideal, and it will be of endless advantage to him to be brought back to the more ordinary and practical interests. There are very few boys of whom it can be said that their intellectual aspirations over-balance their material impulses. As usual he has not only done his work this half entirely to my satisfaction, but has more than repaid any services I can render him by the precious companionship of a fresh and elevated spirit.

"Believe me, dear Lady Randolph,
"Most faithfully yours,
"MAXIMUS D. DERWENTWATER."

A long-drawn breath, which sounded like a sigh, burst from Lucy's breast as she closed this letter. She had, with humility and shrinking, yet with a certain resolution, disclosed to her husband that when the occasion occurred she must do her duty according to her father's will, whether it pleased him or not. She had steeled herself to do this; but she had prayed that the occasion might be slow to come. Nobody but Jock knew anything about these Churchills, and Jock was going back to school, and he was young and perhaps he might forget! But here was another who would not forget. She read all the recommendations of the family and their excellences with a sort of despair. Money, it was evident, could not be better bestowed than in this way. There seemed no opening by which she could escape; no way of thrusting this act away from her. She felt a panic seize her. How was she to disobey Tom, how to do a thing of so much importance, contrary to his will, against his advice? The whole world around her, the solid walls, and the sky that shone in through the great window, swam in Lucy's eyes. She drew her breath hard like a hunted creature; there was a singing in her ears, and a dimness in her sight. Lady Randolph's voice asking with a certain satisfaction, yet sympathy, "What is the matter? I hope it is not anything very bad," seemed to come to her from a distance as from a different world; and when she added, after a moment, soothingly, "You must not vex yourself about it, Lucy, if it is just a piece of folly. Boys are constantly in that way coming to grief:" it was with difficulty that Lucy remembered to what she could refer. Jock! Ah, if it had been but a boyish folly, Sir Tom would have been the first to forgive that; he would have opened his kind heart and taken the offender in, and laughed and persuaded him out of his folly. He would have been like a father to the boy. To feel all that, and how good he was; and yet determinedly to contradict his will and go against him! Oh, how could she do it? and yet what else was there to do?

"It is not about Jock," she answered with a faint voice.

"I beg your pardon, my dear. I was not aware that you knew Jock's tutor well enough for general correspondence. These gentlemen seem to make a great deal of themselves now-a-days, but in my time, Lucy—"

"I do not know him very well, Aunt Randolph. He is only sending me some information. I wish I might ask you a question," she cried suddenly, looking into the Dowager's face with earnest eyes. This lady had perhaps not all the qualities that make a perfect woman, but she had always been very kind to Lucy. She was not unkind to anybody, although there were persons, of whom Jock was one, whom she did not like. And in all circumstances to Lucy, even when there was no immediate prospect that the Randolph family would be any the better for her, she had always been kind.

"As many as you like, my love," she answered, cordially.

"Yes," said Lucy; "but, dear Aunt Randolph, what I want is that you should let me ask, without asking anything in return. I want to know what you think, but I don't want to explain—"

"It is a strange condition," said Lady Randolph; but then she thought in her superior experience that she was very sure to find out what this simple girl meant without explanations. "But I am not inquisitive," she added, with a smile, "and I am quite willing, dear, to tell you anything I know—"

"It is this," said Lucy, leaning forward in her great earnestness; "do you think a woman is ever justified in doing anything which her husband disapproves?"

"Lucy!" cried Lady Randolph, in great dismay, "when her husband is my Tom, and the thing she wants to do is connected with Jock's tutor—"

Lucy's gaze of astonishment, and her wondering repetition of the words, "connected with Jock's tutor!" brought Lady Randolph to herself. In society, such a suspicion being fostered by all the gossips, comes naturally; but though she was a society-woman, and had not much faith in holy ignorance, she paused here, horrified by her own suggestion, and blushed at herself.

"No, no," she said, "that was not what I meant; but perhaps I could not quite advise, Lucy, where I am so closely concerned."

At which Lucy looked at her somewhat wistfully. "I thought you would perhaps remember," she said, "when you were like me, Aunt Randolph, and perhaps did not know so well as you know now—"

This touched the elder lady's heart. "Lucy," she said, "my dear, if you were not as innocent as I know you are, you would not ask your husband's nearest relation such a question. But I will answer you as one woman to another, and let Tom take care of himself. I never was one that was very strong upon a husband's rights. I always thought that to obey meant something different from the common meaning of the word. A child must obey; but even a grown-up child's obedience is very different from what is natural and proper in youth; and a full-grown woman, you know, never could be supposed to obey like a child. No wise man, for that matter, would ever ask it or think of it."

This did not give Lucy any help. She was very willing, for her part, to accept his light yoke without any restriction, except in the great and momentous exception which she did not want to specify.

"I think," Lady Randolph went on, "that to obey means rather—keep in harmony with your husband, pay attention to his opinions, don't take up an opposite course, or thwart him, be united—instead of the obedience of a servant, you know: still less of a slave."

She was a great deal cleverer than Lucy, who was not thinking of the general question at all. And this answer did the perplexed mind little good. Lucy followed every word with curious attention, but at the end slowly shook her head.

"It is not that. Lady Randolph, if there was something that was your duty before you were married, and that is still and always your duty, a sacred promise you had made; and your husband said no, you must not do it—tell me what you would have done? The rest is all so easy," cried Lucy, "one likes what he likes, one prefers to please him. But this is difficult. What would you have done?"

Here Lady Randolph all at once, after giving forth the philosophical view which was so much above her companion, found herself beyond her depth altogether, and incapable of the fathom of that simple soul.

"I don't understand you, Lucy. Lucy, for heaven's sake, take care what you are doing! If it is anything about Jock, I implore of you give way to your husband. You may be sure in dealing with a boy that he knows best."

Lucy sighed. "It is nothing about Jock," she said; but she did not repeat her demand. Lady Randolph gave her a lecture upon the subject of relations which was very wide of the question; and, with a sigh, owning to herself that there was no light to be got from this, Lucy listened very patiently to the irrelevant discourse. The clever dowager cut it short when it was but half over, perceiving the same, and asked herself not without excitement what it was possible Lucy's difficulty could be? If it was not Jock (and a young brother hanging on to her, with no home but hers, an inquisitive young intelligence, always in the way, was a difficulty which anybody could perceive at a glance) what was it? But Lucy baffled altogether this much experienced woman of the world.

And Jock watched all the day for an opportunity to get possession of her, and assail her on the other side of the question. She avoided him as persistently as he sought her, and with a panic which was very different from her usual happy confidence in him. But the moment came when she could elude him no longer. Lady Randolph had gone to her own room after her cup of tea, for that little nap before dinner which was essential to her good looks and pleasantness in the evening. Sir Tom, who was too much disturbed for the usual rules of domestic life, had not come in for that twilight talk which he usually enjoyed; and as Lucy found herself thus plunged into the danger she dreaded, she was hurrying after Lady Randolph, declaring that she heard baby cry, when Jock stepped into her way, and detained her, if not by physical, at least by moral force—

"Lucy," he said, "are you not going to tell me anything? I know you have got the letter, but you won't look at me, or speak a word."

"Oh, Jock, how silly! why shouldn't I look at you? but I have so many things to do, and baby—I am sure I heard baby cry."

"He is no more crying than I am. I saw him, and he was as jolly as possible. I want awfully to know about the Churchills, and what MTutor says."

"Jock, I think Mr. Derwentwater is rather grand in his writing. It looks as if he thought a great deal of himself."

"No, he doesn't," said Jock, hotly, "not half enough. He's the best man we've got, and yet he can't see it. You needn't give me any information about MTutor," added the young gentleman, "for naturally I know all that much better than you. But I want to know about the Churchills. Lucy, is it all right?"

Lucy gave a little shiver though she was in front of the fire. She said, reluctantly, "I think they seem very nice people, Jock."

"I know they are," said Jock, exultantly. "Churchill in college is the nicest fellow I know. He read such a paper at the Poetical Society. It was on the Method of Sophocles; but of course you would not understand that."

"No, dear," said Lucy, mildly; and again she murmured something about the baby crying, "I think indeed, Jock, I must go."

"Just a moment," said the boy, "Now you are satisfied couldn't we drive into Farafield to-morrow and settle about it? I want to go with you, you and I together, and if old Rushton makes a row you can just call me."

"But I can't leave Lady Randolph, Jock," cried Lucy, driven to her wits' end. "It would be unkind to leave her, and a few days cannot do much harm. When she has gone away—"

"I shall be back at school. Let Sir Tom take her out for once. He might as well drive her in his new phaeton that he is so proud of. If it is fine she'll like that, and we can say we have some business."

"Oh! Jock, don't press me so; a few days can't make much difference."

"Lucy," said Jock, sternly, "do you think it makes no difference to keep a set of good people unhappy, just to save you a little trouble? I thought you had more heart than that."

"Oh, let me go, Jock; let me go—that is little Tom, and he wants me," Lucy cried. She had no answer to make him—the only thing she could do was to fly.

## CHAPTER XV

ON BUSINESS

Ten thousand pounds! These words have very different meanings to different people. Many of us can form little idea of what those simple syllables contain. They enclose as in a golden casket, rest, freedom from care, bounty, kindness, an easy existence, and an ending free of anxiety to many. To others they are nothing more than a cipher on paper, a symbol without any connection with themselves. To some it is great fortune, to others a drop in the ocean. A merchant will risk it any day, and think but little if the speculation is a failure. A prodigal will throw it away in a month, perhaps in a night. But the proportion of people to whom its possession would make all the difference between poverty and wealth far transcends the number of those who are careless of it. It is a pleasure to deal with such a sum of money even on paper. To be concerned in giving it away, makes even the historian, who has nothing to do with it, feel magnificent and all-bounteous. Jock, who had as little experience to back him as any other boy of his age, felt a vague elation as he drove in by Lucy's side to Farafield. To confer a great benefit is always sweet. Perhaps if we analyse it, as is the fashion of the day, we will find that the pleasure of giving has a fond of gratified vanity and self-consideration in it; but this weakness is at least supposed to be generous, and Jock was generous to his own consciousness, and full of delight at what was going to be done, and satisfaction with his own share in it. But Lucy's sensations were very different. She went with him with no goodwill of her own, like a culprit being dragged to execution. Duty is not always willing, even when we see it most clearly. Young Lady Randolph had a clear conviction of what she was bound to do, but she had no wish to do it, though she was so thoroughly convinced that it was incumbent upon her. Could she have pushed it out of her own recollection, banished it from her mind, she would have gladly done so. She had succeeded for a long time in doing this—excluding the consideration of it, and forgetting the burden bound upon her shoulders. But now she could forget it no longer—the thongs which secured it seemed to cut into her flesh. Her heart was sick with thoughts of the thing she must do, yet revolted against doing. "Oh, papa, papa!" she said to herself, shaking her head at the grim, respectable house in which her early days had been passed, as they drove past it to Mr. Rushton's office. Why had the old man put such a burden upon her? Why had not he distributed his money himself and left her poor if he pleased, with at least no unnatural charge upon her heart and life?

"Why do you shake your head?" said Jock, who was full of the keenest observation, and lost nothing.

He had an instinctive feeling that she was by no means so much interested in her duty as he was, and that it was his business to keep her up to the mark.

"Don't you remember the old house?" Lucy said, "where we used to live when you were a child? Where poor papa died—where—"

"Of course I remember it. I always look at it when I pass, and think what a little ass I used to be. But why did you shake your head? That's what I want to know."

"Oh, Jock!" Lucy cried; and said no more.

"That throws very little light on the question," said Jock. "You are thinking of the difference, I suppose. Well, there is no doubt it's a great difference. I was a little idiot in those days. I recollect I thought the circus boy was a sort of little prince, and that it was grand to ride along like that with all the people staring—the grandest thing in the world—"

"Poor little circus boy! What a pretty child he was," said Lucy. And then she sighed to relieve the oppression on her breast, and said, "Do you ever wonder, Jock, why people should have such different lots? You and I driving along here in what we once would have thought such state, and look, these people that are crossing the road in the mud are just as good as we are—"

Jock looked at his sister with a philosophical eye, in which for the moment there was some contempt. "It is as easy as a, b, c," said Jock; "it's your money. You might set me a much harder one. Of course, in the way of horses and carriages and so forth, there is nothing that money cannot buy."

This matter-of-fact reply silenced Lucy. She would have asked, perhaps, why did I have all this money? being in a questioning frame of mind; but she knew that he would answer shortly because her father made it, and this was not any more satisfactory. So she only looked at him with wistful eyes that set many much harder ones, and was silent. Jock himself was too philosophical to be satisfied with his own reply.

"You see," he said condescendingly, "Money is the easiest explanation. If you were to ask me why Sir Tom should be Sir Tom, and that man sweep a crossing, I could not tell you."

"Oh," cried Lucy, "I don't see any difficulty about that at all, for Tom was born to it. You might as well say why should baby be born to be the heir."

Jock did not know whether to be indignant or to laugh at this feminine begging of the question. He stared at her for a moment uncertain, and then went on as if she had not spoken. "But money is always intelligible. That's political economy. If you have money, as a matter of course you have everything that money can buy; and I suppose it can buy almost everything?" Jock said, reflectively.

"It cannot buy a moment's happiness," cried Lucy, "nor one of those things one wishes most for. Oh Jock, at your age don't be deceived like that. For my part," she cried, "I think it is just the trouble of life. If it was not for this horrible money—"

She stopped short, the tears were in her eyes, but she would not betray to Jock how great was the difficulty in which she found herself. She turned her head away and was glad to wave her hand to a well known face that was passing, an acquaintance of old times, who was greatly elated to find that Lady Randolph in her grandeur still remembered her. Jock looked on upon all this with a partial comprehension, mingled with disapproval. He did not quite understand what she meant, but he disapproved of her for meaning it all the same.

"Money can't be horrible," he said, "unless it's badly spent: and to say you can't buy happiness with it is nonsense. If it don't make you happy to save people from poverty it will make them happy, so somebody will always get the advantage. What are you so silly about, Lucy? I don't say money is so very fine a thing. I only say it's intelligible. If you ask me why a man should be a great deal better than you or me, only because he took the trouble to be born—"

"I am not so silly, though you think me so silly, as to ask that," said Lucy; "that is so easy to understand. Of course you can only be who you are. You can't make yourself into another person; I hope I understand that."

She looked him so sweetly and seriously in the face as she spoke, and was so completely unaware of any flaw in her reply, that Jock, argumentative as he was, only gasped and said nothing more. And it was in this pause of their conversation that they swept up to Mr. Rushton's door. Mr. Rushton was the town-clerk of Farafield, the most important representative of legal knowledge in the place. He had been the late Mr. Trevor's man of business, and had still the greater part of Lucy's affairs in his hands. He had known her from her childhood, and in the disturbed chapter of her life before her marriage, his wife had taken a great deal of notice, as she expressed it, of Lucy: and young Raymond, who had now settled down in the office as his father's partner (but never half such a man as his father, in the opinion of the community), had done her the honour of paying her his addresses. But all that had passed from everybody's mind. Mrs. Rushton, never very resentful, was delighted now to receive Lady Randolph's invitation, and proud of the character of an old friend. And if Raymond occasionally showed a little embarrassment in Lucy's presence, that was only because he was by nature awkward in the society of ladies, and according to his own description never knew what to say.

"And what can I do for your ladyship this morning?" Mr. Rushton said, rising from his chair. His private room was very warm and comfortable, too warm, the visitors thought, as an office always is to people going in from the fresh air. The fire burned with concentrated heat, and Lucy, in her furs and suppressed agitation, felt her very brain confused. As for Jock, he lounged in the background with his hands in his pockets, reading the names upon the boxes that lined the walls, and now that it had come to the crisis, feeling truly helpless to aid his sister, and considerably in the way.

"It is a very serious business," said Lucy, drawing her breath hard. "It is a thing you have never liked or approved of, Mr. Rushton, nor any one," she added, in a faint voice.

"Dear me, that is very unfortunate," said the lawyer, cheerfully; "but I don't think you have ever been much disapproved of, Lady Randolph. Come, there is nothing you can't talk to me about—an old friend. I was in all your good father's secrets, and I never saw a better head for business. Why, this is Jock, I believe, grown into a man almost! I wonder if he has any of his father's talent? Is it about him you want to consult me? Why, that's perfectly natural, now he's coming to an age to look to the future," Mr. Rushton said.

"Oh, no! it is not about Jock. He is only sixteen, and, besides, it is something that is much more difficult," said Lucy. And then she paused, and cleared her throat, and put down her muff among Mr. Rushton's papers, that she might have her hands free for this tremendous piece of business. Then she said, with a sort of desperation, looking him in the face: "I have come to get you to—settle some money for me in obedience to papa's will."

Mr. Rushton started as if he had been shot. "You don't mean—" he cried, "You don't mean— Come, I dare say I am making a mountain out of a mole-hill, and that what you are thinking of is quite innocent. If not about our young friend here, some of your charities or improvements? You are a most extravagant little lady in your improvements, Lady Randolph. Those last cottages you know—but I don't doubt the estate will reap the advantage, and it's an outlay that pays; oh, yes, I don't deny it's an outlay that pays."

Lucy's countenance betrayed the futility of this supposition long before he had finished speaking. He had been standing with his back to the fire, in a cheerful and easy way. Now his countenance grew grave. He drew his chair to the table and sat down facing her. "If it is not that, what is it?" he said.

"Mr. Rushton," said Lucy, and she cleared her throat. She looked back to Jock for support, but he had his back turned to her, and was still reading the names on the lawyer's boxes. She turned round again with a little sigh. "Mr. Rushton, I want to carry out papa's will. You know all about it. It is codicil F. I have heard of some one who is the right kind of person. I want you to transfer ten thousand pounds—"

The lawyer gave a sort of shriek; he bolted out of his chair, pushing it so far from him that the substantial mahogany shivered and tottered upon its four legs.

"Nonsense!" he said, "Nonsense!" increasing the firmness of his tone until the word thundered forth in capitals, "NONSENSE!—you are going out of your senses; you don't know what you are saying. I made sure we had done with all this folly—"

When it had happened to Lucy to propose such an operation as she now proposed, for the first time, to her other trustee, she had been spoken to in a way which young ladies rarely experience. That excellent man of business had tried to put this young lady—then a very young lady—down, and he had not succeeded. It may be supposed that at her present age of twenty-three, a wife, a mother, and with a modest consciousness of her own place and position, she was not a less difficult antagonist. She was still a little frightened, and grew somewhat pale, but she looked steadfastly at Mr. Rushton with a nervous smile.

"I think you must not speak to me so," she said. "I am not a child, and I know my father's will and what it meant. It is not nonsense, nor folly—it may perhaps have been," she said with a little sigh—"not wise."

"I beg your pardon, Lady Randolph," Mr. Rushton said precipitately, with a blush upon his middle-aged countenance, for to be sure, when you think of it, to tell a gracious young lady with a title, one of your chief clients, that she is talking nonsense, even if you have known her all her life, is going perhaps a little too far. "I am sure you will understand that is what I meant," he cried, "unwise—the very word I meant. In the heat of the moment other words slip out, but no offence was intended."

She made him a little bow; she was trembling, though she would not have him see it. "We are not here," she said, "to criticise my father." Lucy was scarcely half aware how much she had gained in composure and the art of self-command. "I think he would have been more wise and more kind to have done himself what he thought to be his duty; but what does that matter? You must not try to convince me, please, but take the directions, which are very simple. I have written them all down in this paper. If you think you ought to make independent inquiries, you have the right to do that; but you will spare the poor gentleman's feelings, Mr. Rushton. It is all put down here."

Mr. Rushton took the paper from her hand. He smiled inwardly to himself, subduing his fret of impatience. "You will not object to let me talk it over," he said, "first with Sir Tom?"

Lucy coloured, and then she grew pale. "You will remember," she said, "that it has nothing to do with my husband, Mr. Rushton."

"My dear lady," said the lawyer, "I never expected to hear you, who I have always known as the best of wives, say of anything that it has nothing to do with your husband. Surely that is not how ladies speak of their lords?"

Lucy heard a sound behind her which seemed to imply to her quick ear that Jock was losing patience. She had brought him with her, with the idea of deriving some support from his presence; but if Sir Tom had nothing to do with it, clearly on much stronger grounds neither had her brother. She turned round and cast a hurried warning glance at him. She had herself no words ready to reply to the lawyer's gibe. She would neither defend herself as from a grave accusation, nor reply in the same tone. "Mr. Rushton," she said faltering, "I don't think we need argue, need we? I have put down all the particulars. You know about it as well as I do. It is not for pleasure. If you think it is right, you will inquire about the gentleman—otherwise—I don't think there need be any more to say."

"I will talk it over with Sir Tom," said Mr. Rushton, feeling that he had found the only argument by which to manage this young woman. He even chuckled a little to himself at the thought. "Evidently," he said to himself, "she is afraid of Sir Tom, and he knows nothing about this. He will soon put a stop to it." He added aloud, "My dear Lady Randolph, this is far too serious a matter to be dismissed so summarily. You are young and very inexperienced. Of course I know all about it, and so does Sir Thomas. We will talk it over between us, and no doubt we will manage to decide upon some course that will harmonise everything."

Lucy looked at him with grave suspicion. "I don't know," she said, "what there is to be harmonised, Mr. Rushton. There is a thing which I have to do, and I have shrunk from it for a long time; but I cannot do so any longer."

"Look here," said Jock, "it's Lucy's affair, it's nobody else's. Just you look at her paper and do what she says."

"My young friend," said the lawyer blandly, "that is capital advice for yourself: I hope you always do what your sister says."

"Most times I do," said Jock; "not that it's your business to tell me. But you know very well you'll have to do it. No one has got any right to interfere with her. She has more sense than a dozen. She has got the right on her side. You may do what you please, but you know very well you can't stop her—neither you, nor Sir Tom, nor the old lady, nor one single living creature; and you know it," said Jock. He confronted Mr. Rushton with lowering brows, and with an angry sparkle in his deep-set eyes. Lucy was half proud of and half alarmed by her champion.

"Oh hush, Jock!" she cried. "You must not speak; you are only a boy. You must beg Mr. Rushton's pardon for speaking to him so. But, indeed, what he says is quite true; it is no one's duty but mine. My husband will not interfere with what he knows I must do," she said, with a little chill of apprehension. Would he indeed be so considerate for her? It made her heart sick to think that she was not on this point quite certain about Sir Tom.

"In that case there will be no harm in talking it over with him," said the lawyer briefly. "I thought you were far too sensible not to see that was the right way. Oh, never mind about his asking my pardon. I forgive him without that. He has a high idea of his sister's authority, which is quite right; and so have I— and so have all of us. Certainly, certainly, Master Jock, she has the right; and she will arrange it judiciously, of that there is no fear. But first, as a couple of business men, more experienced in the world than you young philanthropists, I will just, the first time I see him, talk it over with Sir Tom. My dear Lady Randolph, no trouble at all. Is that all I can do for you? Then I will not detain you any longer this fine morning," the lawyer said.


## CHAPTER XVI

### AN UNEXPECTED ARRIVAL

They drove away again with scarcely a word to each other. It was a bright, breezy, wintry day. The roads about Farafield were wet with recent rains, and gleamed in the sunshine. The river was as blue as steel, and gave forth a dazzling reflection; the bare trees stood up against the sky without a pretence of affording any shadow. The cold to these two young people, warmly dressed and prosperous, was nothing to object to—indeed, it was not very cold. But they both had a slight sense of discomfiture—a feeling of having suffered in their own opinion. Jock, who was much regarded at school as a fellow high up, and a great friend of his tutor, was not used to such unceremonious treatment, and he was wroth to see that even Lucy was supposed to require the sanction of Sir Tom for what it was clearly her own business to do. He said nothing, however, until they had quite cleared the town, and were skimming along the more open country roads; then he said suddenly—

"That old Rushton has a great deal of cheek. I should have another fellow to manage my affairs, Lucy, if I were you."

"Don't you know, Jock, that I can't? Papa appointed him. He is my trustee; he has always to be consulted. Papa did not mind," said Lucy with a little sigh. "He said it would be good for me to be contradicted, and not to have my own way."

"Don't you have your own way?" said Jock, opening his eyes. "Lucy, who contradicts you? I should like to know who it was, and tell him my mind a bit. I thought you did whatever you pleased. Do you mean to say there is any truth in all that about Sir Tom?"

"In what about Sir Tom?" cried Lucy, instantly on her defence; and then she changed her tone with a little laugh. "Of course I do whatever I please. It is not good for anybody, Jock. Don't you know we must be crossed sometimes, or we should never do any good at all?"

"Now I wonder which she means?" said Jock. "If she does have her own way or if she don't? I begin to think you speak something else than English, Lucy. I know it is the thing to say that women must do what their husbands tell them; but do you mean that it's true like that? and that a fellow may order you to do this or not to do that, with what is your own and not his at all?"

"I don't think I understand you, dear," said Lucy sweetly.

"Oh! you can't be such a stupid as that," said the boy; "you understand right enough. What did he mean by talking it over with Sir Tom? He thought Sir Tom would put a stop to it, Lucy."

"If Mr. Rushton forms such false ideas, dear, what does it matter? That is not of any consequence either to you or me."

"I wish you would give me a plain answer," said Jock, impatiently. "I ask you one thing, and you say another; you never give me any satisfaction."

She smiled upon him with a look which, clever as Jock was, he did not understand. "Isn't that conversation?" she said.

"Conversation!" The boy repeated the word almost with a shriek of disdain: "You don't know very much about that, down here in the country, Lucy. You should hear MTutor; when he's got two or three fellows from Cambridge with him, and they go at it! That's something like talk."

"It is very nice for you, Jock, that you get on so well with Mr. Derwentwater," said Lucy, catching with some eagerness at this way of escape from embarrassing questions. "I hope he will come and see us at Easter, as he promised."

"He may," said Jock, with great gravity, "but the thing is, everybody wants to have him; and then, you see, whenever he has an opportunity he likes to go abroad. He says it freshens one up more than anything. After working his brain all the half, as he does, and taking the interest he does in everything, he has got to pay attention, you know, and not to overdo it; he must have change, and he must have rest."

Lucy was much impressed by this, as she was by all she heard of MTutor. She was quite satisfied that such immense intellectual exertions as his did indeed merit compensation. She said, "I am sure he would get rest with us, Jock. There would be nothing to tire him, and whatever I could do for him, dear, or Sir Tom either, we should be glad, as he is so good to you."

"I don't know that he's what you call fond of the country—I mean the English country. Of course it is different abroad," said Jock doubtfully. Then he came back to the original subject with a bound, scattering all Lucy's hopes. "But we didn't begin about MTutor. It was the other business we were talking of. Is it true that Sir Tom—"

"Jock," said Lucy seriously. Her mild eyes got a look he had never seen in them before. It was a sort of dilation of unshed tears, and yet they were not wet. "If you know any time when Sir Tom was ever unkind or untrue, I don't know it. He has always, always been good. I don't think he will change now. I have always done what he told me, and I always will. But he never told me anything. He knows a great deal better than all of us put together. Of course, to obey him, that is my first duty. And I always shall. But he never asks it—he is too good. What is his will, is my will," she said. She fixed her eyes very seriously on Jock, all the time she spoke, and he followed every movement of her lips with a sort of astonished confusion, which it is difficult to describe. When she had ceased Jock drew a long breath, and seemed to come to the surface again, after much tossing in darker waters.

"I think that it must be true," he said slowly, after a pause, "as people say—that women are very queer, Lucy. I didn't understand one word you said."

"Didn't you, then?" she said, with a smile of gentle benignity; "but what does it matter, when it will all come right in the end? Is that our omnibus, Jock, that is going along with all that luggage? How curious that is, for nobody was coming to-day that I know of. Don't you see it just turning in to the avenue? Now that is very strange indeed," said Lucy, raising herself very erect upon her cushions with a little quickened and eager look. An arrival is always exciting in the country, and an arrival which was quite unexpected, and of which she could form no surmise as to who it could be, stirred up all her faculties. "I wonder if Mrs. Freshwater will know what rooms are best?" she said, "and if Sir Tom will be at home to receive them; or perhaps it may be some friends of Aunt Randolph's, or perhaps—I wonder very much who it can be."

Jock's countenance covered itself quickly with a tinge of gloom.

"Whoever it is, I know it will be disgusting," cried the boy. "Just when we have got so much to talk about! and now I shall never see you any more. Lady Randolph was bad enough, and now here's more of them! I should just as soon go back to school at once," he said, with premature indignation. The servants on the box perceived the other carriage in advance with equal curiosity and excitement. They were still more startled, perhaps, for a profound wonder as to what horses had been sent out, and who was driving them, agitated their minds. The horses, solicited by a private token between them and their driver which both understood, quickened their pace with a slight dash, and the carriage swept along as if in pursuit of the larger and heavier vehicle, which, however, had so much the advance of them, that it had deposited its passengers, and turned round to the servants' entrance with the luggage, before Lady

Randolph could reach the door. Williams the butler wore a startled look upon his dignified countenance, as he came out on the steps to receive his mistress.

"Some one has arrived," said Lucy with a little eagerness. "We saw the omnibus."

"Yes, my lady. A telegram came for Sir Thomas soon after your ladyship left; there was just time to put in the horses—"

"But who is it, Williams?"

Williams had a curious apologetic air. "I heard say, my lady, that it was some of the party that were invited before Mr. Randolph fell ill. There had been a mistake about the letters, and the lady has come all the same—a lady with a foreign title, my lady—"

"Oh!" said Lucy, with English brevity. She stood startled, in the hall, lingering a little, changing colour, not with any of the deep emotions which Williams from his own superior knowledge suspected, but with shyness and excitement. "It will be the lady from Italy, the Contessa— Oh, I hope they have attended to her properly! Was Sir Thomas at home when she came?"

"Sir Thomas, my lady, went to meet them at the station," Williams said.

"Oh, that is all right," cried Lucy, relieved. "I am so glad she did not arrive and find nobody. And I hope Mrs. Freshwater—"

"Mrs. Freshwater put the party into the east wing, my lady. There are two ladies besides the man and the maid. We thought it would be the warmest for them, as they came from the South."

"It may be the warmest, but it is not the prettiest," said Lucy. "The lady is a great friend of Sir Thomas', Williams."

The man gave her a curious look.

"Yes, my lady, I was aware of that," he said.

This surprised Lucy a little, but for the moment she took no notice of it. "And therefore," she went on, "the best rooms should have been got ready. Mrs. Freshwater ought to have known that. However, perhaps she will change afterwards. Jock, I will just run upstairs and see that everything is right."

As she turned towards the great staircase, so saying, she ran almost into her husband's arms. Sir Tom had appeared from a side door, where he had been on the watch, and it was certain that his face bore some traces of the new event that had happened. He was not at his ease as usual. He laughed a little uncomfortable laugh, and put his hand on Lucy's shoulder as she brushed against him. "There," he said, "that will do; don't be in such a hurry," arresting her in full career.

"Oh, Tom!" Lucy for her part looked at her husband with the greatest relief and happiness. There had been a cloud between them which had been more grievous to her than anything else in the world. She had felt hourly compelled to stand up before him and tell him that she must do what he desired her not to do. The consternation and pain and wrath that had risen over his face after that painful interview had not passed away through all the intervening time. There had been a sort of desperation in her mind when she went to Mr. Rushton, a feeling that she so hated the duty which had risen like a ghost between her husband and herself, that she must do it at all hazards and without delay. But this cloud had now departed from Sir Tom's countenance. There was a little suffusion of colour upon it which was unusual to him. Had it been anybody but Sir Tom, it would have looked like embarrassment, shyness mingled with a certain self-ridicule and sense of the ludicrous in the position altogether. He caught his wife in his arms and met her eyes with a certain laughing shamefacedness, "Don't," he said, "be in such a hurry, Lucy. Ces dames have gone to their rooms; they have been travelling all night, and they are not fit to be seen. It is only silly little English girls like you that can bear to be looked at at all times and seasons." And with this he stooped over her and gave her a kiss on her forehead, to Lucy's delight, yet horror—before Williams, who looked on approving, and the footman with the traps, and Jock and all! But what a load it took off her breast! He was not any longer vexed or disturbed or angry. He was indeed conciliatory and apologetic, but Lucy only saw that he was kind.

"Poor lady," cried Lucy, "has she been travelling all night? And I am so sorry she has been put into the east wing. If I had been at home I should have said the blue rooms, Tom, which you know are the nicest—"

"I think they are quite comfortable, my dear," said Sir Tom, with his usual laugh, which was half-mocking half-serious, "you may be sure they will ask for anything they want. They are quite accustomed to making themselves at home."

"Oh, I hope so, Tom," said Lucy, "but don't you think it would be more polite, more respectful, if I were to go and ask if they have everything? Mrs. Freshwater is very well you know, Tom, but the mistress of the house—"

He gave her another little hug, and laughed again. "No," he said, "you may be sure Madame Forno-Populo is not going to let you see her till she has repaired all ravages. It was extremely indiscreet of me to go to the station," he continued, still with that chuckle, leading Lucy away. "I had forgotten all these precautions after a few years of you, Lucy. I was received with a shriek of horror and a double veil."

Lucy looked at him with great surprise, asking: "Why? wasn't she glad to see you?" with incipient indignation and a sense of grievance.

"Not at all," cried Sir Tom, "indeed I heard her mutter something about English savagery. The Contessa expresses herself strongly sometimes. Freshwater and the maid, and the excellent breakfast Williams has ordered, knowing her ways—"

"Does Williams know her ways?" asked Lucy, wondering. There was not the faintest gleam of suspicion in her mind; but she was surprised, and her husband bit his lip for a moment, yet laughed still.

"He knows those sort of people," he said. "I was very much about in society at one time you must know, Lucy, though I am such a steady old fellow now. We knew something of most countries in these days. We were bien vu, he and I, in various places. Don't tell Mrs. Williams, my love." He laughed almost violently at this mild joke, and Lucy looked surprised. But still no shadow came upon her simple countenance. Lucy was like Desdemona, and did not believe that there were such women. She thought it was "fun," such fun as she sometimes saw in the newspapers, and considered as vulgar as it was foolish. Such words could not be used in respect to anything Sir Tom said, but even in her husband it was not good taste, Lucy thought. She smiled at the reference to Mrs. Williams with a kind of quiet disdain, but it never occurred to her that she too might require to be kept in the dark.

"I dare say most of what you are talking is nonsense," she said; "but if Madame Forno —"—Lucy was not very sure of the name, and hesitated—"is really very tired, perhaps it may be kindness not to disturb her. I hope she will go to bed, and get a thorough rest. Did she not get your second letter, Tom? and what a thing it is that dear baby is so much better, and that we can really pay a little attention to her."

"Either she did not get my letter, or I didn't write, I cannot say which it was, Lucy. But now we have got her we must pay attention to her, as you say. You will have to get up a few dinner parties, and ask some people to stay. She will like to see the humours of the wilderness while she is in it."

"The wilderness—but, Tom, everybody says society is so good in the county."

"Everybody does not know the Forno-Populo," cried Sir Tom; and then he burst out into a great laugh. "I wonder what her Grace will say to the Contessa; they have met before now."

"Must we ask the Duchess?" cried Lucy, with awe and alarm, coming a little nearer to her husband's side.

But Sir Tom did nothing but laugh. "I've seen a few passages of arms," he said. "By Jove, you don't know what war is till you see two — at it tooth and nail. Two—what, Lucy? Oh, I mean fine ladies; they have no mercy. Her Grace will set her claws into the fair countess. And as for the Forno-Populo herself—"

"Dear Tom" said Lucy with gentle gravity, "Is it nice to speak of ladies so? If any one called me the Randolph, I should be, oh, so—"

"You," cried her husband with a hot and angry colour rising to his very hair, and then he perceived that he was betraying himself, and paused. "You see, my love, that's different," he said. "Madame di Forno-Populo is—an old stager: and you are very young, and nobody ever thought of you but with—reverence, my dear. Yes, that's the word, Lucy, though you are only a bit of a girl."

"Tom," said Lucy with great dignity, "I have you to take care of me, and I have never been known in the world. But, dear, if this poor lady has no one—and I suppose she is a widow, is she not, Tom?"

He had been listening to her almost with emotion—with a half-abashed look, full of fondness and admiration. But at this question he drew back a little, with a sort of stagger, and burst into a wild fit of laughter. When he came to himself wiping his eyes, he was, there could be no doubt, ashamed of himself. "I beg you ten thousand pardons," he cried. "Lucy, my darling! Yes, yes—I suppose she is a widow, as you say."

Lucy looked at him while he laughed, with profound gravity, without the slightest inclination to join in his merriment, which is a thing which has a very uncomfortable effect. She waited till he was done, with a mixture of wonder and disapproval in her seriousness, looking at his laughter as if at some phenomenon which she did not understand. "I have often heard gentlemen," she said, "talk about widows as if it were a sort of laughable name, and as if they might make their jokes as they pleased. But I did not think you would have done it, Tom. I should feel all the other way," said Lucy. "I should think I could never do enough to make it up, if that were possible, and to make them forget. Is it their fault that they are left desolate, that a man should laugh?" She turned away from her husband with a soft superiority of innocence and true feeling which struck him dumb.

He begged her pardon in the most abject way; and then he left her for a moment quietly, and had his laugh out. But he was ashamed of himself all the same. "I wonder what she will say when she sees the Forno-Populo," he said to himself.

## CHAPTER XVII

### FOREWARNED

Lucy did not see her visitors till the hour of dinner. She had expected them to appear in the afternoon at the mystic hour of tea, which calls an English household together, but when it was represented to her that afternoon tea was not the same interesting institution in Italy, her surprise ceased, and though her expectations were still more warmly excited by this delay, she bore it with becoming patience. There was no doubt, however, that the arrival had made a great commotion in the house, and Lucy perceived without in the least understanding it, a peculiarity in the looks which various of the people around her cast upon her during the course of the day. Her own maid was one of these people, and Mrs. Freshwater, the housekeeper, who explained in a semi-apologetic tone all the preparations she had made for the comfort of the guests, was another. And Williams, though he was always so dignified, thought Lucy could not help feeling an eye upon her. He was almost compassionately attentive to his young mistress. There was a certain pathos in the way in which he handed her the potatoes at lunch. He pressed a little more claret upon her with a fatherly anxiety, and an air that seemed to say, "It will do you good." Lucy was conscious of all this additional attention without realising the cause of it. But it found its culmination in Lady Randolph, in whom a slightly-injured and aggrieved air towards Sir Tom was enhanced by the extreme tenderness of her aspect to Lucy, for whom she could not do too much. "Williams is quite right in giving you a little more wine. You take nothing," she said, "and I am sure you want support. After your long drive, too, my dear: and how cold it has been this morning!"

"Yes, it was cold; but we did not mind, we rather liked it, Jock and I. Poor Madame di Forno-Populo! She must have felt it travelling all night."

"Bravo, Lucy, that is right! you have tackled the name at last, and got through with it beautifully," said Sir Tom with a laugh.

Lucy was pleased to be praised. "I hope I shan't forget," she said, "it is so long: and oh, Tom, I do hope she can talk English, for you know my French."

"I should think she could talk English!" said Lady Randolph, with a little scorn. And what was very extraordinary was that Williams showed a distinct but suppressed consciousness, putting his lips tight as if to keep in what he knew about the matter. "And I don't think you need be so sorry for the lady, Lucy," said the dowager. "No doubt she didn't mean to travel by night. It arose from some mistake or other in Tom's letter. But she does not mind that, you may be sure, now that she has made out her point."

"What point?" said Sir Tom, with some heat. But Lady Randolph made no reply, and he did not press the question. They were both aware that it is sometimes better to hold one's tongue. And the curious thing to all of those well-informed persons was that Lucy took no notice of all their hints and innuendoes. She was in the greatest spirits, not only interested about her unknown visitors and anxious to secure their comfort, but in herself more gay than she had been for some time past. In fact this arrival was a godsend to Lucy. The cloud had disappeared entirely from her husband's brow. Instead of making any inquiries about her visit to Farafield, or resuming the agitating discussion which had ended in what was really a refusal on her part to do what he wished, he was full of a desire to conciliate and please her. The matter which had brought so stern a look to his face, and occasioned her an anxiety and pain far more severe than anything that had occurred before in her married life, seemed to have dropped out of his mind altogether. Instead of that opposition and disapproval, mingled with angry suspicion, which had been in his manner and looks, he was now on the watch to propitiate Lucy; to show a gratitude for which she knew no reason, and a pride in her which was still less comprehensible. What did it all mean, the compassion on one side, the satisfaction on the other? But Lucy scarcely asked herself the question. In her relief at having no new discussion with her husband, and at his apparent forgetfulness of all displeasure and of any question between them, her heart rose with all the glee of a child's. It seemed to her that she had surmounted the difficulties of her position by an intervention which was providential. It even occurred to her innocent mind to make reflections as to the advantage of doing what was right in the face of all difficulties. God, she said to herself, evidently was protecting her. It was known in heaven what an effort it had cost her to do her duty to fulfil her father's will, and now heavenly succour was coming, and the difficulties disappearing out of her way. Lucy would have been ready in any case with the most unhesitating readiness to receive and do any kindness to her husband's friend. No idea of jealousy had come into her unsuspicious soul. She had taken it as a matter of course that this unknown lady should have the best that the Hall could offer her, and that her old alliance with Sir Tom should throw open his doors and his wife's heart. Perhaps it was because Lucy's warm and simple-minded attachment to her husband had little in it of the character of passion that it was thus entirely without any impulse of jealousy. And what was so natural in common circumstances became still more so in the exhilaration and rebound of her troubled heart. Sir Tom was so kind to her in departing from his opposition, in letting her have her way without a word. It was certain that Lucy would not have relinquished her duty for any opposition he had made. But with what a bleeding heart she would have done it, and how hateful would have been the necessity which separated her from his goodwill and assistance! Now she felt that terrible danger was over. Probably he would not ask her what she had been about. He would not give it his approval, which would have been most sweet of all, but if he did not interfere, if he permitted it to be done without opposition, without even demanding of his wife an account of her action, how much that would be, and how cordially, with what a genuine impulse of the heart would she set to work to carry out his wishes—he who had been so generous, so kind to her! This was how it was that her gaiety, the ease and happiness of her look, startled them all so much. That she should have been amiable to the new comers was comprehensible. She was so amiable by nature, and so ignorant and unsuspicious: but that their coming should give her pleasure, this was the thing that confounded the spectators: they could not understand how any other subject should withdraw her from what is supposed to be a wife's master emotion—nay, they could not understand how it was that mere instinct had not enlightened Lucy, and pointed out to her what elements were coming together that would be obnoxious to her peace. Even Sir Tom felt this, with a deepened tenderness for his pure-minded little wife, and pride in her unconsciousness. Was there another woman in England who would have been so entirely generous, so unaware even of the possibility of evil? He admired her for it, and wondered—if it was a little silly (which he had a kind of undisclosed suspicion that it was), yet what a heavenly silliness. There was nobody else who would have been so magnanimous, so confident in his perfect honour and truth.

The only other element that could have added to Lucy's satisfaction was also present. Little Tom was better than usual. Notwithstanding the cold he had been able to go out, and was all the brighter for it, not chilled and coughing as he sometimes was. His mother had found him careering about his nursery in wild glee, and flinging his toys about, in perfectly boyish, almost mannish, altogether wicked, indifference to the danger of destroying them. It was this that brought her downstairs radiant to the luncheon table, where Lady Randolph and Williams were so anxious to be good to her. Lucy was much surprised by the solicitude which she felt to be so unnecessary. She was disposed to laugh at the care they took of her; feeling in her own mind, more triumphant, more happy and fortunate, than she had ever been before.

As for Jock, he took no notice at all of the incident of the day. He perceived with satisfaction, a point on which for the moment he was unusually observant, that Sir Tom showed no intention of questioning them as to their morning's expedition or opposing Lucy. This being the case, what was it to the boy who went or came? A couple of ladies were quite indifferent to him. He did not expect anything or fear anything. His own doings interested him much more. The conversation about this new subject floated over his head. He did not take the trouble to pay any attention to it. As for Williams' significant looks or Lady Randolph's anxieties, Jock was totally unconscious of their existence. He did not pay any attention. When the party was not interesting he had plenty of other thoughts to retire into, and the coming of new people, except in so far as it might be a bore, did not affect him at all.

Lucy went out dutifully for a drive with Lady Randolph after luncheon. It was still very bright, though it was cold, and after a little demur as to the propriety of going out when it was possible her guests might be coming downstairs, Lucy took her place beside the fur-enveloped Dowager with her hot water footstool and mountain of wrappings. They talked about ordinary matters for a little, about the landscape and the improvements, and about little Tom, whose improvement was the most important of all. But it was not possible to continue long upon indifferent matters in face of the remarkable events which had disturbed the family calm.

"I hope," said Lucy, "that Madame di Forno-Populo" (she was very careful about all the syllables) "may not be more active than you think, and come down while we are away."

"Oh, there is not the least fear," said Lady Randolph, somewhat scornfully. "She was always a candle-light beauty. She is not very fond of the eye of day."

"She is a beauty, then?" said Lucy. "I am very glad. There are so few. You know I have always been—rather—disappointed. There are many pretty people: but to be beautiful is quite different."

"That is because you are so unsophisticated, my dear. You don't understand that beauty in society means a fashion, and not much more. I have seen a quantity of beauties in my day. How they came to be so, nobody knew; but there they were, and we all bowed down to them. This woman, however, was very pretty, there was no doubt about it," said Lady Randolph, with reluctant candour. "I don't know what she may be now. She was enough to turn any man's head when she was young—or even a woman's—who ought to have known better."

"Do you think then, Aunt Randolph, that women don't admire pretty people?" It is to be feared that Lucy asked for the sake of making conversation, which it is sometimes necessary to do.

"I think that men and women see differently—as they always do," said Lady Randolph. She was rather fond of discriminating between the ideas of the sexes, as many ladies of a reasonable age are. "There is a gentleman's beauty, you know, and there is a kind of beauty that women love. I could point out the difference to you better if the specimens were before us; but it is a little difficult to describe. I rather think we admire expression, you know. What men care for is flesh and blood. We like people that are good—that is to say, who have the air of being good, for the reality doesn't by any means follow. Perhaps I am taking too much credit to ourselves," said the old lady, "but that is the best description I can hit upon. We like the interesting kind—the pensive kind—which was the fashion when I was young. Your great, fat, golden-haired, red and white women are gentlemen's beauties; they don't commend themselves to us."

"And is Madame di Forno-Populo," said Lucy, in her usual elaborate way, "of that kind?"

"Oh! my dear, she is just a witch," Lady Randolph said. "It does not matter who it is, she can bring them to her feet if she pleases!" Then she seemed to think she had gone too far, and stopped herself: "I mean when she was young; she is young no longer, and I dare say all that has come to an end."

"It must be sad to grow old when one is like that," said Lucy, with a look of sympathetic regret.

"Oh, you are a great deal too charitable, Lucy!" said the old lady: and then she stopped short, putting a sudden restraint upon herself, as if it were possible that she might have said too much; then after a while she resumed: "As you are in such a heavenly frame of mind, my dear, and disposed to think so well of her, there is just one word of advice I will give you—don't allow yourself to get intimate with this lady. She is quite out of your way. If she liked, she could turn you round her little finger. But it is to be hoped she will not like; and, in any case, you must remember that I have warned you. Don't let her, my dear, make a catspaw of you."

"A catspaw of me!" Lucy was amused by these words—not offended, as so many might have been—perhaps because she felt herself little likely to be so dominated; a fact that the much older and more experienced woman by her side was quite unaware of. "But," she said, "Tom would not have invited her, Aunt Randolph, if he had thought her likely to do that—indeed, how could he have been such great friends with her if she had not been nice as well as pretty? You forget there must always be that in her favour to me."

"Oh, Tom!" cried Lady Randolph with indignation. "My dear Lucy," she added after a pause, with subdued exasperation, "men are the most unaccountable creatures! Knowing him as I do, I should have thought she was the very last person—but how can we tell? I dare say the idea amused him. Tom will do anything that amuses him—or tickles his vanity. I confess it is as you say, very, very difficult to account for it; but he has done it. He wants to show off a little to her, I suppose; or else he— There is really no telling, Lucy. It is the last thing in the world I should have thought of; and you may be quite sure, my dear," she added with emphasis, "she never would have been invited at all if he had expected me to be here when she came."

Lucy did not make any answer for some time. Her face, which had kept its gaiety and radiance, grew grave, and when they had driven back towards the hall for about ten minutes in silence, she said quietly "You do not mean it, I am sure; but do you know, Aunt Randolph, you are trying to make me think very badly of my husband; and no one has ever done that before."

"Oh, your husband is just like other people's husbands, Lucy," cried the elder lady impatiently. Then, however, she subdued herself, with an anxious look at her companion. "My dear, you know how fond I am of Tom: and I know he is fond of you; he would not do anything to harm you for the world. I suppose it is because he has such a prodigious confidence in you that he thinks it does not matter; and I don't suppose it does matter. The only thing is, don't be over intimate with her, Lucy; don't let her fix herself upon you when you go to town, and talk about young Lady Randolph as her dearest friend. She is quite capable of doing it. And as for Tom—well, he is just a man when all is said."

Lucy did not ask any more questions. That she was greatly perplexed there is no doubt, and her first fervour of affectionate interest in Tom's friend was slightly damped, or at least changed. But she was more curious than ever; and there was in her mind the natural contradiction of youth against the warnings addressed to her. Lucy knew very well that she herself was not one to be twisted round anybody's little finger. She was not afraid of being subjugated; and she had a prejudice in favour of her husband which neither Lady Randolph nor any other witness could impair. The drive home was more silent than the outset. Naturally, the cold increased as the afternoon went on, and the Dowager shrunk into her furs, and declared that she was too much chilled to talk. "Oh how pleasant a cup of tea will be," she said.

Lucy longed for her part to get down from the carriage and walk home through the village, to see all the cottage fires burning, and quicken the blood in her veins, which is a better way than fur for keeping one's self warm. When they got in, it was exciting to think that perhaps the stranger was coming down to tea; though that, as has been already said, was a hope in which Lucy was disappointed. Everything was prepared for her reception, however—a sort of throne had been arranged for her, a special chair near the fire, shaded by a little screen, and with a little table placed close to it to hold her cup of tea. The room was all in a ruddy blaze of firelight, the atmosphere delightful after the cold air outside, and all the little party a little quiet, thinking that every sound that was heard must be the stranger.

"She must have been very tired," Lucy said sympathetically.

"I dare say," said Lady Randolph, "she thinks a dinner dress will make a better effect."

Lucy looked towards her husband almost with indignation, with eyes that asked why he did not defend his friend. But, to be sure, Sir Tom could not judge of their expression in the firelight, and instead of defending her he only laughed. "One general understands another's tactics," he said.


CHAPTER XVIII

THE VISITORS

Sir Tom paid his wife a visit when she was in the midst of her toilette for dinner. He came in, and looked at her dress with an air of dissatisfaction. It was a white dress, of a kind which suited Lucy very well, and which she was in the habit of wearing for small home parties, at which full dress was unnecessary. He looked at her from head to foot, and gave a little pull to her skirt with a doubtful air. "It doesn't sit, does it?" he said; "can't you pin it, or something, to make it come better?"

This, it need not be said, was a foolish piece of ignorance on Sir Tom's part, and as Miss Fletcher, Lucy's maid, thought, "just like a man." Fletcher was for the moment not well-disposed towards Sir Tom. She said—"Oh no, Sir Thomas, my lady don't hold with pins. Some ladies may that are all for effect; but my lady, that is not her way."

Sir Tom felt that these words inclosed a dart as sharp as any pin, and directed at himself; but he took no notice. He walked round his wife, eyeing her on every side; and then he gave a little pull to her hair as he had done to her dress. "After all," he said, "it is some time since you left school, Lucy. Why this simplicity? I want you to look your best to-night."

"But, dear Tom," said Lucy, "you always say that I am not to be over-dressed."

"I don't want you to be under-dressed; there is plenty of time. Don't you think you might do a little more in the way of toilette? Put on some lace or something; Fletcher will know. Look here, Fletcher, I want Lady Randolph to look very well to-night. Don't you think this get-up would stand improvement? I dare say you could do it with ribbons, or something. We must not have her look like my grandchild, you know."

Upon which Fletcher, somewhat mollified and murmuring that Sir Thomas was a gentleman that would always have his joke, answered boldly that that was not how she would have dressed her lady had she had the doing of it. "But I know my place," Fletcher said, "though to see my lady like this always goes against me, Sir Thomas, and especially with foreigners in the house that are always dressed up to the nines and don't think of nothing else. But if Lady Randolph would wear her blue it could all be done in five minutes, and look far nicer and more like the lady of the house."

This transfer was finally made, for Lucy had no small obstinacies and was glad to please her husband. The "blue" was of the lightest tint of shimmering silk, and gave a little background of colour, upon which Lucy's fairness and whiteness stood out. Sir Thomas always took an interest in his wife's dress; but it was seldom he occupied himself so much about it. It was he who went to the conservatory to get a flower for her hair. He took her downstairs upon his arm "as if they were out visiting," Lucy said, instead of at home in their own house. She was amused at all this form and ceremony, and came down to the drawing-room with a little flush of pleasure and merriment about her, quite different from the demure little Lady Randolph, half frightened and very serious, with the weight on her mind of a strange language to be spoken, who but for Sir Tom's intervention would have been standing by the fire awaiting her visitor. The Dowager was downstairs before her, looking grave enough, and Jock, slim and dark, supporting a corner of the mantelpiece, like a young Caryatides in black. Lucy's brightness, her pretty shimmer of blue, the flower in her hair, relieved these depressing influences. She stood in the firelight with the ruddy irregular glare playing on her, a pretty youthful figure; and her husband's assiduities, and the entire cessation of any apparent consciousness on his part that any question had ever arisen between them, made Lucy's heart light in her breast. She forgot even the possibility of having to talk French in the ease of her mind; and before she had time to remember her former alarm there came gliding through the subdued light of the greater drawing-room two figures. Sir Tom stepped forward to meet the stranger, who gave him her hand as if she saw him for the first time, and Lucy advanced with a little tremor. Here was the Contessa—the Forno-Populo—the foreign great lady and great beauty at last.

She was tall—almost as tall as Sir Tom—and had the majestic grace which only height can give. She was clothed in dark velvet, which fell in long folds to her feet, and her hair, which seemed very abundant, was much dressed with puffs and curlings and frizzings, which filled Lucy with wonder, but furnished a delicate frame-work for her beautiful, clear, high features, and the wonderful tint of her complexion—a sort of warm ivory, which made all brighter colours look excessive. Her eyes were large and blue, with long but not very dark eyelashes; her throat was like a slender column out of a close circle of feathery lace. Lucy, who had a great deal of natural taste, felt on the moment a thrill of shame on account of her blue gown, and an almost disgust of Lady Randolph's old-fashioned openness about the shoulders. The stranger was one of those women whose dress always impresses other women with such a sense of fitness that fashion itself looks vulgar or insipid beside her. She gave Sir Tom her left hand in passing, and then she turned with both extended to Lucy. "So this is the little wife," she said. She did not pause for the modest little word of welcome which Lucy had prepared. She drew her into the light, and gazed at her with benignant but dauntless inspection, taking in, Lucy felt sure, every particular of her appearance—the something too much of the blue gown, the deficiency of dignity, the insignificance of the smooth fair locks, and open if somewhat anxious countenance. "Bel enfant," said the Contessa, "your husband and I are such old friends that I cannot meet you as a stranger. You must let me kiss you, and accept me as one of yours too." The salutation that followed made Lucy's heart jump with mingled pleasure and distaste. She was swallowed up altogether in that embrace. When it was over, the lady turned from her to Sir Tom without another word. "I congratulate you, mon ami. Candour itself, and sweetness, and every English quality"—upon which she proceeded to seat herself in the chair which Lucy had set for her in the afternoon with the screen and the footstool. "How thoughtful some one has been for my comfort," she said, sinking into it, and distributing a gracious smile all round. There was something in the way in which she seized the central place in the scene, and made all the others look like surroundings which bewildered Lucy, who did nothing but gaze, forgetting everything she meant to say, and even that it was she who was the mistress of the house.

"You do not see my aunt, Contessa," said Sir Tom, "and yet I think you ought to know each other."

"Your aunt," said the Contessa, looking round, "that dear Lady Randolph—who is now Dowager. Chère dame!" she added, half rising, holding out again both hands.

Lady Randolph the elder knew the world better than Lucy. She remained in the background into which the Contessa was looking with eyes which she called shortsighted. "How do you do, Madame di Forno-Populo!" she said. "It is a long time since we met. We have both grown older since that period. I hope you have recovered from your fatigue."

The Contessa sank back again into her chair. "Ah, both, yes!" she said, with an eloquent movement of her hands. At this Sir Tom gave vent to a faint chuckle, as if he could not contain himself any longer.

"The passage of time is a myth," he said; "it is a fable; it goes the other way. To look at you—"

"Both!" said the Contessa, with a soft, little laugh, spreading out her beautiful hands.

Lucy hoped that Lady Randolph, who had kept behind, did not hear this last monosyllable, but she was angry with her husband for laughing, for abandoning his aunt's side, upon which she herself, astonished, ranged herself without delay. But what was still more surprising to Lucy, with her old-fashioned politeness, was to see the second stranger who had followed the Contessa into the room, but who had not been introduced or noticed. She had the air of being very young—a dependent probably, and looking for no attention—and with a little curtsey to the company, withdrew to the other side of the table on which the lamp was standing. Lucy had only time to see that there was a second figure, very slim and slight, and that the light of the lamp seemed to reflect itself in the soft oval of a youthful face as she passed behind it; but save for this noiseless movement the young lady gave not the smallest sign of existence, nor did any one notice her. And it was only when the summons came to dinner, and when Lucy called forth the bashful Jock to offer his awkward arm to Lady Randolph, that the unannounced and unconsidered guest came fully into sight.

"There are no more gentlemen, and I think we must go in together," Lucy said.

"It is a great honour for me," said the girl. She had a very slight foreign accent, but she was not in the least shy. She came forward at once with the utmost composure. Though she was a stranger and a dependent without a name, she was a great deal more at her ease than Lucy was, who was the mistress of everything. Lucy for her part was considerably embarrassed. She looked at the girl, who smiled at her, not without a little air of encouragement and almost patronage in return.

"I have not heard your name," Lucy at last prevailed upon herself to say, as they went through the long drawing-room together. "It is very stupid of me; but I was occupied with Madame di Forno-Populo—"

"You could not hear it, for it was never mentioned," said the girl. "The Contessa does not think it worth while. I am at present in the cocoon. If I am pretty enough when I am quite grown up, then she will tell my name—"

"Pretty enough? But what does that matter? one does not talk of such things," said the decorous little matron, startled and alarmed.

"Oh, it means everything to me," said the anonymous. "It is doubtful what I shall be. If I am only a little pretty I shall be sent home; but if it should happen to me—ah! no such luck!—to be beautiful, then the Contessa will introduce me, and everybody says I may go far—farther, indeed, than even she has ever done. Where am I to sit? Beside you?"

"Here, please," said Lucy, trembling a little, and confounded by the ease of this new actor on the scene, who spoke so frankly. She was dressed in a little black frock up to her throat; her hair in great shining bands coiled about her head, but not an ornament of any kind about her. A little charity girl could not have been dressed more plainly. But she showed no consciousness of this, nor, indeed, of anything that was embarrassing. She looked round the table with a free and fearless look. There was not about her any appearance of timidity, even in respect to the Contessa. She included that lady in her inspection as well as the others, and even made a momentary pause before she sat down, to complete her survey. Lucy, who had on ordinary occasions a great deal of gentle composure, and had sat with a Cabinet Minister by her side without feeling afraid, was more disconcerted than it would be easy to say by this young creature, of whom she did not know the name. It was so small a party that a separate little conversation with her neighbour was scarcely practicable, but the Contessa was talking to Sir Tom with the confidential air of one who has a great deal to say, and Lady Randolph on his other side was keeping a stern silence, so that Lucy was glad to make a little attempt at her end of the table.

"You must have had a very fatiguing journey?" she said. "Travelling by night, when you are not used to it—"

"But we are quite used to it," said the girl. "It is our usual way. By land it is so much easier: and even at sea one goes to bed, and one is at the other side before one knows."

"Then you are a good sailor, I suppose—"

"Pas mal," said the young lady. She began to look at Jock, and to turn round from time to time to the elder Lady Randolph, who sat on the other side of her. "They are not dumb, are they?" she asked. "Not once have I heard them speak. That is very English, so like what one reads in books."

"You speak English very well, Mademoiselle," said the Dowager suddenly.

The girl turned round and examined her with a candid surprise. "I am so glad you do," she said calmly: a little mot which brought the colour to Lady Randolph's cheeks.

"A pupil of the Contessa naturally knows a good many languages," she said, "and would be little at a loss wherever she went. You have come last from Florence, Rome, or perhaps some other capital. The Contessa has friends everywhere—still."

This last little syllable caught the Contessa's fine ear, though it was not directed to her. She gave the Dowager a very gracious smile across the table. "Still," she repeated, "everywhere! People are so kind. My invitations are so many it was with difficulty I managed to accept that of our excellent Tom. But I had made up my mind not to disappoint him nor his dear young wife. I was not prepared for the pleasure of finding your ladyship here."

"How fortunate that you were able to manage it! I have been complimenting Mademoiselle on her English. She does credit to her instructors. Tell me, is this your first visit," Lady Randolph said, turning to the young lady "to England?" Even in this innocent question there was more than met the eye. The girl, however, had begun to make a remark to Lucy, and thus evaded it in the most easy way.

"I saw you come home soon after our arrival," she said. "I was at my window. You came with—Monsieur—" She cast a glance at Jock as she spoke, with a smile in her eyes that was not without its effect. There was a little provocation in it, which an older man would have known how to answer. But Jock, in the awkwardness of his youth, blushed fiery red, and turned away his gaze, which, indeed, had been dwelling upon her with an absorbed but shy attention. The boy had never seen anything at all like her before.

"My brother," said Lucy, and the young lady gave him a beaming smile and bow which made Jock's head turn round. He did not know how to reply to it, whether he ought not to get up to answer her salutation; and being so uncertain and abashed and excited, he did nothing at all, but gazed again with an absorption which was not uncomplimentary. She gave him from time to time a little encouraging glance.

"That was what I thought. You drive out always at that early hour in England, and always with—Monsieur?" The girl laughed now, looking at him, so that Jock longed to say something witty and clever. Oh, why was not MTutor here? He would have known the sort of thing to say.

"Oh not, not always with Jock," Lucy answered, with honest matter-of-fact. "He is still at school, and we have him only for the holidays. Perhaps you don't know what that means?"

"The holidays? yes, I know. Monsieur, no doubt, is at one of the great schools that are nowhere but in England, where they stay till they are men."

"We stay," said Jock, making an almost convulsive effort, "till we are nineteen. We like to stay as long as we can."

"How innocent," said the girl with a pretty elderly look of superiority and patronage; and then she burst into a laugh, which neither Lucy nor Jock knew how to take, and turned back again in the twinkling of an eye to Lady Randolph, who had relapsed into silence. "And you drive in the afternoon," she said. "I have already made my observations. And the baby in the middle, between. And Sir Tom always. He goes out and he goes in, and one sees him continually. I already know all the habits of the house."

"You were not so very tired, then, after all. Why did you not come down stairs and join us in what we were doing?"

The young lady did not make any articulate reply, but her answer was clear enough. She cast a glance across the table to the Contessa, and laid her hand upon her own cheek. Lucy was a little mystified by this pantomime, but to Lady Randolph there was no difficulty about it. "That is easily understood," she said, "when one is sur le retour. But the same precautions are not necessary with all."

A smile came upon the girl's lip. "I am sympathetic," she said. "Oh, troppo! I feel just like those that I am with. It is sometimes a trouble, and sometimes it is an advantage." This was to Lucy like the utterance of an oracle, and she understood it not.

"Another time," she said kindly, "you must not only observe us from the window, but come down and share what we are doing. Jock will show you the park and the grounds, and I will take you to the village. It is quite a pretty village, and the cottages are very nice now."

The young stranger's eyes blazed with intelligence. She seemed to perceive everything at a glance.

"I know the village," she said, "it is at the park gates, and Milady takes a great deal of trouble that all is nice in the cottages. And there is an old woman that knows all about the family, and tells legends of it; and a school and a church, and many other objets-de-piété. I know it like that," she cried, holding out the pretty pink palm of her hand.

"This information is preternatural," said Lady Randolph. "You are astonished, Lucy. Mademoiselle is a sorceress. I am sure that Jock thinks so. Nothing save an alliance with something diabolical could have made her so well instructed, she who has never been in England before."

"Do you ask how I know all that?" the girl said laughing. "Then I answer, novels. It is all Herr Tauchnitz and his pretty books."

"And so you really never were in England before—not even as a baby?" Lady Randolph said.

The girl's gaiety had attracted even the pair at the other end of the table, who had so much to say to each other. The Contessa and Sir Tom exchanged a look, which Lucy remarked with a little surprise, and remarked in spite of herself: and the great lady interfered to help her young dependent out.

"How glad I am to give her that advantage, dear lady! It is the crown of the petite's education. In England she finds the most fine manners, as well as villages full of objets-de-piété. It is what is needful to form her," the Contessa said.

## CHAPTER XIX

THE OPENING OF THE DRAMA

"Come and sit beside me and tell me everything," said the Contessa. She had appropriated the little sofa next the fire where Lady Randolph generally sat in the evening. She had taken Lucy's arm on the way from the dining-room, and drew her with her to this corner. Nothing could be more caressing or tender than her manner. She seemed to be conferring the most delightful of favours as she drew towards her the mistress of the house. "You have been married—how long? Six years! But it is impossible! And you have all the freshness of a child. And very happy?" she said smiling upon Lucy. She had not a fault in her pronunciation, but when she uttered these two words she gave a little roll of the "r" as if she meant to assume a defect which she had not, and smiled with a tender benevolence in which there was the faintest touch of derision. Lucy did not make out what it was, but she felt that something lay under the dazzling of that smile. She allowed the stranger to draw her to the sofa, and sat down by her.

"Yes, it is six years," she said.

"And ver—r—y happy?" the Contessa repeated. "I am sure that dear Tom is a model husband. I have known him a very long time. Has he told you about me?"

"That you were an old friend," said Lucy, looking at her. "Oh yes! The only thing is, that we are so much afraid you will find the country dull."

The Contessa replied only with an eloquent look and a pressure of the hand. Her eyes were quite capable of expressing their meaning without words; and Lucy felt that she had guessed her rightly.

"We wished to have a party to meet you," Lucy said, "but the baby fell ill—and I thought as you had kindly come so far to see Tom, you would not mind if you found us alone."

The lady still made no direct reply. She said after a little pause,

"The country is very dull—" still smiling upon Lucy, and allowed a full minute to pass without another word. Then she added, "And Milady?—is she always with you?"—with a slight shrug of the shoulders. She did not even lower her voice to prevent Lady Randolph from hearing, but gave Lucy's hand a special pressure, and fixed upon her a significant look.

"Oh! Aunt Randolph?" cried Lucy. "Oh no; she is only paying her usual Christmas visit."

The Contessa drew a sigh of relief, and laid her other delicate hand upon her breast. "You take a load off my heart," she said; then gliding gracefully from the subject, "And that excellent Tom—? you met him—in society?"

Lucy did not quite like the questioning, or those emphatic pressures of her hand. She said quickly, "We met at Lady Randolph's. I was living there."

"Oh—I see," the stranger said, and she gave vent to a little gentle laugh. "I see!" Her meaning was entirely unknown to Lucy; but she felt an indefinable offence. She made a slight effort to withdraw her hand; but this the Contessa would not permit. She pressed the imprisoned fingers more closely in her own. "You do not like this questioning. Pardon! I had forgotten English ways. It is because I hope you will let me be your friend too."

"Oh yes," cried Lucy, ashamed of her own hesitation, yet feeling every moment more reluctant. She subdued her rising distaste with an effort. "I hope," she said, sweetly, "that we shall be able to make you feel at home, Madame di Forno-Populo. If there is anything you do not like, will you tell me? Had I been at home I should have chosen other rooms for you."

"They are so pretty, those words, 'at home!' so English," the Contessa said, with smiles that were more and more sweet. "But it will fatigue you to call me all that long name."

"Oh no!" cried Lucy, with a vivid blush. She did not know what to say, whether this meant a little derision of her careful pronunciation, or what it was. She went on, after a little pause, "But if you are not quite comfortable the other rooms can be got ready directly. It was the housekeeper who thought the rooms you have would be the warmest."

The Contessa gave her another gentle pressure of the hand. "Everything is perfect," she said. "The house and the wife, and all. I may call you Lucy? You are so fresh and young. How do you keep that pretty bloom after six years—did you say six years? Ah! the English are always those that wear best. You are not afraid of a great deal of light—no? but it is trying sometimes. Shades are an advantage. And he has not spoken to you of me, that dear Tom? There was a time when he talked much of me—oh, much—constantly! He was young then—and," she said with a little sigh—"so was I. He was perhaps not handsome, but he was distinguished. Many Englishmen are so who have no beauty, no handsomeness, as you say, and English women also, though that is more rare. And you are ver-r-y happy?" the Contessa asked again. She said it with a smile that was quite dazzling, but yet had just the faintest touch of ridicule in it, and rippled over into a little laugh. "When we know each other better I will betray all his little secrets to you," she said.

This was so very injudicious on the part of an old friend, that a wiser person than Lucy would have divined some malign meaning in it. But Lucy, though suppressing an instinctive distrust, took no notice, not even in her thoughts. It was not necessary for her to divine or try to divine what people meant; she took what they said, simply, without requiring interpretation. "He has told me a great deal," she said. "I think I almost know his journeys by heart." Then Lucy carried the war into the enemy's country without realising what she was doing. "You will think it very stupid of me," she said, "but I did not hear Mademoiselle,—the young lady's name?"

The Contessa's eyes dwelt meditatively upon Lucy: she patted her hand and smiled upon her, as if every other subject was irrelevant. "And he has taken you into society?" she said, continuing her examination. "How delightful is that English domesticity. You go everywhere together?" She had no appearance of having so much as heard Lucy's question. "And you do not fear that he will find it dull in the country? You have the confidence of being enough for him? How sweet for me to find the happiness of my friend so assured. And now I shall share it for a little. You will make us all happy. Dear child!" said the lady with enthusiasm, drawing Lucy to her and kissing her forehead. Then she broke into a pretty laugh. "You will work for your poor, and I, who am good for nothing—I shall take out my tapisserie, and he will read to us while we work. What a tableau!" cried the Contessa. "Domestic happiness, which one only tastes in England. The Eden before the fall!"

It was at this moment that the gentlemen, i.e. Sir Tom and Jock, appeared out of the dining-room. They had not lingered long after the ladies. Sir Tom had been somewhat glum after they left. His look of amusement was not so lively. He said sententiously, not so much to Jock as to himself, "That woman is bent on mischief," and got up and walked about the room instead of taking his wine. Then he laughed and turned to Jock, who was musing over his orange skins. "When you get a fellow into your house that is not much good—I suppose it must happen sometimes—that knows too much and puts the young ones up to tricks, what do you do with him, most noble Captain? Come, you find out a lot of things for yourselves, you boys. Tell me what you do."

Jock was a little startled by this demand, but he rose to the occasion. "It has happened," he said. "You know, unless a fellow's been awfully bad, you can't always keep him out."

"And what then?" said Sir Tom. "MTutor sets his great wits to work?"

"I hope, sir," cried Jock, "that you don't think I would trouble MTutor, who has enough on his hands without that. I made great friends with the fellow myself. You know," said the lad, looking up with splendid confidence, "he couldn't harm me—"

Sir Tom looked at him with a little drawing of his breath, such as the experienced sometimes feel as they look at the daring of the innocent—but with a smile, too.

"When he tried it on with me, I just kicked him," said Jock, calmly; "once was enough; he didn't do it again; for naturally he stood a bit in awe of me. Then I kept him that he hadn't a moment to himself. It was the football half, when you've not got much time to spare all day. And in the evenings he had poenas and things. When he got with two or three of the others, one of us would just be loafing about, and call out 'Hallo, what's up?' He never had any time to go wrong, and then he got to find out it didn't pay."

"Philosopher! sage!" cried Sir Tom. "It is you that should teach us; but, alas, my boy, have you never found out that even that last argument fails to tell—and that they don't mind even if it doesn't pay?"

He sighed as he spoke; then laughed out, and added, "I can at all events try the first part of your programme. Come along and let's cry, Hallo! what's up? It simplifies matters immensely, though," said Sir Tom, with a serious face, "when you can kick the fellow you disapprove of in that charming candid way. Guard the privilege; it is invaluable, Jock."

"Well," said Jock, "some fellows think it's brutal, you know. MTutor he always says try argument first. But I just want to know how are you to do your duty, captain of a big house, unless it's known that you will just kick 'em when they're beastly. When it's known, even that does a deal of good."

"Every thing you say confirms my opinion of your sense," said Sir Tom, taking the boy by the arm, "but also of your advantages, Jock, my boy. We cannot act, you see, in that straightforward manner, more's the pity, in the world; but I shall try the first part of your programme, and act on your advice," he said, as they walked into the room where the ladies were awaiting them. The smaller room looked very warm and bright after the large, dimly-lighted one through which they had passed. The Contessa, in her tender conference with Lucy, formed a charming group in the middle of the picture. Lady Randolph sat by, exiled out of her usual place, with an illustrated magazine in her hand, and an air of quick watchfulness about her, opposite to them. She was looking on like a spectator at a play. In the background behind the table, on which stood a large lamp, was the Contessa's companion, with her back turned to the rest, lightly flitting from picture to picture, examining everything. She had been entirely careless of the action of the piece, but she turned round at the voices of the new-comers, as if her attention was aroused.

"You are going to take somebody's advice?" said the Contessa. "That is something new; come here at once and explain. To do so is due to your—wife; yes, to your wife. An Englishman tells every thought to his wife; is it not so? Oh yes, mon ami, your sweet little wife and I are the best of friends. It is for life," she said, looking with inexpressible sentiment in Lucy's face, and pressing her hands. Then, was it possible? a flash of intelligence flew from her eyes to those of Sir Tom, and she burst into a laugh and clapped her beautiful hands together. "He is so ridiculous, he makes one laugh at everything," she cried.

Lucy remained very serious, with a somewhat forced smile upon her face, between these two, looking from one to another.

"Nay, if you have come the length of swearing eternal friendship—" said Sir Tom.

Jock did not know what to do with himself. He began by stumbling over Lady Randolph's train, which though carefully coiled about her, was so long and so substantial that it got in his way. In getting out of its way he almost stumbled against the slim, straight figure of the girl, who stood behind surveying the company. She met his awkward apology with a smile. "It doesn't matter," she said, "I am so glad you are come. I had nobody to talk to." Then she made a little pause, regarding him with a bright, impartial look, as if weighing all his qualities. "Don't you talk?" she said. "Do you prefer not to say anything? because I know how to behave: I will not trouble you if it is so. In England there are some who do not say anything?" she added with an inquiring look. Jock, who was conscious of blushing all over from top to toe, ventured a glance at her, to which she replied by a peal of laughter, very merry but very subdued, in which, in spite of himself, he was obliged to join.

"So you can laugh!" she said; "oh, that is well; for otherwise I should not know how to live. We must laugh low, not to make any noise and distract the old ones; but still, one must live. Tell me, you are the brother of Madame—Should I say Milady? In my novels they never do, but I do not know if the novels are just or not."

"The servants say my lady, but no one else," said Jock.

"How fine that is," the young lady said admiringly, "in a moment to have it all put right. I am glad we came to England; we say mi-ladi and mi-lord as if that was the name of every one here; but it is not so in the books. You are, perhaps Sir? like Sir Tom—or you are—"

"I am Trevor, that is all," said Jock with a blush; "I am nobody in particular: that is, here"—he added with a momentary gleam of natural importance.

"Ah!" cried the young lady, "I understand—you are a great person at home."

Jock had no wish to deceive, but he could not prevent a smile from creeping about the corners of his mouth. "Not a great person at all," he said, not wishing to boast.

The young stranger, who was so curious about all her new surroundings, formed her own conclusion. She had been brought up in an atmosphere full of much knowledge, but also of theories which were but partially tenable. She interpreted Jock according to her own ideas, which were not at all suited to his case; but it was impossible that she could know that.

"I am finding people out," she said to him. "You are the only one that is young like me. Let us form an alliance—while the old ones are working out all their plans and fighting it out among themselves."

"Fighting it out! I know some that are not likely to fight," cried Jock, bewildered.

"Was not that right?" said the girl, distressed. "I thought it was an idiotisme, as the French say. Ah! they are always fighting. Look at them now! The Contessa, she is on the war-path. That is an American word. I have a little of all languages. Madame, you will see—ah, that is what you meant!—does not understand, she looks from one to another. She is silent, but Sir Tom, he knows everything. And the old lady, she sees it too. I have gone through so many dramas, I am blasée. It wearies at last, but yet it is exciting too. I ask myself what is going to be done here? You have heard perhaps of the Contessa in England, Mr.—"

"Trevor," said Jock.

"And you pronounce it just like this—Mis-ter? I want to know; for perhaps I shall have to stay here. There is not known very much about me. Nor do I know myself. But if the Contessa finds for me— I am quite mad," said the girl suddenly. "I am telling you—and of course it is a secret. The old lady watches the Contessa to see what it is she intends. But I do not myself know what the Contessa intends—except in respect to me."

Jock was too shy to inquire what that was: and he was confused with this unusual confidence. Young ladies had not been in the habit of opening to him their secrets; indeed he had little experience of these kind of creatures at all. She looked at him as she spoke as if she wished to provoke him to inquiry—with a gaze that was very open and withal bold, yet innocent too. And Jock, on his side, was as entirely innocent as if he had been a Babe in the Wood.

"Don't you want to know what she is going to do with me, and why she has brought me?" the girl said, talking so quickly that he could scarcely follow the stream of words. "I was not invited, and I am not introduced, and no one knows anything of me. Don't you want to know why I am here?"

Jock followed the movements of her lips, the little gestures of her hands, which were almost as eloquent, with eyes that were confused by so great a call upon them. He could not make any reply, but only gazed at her, entranced, as he had never been in his life before, and so anxious not to lose the hurried words, the quick flash of the small white hands against her dark dress, that his mind had not time to make out what she meant.

Lucy on her side sat between her husband and the Contessa for some time, listening to their conversation. That was more rapid, too, than she was used to, and it was full of allusions, understood when they were half-said by the others, which to her were all darkness. She tried to follow them with a wistful sort of smile, a kind of painful homage to the Contessa's soft laugh and the ready response of Sir Tom. She tried too, to follow, and share the brightening interest of his face, the amusement and eagerness of his listening; but by and by she got chilled, she knew not how—the smile grew frozen upon her face, her comprehension seemed to fail altogether. She got up softly after a while from her corner of the sofa, and neither her husband nor her guest took any particular notice. She came across the room to Lady Randolph, and drew a low chair beside her, and asked her about the pictures in the magazine which she was still holding in her hand.

CHAPTER XX

AN ANXIOUS CRITIC

In a few days after the arrival of Madame di Forno-Populo, there was almost an entire change of aspect at the Hall. Nobody could tell how this change had come about. It was involuntary, unconscious, yet complete. The Contessa came quietly into the foreground. She made no demonstration of power, and claimed no sort of authority. She never accosted the mistress of the house without tender words and caresses. Her attitude towards Lucy, indeed, was that of an admiring relation to a delightful and promising child. She could not sufficiently praise and applaud her. When she spoke, her visitor turned towards her with the most tender smiles. In whatsoever way the Contessa was occupied, she never failed when she heard Lucy's voice to turn round upon her, to bestow this smile, to murmur a word of affectionate approval. When they were near enough to each other, she would take her hand and press it with affectionate emotion. The other members of the household, except Sir Tom, she scarcely noticed at all. The Dowager Lady Randolph exchanged with her now and then a few words of polite defiance, but that was all. And she had not been long at the Hall before her position there was more commanding than that of Lady Randolph. Insensibly all the customs of the house changed for her. There was no question as to who was the centre of conversation in the evening. Sir Tom went to the sofa from which she had so cleverly ousted his aunt, as soon as he came in after dinner, and leaning over her with his arm on the mantelpiece, or drawing a chair beside her, would laugh and talk with endless spirit and amusement. When he talked of the people in the neighbourhood who afforded scope for satire, she would tap him with her fan and say, "Why do I not see these originals? bring them to see me," to Lucy's wonder and often dismay. "They would not amuse you at all," Sir Tom would reply, upon which the lady would turn and call Lucy to her. "My little angel! he pretends that it is he that is so clever, that he creates these characters. We do not believe him, my Lucy, do we? Ask them, ask them, cara, then we shall judge."

In this way the house was filled evening after evening. A reign of boundless hospitality seemed to have begun. The other affairs of the house slipped aside, and to provide amusement for the Contessa became the chief object of life. She had everybody brought to see her, from the little magnates of Farafield to the Duchess herself, and the greatest people in the county. The nursery, which had been so much, perhaps too much, in the foreground, regulating the whole great household according as little Tom was better or worse, was thrust altogether into the shadow. If neglect was wholesome, then he had that advantage. Even his mother could do no more than run furtively to him, as she did about a hundred times a day in the intervals of her duties. His little mendings and fallings back ceased to be the chief things in the house. His father, indeed, would play with his child in the mornings when he was brought to Lucy's room; but the burden of his remarks was to point out to her how much better the little beggar got on when there was less fuss made about him. And Lucy's one grievance against her visitor, the only one which she permitted herself to perceive, was that she never took any notice of little Tom. She never asked for him, a thing which was unexampled in Lucy's experience. When he was produced she smiled, indeed, but contemplated him at a distance. The utmost stretch of kindness she had ever shown was to touch his cheek with a finger delicately when he was carried past her. Lucy made theories in her mind about this, feeling it necessary to account in some elaborate way for what was so entirely out of nature. "I know what it must be—she must have lost her own," she said to her husband. Sir Tom's countenance was almost convulsed by one of those laughs, which he now found it expedient to suppress, but he only replied that he had never heard of such an event. "Ah! it must have been before you knew her; but she has never got it out of her mind," Lucy cried. That hypothesis explained everything. At this time it is scarcely necessary to say Lucy was with her whole soul trying to be "very fond," as she expressed it, of the Contessa. There were some things about her which startled young Lady Randolph. For one thing, she would go out shooting with Sir Tom, and was as good a shot as any of the gentlemen. This wounded Lucy terribly, and took her a great effort to swallow. It went against all her traditions. With her bourgeois education she hated sport, and even in her husband with difficulty made up her mind to it; but that a woman should go forth and slay was intolerable.

There were other things besides which were a mystery to her. Lady Randolph's invariably defiant attitude for one, and the curious aspect of the Duchess when suddenly brought face to face with the stranger. It appeared that they were old friends, which astonished Lucy, but not so much as the great lady's bewildered look when Madame di Forno-Populo went up to her. It seemed for a moment as if the shock was too much for her. She stammered and shook through all her dignity and greatness, as she exclaimed. "You! here?" in two distinct outcries, gazing appalled into the smiling and beautiful face before her. But then the Duchess came to, after a while. She seemed to get over her surprise, which was more than surprise. All these things disturbed Lucy. She did not know what to make of them. She was uneasy at the change that had been wrought upon her own household, which she did not understand. Yet it was all perfectly simple, she said to herself. It was Tom's duty to devote himself to the stranger. It was the duty of both as hosts to procure for her such amusement as was to be found. These were things of which Lucy convinced herself by various half unconscious processes of argument. But it was necessary to renew these arguments from time to time, to keep possession of them in order to feel their force as she wished to do. She said nothing to her husband on the subject, with an instinctive sense that it would be very difficult to handle. And Sir Tom, too, avoided it. But it was impossible to pursue the same reticence with Lady Randolph, who now and then insisted on opening it up. When the end of her visit arrived she sent for Lucy into her own room, to speak to her seriously. She said—

"My dear, I am due to-morrow at the Maltravers', as you know. It is a visit I like to pay, they are always so nice; but I cannot bear the thought of going off, Lucy, to enjoy myself and leaving you alone."

"Alone, Aunt Randolph!" cried Lucy, "when Tom is at home!"

"Oh, Tom! I have no patience with Tom," cried the Dowager. "I think he must be mad to let that woman come upon you so. Of course you know very well, my dear, it is of her that I want to speak. In the country it does not so much matter; but you must not let her identify herself with you, Lucy, in town."

"In town!" Lucy said with a little dismay; "but, dear Aunt Randolph, it will be six weeks before we go to town; and, surely, long before that—" She paused, and blushed with a sense of the inhospitality involved in her words, which made Lucy ashamed of herself.

"You think so?" said Lady Randolph, smiling somewhat grimly. "Well, we shall see. For my part, I think she will find Park Lane a very desirable situation, and if you do not take the greatest care— But why should I speak to you of taking care? Of course, if Tom wished it, you would take in all Bohemia, and never say a word—"

"Surely," said Lucy, looking with serene eyes in the elder lady's face, "I do not know what you mean by Bohemia, Aunt Randolph; but if you think it possible that I should object when Tom asks his friends—"

"Oh—his friends! I have no patience with you, either the one or the other," said the old lady. "When Sir Robert was living, do you think it was he who invited my guests? I should think not indeed! especially the women. If that was to be the case, marriage would soon become an impossibility. And is it possible, Lucy, is it possible that you, with your good sense, can like all that petting and coaxing, and the way she talks to you as if you were a child?"

As a matter of fact Lucy had not been able to school herself into liking it; but when the objection was stated so plainly, she coloured high with a vexation and annoyance which were very grievous and hard to bear. It seemed to her that it would be disloyal both to her husband and her guest if she complained, and at the same time Lady Randolph's shot went straight to the mark. She did her best to smile, but it was not a very easy task.

"You have always taught me, Aunt Randolph," she said with great astuteness, "that I ought not to judge of the manners of strangers by my own little rules—especially of foreigners," she added, with a sense of her own cleverness which half comforted her amid other feelings not agreeable. It was seldom that Lucy felt any sense of triumph in her own powers.

"Foreigners?" said Lady Randolph, with disdain. But then she stopped short with a pause of indignation. "That woman," she said, which was the only name she ever gave the visitor, "has some scheme in her head you may be sure. I do not know what it is. It would not do her any good that I can see to increase her hold upon Tom."

"Upon Tom!" cried Lucy. It was her turn now to be indignant. "I don't know what you mean, Aunt Randolph," she said. "I cannot think that you want to make me—uncomfortable. There are some things I do not like in Madame di Forno-Populo. She is—different; but she is my husband's friend. If you mean that they will become still greater friends seeing more of each other, that is natural. For why should you be friends at all unless you like each other? And that Tom likes her must be just a proof that I am wrong. It is my ignorance. Perhaps the wisest way would be to say nothing more about it," young Lady Randolph concluded, briskly, with a sudden smile.

The Dowager looked at her as if she were some wonder in natural history, the nature of which it was impossible to divine. She thought she knew Lucy very well, but yet had never understood her, it being more difficult for a woman of the world to understand absolute straightforwardness and simplicity than it is even for the simple to understand the worldly. She was silent for a moment and stared at Lucy, not knowing what to make of her. At last she resumed as if going on without interruption. "But she has some scheme in hand, perhaps in respect to the girl. The girl is a very handsome creature, and might make a hit if she were properly managed. My belief is that this has been her scheme all through. But partly the presence of Tom—an old friend as you say of her own—and partly the want of opportunity, has kept it in abeyance. That is my idea, Lucy; you can take it for what it is worth. And your home will be the headquarters, the centre from which the adventuress will carry on—"

"Aunt Randolph!" Lucy's voice was almost loud in the pain and indignation that possessed her. She put out her hands as if to stop the other's mouth. "You want to make me think she is a wicked woman," she said. "And that Tom—Tom—"

Lucy had never permitted suspicion to enter her mind. She did not know now what it was that penetrated her innocent soul like an arrow. It was not jealousy. It was the wounding suggestion of a possibility which she would not and could not entertain.

"Lucy, Tom has no excuse at all," said the Dowager solemnly. "You'll believe nothing against him, of course, and I can't possibly wish to turn you against him; but I don't suppose he meant all that is likely to come out of it. He thought it would be a joke—and in the country what could it matter? And then things have never gone so far as that people could refuse to receive her, you know. Oh no! the Contessa has her wits too much about her for that. But you saw for yourself that the Duchess was petrified; and I— not that I am an authority, like her Grace. One thing, Lucy, is quite clear, and that I must say; you must not take upon yourself to be answerable—you so young as you are and not accustomed to society—for that woman, before the world. You must just take your courage in both hands, and tell Tom that though you give in to him in the country, in town you will not have her. She means to take advantage of you, and bring forward her girl, and make a grand coup. That is what she means—I know that sort of person. It is just the greatest luck in the world for them to get hold of some one that is so unexceptionable and so unsuspicious as you."

Lady Randolph insisted upon saying all this, notwithstanding the interruptions of Lucy. "Now I wash my hands of it," she said. "If you won't be advised, I can do no more." It was the day after the great dinner when the Duchess had met Madame di Forno-Populo with so much surprise. The elder lady had been in much excitement all the evening. She had conversed with her Grace apart on several occasions, and from the way in which they laid their heads together, and their gestures, it was clear enough that their feeling was the same upon the point they discussed. All the best people in the county had been collected together, and there could be no doubt that the Contessa had achieved a great success. She sang as no woman had ever been heard to sing for a hundred miles round, and her beauty and her grace and her diamonds had been enough to turn the heads of both men and women. It was remarked that the Duchess, though she received her with a gasp of astonishment, was evidently very well acquainted with the fascinating foreign lady, and though there was a little natural and national distrust of her at first, as a person too remarkable, and who sang too well for the common occasions of life, yet not to gaze at her, watch her, and admire, was impossible. Lucy had been gratified with the success of her visitor. Even though she was not sure that she was comfortable about her presence there at all, she was pleased with the effect she produced. When the Contessa sang there suddenly appeared out of the midst of the crowd a slim, straight figure in a black gown, which instantly sat down at the piano, played the accompaniments, and disappeared again without a word. The spectators thronging round the piano saw that this was a girl, as graceful and distinguished as the Contessa herself, who passed away without a word, and disappeared when her office was accomplished, with a smile on her face, but without lingering for a moment or speaking to any one; which was a pretty bit of mystery too.

All this had happened on the night before Lady Randolph's summons to Lucy. It was in the air that the party at the Hall was to break up after the great entertainment; the Dowager was going, as she had said, to the Maltravers'; Jock was going back to school; and though no limit of Madame di Forno-Populo's visit had been mentioned, still it was natural that she should go when the other people did. She had been a fortnight at the Hall. That is long for a visit at a country house where generally people are coming and going continually. And Lucy had begun to look forward to the time when once more she would be mistress of her own house and actions, with all visitors and interruptions gone. She had been looking forward to the happy old evenings, the days in which baby should be set up again on his domestic throne. The idea that the Contessa might not be going away, the suggestion that she might still be there when it was time to make the yearly migration to town, chilled the very blood in her veins. But it was a thought that she would not dwell upon. She would not betray her feeling in this respect to any one. She returned the kiss which old Lady Randolph bestowed upon her at the end of their interview, very affectionately; for, though she did not always agree with her, she was attached to the lady who had been so kind to her when she was a friendless little girl. "Thank you, Aunt Randolph, for telling me," she said very sweetly, though, indeed, she had no intention of taking the Dowager's advice. Lady Randolph went off in the afternoon of the next day, for it was a very short journey to the Maltravers', where she was going. All the party came out into the hall to see her away, the Contessa herself as well as the others. Nothing, indeed, could be more cordial than the Contessa. She caught up a shawl and wound it round her, elaborately defending herself against the cold, and came out to the steps to share in the last farewells.

When Lady Randolph was in the carriage with her maid by her side, and her hot-water footstool under her feet, and the coachman waiting his signal to drive away, she put out her hand amid her furs to Lucy. "Now remember!" Lady Randolph said. It was almost as solemn as the mysterious reminder of the dying king to the bishop. But unfortunately, what is solemn in certain circumstances may be ludicrous in others. The party in the Hall scarcely restrained its merriment till the carriage had driven away.

"What awful compact is this between you, Lucy?" Sir Tom said. "Has she bound you by a vow to assassinate me in my sleep?"

The Contessa unwound herself out of her shawl, and putting her arm caressingly round Lucy, led her back to the drawing-room. "It has something to do with me," she said. "Come and tell me all about it." Lucy had been disconcerted by Lady Randolph's reminder. She was still more disconcerted now.

"It is—something Aunt Randolph wishes me to do in the spring, when we go to town," she said.

"Ah! I know what that is," said the Contessa. "They see that you are too kind to your husband's friend. Milady would wish you to be more as she herself is. I understand her very well. I understand them all, these women. They cannot endure me. They see a meaning in everything I do. I have not a meaning in everything I do," she added, with a pathetic look, which went to Lucy's heart.

"No, no, indeed you are mistaken. It was not that. I am sure you have no meaning," said Lucy, vehement and confused.

The Contessa read her innocent distraite countenance like a book, as she said—or at least she thought so. She linked her own delicate arm in hers, and clasped Lucy's hand. "One day I will tell you why all these ladies hate me, my little angel," she said.


CHAPTER XXI

AN UNEXPECTED ENCOUNTER

In the meantime something had been going on behind-backs of which nobody took much notice. It had been discovered long before this, in the family, that the Contessa's young companion had a name like other people—that is to say, a Christian name. She was called by the Contessa, in the rare moments when she addressed her, Bice—that is to say, according to English pronunciation, Beeshée (you would probably call it Beetchee if you learned to speak Italian in England, but the Contessa had the Tuscan tongue in a Roman mouth, according to the proverb), which, as everybody knows, is the contraction of Beatrice. She was called Miss Beachey in the household, a name which was received—by the servants at least—as a quite proper and natural name; a great deal more sensible than Forno-Populo. Her position, however, in the little party was a quite peculiar one. The Contessa took her for granted in a way which silenced all inquisitive researches. She gave no explanation who she was, or what she was, or why she carried this girl about with her. If she was related to herself, if she was a dependent, nobody knew; her manner gave no clue at all to the mystery. It was very seldom that the two had any conversation whatsoever in the presence of the others. Now and then the Contessa would send the girl upon an errand, telling her to bring something, with an absence of directions where to find it that suggested the most absolute confidence in her young companion. When the Contessa sang, Bice, as a matter of course, produced herself at the right moment to play her accompaniments, and got herself out of the way, noiselessly, instantly, the moment that duty was over. These accompaniments were played with an exquisite skill and judgment, an exact adaptation to the necessities of the voice, which could only have been attained by much and severe study; but she never, save on these occasions, was seen to look at a piano. For the greater part of the time the girl was invisible. She appeared in the Contessa's train, always in her closely-fitting, perfectly plain, black frock, without an ornament, at luncheon and dinner, and was present all the evening in the drawing-room. But for the rest of the day no one knew what became of this young creature, who nevertheless was not shy, nor showed any appearance of feeling herself out of place, or uncomfortable in her strange position. She looked out upon them all with frank eyes, in which it was evident there was no sort of mist, either of timidity or ignorance, understanding everything that was said, even allusions which puzzled Lucy; always intelligent and observant, though often with a shade of that benevolent contempt which the young with difficulty prevent themselves from feeling towards their elders. The littleness of their jokes and their philosophies was evidently quite apparent to this observer, who sat secure in the superiority of sixteen taking in everything; for she took in everything, even when she was not doing the elder people the honour of attending to what they were saying, with a faculty which belongs to that age. Opinions were divided as to Bice's beauty. The simpler members of the party, Lucy and Jock, admired her least; but such a competent critic as Lady Randolph, who understood what was effective, had a great opinion and even respect for her, as of one whose capabilities were very great indeed, and who might "go far," as she had herself said. As there was so much difference of opinion it is only right that the reader should be able to judge, as much as is possible, from a description. She was very slight and rather tall, with a great deal of the Contessa's grace, moving lightly as if she scarcely touched the ground, but like a bird rather than a cat. There was nothing in her of the feline grace of which we hear so much. Her movements were all direct and rapid; her feet seemed to skim, not to tread, the ground with an airy poise, which even when she stood still implied movement, always light, untiring, full of energy and impulse. Her eyes were gray—if it is possible to call by the name of the dullest of tints those two globes of light, now dark, now golden, now liquid with dew, and now with flame. Her hair was dusky, of no particular colour, with a crispness about the temples; but her complexion—ay, there was the rub. Bice had no complexion at all. By times in the evening, in artificial light, or when she was excited, there came a little flush to her cheeks, which miraculously chased away the shadows from her paleness, and made her radiant; but in daylight there could be no doubt that she was sallow, sometimes almost olive, though with a soft velvety texture which is more often seen on the dark-complexioned through all its gradations than on any but the most delicate of white skins. A black baby has a bloom upon its little dusky cheek like a purple peach, and this was the quality which gave to Bice's sallowness a certain charm. Her hands and arms were of the same indefinite tint—not white, whatever they might be called. Her throat was slender and beautifully-formed, but shared the same deficiency of colour. It is impossible to say how much disappointed Lucy was in the young stranger's appearance after the first evening. She had thought her very pretty, and she now thought her plain. To remember what the girl had said of her chances if she turned out beautiful filled her with a sort of pitying contempt.

But the more experienced people were not of Lucy's opinion. They thought well, on the contrary, of Bice's prospects. Lady Randolph, as has been said, regarded her with a certain respectfulness. She was not offended by the saucy speeches which the girl might now and then make. She went so far as to say even that if introduced under other auspices than those of the Contessa, there was no telling what such a girl might do. "But the chances now are that she will end on the stage," Lady Randolph said.

This strange girl unfolded herself very little in the family. When she spoke, she spoke with the utmost frankness, and was afraid of nobody. But in general she sat in the regions behind the table, with its big lamp, and said little or nothing. The others would all be collected about the fire, but Bice never approached the fire. Sometimes she read, sitting motionless, till the others forgot her presence altogether. Sometimes she worked at long strips of Berlin-wool work, the tapisserie to which, by moments, the Contessa would have recourse. But she heard and saw everything, as has been said, whether she attended or not, in the keenness of her youthful faculties. When the Contessa rose to sing, she was at the piano without a word; and when anything was wanted she gave an alert mute obedience to the lady who was her relation or her patroness, nobody knew which, almost without being told what was wanted. Except in this way, however, they seldom approached or said a word to each other that any one saw. During the long morning, which the Contessa spent in her room, appearing only at luncheon, Bice too was invisible. Thus she lived the strangest life of retirement and seclusion, such as a crushed dependent would find intolerable in the midst of a family, but without the least appearance of anything but enjoyment, and a perfect and dauntless freedom.

Bice, however, had one confidant in the house, and this, as is natural, was the very last person who would have seemed probable—it was Jock. Jock, it need scarcely be said, had no tendency at all to the society of girls. Deep as he was in MTutor's confidence, captain of his house, used to live in a little male community, and to despise (not unkindly) the rest of the world, it is not likely that he would care much for the antagonistic creatures who invariably interfered, he thought, with talk and enjoyment wherever they appeared. Making an exception in favour of Lucy and an older person now and then, who had been soothing to him when he was ill or out of sorts, Jock held that the feminine part of the creation was a mistake, and to be avoided in every practicable way. He had been startled by the young stranger's advances to him on the first evening, and her claim of fellowship on the score that he was young like herself. But when Bice first appeared suddenly in his way, far down in the depths of the winterly park, the boy's impulse would have been, had that been practicable, to turn and flee. She was skimming along, singing to herself, leaping lightly over fallen branches and the inequalities of the humid way, when he first perceived her; and Jock had a moment's controversy with himself as to what he ought to do. If he took to flight across the open park she would see him and understand the reason why— besides, it would be cowardly to fly from a girl, an inferior creature, who probably had lost her way, and would not know how to get back again. This reflection made him withdraw a little deeper into the covert, with the intention of keeping her in sight lest she should wander astray altogether, but yet keeping out of the way, that he might exercise this secret protecting charge of his, which Jock felt was his natural attitude even to a girl without the embarrassment of her society. He tried to persuade himself that she was a lower boy, of an inferior kind no doubt, but yet possessing claims upon his care; for MTutor had a great idea of influence, and had imprinted deeply upon the minds of his leading pupils the importance of exercising it in the most beneficial way for those who were under them.

Jock accordingly stayed among the brushwood watching where she went. How light she was! her feet scarcely made a dint upon the wet and spongy grass, in which his own had sunk. She went over everything like a bird. Now and then she would stop to gather a handful of brown rustling brambles, and the stiff yellow oak leaves, and here and there a rusty bough to which some rays of autumn colour still hung, which at first Jock supposed to mean botany, and was semi-respectful of, until she took off her hat and arranged them in it, when he was immediately contemptuous, saying to himself that it was just like a girl. All the same, it was interesting to watch her as she skipped and skimmed along with an air of enjoyment and delight in her freedom, which it was impossible not to sympathise with. She sang, not loudly, but almost under her breath, for pure pleasure, it seemed, but sometimes would break off and whistle, at which Jock was much shocked at first, but gradually got reconciled to, it was so clear and sweet. After awhile, however, he made an incautious step upon the brushwood, and the crashing of the branches betrayed him. She stopped suddenly with her head to the wind like a fine hound, and caught him with her keen eyes. Then there occurred a little incident which had a very strange effect—an effect he was too young to understand—upon Jock. She stood perfectly still, with her face towards the bushes in which he was, her head thrown high, her nostrils a little dilated, a flush of sudden energy and courage on her face. She did not know who he was or what he wanted watching her from behind the covert. He might be a tramp, a violent beggar, for anything she knew. These things are more tragic where Bice came from, and it was likely enough that she took him for a brigand. It was a quick sense of alarm that sprang over her, stringing all her nerves, and bringing the colour to her cheeks. She never flinched or attempted to flee, but stood at bay, with a high valour and proud scorn of her pursuer. Her attitude, the flush which made her fair in a moment, the expanded nostrils, the fulness which her panting breath of alarm gave to her breast, made an impression upon the boy which was ineffable and beyond words. It was his first consciousness that there was something in the world—not boy, or man, or sister, something which he did not understand, which feared yet confronted him, startled but defiant. He too paused for a moment, gazing at her, getting up his courage. Then he came slowly out from under the shade of the bushes and went towards her. There were a few yards of the open park to traverse before he reached her, so that he thought it necessary to relieve her anxiety before they met. He called out to her, "Don't be afraid, it is only me." For a moment more that fine poise lasted, and then she clapped her hands with a peal of laughter that seemed to fill the entire atmosphere and ring back from the clumps of wintry wood. "Oh," she cried, "it is you!" Jock did not know whether to be deeply affronted or to laugh too.

"I—thought you might have lost your way," he said, knitting his brows and looking as forbidding as he knew how, by way of correcting the involuntary sentiment that had stolen into his boyish heart.

"Then why did not you come to me?" she said, "is not that what you call to spy—to watch when one does not know you are there?"

Jock's countenance flushed at this word. "Spy! I never spied upon any one. I thought perhaps you might not be able to get back—so I would not go away out of reach."

"I see," she cried, "you meant to be kind but not friendly. Do I say it right? Why will not you be friendly? I have so many things I want to say, and no one, no one! to say them to. What harm would it do if you came out from yourself, and talked with me a little? You are too young to make it any—inconvenience," the girl said. She laughed a little and blushed a little as she said this, eyeing him all the time with frank, open eyes. "I am sixteen; how old are you?" she added, with a quick breath.

"Sixteen past," said Jock, with a little emphasis, to show his superiority in age as well as in other things.

"Sixteen in a boy means no more than nine or so," she said, with a light disdain, "so you need not have any fear. Oh, come and talk! I have a hundred and more of things to say. It is all so strange. How would you like to plunge in a new world like the sea, and never say what you think of it, or ask any questions, or tell when it makes you laugh or cry?"

"I should not mind much. I should neither laugh nor cry. It is only girls that do," said Jock, somewhat contemptuous too.

"Well! But then I am a girl. I cannot change my nature to please you," she said. "Sometimes I think I should have liked better to be a boy, for you have not to do the things we have to do—but then when I saw how awkward you were, and clumsy, and not good for anything"—she pointed these very plain remarks with a laugh between each and a look at Jock, by which she very plainly applied what she said. He did not know at all how to take this. The instinct of a gentleman to betray no angry feeling towards a girl, who was at the same time a lady, contrasted in him with the instinct of a child, scarcely yet aware of the distinctions of sex, to fight fairly for itself; but the former prevailed. And then it was scarcely possible to resist the contagion of the laugh which the damp air seemed to hold suspended, and bring back in curls and wreaths of pleasant sound. So Jock commanded himself and replied with an effort—

"We are just as good for things that we care about as you—but not for girls' things," he added, with another little fling of the mutual contempt which they felt for each other. Then after a pause: "I suppose we may as well go home, for it is getting late; and when it is dark you would be sure to lose your way—"

"Do you think so?" she said. "Then I will come, for I do not like to be lost. What should you do if we were lost? Build me a hut to take shelter in? or take off your coat to keep me warm and then go and look for the nearest village? That is what happens in some of the Contessa's old books—but, ah, not in the Tauchnitz now. But it would be nonsense, of course, for there are the red chimneys of the Hall staring us in the face, so how could we be lost?"

"When it is dark," said Jock, "you can't see the red always; and then you go rambling and wandering about, and hit yourself against the trees, and get up to the ankles in the wet grass and—don't like it at all." He laughed himself a little, with a laugh that was somewhat like a growl at his own abrupt conclusion, to which Bice responded cordially.

"How nice it is to laugh," she said, "it gets the air into your lungs and then you can breathe. It is to breathe I want—large—a whole world full," she cried, throwing out her arms and opening her mouth. "Because you know the rooms are small here, and there is so much furniture, the windows closed with curtains, the floors all hot with carpets. Do they shut you up as if in a box at night, with the shutters shut and all so dark? They do me. But as soon as they are gone I open. I like far better our rooms with big walls, and marble that is cool, and large, large windows that you can lie and look out at, when you wake, all painted upon the sky."

"I should think," said Jock, with the impulse of contradiction, "they would not be at all comfortable—"

"Comfortable," she cried in high disdain, "does one want to be comfortable? One wants to live, and feel the air, and everything that is round."

"That's what we do at school," said Jock, waking up to a sense of the affinities as he had already done to the diversities between them.

"Tell me about school," she cried, with a pretty imperious air; and Jock, who never desired any better, obeyed.

## CHAPTER XXII

### A PAIR OF FRIENDS

After this it came to be a very common occurrence that Jock and Bice should meet in the afternoon. He for one thing had lost his companionship with Lucy, and had been straying forth forlorn not knowing what to do with himself, taking long walks which he did not care for, and longing for the intellectual companionship of MTutor, or even of the other fellows who, if not intellectual, at least were acquainted with the same things, and accustomed to the same occupations as himself. It worked in him a tremor and commotion of a kind in which he was wholly inexperienced, when he saw the slim figure of the girl approaching him, through the paths of the shrubberies, or across the glades of the park. He said to himself once or twice, "What a bore;" but those words did not express his feelings. It was not a bore, it was something very different. He could not explain the mingled reluctance and pleasure of his own mood, the little tumult that arose in him when he saw her. He wanted to turn his back and rush away, and yet he wanted to be there waiting for her, seeing her approach step by step. He had no notion what his own mingled sentiments meant. But Bice to all appearance had neither the reluctance nor the excitement. She came running to her playmate whenever she saw him with frank satisfaction. "I was looking for you," she would say, "Let us go out into the park where nobody can see us. Run, or some one will be coming," and then she would fly over stock and stone, summoning him after her. There were many occasions when Jock did not approve, but he always followed her, though with internal grumblings, in which he indulged consciously, making out his own annoyance to be very great. "Why can't she let me alone?" he said to himself; but when it occurred that Bice did leave him alone, and made no appearance, his sense of injury was almost bitter. On such occasions he said cutting things within himself, and was very satirical as to the stupidity of girls who were afraid to wet their feet, and estimated the danger of catching a cold as greater than any natural advantage. For Jock had all that instinctive hostility to womankind, which is natural to the male bosom, except perhaps at one varying period of life. They had no place in the economy of his existence at school, and he knew nothing of them nor wanted to know. But Bice, though, when he was annoyed with her, she became to him the typical girl, the epitome of offending woman, had at other times a very different position. It stirred his entire being, he did not know how, when she roamed with him about the woods talking of everything, from a point of view which was certainly different from Jock's. Occasionally, even, he did not understand her any more than if she had been speaking a foreign language. She had never any difficulty in penetrating his meaning as he had in penetrating hers, but there were times when she did not understand him any more than he understood her. She was by far the easiest in morals, the least Puritanical. It was not easy to shock Bice, but it was not at all difficult to shock Jock, brought up as he was in the highest sentiments under the wing of MTutor, who believed in moral influence. But the fashion of the intercourse held between these two, was very remarkable in its way. They were like brother and sister, without being brother and sister. They were strangers to each other, yet living in the most entire intimacy, and likely to be parted for ever to-morrow. They were of the same age, yet the girl was, in experience of life, a world in advance of the boy, who, notwithstanding, had the better of her in a thousand ways. In short, they were a paradox, such as youth, more or less, is always, and the careless close companionship that grew up between them was at once the most natural and the most strange alliance. They told each other everything by degrees, without being at all aware of the nature of their mutual confidence; Bice revealing to Jock the conditions on which she was to be brought out in England, and Jock to Bice the unusual features of his own and his sister's position, to the unbounded astonishment and scepticism of each.

"Beautiful?" said Jock, drawing a long breath. "But beautiful's not a thing you can go in for, like an exam: You're born so, or you're born not so; and you know you're not—I mean, you know you're— Well, it isn't your fault. Are you going to be sent away for just being—not pretty?"

"I told you," said the girl, with a little impatience. "Being pretty is of no consequence. I am pretty, of course," she added regretfully. "But it is only if I turn out beautiful that she will take the trouble. And at sixteen, I am told, one cannot yet know."

"But—" cried Jock with a sort of consternation, "you don't mind, do you? I don't mean anything unkind, you know; I don't think it matters—and I am sure it isn't your fault; you are not even—good-looking," candour compelled the boy to say, as to an honest comrade with whom sincerity was best.

"Ah!" cried Bice, with a little excitement. "Do you think so? Then perhaps there is more hope."

Jock was confounded by this utterance, and he began to feel that he had been uncivil. "I don't mean," he said, "that you are not—I mean that it is not of the least consequence. What does it matter? I am sure you are clever, which is far better. I think you could get up anything faster than most fellows if you were to try."

"Get up! What does that mean? And when I tell you that it does matter to me—oh much,—very much!" she cried. "When you are beautiful, everything is before you—you marry, you have whatever you wish, you become a great lady; only to be pretty—that does nothing for you. Ugly, however," said the girl reflectively; "if I am ugly, then there is some hope."

"I did not say that," cried Jock, shocked at the suggestion. "I wouldn't be so uncivil. You are—just like other people," he added encouragingly, "not much either one way or another—like the rest of us," Jock said, with the intention of soothing her ruffled feelings. At sixteen decorum is not always the first thing we think of; and though Bice was not an English girl, she was very young. She threw out a vigorous arm and pushed him from her, so that the astonished critic, stumbling over some fallen branches, measured his length upon the dewy sod.

"That was not I," she said demurely, as he picked himself up in great surprise—drawing a step away, and looking at him with wide-open eyes, to which the little fright of seeing him fall, and the spark of malice that took pleasure in it, had given sudden brilliancy. Jock was so much astonished that he uttered no reproach, but went on by her side, after a moment, pondering. He could not see how any offence could have lurked in the encouraging and consolatory words he had said.

But when they reached the other chapter, which concerned his fortunes, Bice was not more understanding. Her gray eyes absolutely flamed upon him when he told her of his father's will, and the conditions upon which Lucy's inheritance was held. "To give her money away! But that is impossible—it would be to prove one's self mad," the girl said.

"Why? You forget it's my father you're speaking of. He was not mad, he was just," said Jock, reddening. "What's mad in it? You've got a great fortune—far more than you want. It all came out of other people's pockets somehow. Oh, of course, not in a dishonest way. That is the worst of speaking to a girl that doesn't understand political economy and the laws of production. Of course it must come out of other people's pockets. If I sell anything and get a profit (and nobody would sell anything if they didn't get a profit), of course that comes out of your pocket. Well, now, I've got a great deal more than I want, and I say you shall have some of it back."

"And I say," cried Bice, making him a curtsey, "Merci Monsieur! Grazia Signor! oh thank you, thank you very much—as much as you like, sir, as much as you like! but all the same I think you are mad. Your money! all that makes you happy and great—"

"Money," said Jock, loftily, "makes nobody happy. It may make you comfortable. It gives you fine houses, horses and carriages, and all that sort of thing. So it will do to the other people to whom it goes; so it is wisdom to divide it, for the more good you can get out of it the better. Lucy has money lying in the bank—or somewhere—that she does not want, that does her no good; and there is some one else" (a fellow I know, Jock added in a parenthesis), "who has not got enough to live upon. So you see she just hands over what she doesn't want to him, and that's better for both. So far from being mad, it's"—Jock paused for a word—"it's philosophy, it's wisdom, it's statesmanship. It is just the grandest way that was ever invented for putting things straight."

Bice looked at him with a sort of incredulous cynical gaze—as if asking whether he meant her to believe this fiction—whether perhaps he was such a fool as to think that she could be persuaded to believe it. It was evident that she did not for a moment suppose him to be serious. She laughed at last in ridicule and scorn. "You think," she said, "I know so little. Ah, I know a great deal more than that. What are you without money? You are nobody. The more you have, so much more have you everything at your command. Without money you are nobody. Yes, you may be a prince or an English milord, but that is nothing without money. Oh yes! I have known princes that had nothing and the people laughed at them. And a milord who is poor—the very donkey-boys scorn him. You can do nothing without money," the girl said with almost fierce derision, "and you tell me you will give it away!" She laughed again angrily, as if such a brag was offensive and insulting to her own poverty. The boy who had never in his life known what it was to want anything that money could procure for him, treated the whole question lightly, and undervalued its importance altogether. But the girl who knew by experience what was involved in the want of it, heard with a sort of wondering fury this slighting treatment of what was to her the universal panacea. Her cynicism and satirical unbelief grew into indignation. "And you tell me it is wise to give it away!"

"Lucy has got to do it, whether it is wise or not," said Jock, almost overawed by this high moral disapproval. "We went to the lawyer about it the day you came. He is settling it now. She is giving away—well, a good many thousand pounds."

"Pounds are more than francs, eh?" said Bice quickly.

"More than francs! just twenty-five times more," cried Jock, proud of his knowledge, "a thousand pounds is—"

"Then I don't believe you!" cried the girl in an outburst of passion, and she fled from him across the park, catching up her dress and running at a pace which even Jock with his long legs knew he could not keep up with. He gazed with surprise, standing still and watching her with the words arrested on his lips. "But she can't keep it up long like that," after a moment Jock said.

The time, however, approached when the two friends had to part. Jock left the Hall a few days after Lady Randolph, and he was somehow not very glad to go. The family life had been less cheerful lately, and conversation languished when the domestic party were alone together. When the Contessa was present she kept up the ball, maintaining at least with Sir Tom an always animated and lively strain of talk; but at breakfast there was not much said, and of late a little restraint had crept even between the master and mistress of the house, no one could tell how. The names of the guests were scarcely mentioned between them. Sir Tom was very attentive and kind to his wife, but he was more silent than he used to be, reading his letters and his newspapers. Lucy had been quite satisfied when he said, though it must be allowed with a laugh not devoid of embarrassment, that it was more important he should master all the papers and see how public opinion was running, now when it was so near the opening of Parliament. But a little veil of silence had fallen over Lucy too. It cost her an effort to speak even to Jock of common subjects and of his going away. She had thought him looking a little disturbed, however, on the last morning, and with the newspaper forming a sort of screen between them and Sir Tom, Lucy made an attempt to talk to her brother as of old.

"I shall miss you very much, Jock. We have not had so much time together as we thought."

"We have had no time together, Lucy."

"You must not say that, dear. Don't you recollect that drive to Farafield? We have not had so many walks, it is true; but then I have been—occupied."

"Is it ever finished yet, that business?" Jock said suddenly.

It was all Lucy could do not to give him a warning look. "I have had some letters about it. A thing cannot be finished in a minute like that." Instinctively she spoke low to escape her husband's ear; he had never referred to the subject, and she avoided it religiously. It gave her a thrill of alarm to have it thus reintroduced. To escape it, she said, raising her voice a little: "The Contessa's letters have not been sent to her. You must ring the bell, Jock. There are a great many for her." The name of the Contessa always moved Sir Tom to a certain attention. He seemed to be on the alert for what might be said of her. He looked round the corner of the paper with a short laugh, and said, jocularly, with mock gravity—

"It is a great thing to keep up your correspondence, Lucy. You never can know when it may prove serviceable. If it had not been for that, she most likely never would have come here."

Lucy smiled, though with a little restraint. "Perhaps she is sorry now," she said, "for it must be dull." Then she hurriedly changed the subject, afraid lest she might seem ill-natured. "Poor Miss Bice has never any letters," she said; "she must have very few friends."

"Oh, she has nobody at all," said Jock, "She hasn't got a relation. She has always lived like this, in different places; and never been to school, or—anywhere; though she has been nearly round the world."

"Poor little thing! and she is fond of children too," said Lucy. "I found her one day with baby on her shoulder, a wet day when he could not get out, racing up and down the long gallery with him crowing and laughing. It was so pretty to see him—"

"Or to see her, Lucy, most people would say," said Sir Tom, interrupting again.

"Would they? Oh, yes. But I thought naturally of baby," said the young mother. Then she made a pause and added softly, "I hope—they—are always kind to her."

There was a little silence. Sir Tom was behind his newspaper. He listened, but he did not say anything, and Jock was not aware that he was listening.

"Oh, I don't think she minds," said Jock. "She is rather jolly when you come to know her. I say, Lucy, it will be awfully dull for her, you know, when—"

"When what, Jock?"

"When I am gone," the boy intended to have said, but some gleam of consciousness came over him that made him pause. He did not say this, but grew a little red in the effort to think of something else that he could say.

"Well, I mean here," he said, "for she hasn't been used to it. She has been in places where there was always music playing and that sort of thing. She never was in the country. There's plenty of books, to be sure; but she's not very fond of reading. Few people, are, I think. You never open a book—"

"Oh yes, Jock! I read the books from Mudie's," Lucy said, with some spirit, "and I always send them upstairs."

Jock had it on his lips to say something derogatory of the books from Mudie's; but he checked himself, for he remembered to have seen MTutor with one of those frivolous volumes, and he refrained from snubbing Lucy. "I believe she can't read," he said. "She can do nothing but laugh at one. And she thinks she's pretty," he added, with a little laugh yet sense of unfaithfulness to the trust reposed in him, which once more covered his face with crimson.

Lucy laughed too, with hesitation and doubt. "I cannot see it," she said, "but that is what Lady Randolph thought. It is strange that she should talk of such things; but people are very funny who have been brought up abroad."

"All girls are like that," said Jock, authoritatively. "They think so much of being pretty. But I tell her it doesn't matter. What difference could it make? Nobody will suppose it was her fault. She says—"

"Hallo, young man," said Sir Tom. "It is time you went back to school, I think. What would MTutor say to all these confidences with young ladies, and knowledge of their ways!"

Jock gave his brother-in-law a look, in which defiant virtue struggled with a certain consciousness; but he scorned to make any reply.

## CHAPTER XXIII

Lucy found her life much changed when Jock had gone, and she was left alone to face the change of circumstances which had tacitly taken place. The Contessa said not a word of terminating her visit. The departure of Lady Randolph apparently suggested nothing to her. She could scarcely have filled up the foreground more entirely than she did before—but she was now uncriticised, unremarked upon. There seemed even to be no appropriation of more than her due, for it was very natural that a person of experience and powers of conversation like hers should take the leading place, and simple Lucy, so much younger and with so much less acquaintance with the world, fall into the background. And accordingly this was what happened. Madame di Forno-Populo knew everybody. She had a hundred mutual acquaintances to tell Sir Tom about, and they seemed to have an old habit of intercourse, which by this time had been fully resumed. The evenings were the time when this was most apparent. Then the Contessa was at her brightest. She had managed to introduce shades upon all the lamps, so as to diffuse round her a softened artificial illumination such as is favourable to beauty that has passed its prime: and in this ruddy gloom she sat half seen, Sir Tom sometimes standing by her, sometimes permitted to take the other corner of her sofa—and talked to him, sometimes sinking her voice low as her reminiscences took some special vein, sometimes calling sweetly to her pretty Lucy to listen to this or that. These extensions of confidence, generally, were brought in to make up for a long stretch of more private communications, and the aspect of the little domestic circle was on such occasions curious enough. By the table, in a low chair, with the full light of the lamp upon her, sat Lucy, generally with some work in her hands; she did not read or write (exercises to which, to tell the truth, she was not much addicted) out of politeness, lest she should seem to be withdrawing her attention from her guest, but sat there with her slight occupation, so as to be open to any appeal, and ready if she were wanted. On the other side of the table, the light making a sort of screen and division between them, sat Bice, generally with a book before her, which, as has been said, did not at all interfere with her power of giving a vivid attention to what was going on around her. These two said nothing to each other, and were often silent for the whole evening, like pieces of still life. Bice sat with her book upon the table, so that only the open page and the hands that held the book were within the brightness of the light, which on the other side streamed down upon Lucy's fair shoulders and soft young face, and upon the work in her hands. In the corner was the light continuous murmur of talk; the half-seen figure of the Contessa, generally leaning back, looking up to Sir Tom, who stood with his arm on the mantelpiece with much animation, gesticulation of her hands and subdued laughter, the most lively current of sound, soft, intensified by little eloquent breaks, by emphatic gestures, by sentences left incomplete, but understood all the better for being half said. There were many evenings in which Lucy sat there with a little wonder, but no other active feeling in her mind. It is needless to say that it was not pleasant to her. She would sit and wonder wistfully whether her husband had forgotten she was there, but then reminded herself that of course it was his duty to think of the Contessa first, and consoled herself that by and by the stranger would go away, and all would be as it had been. As time went on, the desire that this should happen, and longing to have possession of her home again, grew so strong that she could scarcely subdue it, and it was with the greatest difficulty that she kept all expression of it from her lips. And by and by, the warmth of this restrained desire so absorbed Lucy that she scarcely dared allow herself to speak lest it should burst forth, and there seemed to herself to be continually going on in her mind a calculation of the chances, a scrutiny of everything the Contessa said which seemed to point at such a movement. But, indeed, the Contessa said very little upon which the most sanguine could build. She said nothing of her arrangements at all, nor spoke of what she was going to do, and answered none of Lucy's ardent and innocent fishings after information. The evenings became more and more intolerable to Lady Randolph as they went on. She was glad that anybody should come, however little she might care for their society, to break these private conferences up.

And this was not all, nor even perhaps the worst, of the vague evils not yet defined in her mind, and which she was so very reluctant to define, which Lucy had to go through. At breakfast, when she was alone with her husband, matters were almost worse. Sir Tom, it was evident, began to feel the tête-à-tête embarrassing. He did not know what to say to his little wife when they were alone. The presence of the Dowager and Jock had freed him from any necessity of explanation, had kept him in his usual easy way; but now that Lucy alone sat opposite to him, he was more silent than his wont, and with no longer any of the little flow of simple observations which had once been so delightful to her. Sir Tom was more uneasy than if she had been a stern and jealous Eleanor, a clear-sighted critic seeing through and through him. The contest was so unequal, and the weaker creature so destitute of any intention or thought of resistance, that he felt himself a coward and traitor for thus deserting her and overclouding her home and her life. Then he took to asking himself, Did he overcloud her? Was she sensible of any difference? Did she know enough to know that this was not how she ought to be treated, or was she not quite contented with her secondary place? Such a simple creature, would she not cry—would she not show her anger if she was conscious of anything to be grieved or angry about? He took refuge in those newspapers which, he gave out, it was so necessary he should study, to understand the mind of the country before the opening of Parliament. And thus they would sit, Lucy dutifully filling out the tea, taking care that he had the dish he liked for breakfast, swallowing her own with difficulty yet lingering over it, always thinking that perhaps Tom might have something to say. While he, on the other hand, kept behind his newspaper, feeling himself guilty, conscious that another sort of woman would make one of those "scenes" which men dread, yet despising Lucy a little in spite of himself for the very quality he most admired in her, and wondering if she were really capable of feeling at all. Sometimes little Tom would be brought downstairs to roll about the carpet and try his unsteady little limbs in a series of clutches at the chairs and table; and on these occasions the meal was got through more easily. But little Tom was not always well enough to come downstairs, and sometimes Lucy thought that her husband might have something to say to her which the baby's all-engrossing presence hindered. Thus it came about that the hours in which the Contessa was present and in the front of everything, were really less painful than those in which the pair were alone with the shadow of the intruder, more powerful even than her presence holding them apart.

One of these mornings, however, Lucy's anticipations and hopes seemed about to be realised. Sir Tom laid down his paper, looked at her frankly without any shield, and said, as she had so often imagined him saying, "I want to talk to you, Lucy." How glad she was that little Tom was not downstairs that morning!

She looked at him across the table with a brightening countenance, and said, "Yes, Tom!" with such warm eagerness and sudden pleasure that her look penetrated his very heart. It implied a great deal more than Sir Tom intended and thought, and he was a man of very quick intelligence. The expectation in her eyes touched him beyond a thousand complaints.

"I had an interview yesterday, in which you were much concerned," he said; then made a pause, with such a revolution going on within him as seldom happens in a mature and self-collected mind. He had begun with totally different sentiments from those which suddenly came over him at the sight of her kindling face. When he said, "I want to talk to you, Lucy," he had meant to speak of her interview with Mr. Rushton, to point out to her the folly of what she was doing, and to show her how it was that he should be compelled to do everything that was in his power to oppose her. He did not mean to go to the root of the matter, as he had done before, when he was obliged to admit to himself that he had failed— but to address himself to the secondary view of the question, to the small prospect there was of doing any good. But when he caught her eager, questioning look, her eyes growing liquid and bright with emotion, her face full of restrained anxiety and hope, Sir Tom's heart smote him. What did she think he was going to say? Not anything about money, important as that subject was in their life—but something far more important, something that touched her to the quick, a revelation upon which her very soul hung. He was startled beyond measure by this disclosure. He had thought she did not feel, and that her heart unawakened had regarded calmly, with no pain to speak of, the new state of affairs of which he himself was guiltily conscious; but that eager look put an end in a moment to his delusion. He paused and swerved mentally as if an angel had suddenly stepped into his way.

"It is about—that will of your father's," he said.

Lucy, gazing at him with such hope and expectation, suddenly sank, as it were, prostrate in the depth of a disappointment that almost took the life out of her. She did not indeed fall physically or faint, which people seldom do in moments of extreme mental suffering. It was only her countenance that fell. Her brightening, beaming, hopeful face grew blank in a moment, her eyes grew utterly dim, a kind of mist running over them: a sound—half a sob, half a sigh, came from her breast. She put up her hand trembling to support her head, which shook too with the quiver that went over her. It took her at least a minute to get over the shock of the disappointment. Then commanding herself painfully, but without looking at him, which, indeed, she dared not do, she said again, "Yes, Tom?" with a piteous quiver of her lip.

It did not make Sir Tom any the less kind, and full of tender impulses, that he was wounding his wife in the profoundest sensibilities of her heart. In this point the greater does not include the lesser. He was cruel in the more important matter, without intending it indeed, and from what he considered a fatality, a painful combination of circumstances out of which he could not escape; but in the lesser particulars he was as kind as ever. He could not bear to see her suffering. The quiver in her lip, the failure of the colour in her cheeks affected him so that he could scarcely contain himself.

"My dear love," he cried, "my little Lucy! you are not afraid of what I am going to say to you?" These words came to his lips naturally, by the affectionate impulse of his kind nature. But when he had said them, an impulse, which was perhaps more crafty than loving, followed. Quick as thought he changed his intention, his purpose altogether. He could not resist the appeal of Lucy's face; but he slipped instinctively from the more serious question that lay between them, and resolved to sacrifice the other, which was indeed very important, yet could be treated in an easier way and without involving anything more painful. Sir Tom was at an age when money has a great value, and the mere sense of possession is pleasant; and there was a principle involved which he had determined a few weeks ago not to relinquish. But the position in which he found himself placed was one out of which some way of escape had to be invented at once. "Lucy," he said, "you are frightened; you think I am going to cross you in the matter that lies so near your heart. But you mistake me, my dear. I think I ought to be your chief adviser in that as in all matters. It is my duty: but I hope you never thought that I would exercise any force upon you to put a stop to—what you thought right."

Lucy had overcome herself, though with a painful effort. She followed with a quivering humility what he was saying. She acknowledged to herself that this was, indeed, the great thing in her life, and that it was only her childishness and foolishness which had made her place other matters in the chief place. Most likely, she said to herself, Tom was not aware of anything that required explanation; he would never think it possible that she could be so ungracious and unkind as to grudge his guests their place in his house. She gathered herself up hastily to meet him when he entered upon the great question which was far more important, which was indeed the only question between them. "I know," she said, "that you were always kind, Tom. If I did not ask you first it was because—"

"We need not enter upon that, my dear. I was angry, and went too far. At the same time, Lucy, it is a mad affair altogether. Your father himself, had he realised the difficulty of carrying it out, would have seen this. I only say so to let you know my opinion is unchanged. And you know your trustees are of the same mind. But if you think this is your duty, as I am sure you do—"

It seemed to Lucy that her duty had sailed far away from her on some sea of strange distance and dullness where she could scarcely keep it in sight. Her own very voice seemed strange and dull to her and far away, as she said almost mechanically: "I do think it is my duty—to my father—"

"I am aware that you think so, my love. As you get older you will, perhaps, see as I do—that to carry out the spirit of your father's will would be better than to follow so closely the letter of it. But you are still very young, and Jock is younger; and, fortunately, you can afford to indulge a freak of this sort. I shall let Mr. Rushton know that I withdraw all opposition. And now, give me a kiss, and let us forget that there ever was any controversy between us—it never went further than a controversy, did it, darling?" Sir Tom said.

Lucy could not speak for the moment. She looked up into his face with her eyes all liquid with tears, and a great confusion in her soul. Was this all? as he kissed her, and smiled, leaning over her in the old kind way, with a tenderness that was half-fatherly and indulgent to her weakness, she did not seem at all sure what it was that had moved like a ghost between him and her; was it in reality only this—this and no more? She almost thought so as she looked up into his kind face. Only this! How glad it would have made her three weeks ago to have his sanction for the thing she was so reluctant to attempt, which it was so much her duty to do, which Jock urged with so much pertinacity, and which her father from his grave enjoined. If it affected her but dully now, whose was the fault? Not Tom's, who was so generously ready to yield to her, although he disapproved. When he retired behind his newspaper once more with a kind smile at her, to end the matter, Lucy sat quite still in a curious stunned confusion trying to account for it all to herself. There could be no doubt, she thought, that it was she who was in the wrong. She it was who had created the embarrassment altogether. He was not even aware of any other cause. It had never occurred to his greater mind that she could be so petty as to fret under the interruption which their visitors had made in her life. He had thought that the other matter was the cause of her dullness and silence, and generously had put an end to it, not by requiring any sacrifice from her, but by making one in his own person. She sat silent trying to realise all this, but unable to get quite free from the confusion and dimness that had invaded her soul.


CHAPTER XXIV

THE ORACLE SPEAKS

Lucy went up to the nursery when breakfast was over. It was her habit to go and take counsel of little Tom when her heart was troubled or heavy. He was now eighteen months old, an age at which you will say the judicial faculties are small; but a young mother has superstitions, and there are many dilemmas in life in which it will do a woman, though the male critic may laugh, great good to go and confide it all to her baby, and hold that little bundle of white against her heart to conquer the pain of it. When little Tom was lively and well, when he put his arms about her neck and dabbed his velvety mouth against her cheek, Lucy felt that she was approved of and her heart rose. When he was cross and cried and pushed her away from him, as sometimes happened, she ceased to be sure of anything, and felt dissatisfied with herself and all the world. It was with a great longing to consult this baby oracle and see what heaven might have to say to her through his means, that she ran upstairs, neglecting even Mrs. Freshwater, who advanced ceremoniously from her own retirement with her bill of fare in her hand, as Lucy darted past. "Wait a little and I will come to you," she cried. What was the dinner in comparison? She flew up to the nursery only to find it vacant. The morning was clingy and damp, no weather for the delicate child to go out, and Lucy was not alarmed but knew well enough where to find him. The long picture gallery which ran along the front of the house was his usual promenade on such occasions, and there she betook herself hurriedly. There could not be much doubt as to little Tom's whereabouts. Shrieks of baby fun were audible whenever she came within hearing, and the sound of a flying foot careering from end to end of the long space, which certainly was not the foot of Tom's nurse, whose voice could be heard in cries of caution, "Oh, take care, Miss! Oh, for goodness sake—oh, what will my lady say to me if you should trip with him!" Lucy paused suddenly, checked by the sound of this commotion. Once before she had surprised a scene of the kind, and she knew what it meant. She stopped short, and stood still to get possession of herself. It was a circumstance which pulled her up sharply and changed the current of her mind. Her first feeling was one of disappointment and almost irritation. Could she not even have the baby to herself, she murmured? But there was in reality so little of the petty in Lucy's disposition that this was but a momentary sentiment. It changed, however, the manner of her entrance. She came in quietly, not rushing to seize her boy as she had intended, but still with her superstition strong in her heart, and as determined to resort to the Sortes Tomianae as ever. The sight she saw was one to make a picture of. Skimming along the long gallery with that free light step which scarcely seemed to touch the ground was Bice, a long stream of hair flying behind her, the child seated on her shoulder, supported by one raised arm, while the other held aloft the end of a red scarf which she had twisted round him. Little Tom had one hand twisted in her hair, and with his small feet beating upon her breast, and his little chest expanded with cries of delight, encouraged his steed in her wild career. The dark old pictures, some full-length Randolphs of an elder age, good for little but a background, threw up this airy group with all the perfection of contrast. They flew by as Lucy came in, so joyous, so careless, so delightful in pose and movement, that she could not utter the little cry of alarm that came to her lips. Bice had never in her life looked so near that beauty which she considered as so serious a necessity. She was flushed with the movement, her fine light figure, too light and slight as yet for the full perfection of feminine form, was the very impersonation of youth. She flew, she did not glide nor run—her elastic foot spurned the floor. She was like a runner in a Greek game. Lucy stood breathless between admiration and pleasure and alarm, as the animated figure turned and came fast towards her in its airy career. Little Tom perceived his mother as they came up. He was still more daring than his bearer. He detached himself suddenly from Bice's shoulder, and with a shout of pleasure threw himself upon Lucy. The oracle had spoken. It almost brought her to her knees indeed, descending upon her like a little thunderbolt, catching her round the throat and tearing off with a hurried clutch the lace upon her dress; while the flying steed, suddenly arrested, came to a dead stop in front of her, panting, blushing, and disconcerted. "There was no fear," she cried, with involuntary self-defence, "I held him fast." Bice forgot even in the surprise how wildly she stood with her hair floating, and the scarf in her hand still knotted round the baby's waist.

"There was no danger, my lady. I was watching every step; and it do Master Tom a world of good," cried the nurse, coming to the rescue.

"Why should you think I am afraid?" said Lucy. "Don't you know I am most grateful to you for being so kind to him? and it was pretty to see you. You looked so bright and strong, and my boy so happy."

"Miss is just our salvation, my lady," said the nurse; "these wet days when we can't get out, I don't know what I should do without her. Master Tom, bless him, is always cross when he don't get no air; but once set on Miss' shoulder he crows till it do your heart good to hear him," the woman cried.

Bice stood with the colour still in her face, her head thrown back a little, and her breath coming less quickly. She laughed at this applause. "I like it," she said. "I like him; he is my only little companion. He is pleased when he sees me."

This went to Lucy's heart. "And so are we all," she said; "but you will not let me see you. I am often alone, too. If you will come and—and give me your company—"

Bice gave her a wistful look; then shook her head.

"I know you do not wish for us here; and why should you?" she said.

"My dear!" cried Lucy in alarm, with a glance at the woman who stood by, all ears. And now it was that little Tom at eighteen months showed that precocious judgment in which his mother had an instinctive belief. He had satisfied himself with the destruction of Lucy's lace, and with printing the impression of his mouth all over her cheeks. That little wet wide open mouth was delicious to Lucy. No trouble had befallen her yet that could not be wiped out by its touch. But now a new distraction was necessary for the little hero; and his eye caught the red sash which still was round his waist. He transferred all his thoughts to it with an instant revolution of idea, and holding on by it like a little sailor on a rope, drew Bice close till he could succeed in the arduous task, not unattended by danger, of flinging himself from one to another. This game enchanted Master Tom. Had he been a little older it would have been changed into that daring faltering hop from one eminence, say a footstool, to another, which flutters the baby soul. He was too insecure in possession of those aimless little legs to venture on any such daring feat now; but, with a valour more desperate still, he flung himself across the gulf from Lucy's arms to those of Bice and back again, with cries of delight. These cries, it must be allowed, were not very articulate, but they soon became urgent, with a demand which the little tyrant insisted upon with increasing vehemence.

"Oh, my lady," cried the nurse, "it is as plain as if he said it, and he is saying of it, the pet, as pretty!— He wants you to kiss Miss, he do. Ain't that it, my own? Nursey knows his little talk. Ain't that it, my darling lamb?"

There was a momentary pause in the strange little group linked together by the baby's clutches. The young mother and the girl with their heads so near each other, looked in each other's faces. In Lucy's there was a kind of awe, in Bice's a sort of wondering wistfulness mingled with incipient defiance. They were not born to be each other's friends. They were different in everything; they were even on different sides in this house—the one an intruder, belonging to the party which was destroying the other's domestic peace. It would be vain to say that there was not a little reluctance in Lucy's soul as she gazed at the younger girl, come from she knew not where, established under her roof she knew not how. She hesitated for one moment, then she bent forward almost with solemnity and kissed Bice's cheek. She seemed to communicate her own agitation to the girl who stood straight up with her head a little back, half eager, half defiant. When Bice felt the touch of Lucy's lips, however, she melted in a moment. Her slight figure swayed, she took Lucy's disengaged hand with her own, and, stooping over it, kissed it with lips that quivered. There was not a word said between them; but a secret compact was thus made under little Tom's inspiration. The little oracle clambered up upon his mother afterwards, and laid down his head upon her shoulder and dropped off to sleep with that entire confiding and abandonment of the whole little being which is one of the deepest charms of childhood. Who is there with any semblance of a heart in his, much more her, bosom, who is not touched in the tenderest part when a child goes to sleep in his arms? The appeal conveyed in the act is one which scarcely a savage could withstand. The three women gathered round to see this common spectacle, so universal, so touching. Bice, who was almost too young for the maternal sentiment, and who was a stern young Stoic by nature, never shedding a tear, could not tell how it was that her eyes moistened. But Lucy's filled with an emotion which was sharp and sore with alarm. "Oh, nurse, don't call my boy a little angel!" she said, with a sentiment which a woman will understand.

This baby scene upstairs was balanced by one of a very different character below. Sir Tom had gone into his own room a little disturbed and out of sorts. Circumstances had been hard upon him, he felt. The Contessa's letter offering her visit had been a jest to him. He was one of those who thought the best of the Contessa. He had seen a good deal of her one time and another in his life, and she held the clue to one or two matters which it would not have pleased him, at this mature period of his existence, to have published abroad. She was an adventuress, he knew, and her friends were not among the best of humanity. She had led a life which, without being positively evil, had shut her out from the sympathies of many good people. When a woman has to solve the problem how to obtain all the luxuries and amusements of life without money, it is to be expected that her attempts to do so should lead her into risky places, where the footing was far from sure. But she had never, as Lady Randolph acknowledged, gone so far as that society should refuse to receive her, and Sir Tom was always an indulgent critic. If she were coming to England, as she gave him to understand, he saw no reason why she should not come to the Hall. For himself, it would be rather amusing than otherwise, and Lucy would take no harm—even if there was harm in the Forno-Populo (which he did not believe), his wife was far too innocent even to suspect it. She would not know evil if she saw it, he said to himself proudly; and then there was no chance that the Contessa, who loved merriment and gaiety, could long be content with anything so humdrum as his quiet life in the country. Thus it will be seen that Sir Tom had got himself innocently enough into this imbroglio. He had meant no particular harm. He had meant to be kind to a poor woman, who after all needed kindness much; and if the comic character of the situation touched his sense of humour, and he was not unwilling in his own person to get a little amusement out of it, who could blame him? This was the worst that Sir Tom meant. To amuse himself partly by the sight of the conventional beauty and woman of the world in the midst of circumstances so incongruous, and partly by the fluttering of the dovecotes which the appearance of such an adventuress would cause. He liked her conversation too, and to hear all about the more noisy company, full of talk and diversion in which he had wasted so much of his youth. But there were two or three things which Sir Tom did not take into his calculations. The first was the sort of fascination which that talk, and all the associations of the old world, and the charms of the professional sorceress, would exercise upon himself after his settling down as the head of a family and pillar of the State. He had not thought how much amused he would be, how the contrast even would tickle his fancy and affect (for the moment) his life. He laughed within himself at the transparent way in which his old friend bade for his sympathy and society. She was the same as ever, living upon admiration, upon compliments whether fictitious or not, and demanding a show of devotion, somebody always at her feet. She thought, no doubt, he said to himself, that she had got him at her feet, and he laughed to himself when he was alone at the thought. But, nevertheless, it did amuse him to talk to the Contessa, and before long, what with skilful reminders of the past, what with hints and reference to a knowledge which he would not like extended to the world, he had begun by degrees to find himself in a confidential position with her. "We know each other's secrets," she would say to him with a meaning look. He was caught in her snare. On the other hand an indefinite visit prolonged and endless had never come within his calculation. He did not know how to put an end to the situation— perhaps as it was an amusement for his evenings to see the siren spread her snares, and even to be more or less caught in them, he did not sincerely wish to put an end to it as yet. He was caught in them more or less, but never so much as to be unaware of the skill with which the snares were laid, which would have amused him whatever had been the seriousness of the attendant circumstances. He did not, however, allow that he had no desire to make an end of these circumstances, but only said to himself, with a shrug of his shoulders, how could he do it? He could not send his old friend away. He could not but be civil and attentive to her so long as she was under his roof. It distressed him that Lucy should feel it, as this morning's experience proved her to do, but how could he help it? He made that other sacrifice to Lucy by way of reconciling her to the inevitable, but he could do no more. When you invite a friend to be your guest, he said to himself, you must be more or less at the mercy of that friend. If he (or she) stays too long, what can you do? Sir Tom was not the sort of man to be reduced to helplessness by such a difficulty. Yet this was what he said to himself.

It vexed him, however, that Lucy should feel it so much. He could not throw off this uneasy feeling. He had stopped her mouth as one might stop a child's mouth with a sugar plum; but he could not escape from the consciousness that Lucy felt her domain invaded, and that her feeling was just. He had thrown himself into the great chair, and was pondering not what to do, but the impossibility of doing anything, when Williams, his confidential man, who knew all about the Contessa almost as well as he did, suddenly appeared before him. Williams had been all over the world with Sir Tom before he settled down as his butler at the Hall. He was, therefore, not one who could be dismissed summarily if he interfered in any matter out of his sphere. He appeared on the other side of Sir Tom's writing-table with a face as long as his arm, the face with which Sir Tom was so well acquainted—the same face with which he had a hundred times announced the failure of supplies, the delay of carriages, the general hopelessness of the situation. There was tragedy in it of the most solemn kind, but there was a certain enjoyment too.

"What is the matter?" said Sir Tom; and then he jumped to his feet. "Something is wrong with the baby," he cried.

"No, Sir Thomas; Mr. Randolph is pretty well, thank you, Sir Thomas. It is about something else that I made so bold. There is Antonio, sir, in the servants' hall; Madame the Countess' man."

"Oh, the Countess," cried Sir Tom, and he seated himself again; then said, with the confidence of a man to the follower who has been his companion in many straits, "You gave me a fright, Williams. I thought that little shaver— But what's the matter with Antonio? Can't you keep a fellow like that in order without bothering me?"

"Sir Thomas," said Williams, solemnly, "I am not one as troubles my master when things are straightforward. But them foreigners, you never know when you have 'em. And an idle man about an establishment, that is, so to speak, under nobody, and for ever a-kicking of his heels, and following the women servants about, and not a blessed hand's turn to do"—a tone of personal offence came into Williams' complaint; "there is a deal to do in this house," he added, "and neither me nor any of the men haven't got a moment to spare. Why, there's your hunting things, Sir Thomas, is just a man's work. And to see that fellow loafing, and a-hanging on about the women—I don't wonder, Sir Thomas, that it's more than any man can stand," said Williams, lighting up. He was a married man himself, with a very respectable family in the village, but he was not too old to be able to understand the feelings of John and Charles, whose hearts were lacerated by the success of the Italian fellow with his black eyes.

"Well, well, don't worry me," said Sir Tom, "take him by the collar and give him a shake. You're big enough." Then he laughed unfeelingly, which Williams did not expect. "Too big, eh, Will? Not so ready for a shindy as we used to be." This identification of himself with his factotum was mere irony, and Williams felt it; for Sir Tom, if perhaps less slim than in his young days, was still what Williams called a "fine figger of a man;" whereas the butler had widened much round the waist, and was apt to puff as he came upstairs, and no longer contemplated a shindy as a possibility at all.

"Sir Thomas," he said, with great gravity, "if I'm corpulent, which I don't deny, but never thought to have it made a reproach, it's neither over-feeding nor want of care, but constitootion, as derived from my parents, Sir Thomas. There is nothing," he added with a pensive superiority, "as is so gen'rally misunderstood." Then Williams drew himself up to still greater dignity, stimulated by Sir Tom's laugh. "If this fellow is to be long in the house, Sir Thomas, I won't answer for what may happen; for he's got the devil's own temper, like all of them, and carries a knife like all of them."

"What do you want of me, man? Say it out! Am I to represent to Madame di Forno-Populo that three great hulking fellows of you are afraid of her slim Neapolitan?" Sir Tom cried impatiently.

"Not afraid, Sir Thomas, of nothing, but of breaking the law," said Williams, quickly. Then he added in an insinuating tone: "But I tell them, ladies don't stop long in country visits, not at this time of the year. And a thing can be put up with for short that any man'd kick at for long. Madame the Countess will be moving on to pay her other visits, Sir Thomas, if I might make so bold? She is a lady as likes variety; leastways she was so in the old times."

Sir Thomas stared at the bold questioner, who thus went to the heart of the matter. Then he burst into a hearty laugh. "If you knew so much about Madame the Countess," he cried, "my good fellow, what need have you to come and consult me?"


CHAPTER XXV

THE CONTESSA'S BOUDOIR

The east rooms in which Madame di Forno-Populo had been placed on her arrival at the Hall were handsome and comfortable, though they were not the best in the house, and they were furnished as English rooms generally are, the bed forming the principal object in each chamber. The Contessa had looked around her in dismay when first ushered into the spacious room with its huge couch, and wardrobes, and its unmistakable destination as a sleeping-room merely: and it was only the addition of a dressing-room of tolerable proportions which had made her quarters so agreeable to her as they proved. The transformation of this room from a severe male dressing-room into the boudoir of a fanciful and luxurious woman, was a work of art of which neither the master nor the mistress of the house had the faintest conception. The Contessa was never at home; so that she was—having that regard for her own comfort which is one of the leading features in such a life as hers—everywhere at home, carrying about with her wherever she went the materials for creating an individual centre (a chez soi, which is something far more intimate and personal than a home), in which everything was arranged according to her fancy. Had Lucy, or even had Sir Tom, who knew more about such matters, penetrated into that sacred retirement, they would not have recognised it for a room in their own house. Out of one of the Contessa's boxes there came a paraphernalia of decoration such as would turn the head of the aesthetic furnisher of the present day. As she had been everywhere, and had "taste," when it was not so usual to have taste as it is now, she had "picked up" priceless articles, in the shape of tapestries, embroideries, silken tissues no longer made, delicate bits of Eastern carpet, soft falling drapery of curtains, such as artistically arranged in almost any room, impressed upon it the Contessa's individuality, and made something dainty and luxurious among the meanest surroundings. The Contessa's maid, from long practice, had become almost an artist in the arrangement of these properties, without which her mistress could not live; and on the evening of the first day of their arrival at the Hall, when Madame di Forno-Populo emerged from the darkness of the chamber in which she had rested all day after her journey, she stepped into a little paradise of subdued colour and harmonious effect. Antonio and Marietta were the authors of these wonders. They took down Mrs. Freshwater's curtains, which were of a solid character adapted to the locality, and replaced them by draperies that veiled the light tenderly and hung with studied grace. They took to pieces the small bed and made a divan covered with old brocade of the prosaic English mattress. They brought the finest of the furniture out of the bedchamber to add to the contents of this, and covered tables with Italian work, and veiled the bare wall with tapestry. This made such a magical change that the maids who penetrated by chance now and then into this little temple of the Graces could only stand aghast and gaze with open mouths; but no profane hand of theirs was ever permitted to touch those sacred things. There were even pictures on the wall, evolved out of the depths of that great coffer, which, more dear to the Contessa even than her wardrobe, went about with her everywhere—and precious pieces of porcelain: Madame di Forno-Populo, it need not be said, being quite above the mean and cheap decoration made with fans or unmeaning scraps of colour. The maids aforesaid, who obtained perilous and breathless glimpses from time to time of all these wonders, were at a loss to understand why so much trouble should be taken for a room that nobody but its inmate ever saw. The finer intelligence of the reader will no doubt set it down as something in the Contessa's favour that she could not live, even when in the strictest privacy, without her pretty things about her. To be sure it was not always so; in other regions, where other habits prevailed, this shrine so artistically prepared was open to worshippers; but the Contessa knew better than to make any such innovation here. She intended, indeed, nothing that was not entirely consistent with the strictest propriety. Her objects, no doubt, were her own interest and her own pleasure, which are more or less the objects of most people; but she intended no harm. She believed that she had a hold over Sir Tom which she could work for her advantage, but she did not mean to hurt Lucy. She thought that repose and a temporary absence from the usual scenes of her existence would be of use to her, and she thought also that a campaign in London under the warrant of the highest respectability would further her grand object. It amused her besides, perhaps, to flutter the susceptibilities of the innocent little ingénue whom Sir Tom had married; but she meant no harm. As for seizing upon Sir Tom in the evenings, and occupying all his attention, that was the most natural and simple of proceedings. She did this as another woman played bezique. Some entertainment was a necessity, and everybody had something. There were people who insisted upon whist—she insisted only upon "some one to talk to." What could be more natural? The Contessa's "some one" had to be a man and one who could pay with sense and spirit the homage to which she was accustomed. It was her only stipulation—and surely it must be an ungracious hostess indeed who could object to that.

She had just finished her breakfast on one of those gray mornings—seated before the fire in an easy-chair, which was covered with a shawl of soft but bright Indian colouring. She had her back to the light, but it was scarcely necessary even had there been any eyes to see her save those of Marietta, who naturally was familiar with her aspect at all times. Marietta made the Contessa's chocolate, as well as arranged and kept in order the Contessa's boudoir. To such a retainer nothing comes amiss. She would sit up till all hours, and perform marvels of waiting, of working, service of every kind. It never occurred to her that it "was not her place" to do anything that her mistress required. Antonio was her brother, which was insipid, but she generally managed to indemnify herself, one way or another, for the loss of this legitimate method of flirtation. She had not great wages, and she had a great deal of work, but Marietta felt her life amusing, and did not object to it. Here in England the excitement indeed flagged a little. Williams was stout and married, and the other men had ties of the heart with which, as has been seen, Antonio ruthlessly interfered. Marietta was not unwilling to give to Charles the footman, who was a handsome young fellow, the means of avenging himself, but as yet this expedient for a little amusement had not succeeded, and there had been a touch of peevishness in the tone with which she asked whether it was true that the Contessa intended remaining here. Madame di Forno-Populo was a woman who disliked the bondage of question and reply.

"You do not amuse yourself, Marietta mia?" said the Contessa. She spoke Italian with her servants, and she was always caressing, fond of tender appellatives. "Patience! the country even in England is very good for the complexion, and in London there is a great deal that is amusing. Wheel this table away and give me the other with my writing things. The cushion for my elbow. Thanks! You forget nothing. My Marietta, you will have a happy life."

"Do you think so, Signora Contessa?" said the girl, a little wistfully.

The Contessa smiled upon her and said "Cara!" with an air of tenderness that might have made any one happy. Then she addressed herself to her correspondence, while Marietta removed into the other room not only the tray but the table with the tray which her mistress had used. The Contessa did not like to know or see anything of the processes of readjustment and restoration. She glanced over her morning's letters again with now and then a smile of satisfaction, and addressed herself to the task of answering them with apparent pleasure. Indeed, her own letters amused her even more than the others had done. When she had finished her task she took up a silver whistle and blew into it a long melodious note. She made the most charming picture, leaning back in her chair, in a white cashmere dressing-gown covered with lace, and a little cap upon her dark locks. All the accessories of her toilette were exquisite, as well as the draperies about her that relieved and set off her whiteness. Her shoes were of white plush with a cockade of lace to correspond. Her sleeves, a little more loose than common, showed her beautiful arms through a mist of lace. She was not more carefully nor more elegantly dressed when she went downstairs in all her panoply of conquest. What a pity there was no one to see it! but the Contessa did not even think of this. In other circumstances, no doubt, there might have been spectators, but in the meantime she pleased herself, which after all is the first object with every well-constituted mind. She leaned back in her chair pleased with herself and her surroundings, in a gentle languor after her occupation, and conscious of a yellow novel within reach should her young companion be slow of appearing. But Bice she knew had the ears of a savage, and would hear her summons wherever she might be.

Bice at this moment was in a very different scene. She was in the large gallery, which was a little chill and dreary of a morning when all the windows were full of a gray, indefinable mist instead of light, and the ancestors were indistinguishable in their frames. She had just been going through her usual exercise with the baby, and had joined Lucy at the upper end of the gallery, that sport being over, and little Tom carried off to his mid-day sleep. There was a fire there, in the old-fashioned chimney, and Lucy had been sitting beside it watching the sport. Bice seated herself on a stool at a little distance. She had a half affection half dislike for this young woman, who was most near her in age of any one in the house. For one thing they were on different sides and representing different interests; and Bice had been trained to dislike the ordinary housekeeping woman. They had been brought together, indeed, in a moment of emotion by the instrumentality of the little delicate child, for whom Bice had conceived a compassionate affection. But the girl felt that they were antagonistic. She did not expect understanding or charity, but to be judged harshly and condemned summarily by this type of the conventional and proper. She believed that Lucy would be "shocked" by what she said, and horrified by her freedom and absence of prejudice. Yet, notwithstanding all this, there was an attraction in the candid eyes and countenance of little Lady Randolph which drew her in spite of herself. It was of her own will, though with a little appearance of reluctance, that she drew near, and soon plunged into talk—for to tell the truth, now that Jock was gone, Bice felt occasionally as if she must talk to the winds and trees, and could not at the hazard of her life keep silence any more. She could scarcely tell how it was that she was led into confessions of all kinds and descriptions of the details of her past life.

"We are a little alike," said Lucy. "I was not much older than you are when my father died, and afterwards we had no real home: to be sure, I had always Jock. Even when papa was living it was not very homelike, not what I should choose for a girl. I felt how different it was when I went to Lady Randolph, who thought of everything—"

Bice did not say anything for some time, and then she laughed. "The Contessa does not think of everything," she said.

Lucy looked at her with a question in her eyes. She wanted to ask if the Contessa was kind. But there was a certain domestic treachery involved in asking such a question.

"People are different," she said, with a certain soothing tone. "We are not made alike, you know; one person is good in one way and one in another." This abstract deliverance was not at all in Lucy's way. She returned to the particular point before them with relief. "England," she said, "must seem strange to you after your own country. I suppose it is much colder and less bright?"

"I have no country" said Bice; "everywhere is my country. We have a house in Rome, but we travel; we go from one place to another—to all the places that are what you call for pleasure. We go in the season. Sometimes it is for the waters, sometimes for the sports or the games—always festa wherever we go."

"And you like that? To be sure, you are so very young; otherwise I should think it was rather tiresome," Lucy said.

"No, it is not rather tiresome," said Bice, with a roll of her "r," "it is horrible! When we came here I did not know why it was, but I rejoiced myself that there was no band playing. I thought at first it was merely jour de relâche: but when morning after morning came and no band, that was heavenly," she said, drawing a long breath.

"A band playing!" Lucy's laugh at the absurdity of the idea rang out with all the gaiety of a child. It amused her beyond measure, and Bice, always encouraged by approbation, went on.

"I expected it every morning. The house is so large. I thought the season, perhaps, was just beginning, and the people not arrived yet. Sometimes we go like that too soon. The rooms are cheaper. You can make your own arrangement."

Lucy looked at her very compassionately. "That is why you pass the mornings in your own room," she said, "were you never then in a country house before?"

"I do not know what is a country house. We have been in a great castle where there was the chase every day. No, that is not what la chasse means in England—to shoot I would say. And then in the evening the theatre, tableaux, or music. But to be quiet all day and all night too, that is what I have never seen. We have never known it. It is confusing. It makes you feel as if all went on without any division; all one day, all one night."

Bice laughed, but Lucy looked somewhat grave. "This is our natural life in England," she said; "we like to be quiet; though I have not thought we were very quiet, we have had people almost every night."

To this Bice made no reply. But at Lucy's next question she stared, not understanding what it meant. "You go everywhere with the Contessa," she said; "are you out?"

"Out!" Bice's eyes opened wide. She shook her head. "What is out?" she said.

"It is when a girl begins to go to parties—when she comes out of her home, out of the schoolroom, from being just a little girl—"

"Ah, I know! From the Convent," said Bice; "but I never was there."

"And have you always gone to parties—all your life?" asked Lucy, with wondering eyes.

Bice looked at her, wondering too. "We do not go to parties. What is a party?" she said. "We go to the rooms—oh yes, and to the great receptions sometimes, and at hotels. Parties? I don't know what that means. Of course, I go with the Contessa to the rooms, and to the tables d'hôte. I give her my arm ever since I was tall enough. I carry her fan and her little things. When she sings I am always ready to play. They call me the shadow of the Contessa, for I always wear a black frock, and I never talk except when some one talks to me. It is most amusing how the English look at me. They say, Miss—? and then stop that I may tell them my name."

"And don't you?" said Lucy. "Do you know; though it is so strange to say it, I don't even know your name."

Bice laughed, but she made no attempt to supply the omission. "The Contessa thinks it is more piquant," she said. "But nothing is decided about me, till it is known how I turn out. If I am beautiful the Contessa will marry me well, and all will be right."

"And is that what you—wish?" said Lucy, in a tone of horror.

"Monsieur, your brother," said Bice, with a laugh, "says I am not pretty, even. He says it does not matter. How ignorant men are, and stupid! And then suddenly they are old, old, and sour. I do not know which is the worst. I do not like men."

"And yet you think of being married, which it is not nice to speak of," said Lucy, with disapproval.

"Not—nice? Why is that? Must not girls be married? and if so, why not think of it?" said Bice, gravely. There was not the ghost of a blush upon her cheek. "If you might live without being married that would understand itself; but otherwise—"

"Indeed," cried Lucy, "you can, indeed you can! In England, at least. To marry for a living, that is terrible."

"Ah!" cried Bice, with interest, drawing her chair nearer, "tell me how that is to be done."

There was the seriousness of a practical interest in the girl's manner. The question was very vital to her. There was no other way of existence possible so far as she knew; but if there was it was well worth taking into consideration.

Lucy felt the question embarrassing when it was put to her in this very decisive way. "Oh," she cried with an Englishwoman's usual monosyllabic appeal for help to heaven and earth: "there are now a great number of ways. There are so many things that girls can do; there are things open to them that never used to be—they can even be doctors when they are clever. There are many ways in which they can maintain themselves."

"By trades?" cried Bice, "by work?" She laughed. "We hear of that sometimes, and the doctors; everybody laughs; the men make jokes, and say they will have one when they are ill. If that is all, I do not think there is anything in it. I should not like to work even if I were a man, but a woman—! that gets no money, that is mal vu. If that is all! Work," she said, with a little oracular air, "takes up all your time, and the money that one can earn is so small. A girl avoids saying much to men who are like this. She knows how little they can have to offer her; and to work herself, why, it is impossible. What time would you have for anything?" cried the girl, with an impatient sense of the fatuity of the suggestion. Lucy was so much startled by this view of the subject that she made no reply.

"There is no question of working," said Bice with decision, "neither for women, neither for men. That is not in our world. But if I am only pretty, no more," she added, "what will become of me? It is not known. I shall follow the Contessa as before. I will be useful to her, and afterwards— I prefer not to think of that. In the meantime I am young. I do not wish for anything. It is all amusing. I become weary of the band playing, that is true; but then sometimes it plays not badly, and there is something always to laugh at. Afterwards, if I marry, then I can do as I like," the girl said.

Lucy gave her another look of surprised awe, for it was really with that feeling that she regarded this strange little philosopher. But she did not feel herself able to pursue the subject with so enlightened a person. She said: "How very well you speak English. You have scarcely any accent, and the Contessa has none at all. I was afraid she would speak only French, and my French is so bad."

"I have always spoken English all my life. When the Contessa is angry she says I am English all over; and she—she is of no country—she is of all countries; we are what you call vagabonds," the girl cried, with a laugh. She said it so calmly, without the smallest shadow of shame or embarrassment, that Lucy could only gaze at her and could not find a word to say. Was it true? It was evident that Bice at least believed so, and was not at all afraid to say it. This conversation took place, as has been said, in the picture gallery, where Lady Randolph and her young visitor had first found a ground of amity. The rainy weather had continued, and this place had gradually become the scene of a great deal of intercourse between the young mistress of the house and her guest. They scarcely spoke to each other in the evening. But in the morning after the game of romps with little Tom, by which Bice indemnified herself for the absence of other society, Lucy would join the party, and after the child had been carried off for his mid-day sleep, the others left behind would have many a talk. To Lucy the revelations thus made were more wonderful than any romance—so wonderful that she did not half take in the strange life to which they gave a clue, nor realise how perfectly right was Bice's description of herself and her patroness. They were vagabonds, as she said; and like other vagabonds, they got a great deal of pleasure out of their life. But to Lucy it seemed the most terrible that mind could conceive. Without any home, without any retirement or quietness, with a noisy band always playing, and a series of migrations from one place to another—no work, no duties, nothing to represent home occupations but a piece of tapisserie. She put her hand very tenderly upon Bice's shoulder. There had been prejudices in her mind against this girl— but they all melted away in a womanly pity. "Oh," she said, "Cannot I help you in any way? Cannot Sir Tom—" But here she paused. "I am afraid," she said, "that all we could think of would be an occupation for you; something to do, which would be far, far better, surely, than this wandering life."

Bice looked at her for a moment with a doubtful air. "I don't know what you mean by occupation," she said.

And this, to Lucy's discomfiture, she found to be true. Bice had no idea of occupation. Young Lady Randolph, who was herself not much instructed, made a conscientious effort at least to persuade the strange girl to read and improve her mind. But she flew off on all such occasions with a laugh that was half mocking and half merry. "To what good?" she said, with that simplicity of cynicism which is a quality of extreme youth. "If I turn out beautiful, if I can marry whom I will, I will then get all I want without any trouble."

"But if not?" said Lucy, too careful of the other's feelings to express what her own opinions were on this subject.

"If not it will be still less good," said Bice, "for I shall never then do anything or be of any importance at all; and why should I tr-rouble?" she said, with that rattle of the r's which was about the only sign that English was not her native speech. This was very distressing to Lucy, who wished the girl well, and altogether Lady Randolph was anxious to interfere on Bice's behalf, and put her on a more comprehensible footing.

"It will be very strange when you go among other people in London," she said. "Madame di Forno-Populo does not know England. People will want to know who you are. And if you were to be married, since you will talk of that," Lucy added with a blush, "your name and who you are will have to be known. I will ask Sir Tom to talk to the Contessa—or," she said with reluctance, "I will speak to her if you think she will listen to me."

"I am called," said Bice, making a sweeping curtsey, and waving her hand as she darted suddenly away, leaving Lucy in much doubt and perplexity. Was she really called? Lucy heard nothing but a faint sound in the distance, as of a low whistle. Was this a signal between the strange pair who were not mother and daughter, nor mistress and servant, and yet were so linked together. It seemed to Lucy, with all her honest English prejudices, that to train so young a girl (and a girl so fond of children, and, therefore, a good girl at bottom, whatever her little faults might be) to such a wandering life, and to put her up as it were to auction for whoever would bid highest, was too terrible to be thought of. Better a thousand times to be a governess, or a sempstress, or any honest occupation by which she could earn her own bread. But then to Bice any such expedient was out of the question. Her incredulous look of wonder and mirth came back to Lucy with a sensation of dumb astonishment. She had no right feelings, no sense of the advantages of independence, no horror of being sold in marriage. Lady Randolph did not know what to think of a creature so utterly beyond all rules known to her. She was in such a condition of mind, unsettled, unhinged, feeling all her old landmarks breaking up, that a new interest was of great importance to her. It withdrew her thoughts from the Contessa, and the irksomeness of her sway, when she thought of Bice and what could be done for her. The strange thing was that the girl wanted nothing done for her. She was happy enough so far as could be seen. In her close confinement and subjection she was so fearless and free that she might have been thought the mistress of the situation. It was incomprehensible altogether. To state the circumstances from one side was to represent a victim of oppression. A poor girl stealing into a strange house and room in the shadow of her patroness; unnamed, unnoticed, made no more account of than the chair upon which she sat, held in a bondage which was almost slavery, and intended to be disposed of when the moment came without a reference to her own will and affections. Lucy felt her blood boil when she thought of all this, and determined that she would leave no expedient untried to free this white slave, this unfortunate thrall. But the other side was one which could not pass without consideration. The girl was careless and fearless and free, without an appearance of bondage about her. She scoffed at the thought of escaping, of somehow earning a personal independence—such was not for persons in her world, she said. She was not horrified by her own probable fate. She was not unhappy, but amused and interested in her life, and taking everything gaily, both the present quiet and the tumult of the many "seasons" in watering-places and other resorts of gaiety through which, young as she was, she had already gone. She had looked at Lucy with a smile, which was half cynical, and altogether decisive, when the anxious young matron had pointed out to her the way of escaping from such a sale and bargain. She did not want to escape. It seemed to her right and natural. She walked as lightly as a bird with this yoke upon her shoulders. Lucy had never met anything of this kind before, and it called forth a sort of panic in her mind. She did not know how to deal with it; but neither would she give it up. She had something else to think upon, when the Contessa, lying back on her sofa, almost going to sleep before Sir Tom entered, roused herself on the moment to occupy and amuse him all the evening. Instead of thinking of that and making herself unhappy, Lucy looked the other way at Bice reading a novel rapidly at the other side of the table, with all her young savage faculties about her to see and hear everything. How to get her delivered from her fate! To make her feel that deliverance was necessary, to save her before she should be sacrificed, and take her out of her present slavery. It was very strange that it never occurred to Lucy to free the girl by making her one of the recipients of the money she had to give away. She was very faithful to the letter of her father's will, and he had excluded foreigners. But even that was not the reason. The reason was that it did not occur to her. She thought of every way of relieving the too-contented thrall before her except that way. And in the meantime the time wore on, and everything fell into a routine, and not a word was said of the Contessa's plans. It was evident, for the time being at least, that she meant to make no change, but was fully minded, notwithstanding the dullness of the country, to remain where she was.


CHAPTER XXVI

THE TWO STRANGERS

The Contessa did not turn her head or change her position when Bice entered. She said, "You have not been out?" in a tone which was half question and half reproof.

"It rained, and there is nothing to breathe but the damp and fog."

"What does it matter? it is very good for the complexion, this damp; it softens the skin, it clears your colour. I see the improvement every day."

"Do you think so?" said Bice, going up to the long mirror which had been established in a sort of niche against the wall, and draped as everything was draped, with graceful hangings. She went up to it and put her face close, looking with some anxiety at the image which she found there. "I do not see it," she said. "You are too sanguine. I am no better than I was. I have been racing in the long gallery with the child; that makes one's blood flow."

"You do well," said the Contessa, nodding her head. "I cannot take any notice of the child; it is too much for me. They are odious at that age."

"Ah! they are delightful," said Bice. "They are so good to play with, they ask no questions, and are always pleased. I put him on my shoulder and we fly. I wish that I might have a gymnastique, trapeze, what-you-call it, in that long gallery; it would be heaven."

The Contessa uttered an easy exclamation meaning nothing, which translated into English would have been a terrible oath. "Do not do it, in the name of—they will be shocked, oh, beyond everything."

Bice, still standing close to the glass, examining critically her cheek which she pinched, answered with a laugh. "She is shocked already. When I say that you will marry me well, if I turn out as I ought, she is full of horror. She says it is not necessary in England that a young girl should marry, that there are other ways."

The Contessa started to her feet. "Giove!" she cried, "Baccho! that insipidity, that puritan. And I who have kept you from every soil. She speak of other ways. Oh, it is too much!"

Bice turned from the glass to address a look of surprise to her patroness. "Reassure yourself, Madama," she said. "What Milady said was this, that I might work if I willed, and escape from marrying—that to marry was not everything. It appears that in England one may make one's living as if (she says) one were a man."

"As if one were a man!"

"That is what Milady said," Bice answered demurely. "I think she would help me to work, to get something to do. But she did not tell me what it would be; perhaps to teach children; perhaps to work with the needle. I know that is how it happens in the Tauchnitz. You do not read them, and, therefore, do not know; but I am instructed in all these things. The girl who is poor like me is always beautiful; but she never thinks of it as we do. She becomes a governess, or perhaps an artiste; or even she will make dresses, or at the worst tapisserie."

"And this she says to you—to you!" cried the Contessa, with flaming eyes.

"Oh, restrain yourself, Madama! It does not matter at all. She makes the great marriage just the same. It is not Milady who says this, it is in the Tauchnitz. It is the English way. Supposing," said Bice, "that I remain as I am? Something will have to be done with me. Put me, then, as a governess in a great family where there is a son who is a great nobleman, or very rich; and you shall see it will so happen, though I never should be beautiful at all."

"My child," said the Contessa, "all this is foolishness. You will not remain as you are. I see a little difference every day. In a little time you will be dazzling; you will be ready to produce. A governess! It is more likely that you will be a duchess; and then you will laugh at everybody—except me," said Madame di Forno-Populo, tapping her breast with her delicate fingers, "except me."

Bice looked at her with a searching, inquiring look. "I want to ask something," she said. "If I should be beautiful, you were so before me—oh, more, more!—you we—are very lovely, Madama."

The Contessa smiled—who would not smile at such a speech? made with all the sincerity and simplicity possible—simplicity scarcely affected by the instinct which made Bice aware before she said it, that to use the past tense would spoil all. The Contessa smiled. "Well," she said, "and then?"

"They married you," said Bice with a curious tone between philosophical remark and interrogation.

"Ah!" the Contessa said. She leaned back in her chair making herself very comfortable, and shook her head. "I understand. You think then it has been a—failure in my case? Yes, they married me—that is to say there was no they at all. I married myself, which makes a great difference. Ah, yes, I follow your reasoning very well. This woman you say was beautiful, was all that I hope to be, and married; and what has come of it? It is quite true. I speak to you as I speak to no one, Bice mia. The fact was we deceived each other. The Conte expected to make his fortune by me, and I by him. I was English, you perceive, though no one now remembers this. Poor Forno-Populo! He was very handsome; people were pleased to say we were a magnificent pair—but we had not the sous: and though we were fond of each other, he proceeded in one direction to repair his fortunes, and I—on another to—enfin to do as best I could. But no such accident shall happen in your case. It is not only your interest I have in hand; it is my own. I want a home for my declining years."

She said this with a smile at the absurdity of the expression in her case, but Bice at sixteen naturally took the words au pied de la lettre, and did not see any absurdity in them. To her forty was very much the same as seventy. She nodded her head very seriously in answer to this, and turning round to the glass surveyed herself once more, but not with that complacency which is supposed to be excited in the feminine bosom by the spectacle. She was far too serious for vanity—the gaze she cast upon her own youthful countenance was severely critical, and she ended by a shrug of her shoulders, as she turned away. "The only thing is," she said, "that perhaps the young brother is right, and at present I am not even pretty at all."

The Contessa had a great deal to think of during this somewhat dull interval. The days flowed on so regular, and with so little in them, that it was scarcely possible to take note of the time at all. Lucy was always scrupulously polite and sometimes had little movements of anxious civility, as if to make up for impulses that were less kind. And Sir Tom, though he enjoyed the evenings as much as ever, and felt this manner of passing the heavy hours to retain a great attraction, was at other times a little constrained, and made furtive attempts to find out what the Contessa's intentions were for the future, which betrayed to a woman who had always her wits about her, a certain strain of the old bonds, and uneasiness in the indefinite length of her visit. She had many reasons, however, for determining to ignore this uneasiness, and to move on upon the steady tenor of her way as if unconscious of any reason for change, opposing a smiling insensibility to all suggestions as to the approaching removal of the household to London. It seemed to the Contessa that the association of her débutante with so innocent and wealthy a person as Lady Randolph would do away with all the prejudices which her own dubious antecedents might have provoked; while the very dubiousness of those antecedents had procured her friends in high quarters and acquaintances everywhere, so that both God and Mammon were, so to speak, enlisted in her favour, and Bice would have all the advantage, without any of the disadvantage, of her patroness' position, such as it was. This was so important that she was quite fortified against any pricks of offence, or intrusive consciousness that she was less welcome than might have been desired. And in the end of January, when the entire household at the Hall had begun to be anxious to make sure of her departure, an event occurred which strengthened all her resolutions in this respect, and made her more and more determined, whatever might be the result, to cling to her present associations and shelter.

This was the arrival of a visitor, very unexpected and unthought of, who came in one afternoon after the daily drive, often a somewhat dull performance, which Lucy, when there was nothing more amusing to do, dutifully took with her visitor. Madame di Forno-Populo was reclining in the easiest of chairs after the fatigue of this expedition. There had been a fresh wind, and notwithstanding a number of veils, her delicate complexion had been caught by the keen touch of the breeze. Her cheeks burned, she declared, as she held up a screen to shield her from the glow of the fire. The waning afternoon light from the tall window behind threw her beautiful face into shadow, but she was undeniably the most important person in the tranquil domestic scene, occupying the central position, so that it was not wonderful that the new comer suddenly ushered in, who was somewhat timid and confused, and advanced with the hesitating step of a stranger, should without any doubt have addressed himself to her as the mistress of the house. Lucy, little and young, who was moving about the room, with her light step and in the simple dress of a girl, appeared to Mr. Churchill, who had many daughters of his own, to be (no doubt) the eldest, the mother's companion. He came in with a slightly embarrassed air and manner. He was a man beyond middle age, gray haired, stooping, with the deprecating look of one who had been obliged in many ways to propitiate fate in the shape of superiors, officials, creditors, all sorts of alien forces. He came up with his hesitating step to the Contessa's chair. "Madam," he said, with a voice which had a tremor in it, "my name will partly tell you the confused feelings that I don't know how to express. I am come in a kind of bewilderment, scarcely able to believe that what I have heard is true—"

The Contessa gazed at him calmly from the depths of her chair. The figure before her, thin, gray haired, submissive, with the long clerical coat and deprecating air, did not promise very much, but she had no objection to hear what he had to say in the absolute dearth of subjects of interest. Lucy, to whom his name seemed vaguely familiar, without recalling any distinct idea, and who was a little startled by his immediate identification of the Contessa, came forward a little and put a chair for him, then withdrew again, supposing his business to be with her guest.

"I will not sit down," Mr. Churchill said, faltering a little, "till I have said what I have no words to say. If what I am told is actually true, and your ladyship means to confer upon me a gift so—so magnificent— oh! pardon me—I cannot help thinking still that there must be some extraordinary mistake."

"Oh!" Lucy began, hurriedly making a step forward again; but the Contessa, to her surprise, accepted the address with great calm.

"Be seated, sir," Madame di Forno-Populo said, with a dignity which Lucy was far from being able to emulate. "And pray do not hesitate to say anything which occurs to you. I am already interested—" She waved her hand to him with a sort of regal grace, without moving in any other way. She had the air of a princess not deeply concerned indeed, but benevolently willing to listen. It was evident that this reception of him confused the stranger more and more. He became more deeply embarrassed in sight of the perfect composure with which he was contemplated, and cleared his throat nervously three or four times.

"I think," he said, "that there must be some mistake. It was, indeed, impossible that it should be true; but as I heard it from two quarters at once—and it was said to be something in the nature of a trust—But," he added, looking with a nervous intentness at the unresponsive face which he could with difficulty see, "it must be, since your ladyship does not recognise my name, a—mistake. I felt it was so from the beginning. A lady of whom I know nothing!—to bestow what is really a fortune—upon a man with no claim—"

He gave a little nervous laugh as he went on—the disappointment, after such a dazzling giddy hope, took away every vestige of colour from his face. "I will sit down for a moment, if you please," he said suddenly. "I—am a little tired with the walk—you will excuse me, Lady Randolph—"

"Oh, sir," cried Lucy, coming forward, "forgive me that I did not understand at once. It is no mistake at all. Oh, I am afraid you are very much fatigued, and I ought to have known at once when I heard your name."

He put out his hand in his deprecating way as she came close to the chair into which he had dropped. "It is nothing—nothing—my dear young lady: in a moment," he said.

"My Lucy," said the Contessa, "this is one of your secret bounties. I am quite interested. But do not interrupt; let us hear it out."

"It is something which is entirely between Mr. Churchill and me," cried Lucy. "Indeed, it would not interest you at all. But, pray, don't think it is a mistake," she said, earnestly turning to him. "It is quite right—it is a trust—there is nothing that need distress you. I am obliged to do it, and you need not mind. Indeed, you must not mind. I will tell you all about it afterwards."

"My dear young lady!" the clergyman said. He was relieved, but he was perplexed; he turned still towards the stately lady in the chair—"If it is really so, which I scarcely can allow myself to believe, how can I express my obligation? It seems more than any man ought to take; it is like a fairy tale. I have not ventured to mention it to my children, in case,— Thanks are nothing," he cried, with excitement; "thanks are for a trifle, a little every-day service; but this is a fortune; it is something beyond belief. I have been a poor man all my life, struggling to do my best for my children; and now, what I have never been able to do with all my exertions, you—put me in a position to do in a moment. What am I to say to you? Words can't reach such a case. It is simply unspeakable—incredible; and why out of all the world you should have chosen me—"

He had to stop, his emotion getting the better of him. Bice had come into the room while this strange scene was going on, and she stood in the shadow, unseen by the speaker, listening too.

"Pray compose yourself," said the Contessa, in her most gracious voice. "Your expressions are full of feeling. To have a fortune given to one must be very delightful; it is an experience that does not often happen. Probably a little tea, as I hear tea is coming, will restore Mr. — Pardon me, they are a little difficult to catch those, your English names."

The Contessa produced a curious idiom now and then like a work of art. It was almost the only sign of any uncertainty in her English; and while the poor clergyman, not quite understanding in his own emotion what she was saying, made an effort to gulp it down and bring himself to the level of ordinary life, the little stir of the bringing-in of tea suddenly converted everything into commonplace. He sat in a confusion that made all dull to him while this little stir went on. Then he rose up and said, faltering: "If your ladyship will permit me, I will go out into the air a little. I have got a sort of singing in my ears. I am—not very strong; I shall come back presently if you will allow me, and try to make my acknowledgments—in a less confused way."

Lucy followed him out of the room; he was not confused with her. "My dear young lady," he said, "my head is going round and round. Perhaps you will explain it all to me." He looked at her with a helpless, appealing air. Lucy had the appearance of a girl of his own. He was not afraid to ask her anything. But the great lady, his benefactress, who spoke so regally and responded so little to his emotion, alarmed him. Lucy, too, on her side, felt as if she had been a girl of his own. She put her arm within his, and led him to the library, where all was quiet, and where she felt by instinct—though she was not bookish— that the very backs of the books would console him and make him feel himself at home.

"It is very easy to explain," she said. "It is all through my brother Jock and your son, who is at school with him. And it is I who am Lady Randolph," she said, smiling, supporting him with her arm through his. The shock would have been almost too much for poor Mr. Churchill if she had not been so like a child of his own.

The moment this pair had left the room the Contessa raised herself eagerly from the chair. She looked round to Bice in the background with an imperative question. "What does this all mean?" she said, in a voice as different from the languor of her former address as night from day. "Who is it that gives away fortunes, that makes a poor man rich? Did you know all that? Is it that chit of a girl, that piece of simplicity—that—Giove! You have been her friend; you know her secrets. What does it mean?"

"She has no secrets," said Bice, coming slowly forward. "She is not like us, she is like the day."

"Fool!" the Contessa said, stamping her foot—"don't you see there must be something in it. I am thinking of you, though you are so ungrateful. One knows she is rich, all the money is hers; but I thought it had gone to Sir Tom. I thought it was he who could— ... Happily, I have always kept her in hand; and you, you have become her friend—"

"Madama," said Bice, with ironical politeness, "since it happens that Milady is gone, shall I pour out for you your cup of tea?"

"Oh, tea! do I care for tea? when there are possibilities—possibilities!" said the Contessa. She got up from her chair and began to pace about the room, a grand figure in the gathering twilight. As for Bice, some demon of perversity possessed her. She began to move about the tea-table, making the china ring, and pouring out the tea as she had said, betook herself to the eating of cake with a relish which was certainly much intensified by the preoccupation of her patroness. She remembered well enough, very well, what Jock had told her, and her own incredulity; but she would have died rather than give a sign of this—and there was a tacit defiance in the way in which she munched her cake under the Contessa's excited eyes, but this was only a momentary perversity.

## CHAPTER XXVII

AN ADVENTURESS

"When he told me first, I was angry like you, I would not believe it. Money! that is a thing to keep, I said, not to give away."

"To give away!" Few things in all her life, at least in all her later life, had so moved the Contessa. She was walking about the pretty room in an excitement which was like agitation, now sitting down in one place, now in another, turning over without knowing it the things on the table, arranging a drapery here and there instinctively. To how few people in the world would it be a matter of indifference that money, so to speak, was going begging, and might fall into their hands as well as another's! The best of us on this argument would prick up our ears. Nobody cared less for money in itself than Madame di Forno-Populo. She liked not to spend it only, but to squander—to make it fly on all hands. To be utterly extravagant one must be poor, and the money hunger which belongs to poverty is almost, one might say, a disinterested quality, so little is it concerned with the possession of the thing coveted. "Oh," she said, "this is too wonderful! and you are sure you have not been deceived by the language? You know English so well—are you sure that you were not deceived?"

Bice did not deign any reply to this question. She gave her head a slight toss of scorn. The suggestion that she could be mistaken was unworthy of an answer, and indeed was not put in seriousness, nor did the Contessa wait for a reply. "What then," the Contessa went on, "is the position of Sir Tom? Has he no control? Does he permit this? To have it taken away from himself and his family, thrown into the sea, parted with—Oh, it is too much! But how can it be done? I was aware that settlements were very troublesome, but I had not thought it possible—Bice! Bice! this is very exciting, it makes one's heart beat! And you are her friend."

"I am her—friend?" Bice turned one ear to her patroness with a startled look of interrogation.

"Oh!" cried the Contessa once more; by which exclamation, naturally occurring when she was excited, she proved that she was of English race. "What difficulty is there in my meaning? You have English enough for that. What! do you feel no impatience when you hear of money running away?—going into a different channel—to strangers—to people that have nothing to do with it—that have no right to it—anybody—a clergyman, a—"

Her feelings were too much for her. She threw herself into a chair, out of breath.

"He looked a very good man," said Bice, with that absolute calm which is so exasperating to an excited woman, "and what does it matter, if it has to be given away, who gets it? I should give it to the beggars. I should fling it for them, as you do the bajocchi when you are out driving."

"You are a fool! you are a fool!" cried the Contessa, "or rather you are a child, and don't understand anything. Fling it to the beggars? Yes, if it was in shillings or even sovereigns. You don't understand what money is."

"That is true, Madama, for I never had any," cried the girl, with a laugh. She was perfectly unmoved—the desire of money was not in her as yet, though she was far more enlightened as to its uses than most persons of her age. It amused her to see the excitement of her companion; and she knew very well what the Contessa meant, though she would not betray any consciousness of it. "If I marry," she said, "then perhaps I shall know."

"Bice! you are not a fool—you are very sharp, though you choose not to see. Why should not you have this as well as another?—oh, much better than another! I can't stand by and see it all float into alien channels, while you—it would not be doing my duty while you— Oh, don't look at me with that blank face, as if it did not move you in the least! Would it be nothing to have it in your power to dress as you like, to do as you like, to go into the world, to have a handsome house, to enjoy life?—"

"But, yes!" said Bice, "is it necessary to ask?" She was still as calm as if the question they were discussing had been of the very smallest importance. "But we are not good poor people that will spend the money comme il faut. If we had it we should throw it away. Me also—I would throw it away. It would be for nothing good; why should it be given to us? Oh no, Madama. The good old clergyman had many children. He will not waste the money—which we should. What do you care for money, but to spend it fast, fast; and I too—"

"You are a child," said the Contessa. "No, perhaps I am not what people call good, though I am poor enough—but you are a child. If it was given to you it would be invested; you would have power over the income only. You could not throw it away, nor could I, which, perhaps, is what you are thinking of. You are just the person she wants, so far as I can see. She objects to my plan of putting you out in the world; she says it would be better if you were to work; but this is the best of all. Let her provide for you, and then it will not need that you should either marry or work. This is, beyond all description, the best way. And you are her friend. Tell me, was it before or after the boy informed you of this that you advised yourself to become her friend?"

"Contessa!" cried Bice, with a shock of angry feeling which brought the blood to her face. She was not sensitive in many matters which would have stung an English girl; but this suggestion, which was so undeserved, moved her to passion. She turned away with an almost tragic scorn, and seizing the tapisserie, which was part of the Contessa's mise en scene, flung a long strip of the many-coloured embroidery over her arm, and began to work with a sort of savage energy. The Contessa watched her movements with a sudden pause in her own excitement. She stopped short in the eagerness of her own thoughts, and looked with keen curiosity at the young creature upon whom she had built so many expectations. She was not an ungenerous or mercenary woman, though she had many faults, and as she gazed a certain compunction awoke within her, mingled with amusement. She was sorry for the unworthy suggestion she had made, but the sight of the girl in her indignation was like a scene in a play to this woman of the world. Her youthful dignity and wrath, her silent scorn, the manner in which she flung her needle through the canvas, working out her rage, were full of entertainment to the Contessa. She was not irritated by the girl's resentment; it even took off her thoughts from the primary matter to watch this exhibition of feeling. She gave vent to a little laugh as she noted how the needle flew.

"Cara! I was nasty when I said that. I did not mean it. I suffered myself to talk as one talks in the world. You are not of the world—it is not applicable to you."

"Yes, Madama, I am of the world," cried Bice. "What have I known else? But I did not mean to become Milady's friend, as you say. It was by accident. I was in the gallery only to amuse myself, and she came—it was not intention. I think that Milady is—"

Here Bice stopped, looked up from the sudden fervour of her working, threw back her head, and said nothing more.

"That Milady is—what?" the Contessa cried.

A laugh so joyous, so childish, that no one could have refused to be sympathetic, burst from Bice's lips. She gave her patroness a look of merriment and derision, in which there was something tender and sweet. "Milady is—sorry for me," she said.

This speech had a strange effect upon the Contessa. She coloured, and the tears seemed to flood in a moment to her eyes. "Poor child!" she said—"poor child! She has reason. But that amuses you, Bice mia," she said, in a voice full of the softest caressing, looking at her through those sudden tears. The Contessa was an adventuress, and she had brought up this girl after her own traditions; but it was clear as they looked at each other that they loved each other. There was perfect confidence between them. Bice looked with fearless laughing eyes, and a sense of the absurdity of the fact that some one was sorry for her, into the face of her friend.

"She thinks I would be happier if I worked. To give lessons to little children and be their slave would be better, she thinks. To know nothing and see nothing, but live far away from the world and be independent, and take no trouble about my looks, or, if I please—that is Milady's way of thinking," Bice said.

The Contessa's face softened more and more as she looked at the girl. There even dropped a tear from her full eyes. She shook her head. "I am not sure," she said, "dear child, that I am not of Milady's opinion. There are ways in which it is better. Sometimes I think I was most happy when I was like that—without money, without experience, with no wishes."

"No wishes, Madama! Did you not wish to go out into the beautiful bright world, to see people, to hear music, to talk, to please? It is impossible. Money, that is different, and experience that is different: but to wish, every one must do that."

"Bice, you have a great deal of experience for so young a girl. You have seen so much. I ought to have brought you up otherwise, perhaps, but how could I? You have always shared with me, and what I had I gave you. And you know besides how little satisfaction there is in it—how sick one becomes of a crowd of faces that are nothing to you, and of music that goes on just the same whatever you are feeling—and this to please, as you call it! Whom do I please? Persons who do not care at all for me except that I amuse them sometimes—who like me to sing; who like to look at me; who find themselves less dull when I am there. That is all. And that will be all for you, unless you marry well, my Bice, which it is the object of my life to make you do."

"I hope I shall marry well," said the girl, composedly. "It would be very pleasant to find one's self above all shifts, Madama. Still that is not everything; and I would much rather have led the life I have led, and enjoyed myself and seen so much, than to have been the little governess of the English family—the little girl who is always so quiet, who walks out with the children, and will not accept the eldest son even when he makes love to her. I should have laughed at the eldest son. I know what they are like—they are so stupid; they have not a word to say; that would have amused me; but in the Tauchnitz books it is all honour and wretchedness. I am glad I know the world, and have seen all kinds of people, and wish for everything that is pleasant, instead of being so good and having no wishes as you say."

The Contessa laughed, having got rid of all her incipient tears. "There is more life in it," she said. "You see now what it is—this life in England; one day is like another, one does the same things. The newspaper comes in the morning, then luncheon, then to go out, then tea, dinner; there is no change. When we talk in the evening, and I remind Sir Tom of the past when I lived in Florence, and he was with me every day,"—the Contessa once more uttered that easy exclamation which would sound so profane in English. "Quelle vie!" she cried, "how much we got out of every day. There were no silences! They came in one after another with some new thing, something to see and to do. We separated to dress, to make ourselves beautiful for the evening, and then till the morning light came in through the curtains, never a pause or a weariness. Yes! sometimes one had a terrible pang. There would be a toilette, which was ravishing, which was far superior to mine—for I never had money to dress as I wished—or some one else would have a success, and attract all eyes. But what did that matter?" the Contessa cried, lighting up more and more. "One did not really grudge what lasted only for a time; for one knew next day one would have one's turn. Ah!" she said, with a sigh, "I knew what it was to be a queen, Bice, in those days."

"And so you do still, Madama," said the girl, soothingly.

Madama di Forno-Populo shook her head. "It is no longer the same," she said. "You have known only the worst side, my poverina. It is no longer one's own palace, one's own people, and the best of the strangers, the finest company. You saw the Duchess at Milady's party the other day. To see me made her lose her breath. She could not refuse to speak to me—to salute me—but it was with a consternation! But, Bice, that lady was only too happy to be invited to the Palazzo Populino. To make one of our expeditions was her pride. I believe in my soul," cried the Contessa, "that when she looks back she remembers those days as the most bright of her life."

Bice's clear shining eyes rested upon her patroness with a light in them which was keen with indignation and wonder. She cried, "And why the change—and why the change, Madama?" with a high indignant tone, such as youth assumes in presence of ingratitude and meanness. Bice knew much that a young girl does not usually know; but the reason why her best friend should be thus slighted was not one of these things.

The Contessa shrank a little from her gaze. She rose up again and went to the window and looked out upon the wintry landscape, and standing there with her face averted, shrugged her shoulders a little and made answer in a tone of levity very different from the sincerer sound of her previous communications. "It is poverty, my child, poverty, always the easiest explanation! I was never rich, but then there had been no crash, no downfall. I was in my own palace. I had the means of entertaining. I was somebody. Ah! very different; it was not then at the baths, in the watering-places, that the Contessa di Forno-Populo was known. It is this, my Bice, that makes me say that sometimes I am of Milady's opinion; that to have no wishes, to know nothing, to desire nothing—that is best. When I knew the Duchess first I could be of service to her. Now that I meet her again it is she only that can be of service to me."

"But—" Bice began and stopped short. She was, as has been said, a girl of many experiences. When a very young creature is thus prematurely introduced to a knowledge of human nature she approaches the subject with an impartiality scarcely possible at an older age. She had seen much. She had been acquainted with those vicissitudes that occur in the lives of the seekers of pleasure almost since ever she was born. She had been acquainted with persons of the most gay and cheerful appearance, who had enjoyed themselves highly, and called all their acquaintances round them to feast, and who had then suddenly collapsed and after an interval of tears and wailings had disappeared from the scene of their downfall. But Bice had not learnt the commonplace lesson so deeply impressed upon the world from the Athenian Timon downwards, that a downfall of this kind instantly cuts all ties. She was aware, on the contrary, that a great deal of kindness, sympathy, and attempts to aid were always called forth on such occasions; that the women used to form a sort of rampart around the ruined with tears and outcries, and that the men had anxious meetings and consultations and were constantly going to see some one or other upon the affairs of the downfallen. Bice had not seen in her experience that poverty was an argument for desertion. She was so worldly wise that she did not press her question as a simple girl might have done. She stopped short with an air of bewilderment and pain, which the Contessa, as her head was turned, did not see. She gave up the inquiry; but there arose in her mind a suspicion, a question, such as had not ever had admission there before.

"Ah!" cried the Contessa, suddenly turning round, clasping her hands, "it was different indeed when my house was open to all these English, and they came as they pleased. But now I do not know, if I am turned out of this house, this dull house in which I have taken refuge, where I shall go. I don't know where to go!"

"Madama!" Bice sprang to her feet too, and clasped her hands.

"It is true—it is quite true. We have spent everything. I have not the means to go even to a third-rate place. As for Cannes it is impossible. I told you so before we came here. Rome is impossible—the apartment is let, and without that I could not live at all. Everything is gone. Here one may manage to exist a little while, for the house is good, and Sir Tom is rather amusing. But how to get to London unless they will take us I know not, and London is the place to produce you, Bice. It is for that I have been working. But Milady does not like me; she is jealous of me, and if she can she will send us away. Is it wonderful, then, that I am glad you are her friend? I am very glad of it, and I should wish you to let her know that to no one could she give her money more fitly. You see," said the Contessa, with a smile, resuming her seat and her easy tone, "I have come back to the point we started from. It is seldom one does that so naturally. If it is true (which seems so impossible) that there is money to give away, no one has a better right to it than you."

Bice went away from this interview with a mind more disturbed than it had ever been in her life before. Naturally, the novel circumstances which surrounded her awakened deeper questions as her mind developed, and she began to find herself a distinct personage. They set her wondering. Madame di Forno-Populo had been of a tenderness unparalleled to this girl, and had sheltered her existence ever since she could remember. It had not occurred to her mind as yet to ask what the relations were between them, or why she had been the object of so much affection and thought. She had accepted this with all the composure of a child ever since she was a child. And the prospect of achieving a marriage should she turn out beautiful, and thus being in a position to return some of the kindness shown her, seemed to Bice the most natural thing in the world. But the change of atmosphere had done something, and Lucy's company, and the growth, perhaps, of her own young spirit. She went away troubled. There seemed to be more in the world and its philosophy than Bice's simple rules could explain.

CHAPTER XXVIII

THE SERPENT AND THE DOVE

On the very next day after this conversation took place a marked change occurred in the manner of the Contessa. She had been always caressing to Lucy, calling her by pretty names, and using a hundred tender expressions as if to a child; but had never pretended to talk to her otherwise than in a condescending way. On this occasion, however, she exerted herself to a most unusual extent during their drive to captivate and charm Lady Randolph; and as Lucy was very simple and accessible to everything that seemed kindness, and the Contessa very clever and with full command of her powers, it is not wonderful that her success was easy. She led her to talk of Mr. Churchill, who had been kept to dinner on the previous night, and to whom Sir Tom had been very polite, and Lucy anxiously kind, doing all that was possible to put the good man at his ease, though with but indifferent success. For the thought of such an obligation was too great to be easily borne, and the agitation of his mind was scarcely settled, even by the commonplaces of the dinner, and the devotion which young Lady Randolph showed him. Perhaps the grave politeness of Sir Tom, which was not very encouraging, and the curiosity of the great lady, whom he had mistaken for his benefactress, counterbalanced Mr. Churchill's satisfaction, for he did not regain his confidence, and it was evidently with great relief of mind that he got up from his seat when the carriage was announced to take him away. The Contessa had given her attention to all he said and did, with a most lively and even anxious interest, and it was from this that she had mastered so many details which Bice had reluctantly confirmed by her report of the information she had derived from Jock. It was not long before Madame di Forno-Populo managed to extract everything from Lucy. Lady Randolph was not used to defend herself against such inquiries, nor was there any reason why she should do so. She was glad indeed when she saw how sweetly her companion looked, and how kind were her tones, to talk over her own difficult position with another woman, one who was interested, and who did not express her disapproval and horror as most people did. The Contessa, on the contrary, took a great deal of interest. She was astonished, indeed, but she did not represent to Lucy that what she had to do was impossible or even vicious, as most people seemed to suppose. She listened with the gravest attention; and she gave a soothing sense of sympathy to Lucy's troubled soul. She was so little prepared for sympathy from such a quarter that the unexpectedness of it made it more soothing still.

"This is a great charge to be laid upon you," the Contessa said, with the most kind look. "Upon you so young and with so little experience. Your father must have been a man of very original mind, my Lucy. I have heard of a great many schemes of benevolence, but never one like this."

"No?" said Lucy, anxiously watching the Contessa's eye, for it was so strange to her to have sympathy on this point, that she felt a sort of longing for it, and that this new critic, who treated the whole matter with more moderation and reasonableness than usual, should approve.

"Generally one endows hospitals or builds churches; in my country there is a way which is a little like yours; it is to give marriage portions—that is very good I am told. It is done by finding out who is the most worthy. And it is said also that not the most worthy is always taken. Don't you remember there is a Rosiere in Barbe Bleue? Oh, I believe you have never heard of Barbe Bleue."

"I know the story," said Lucy, with a smile, "of the many wives, and the key, and sister Anne—sister Anne."

"Ah! that is not precisely what I mean; but it does not matter. So it is this which makes you so grave, my pretty Lucy. I do not wonder. What a charge for you! To encounter all the prejudices of the world which will think you mad. I know it. And now your husband—the excellent Tom—he," said the Contessa, laying a caressing and significant touch upon Lucy's arm, "does not approve?"

"Oh, Madame di Forno-Populo, that is the worst of it," cried Lucy, whose heart was opened, and who had taken no precaution against assault on this side; "but how do you know? for I thought that nobody knew."

The Contessa this time took Lucy's hand between hers, and pressed it tenderly, looking at her all the time with a look full of meaning. "Dear child," she said, "I have been a great deal in the world. I see much that other people do not see. And I know his face, and yours, my little angel. It is much for you to carry upon those young shoulders. And all for the sake of goodness and charity."

"I do not know," said Lucy, "that it is right to say that; for, had it been left to me, perhaps I should never have thought of it. I should have been content with doing just what I could for the poor. No one," said Lucy, with a sigh, "objects to that. When people are quite poor it is natural to give them what they want; but the others—"

"Ah, the others," said the Contessa. "Dear child, the others are the most to be pitied. It is a greater thing, and far more difficult to give to this good clergyman enough to make his children happy, than it is to supply what is wanted in a cottage. Ah yes, your father was wise, he was a person of character. The poor are always cared for. There are none of us, even when we are ourselves poor, who do not hold out a hand to them. There is a society in my Florence which is like you. It is for the Poveri Vergognosi. You don't understand Italian? That means those who are ashamed to beg. These are they," said the Contessa impressively, "who are to be the most pitied. They must starve and never cry out; they must conceal their misery and smile; they must put always a fair front to the world, and seem to want nothing, while they want everything. Oh!" The Contessa ended with a sigh, which said more than words. She pressed Lucy's hand, and turned her face away. Her feelings were too much for her, and on the delicate cheek, which Lucy could see, there was the trace of a tear. After a moment she looked round again, and said, with a little quiver in her voice: "I respect your father, my Lucy. It was a noble thought, and it is original. No one I have ever heard of had such an intention before."

Lucy, at this unlooked-for applause, brightened with pleasure; but at the same time was so moved that she could only look up into her companion's face and return the pressure of her hand. When she recovered a little she said: "You have known people like that?"

"Known them? In my country," said the Contessa (who was not an Italian at all), "they are as plentiful as in England—blackberries. People with noble names, with noble old houses, with children who must never learn anything, never be anything, because there is no money. Know them! dear child, who can know better? If I were to tell you my history! I have for my own part known—what I could not trouble your gentle spirit to hear."

"But, Madame di Forno-Populo, oh! if you think me worthy of your confidence, tell me!" cried Lucy. "Indeed, I am not so insensible as you may think. I have known more than you suppose. You look as if no harm could ever have touched you," Lucy cried, with a look of genuine admiration. The Contessa had found the right way into her heart.

The Contessa smiled with mournful meaning and shook her head. "A great deal of harm has touched me," she said; "I am the very person to meet with harm in the world. A solitary woman without any one to take care of me, and also a very silly one, with many foolish tastes and inclinations. Not prudent, not careful, my Lucy, and with very little money; what could be more forlorn? You see," she said, with a smile "I do not put all this blame upon Providence, but a great deal on myself. But to put me out of the question—"

Lucy put a hand upon the Contessa's arm. She was much moved by this revelation.

"Oh! don't do that," she said; "it is you I want to hear of."

Madame di Forno-Populo had an object in every word she was saying, and knew exactly how much she meant to tell and how much to conceal. It was indeed a purely artificial appeal that she was making to her companion's feelings; and yet, when she looked upon the simple sympathy and generous interest in Lucy's face, her heart was touched.

"How good you are," she said; "how generous! though I have come to you against your will, and am staying—when I am not wanted."

"Oh! do not say so," cried Lucy with eagerness; "do not think so—indeed, it was not against my will. I was glad, as glad as I could be, to receive my husband's friend."

"Few women are so," said the Contessa gravely. "I knew it when I came. Few, very few, care for their husband's friend—especially when she is a woman—"

Lucy fixed her eyes upon her with earnest attention. Her look was not suspicious, yet there was investigation in it.

"I do not think I am like that," she said simply.

"No, you are not like that," said the Contessa. "You are the soul of candour and sweetness; but I have vexed you. Ah, my Lucy, I have vexed you. I know it—innocently, my love—but still I have done it. That is one of the curses of poverty. Now look," she said, after a momentary pause, "how truth brings truth! I did not intend to say this when I began" (and this was perfectly true), "but now I must open my heart to you. I came without caring much what you would think, meaning no harm—Oh, trust me, meaning no harm! but since I have come all the advantages of being here have appeared to me so strongly that I have set my heart upon remaining, though I knew it was disagreeable to you."

"Indeed:" cried Lucy, divided between sincerity and kindness: "if it was ever so for a moment, it was only because I did not understand."

"My sweetest child! this I tell you is one of the curses of poverty. I knew it was disagreeable to you; but because of the great advantage of being in your house, not only for me, but for Bice, for whom I have sworn to do my best—Lucy, pardon me—I could not make up my mind to go away. Listen! I said to myself, I am poor, I cannot give her all the advantages; and they are rich; it is nothing to them—I will stay, I will continue, though they do not want me, not for my sake, for the sake of Bice. They will not be sorry afterwards to have made the fortune of Bice. Listen, dear one; hear me out. I had the intention of forcing myself upon you—oh no! the words are not too strong—in London, always for Bice's sake, for she has no one but me; and if her career is stopped— I am not a woman," said the Contessa, with dignity, "who am used to find myself de trop. I have been in my life courted, I may say it, rather than disagreeable; yet this I was willing to bear—and impose myself upon you for Bice's sake—"

Lucy listened to this moving address with many differing emotions. It gave her a pang to think that her hopes of having her house to herself were thus permanently threatened. But at the same time her heart swelled, and all her generous feelings were stirred. Was she indeed so poor a creature as to grudge to two lonely women the shelter and advantage of her wealth and position? If she did this, what did it matter if she gave money away? This would indeed be keeping to the letter of her father's will, and abjuring its meaning. She could not resist the pathos, the dignity, the sweetness of the Contessa's appeal, which was not for herself but for Bice, for the girl who was so good to baby, and whom that little oracle had bound her to with links of gratitude and tenderness. "Oh," Lucy said to herself, "if I should ever have to appeal to any one for kindness to him!" And Bice was the Contessa's child—the child of her heart, at least—the voluntary charge which she had taken upon her, and to which she was devoting herself. Was it possible that only because she wanted to have her husband to herself in the evenings, and objected to any interruption of their privacy, a woman should be made to suffer who was a good woman, and to whom Lucy could be of use? No, no, she cried within herself, the tears coming to her eyes; and yet there was a very real pang behind.

"But reassure yourself, dear child," said the Contessa, "for now that I see what you are doing for others, I cannot be so selfish. No; I cannot do it any longer. In England you do not love society; you love your home unbroken; you do not like strangers. No, my Lucy, I will learn a lesson from your goodness. I too will sacrifice—oh, if it was only myself and not Bice!"

"Contessa," said Lucy with an effort, looking up with a smile through some tears, "I am not like that. It never was that you were—disagreeable. How could you be disagreeable? And Bice is—oh, so kind, so good to my boy. You must never think of it more. The town house is not so large as the Hall, but we shall find room in it. Oh, I am not so heartless, not so stupid, as you think! Do you suppose I would let you go away after you have been so kind as to open your heart to me, and let me know that we are really of use? Oh, no, no! And I am sure," she added, faltering slightly, "that Tom—will think the same."

"It is not Tom—excellent, cher Tom! that shall be consulted," cried the Contessa. "Lucy, my little angel! if it is really so that you will give my Bice the advantage of your protection for her début— But that is to be an angel indeed, superior to all our little, petty, miserable— Is it possible, then," cried the Contessa, "that there is some one so good, so noble in this low world?"

This gratitude confused Lucy more than all the rest. She did her best to deprecate and subdue; but in her heart she felt that it was a great sacrifice she was making. "Indeed, it is nothing," she said faintly. "I am fond of her, and she has been so good to baby; and if we can be of any use—but oh, Madame di Forno-Populo," Lady Randolph cried, taking courage. "Her début? do you really mean what she says that she must marry—"

"That I mean to marry her," said the Contessa, "that is how we express it," with a very concise ending to her transports of gratitude. "Sweet Lucy," she continued, "it is the usage of our country. The parents, or those who stand in their place, think it their duty. We marry our children as you clothe them in England. You do not wait till your little boy can choose. You find him what is necessary. Just so do we. We choose so much better than an inexperienced girl can choose. If she has an aversion, if she says I cannot suffer him, we do not press it upon her. Many guardians will pay no attention, but me," said the Contessa, putting forth a little foreign accent, which she displayed very rarely—"I have lived among the English, and I am influenced by their ways. Neither do I think it right," she added, with an air of candour, "to offer an old person, or one who is hideous, or even very disagreeable. But, yes, she must marry well. What else is there that a girl of family can do?"

Lucy was about to answer with enthusiasm that there were many things she could do; but stopped short, arrested by these last words. "A girl of family,"—that, no doubt, made a difference. She paused, and looked somewhat wistfully in her companion's face. "We think," she said, "in England that anything is better than a marriage without—"

The Contessa put up her hand to stay the words. "Without love— I know what you are going to say; but, my angel, that is a word which Bice has never heard spoken. She knows it not. She has not the habit of thinking it necessary—she is a good girl, and she has no sentiment. Besides, why should we go so fast? If she produces the effect I hope— Why should not some one present himself whom she could also love? Oh yes; fall in love with, as you say in English—such an innocent phrase; let us hope that, when the proper person comes who satisfies my requirements, Bice—to whom not a word shall be said—will fall in love with him comme il faut!"

Lucy did not make any reply. She was troubled by the light laugh with which the Contessa concluded, and with the slight change of tone which was perceptible. But she was still too much moved by her own emotion to have got beyond its spell, and she had committed herself beyond recall. While the Contessa talked on with—was it a little, little change?—a faint difference, a levity that had not been in her voice before? Lucy's thoughts went back upon what she had done with a little tremor. Not this time as to what Tom might say, but with a deeper wonder and pang as to what might come of it; was she going voluntarily into new danger, such as she had no clue to, and could not understand? After a little while she asked almost timidly—

"But if Bice should not see any one—"

"You mean if no one suitable should present himself?" The Contessa suddenly grew very grave. She put her hands together with a gesture of entreaty. "My sweet one, let us not think of that. When she is dressed as I shall dress her, and brought out—as you will enable me to bring her out. My Lucy, we do not know what is in her. She will shine, she will charm. Even now, if she is excited, there are moments in which she is beautiful. If she fails altogether— Ah, my love, as I tell you, there is where the curse of poverty comes in. Had she even a moderate fortune, poor child; but alas, orphan, with no one but me—"

"Is she an orphan?" said Lucy, feeling ashamed of the momentary failure of her interest, "and without relations—except—"

"Relations?" said the Contessa; there was something peculiar in her tone which attracted Lucy's attention, and came back to her mind in other days. "Ah, my Lucy, there are many things in this life which you have never thought of. She has relations who think nothing of her, who would be angry, be grieved, if they knew that she existed. Yes, it is terrible to think of, but it is true. She is, on one side, of English parentage. But pardon me, my sweetest, I did not mean to tell you all this: only, my Lucy, you will one time be glad to think that you have been kind to Bice. It will be a pleasure to you. Now let us think of it no more. Marry; yes, she must marry. She has not even so much as your poor clergyman; she has nothing, not a penny. So I must marry her, there is nothing more to be said."


## CHAPTER XXIX

## THE CONTESSA'S TRIUMPH

And it was with very mingled sensations that Sir Tom heard from Lucy (for it was from her lips he heard it) the intimation that Madame di Forno-Populo was going to be so good as to remain at the Hall till they moved to London, and then to accompany them to Park Lane. Sir Tom was taken entirely by surprise. He was not a man who had much difficulty in commanding himself, or showing such an aspect as he pleased to the general world; but on this occasion he was so much surprised that his very jaw dropped with wonder and astonishment. It was at luncheon that the intimation was made, in the Contessa's presence, so that he did not venture to let loose any expression of his feelings. He gave a cry, only half uttered, of astonishment, restrained by politeness, turning his eyes, which grew twice their size in the bewilderment of the moment, from Lucy to the Contessa and back again. Then he burst into a breathless laugh—a twinkle of humour lighted in those eyes which were big with wonder, and he turned a look of amused admiration towards the Contessa. How had she done it? There was no fathoming the cleverness of women, he said to himself, and for the rest of the day he kept bursting forth into little peals of laughter all by himself. How had she managed to do it? It was a task which he himself would not have ventured to undertake. He would not, he said to himself, have had the slightest idea how to bring forward such a proposition. On the contrary, had not his sense that Lucy had much to forgive in respect to this invasion of her home and privacy induced him to make a great sacrifice, to withdraw his opposition to those proceedings of hers of which he so much disapproved? And yet in an afternoon, in one interview, the Contessa had got the upper hand! Her cleverness was extraordinary. It tickled him so that he could not take time to think how very little satisfied he was with the result. He, too, had fallen under her enchantments in the country, in the stillness, if not dulness, of those long evenings, and he had been very willing to be good to her for the sake of old times, to make her as comfortable as possible, to give her time to settle her plans for her London campaign. But that she should begin that campaign under his own roof, and that Lucy, his innocent and simple wife, should be visible to the world as the friend and ally of a lady whose name was too well known to society, was by no means satisfactory to Sir Tom. When his first astonishment and amazement was over, he began to look grave; but what was he to do? He had so much respect for Lucy that when the idea occurred to him of warning her that the Contessa's antecedents were not of a comfortable kind, and that her generosity was mistaken, he rejected it again with a sort of panic, and did not dare, experienced and courageous as he was, to acknowledge to his little wife that he had ventured to bring to her house a woman of whom it could be said that she was not above suspicion. Sir Tom had dared a great many perils in his life, but he did not venture to face this. He recoiled from before it, as he would not have done from any lion in the way. He could not even suggest to her any reticence in her communications, any reserve in showing herself at the Contessa's side, or in inviting other people to meet her. If all his happiness depended upon it, he felt that he could not disturb Lucy's mind by any such warning. Confess to her that he had brought to her a woman with whom scandal had been busy, that he had introduced to her as his friend, and recommended to honour and kindness, one whose name had been in all men's mouths! Sir Tom ran away morally from this suggestion as if he had been the veriest coward; he could not breathe a word of it in Lucy's ear. How could he explain to her that mixture of amazement at the woman's boldness, and humorous sense of the incongruity of her appearance in the absolute quiet of an English home, without company, which, combined with ancient kindness and careless good humour, had made him sanction her first appearance? Still less, how could he explain the mingling of more subtle sensations, the recollections of a past which Sir Tom could not himself much approve of, yet which was full of interest still, and the formation of an intercourse which renewed that past, and brought a little tingling of agreeable excitement into life when it had fallen to too low an ebb to be agreeable in itself? He would not say a word of all this to Lucy. Her purity, her simplicity, even her want of imagination and experience, her incapacity to understand that debatable land between vice and virtue in which so many men find little harm, and which so many women regard with interest and curiosity, closed his mouth. And then he comforted himself with the reflection that, as his aunt herself had admitted, the Contessa had never brought herself openly within the ban. Men might laugh when the name of La Forno-Populo was introduced, and women draw themselves up with indignation, or stare with astonishment not unmingled with consternation as the Duchess had done; but they could not refuse to recognise her, nor could any one assert that there was sufficient reason to exclude her from society. Not even when she was younger, and surrounded by worshippers, could this be said. And now when she was less— But here Sir Tom paused to ask himself, was she less attractive than of old? When he came to consider the question he was obliged to allow that he did not think so; and if she really meant to bring out that girl— Did she mean to bring out that girl? Could she make up her mind to exhibit beside her own waning (if they were waning) charms the first flush of this young beauty? Sir Tom, who thought he knew women (at least of the kind of La Forno-Populo), shook his head and felt it very doubtful whether the Contessa was sincere, or if she could indeed make up her mind to take a secondary place. He thought with a rueful anticipation of the sort of people who would flock to Park Lane to renew their acquaintance with La Forno-Populo. "By Jove! but shall they though? Not if I know it," said Sir Tom firmly to himself.

Williams, the butler, was still more profoundly discomposed. He had opened his mind to Mrs. Freshwater on various occasions when his feelings were too many for him. Naturally, Williams gave the Contessa the benefit of no doubt as to her reputation. He was entirely convinced, as is the fashion of his class, that all that could have been said of her was true, and that she was as unfit for the society of the respectable as any wretched creature could be. "That foreign madam" was what he called her, in the privacy of the housekeeper's room, with many opprobrious epithets. Mrs. Freshwater, who was, perhaps, more good-natured than was advantageous to the housekeeper and manager of a large establishment, was melted whenever she saw her, by the Contessa's gracious looks and ways, but Williams was immovable. "If you'd seen what I've seen," he said, shaking his head. The women, for Lucy's maid Fletcher sometimes shared these revelations, were deeply excited by this—longing, yet fearing to ask what it was that Williams had seen. "And when I think of my lady, that is as innocent as the babe unborn," he said, "mixed up in all that— You'll see such racketing as never was thought of," cried Williams. "I know just how things will go. Night turned into day, carriages driving up at all hours, suppers going on after the play all the night through, masks and dominoes arriving;—no—to be sure this is England. There will be no veglionis, at least—which in England, ladies, would be masked balls—with Madam the Countess and her gentlemen—and even ladies too, a sort of ladies—in all sorts of dresses."

"O-oh!" the women cried.

They were partially shocked, as they were intended to be, but partially their curiosity was excited, and a feeling that they would like to see all these gaieties and fine dresses moved their minds. The primitive intelligence always feel certain that "racketing" and orgies that go on all night, must be at least guiltily delightful, exciting, and amusing, if nothing else. They were not of those who "held with" such dissipation; still for once in a way to see it, the responsibility not being theirs, would be something. They held their breath, but it was not altogether in horror; there was in it a mixture of anticipation too.

"And I know what will come of it," said Williams. "What has come afore: the money will have to come out o' some one's pocket; and master never knew how to keep his to himself, never, as long as I've known him. To be sure, he hadn't got a great deal in the old days. But I know what'll happen; he'll just have to pay up now—he's that soft," said Williams; "a man that can't say no to a woman. Not that I care for the money. I'd a deal sooner he gave her an allowance, or set her up in some other place, or just give her a good round sum—as he could afford to do—and get shut of her. That is what I should advise. Just a round sum and get shut of her."

"I've always heard," said Miss Fletcher, "as the money was my lady's, and not from the Randolph side at all."

"What's hers is his," said Williams; "what's my lady's is her husband's; and a good bargain too—on her side."

"I declare," cried Fletcher energetically, stung with that sense of wrong to her own side which gives heat to party feeling—"I declare if any man took my money to keep up his—his—his old sweetheart, I'd murder him. I'd take his life, that's what I should do."

"Poor dear," said Mrs. Freshwater, wiping her eyes with her apron. "Poor dear! She'll never murder no one, my lady. Bless her innocent face. I only hope as she'll never find it out."

"Sooner than she don't find it out I'll tell her myself," cried Williams. "Now I don't understand you women. You'd let my lady be deceived and made game of, rather than tell her."

"Made game of!" cried Fletcher, with a shriek of indignation. "I should like to see who dared to do that."

"Oh, they'll dare do it, soon enough, and take their fun out of her—it's just what them foreigners are fond of," said Williams, who knew them and all their tricks down to the ground, as he said. Still, however, notwithstanding his evil reports, good Mrs. Freshwater, who was as good-natured as she was fat, could scarcely make up her mind to believe all that of the Contessa. "She do look so sweet, and talk so pretty, not as if she was foreign at all," the housekeeper said.

That evening, however, the Contessa herself took occasion to explain to Sir Tom what her intentions were. She had thought the subject all over while she dressed for dinner, with a certain elation in her success, yet keen clear-mindedness which never deserted her. And then, to be sure, her object had not been entirely the simple one of getting an invitation to Park Lane. She had intended something more than this. And she was not sure of success in that second and still more important point. She meant that Lady Randolph should endow Bice largely, liberally. She intended to bring every sort of motive to bear— even some that verged upon tragedy—to procure this. She had no compunction or faltering on the subject, for it was not for herself, she said within herself, that she was scheming, and she did not mean to be foiled. In considering the best means to attain this great and final object, she decided that it would be well to go softly, not to insist too much upon the advantages she had secured, or to give Lucy too much cause to regret her yielding. The Contessa had the soul of a strategist, the imagination of a great general. She did not ignore the feelings of the subject of her experiment. She even put herself in Lucy's place, and asked herself how she could bear this or that. She would not oppose or overwhelm the probable benefactress to whom she, or at least Bice, might afterwards owe so much. When Sir Tom approached her chair in the evening when he came in after dinner, as he always did, she made room for him on the sofa beside her. "I am going to make you my confidant," she said in her most charming way, with that air of smiling graciousness which made Sir Tom laugh, yet fascinated him in spite of himself. He knew that she put on the same air for whomsoever she chose to charm; but it had a power which he could not resist all the same. "But perhaps you don't care to be taken into my confidence," she added, smiling, too, as if willing to admit all he could allege as to her syren graces. She had a delightful air of being in the joke which entirely deceived Sir Tom.

"On the contrary," he said. "But as we have just heard your plans from my wife—"

The Contessa kissed her hand to Lucy, who occupied her usual place at the table.

"I wonder," she said, "if you understand, being only a man, what there is in that child; for she is but a child. You and I, we are Methuselahs in comparison."

"Not quite so much as that," he said, with a laugh.

"Methuselahs," she said reflectively. "Older, if that is possible; knowing everything, while she knows nothing. She is our good angel. It is what you would not have dared to offer, you who know me—yes, I believe it—and like me. Oh no, I do not go beyond that English word, never! You like the Forno-Populo. I know how you men speak. You think that there is amusement to be got from her, and you will do me the honour to say, no harm. That is, no permanent harm. But you would not offer to befriend me, no, not the best of you. But she who by nature is against such women as I am—Sweet Lucy! Yes it is you I am talking of," the Contessa said, who was skilful to break any lengthened speeches like this by all manner of interruptions, so that it should never tire the person to whom it was addressed. "She, who is not amused by me, who does not like me, whose prejudices are all against me, she it is who offers me her little hand to help me. It is a lovely little hand, though she is not a beauty—"

"My wife is very well," said Sir Tom, with a certain hauteur and abruptness, such as in all their lengthened conversations he had never shown before.

The Contessa gave him a look in which there was much of that feminine contempt at which men laugh as one of the pretences of women. "I am going to be good to her as she is to me," she said. "The Carnival will be short this year, and in England you have no Carnival. I will find myself a little house for the season. I will not too much impose upon that angel. There, now, is something good for you to relieve your mind. I can read you, mon ami, like a book. You are fond of me—oh yes!—but not too long; not too much. I can read you like a book."

"Too long, too much, are not in my vocabulary," said Sir Tom; "have they a meaning? not certainly that has any connection with a certain charming Contessina. If that lady has a fault, which I doubt, it is that she gives too little of her gracious countenance to her friends."

"She does not come down to breakfast," said the Contessa, with her soft laugh, which in itself was a work of art. "She is not so foolish as to put herself in competition with the lilies and the roses, the English flowers. Poverina! she keeps herself for the afternoon which is charitable, and the light of the lamps which is flattering. But she remembers other days—alas! in which she was not afraid of the sun himself, not even of the mid-day, nor of the dawn when it comes in above the lamps. There was a certain bal costumé in Florence, a year when many English came to the Populino palace. But why do I talk of that? You will not remember—"

There was something apparently in the recollection that touched Sir Tom. His eye softened. An unaccustomed colour came to his middle-aged cheek. "I! not remember? I remember every hour, every moment," he said, and then their voices sank lower, and a murmur of reminiscences, one filling up another, ensued between the pair. Their tone softened, there were broken phrases, exclamations, a rapid interchange which was far too indistinct to be audible. Lucy sat by her table and worked, and was vaguely conscious of it all. She had said to herself that she would take no heed any more, that the poor Contessa was too open-hearted, too generous to harm her, that they were but two old friends talking of the past. And so it was; but there was a something forlorn in sitting by at a distance, out of it all, and knowing that it was to go on and last, alas! by her own doing, who could tell how many evenings, how many long hours to come!

CHAPTER XXX

DIFFERENT VIEWS

The time after this seemed to fly in the great quiet, all the entertainments of the Christmas season being over, and the houses in the neighbourhood gradually emptying of guests. The only visitors at the Hall were the clergyman, the doctor, an odd man now and then whom Sir Tom would invite in the character of a "native," for the Contessa's amusement; and Mr. Rushton, who came from Farafield two or three times on business, at first with a very keen curiosity, to know how it was that Lucy had subdued her husband and got him to relinquish his objection to her alienation of her money. This had puzzled the lawyer very greatly. There had been no uncertainty about Sir Tom's opinion when the subject was mooted to him first. He had looked upon it with very proper sentiments. It had seemed to him ridiculous, incredible, that Lucy should set up her will against his, or take her own way, when she knew how he regarded the matter. He had told the lawyer that he had little doubt of being able to bring her to hear reason. And then he had written to say that he withdrew his objection! Mr. Rushton felt that there must be some reason here more than met the eye. He made a pretence of business that he might discover what it was, and he had done so triumphantly, as he thought. Sir Tom, as everybody knew, had been "a rover" in his youth, and the world was charitable enough to conclude that in that youth there must be many things which he would not care to expose to the eye of day. When Mr. Rushton beheld at luncheon the Contessa, followed by the young and slim figure of Bice, it seemed to him that everything was solved. And Lady Randolph, he thought, did not look with very favourable eyes upon the younger lady. What doubt that Sir Tom had bought the assent of his wife to the presence of the guests by giving up on his side some of his reasonable rights?

"Did you ever hear of an Italian lady that Sir Tom was thick with before he married?" he asked his wife when he came home.

"How can you ask me such a question," said that virtuous woman, "when you know as well as I do that there were half-a-dozen?"

"Did you ever hear the name of Forno-Populo?" he asked.

Mrs. Rushton paused and did her best to look as if she was trying to recollect. As a matter of fact all Italian names sounded alike to her, as English names do to foreign ears. But after a moment she said boldly: "Of course I have heard it. That was the lady from Naples, or Venice, or some of those places, that ran away with him. You heard all about it at the time as well as I."

And upon this Mr. Rushton smote upon his thigh, and made a mighty exclamation. "By George!" he said, "he's got her there, under his wife's very nose; and that's why he has given in about the money." Nothing could have been more clearly reasoned out—there could be no doubt upon that subject. And the presence of Bice decided the question. Bice must be—they said, to be sure! Dates and everything answered to this view of the question. There could be no doubt as to who Bice was. They were very respectable, good people themselves, and had never given any scandal to the world; but they never hesitated for a moment or thought there was anything unnatural in attributing the most shameful scandal and domestic treachery to Sir Tom. In fact it would be difficult to say that they thought much less of him in consequence. It was Lucy, rather, upon whom their censure fell. She ought to have known better. She ought never to have allowed it. To pretend to such simplicity was sickening, Mrs. Rushton thought.

It was early in February when they all went to London—a time when society is in a sort of promissory state, full of hopes of dazzling delights to come, but for the present not dazzling, parliamentary, residential, a society made up of people who live in London, who are not merely gay birds of fashion, basking in the sunshine of the seasons. There was only a week or two of what the Contessa called Carnival, which indeed was not Carnival at all, but a sober time in which dinner parties began, and the men began to gather at the clubs. The Contessa did not object to this period of quiet. She acquainted Lucy with all she meant to do in the meantime, to the great confusion of that ingenious spirit. "Bice must be dressed," the Contessa said, "which of itself requires no little time and thought. Unhappily M. Worth is not in London. Even with M. Worth I exert my own faculties. He is excellent, but he has not the intuitions which come when one is very much interested in an object. Sweet Lucy! you have not thought upon that matter. Your dress is as your dressmaker sends it to you. Yes; but, my angel, Bice has her career before her. It is different."

"Oh, Madame di Forno-Populo," said Lucy, "do you still think in that way—must it still be exhibiting her, marrying her?"

"Marriage is honourable," said the Contessa. "It is what all girls are thinking of; but me, I think it better that their parents should take it in hand instead of the young ladies. There is something in Bice that is difficult, oh, very difficult. If one chooses well for her, one will be richly repaid; but if, on the contrary, one leaves it to the conventional, the ordinary—My sweetest! your pretty white dresses, your blues are delightful for you; but Bice is different, quite different. And then she has no fortune. She must be piquant. She must be striking. She must please. In England you take no trouble for that. It is not comme il faut here; but it is in our country. Each of us we like the ways of our country best."

"I have often wondered," said Lucy, "to hear you speak such perfect English, and Bice too. It is, I suppose, because you are so musical and have such good ears—"

"Darling!" said the Contessa sweetly. She said this or a similar word when nothing else occurred to her. She had her room full of lovely stuffs, brought by obsequious shopmen, to whom Lady Randolph's name was sufficient warrant for any extravagance the Contessa might think of. But she said to herself that she was not at all extravagant; for Bice's wardrobe was her stock-in-trade, and if she did not take the opportunity of securing it while in her power, the Contessa thought she would be false to Bice's interests. The girl still wore nothing but her black frock. She went out in the park early in the morning when nobody was there, and sometimes had riding lessons at an unearthly hour, so that nobody should see her. The Contessa was very anxious on this point. When Lucy would have taken Bice out driving, when she would have taken her to the theatre, her patroness instantly interfered. "All that will come in its time," she said. "Not now. She must not appear now. I cannot have her seen. Recollect, my Lucy, she has no fortune. She must depend upon herself for everything." This doctrine, at which Lucy stood aghast, was maintained in the most matter-of-fact way by the neophyte herself. "If I were seen," she said, "now, I should be quite stale when I appear. I must appear before I go anywhere. Oh yes, I love the theatre. I should like to go with you driving. But I should forestall myself. Some persons do and they are never successful. First of all, before anything, I must appear."

"Oh my child," Lucy cried, "I cannot bear to hear of all this. You should not calculate so at your age. And when you appear, as you call it, what then, Bice? Nobody will take any particular notice, perhaps, and you will be so disappointed you will not know what to do. Hundreds of girls appear every season and nobody minds."

Bice took no notice of these subduing and moderating previsions. She smiled and repeated what the Contessa said. "I must do the best for myself, for I have no fortune."

No fortune! and to think that Lucy, with her mind directed to other matters, never once realised that this was a state of affairs which she could put an end to in a moment. It never occurred to her—perhaps, as she certainly was matter of fact, the recollection that there was a sort of stipulation in the will against foreigners turned her thoughts into another channel.

It was, however, during this time of preparation and quiet that the household in Park Lane one day received a visit from Jock, accompanied by no less a person than MTutor, the leader of intellectual life and light of the world to the boy. They came to luncheon by appointment, and after visiting some museum on which Jock's mind was set, came to remain to dinner and go to the theatre. MTutor had a condescending appreciation of the stage. He thought it was an educational influence, not perhaps of any great utility to the youths under such care as his own, but of no small importance to the less fortunate members of society; and he liked to encourage the efforts of conscientious actors who looked upon their own calling in this light. It was rather for this purpose than with the idea of amusement that he patronised the play, and Jock, as in duty bound, though there was in him a certain boyish excitement as to the pleasure itself, did his best to regard the performance in the same exalted light. MTutor was a young man of about thirty, slim and tall. He was a man who had taken honours at college, though his admirers said not such high honours as he might have taken; "For MTutor," said Jock, "never would go in for pot-hunting, you know. What he always wanted was to cultivate his own mind, not to get prizes." It was with heartfelt admiration that this feature in his character was dwelt upon by his disciples. Not a doubt that he could have got whatever he liked to go in for, had he not been so fastidious and high-minded. He was fellow of his college as it was, had got a poetry prize which, perhaps, was not the Newdigate; and smiled indulgently at those who were more warm in the arena of competition than himself. On other occasions when "men" came to luncheon, the Contessa, though quite ready to be amused by them in her own person, sternly forbade the appearance of Bice, the effect of whose future was not, she was determined, to be spoilt by any such preliminary peeps; but the Contessa's vigilance slackened when the visitors were of no greater importance than this. She was insensible to the greatness of MTutor. It did not seem to matter that he should be there sitting grave and dignified by Lucy's side, and talking somewhat over Lucy's head, any more than it mattered that Mr. Rushton should be there, or any other person of an inferior level. It was not upon such men that Bice's appearance was to tell. She took no precautions against such persons. Jock himself at sixteen was not more utterly out of the question. And the Contessa herself, as it happened, was much amused by MTutor; his great ideas of everything, the exalted ideal that showed in all he did or said, gave great pleasure to this woman of the world. And when they came to the question of the educational influence of the stage, and the conscientious character of the actors' work, she could not conceal her satisfaction. "I will go with you, too," she said, "this evening." "We shall all go," said Sir Tom, "even Bice. There is a big box, and behind the curtain nobody will see her." To this the Contessa demurred, but, after a little while, being in a yielding humour, gave way. "It is for the play alone," she said in an undertone, raising her finger in admonition, "You will remember, my child, for the play alone."

"We are all going for the play alone," said Sir Tom, cheerfully. "Here is Lucy, who is a baby for a play. She likes melodrama best, disguises and trap-doors and long-lost sons, and all the rest of it."

"It is a taste that is very general," said MTutor, indulgently; "but I am sure Lady Randolph appreciates the efforts of a conscientious interpreter—one who calls all the resources of art to his aid—"

"I don't care for the play alone," said Bice to Jock in an undertone. "I want to see the people. They are always the most amusing. I have seen nobody yet in London. And though I must not be seen, I may look, that will do no harm. Then there will be the people who come into the box."

"The people who come into the box! but you know us all," said Jock, astonished, "before we go—"

"You all?" said Bice, with some disdain. "It is easy to see you; that is not what I mean; this will be the first time I put my foot into the world. The actors, that is nothing. Is it the custom in England to look much at the play? No, you go to see your friends."

MTutor was on the other side of this strange girl in her black frock. He took it upon him to reply. He said: "That is the case in some countries, but not here. In England the play is actually thought of. English actors are not so good as the French, nor even the Italian. And the Germans are much better trained. Nevertheless, we do what perhaps no other nation does. We give them our attention. It is this which makes the position of the actors more important, more interesting in England."

"Stop a little, stop a little!" cried Sir Tom; "don't let me interrupt you, Derwentwater, if you are instructing the young ones; but don't forget the Comédie Française and the aristocracy of art."

"I do not forget it," said Mr. Derwentwater; "in that point of view we are far behind France; still I uphold that nowhere else do people go to the theatre for the sake of the play as we do; and it is this," he said, turning to Bice, "that makes it possible that the theatre may be an influence and a power."

Bice lifted her eyes upon this man with a wondering gaze of contempt. She gave him a full look which abashed him, though he was so much more important, so much more intellectual, than she. Then, without deigning to take any notice, she turned to Jock at her other side. "If that is all I do not care for going," she said. "I have seen many plays—oh, many! I like quite as well to read at home. It is not for that I wish to go; but to see the world. The world, that is far more interesting. It is like a novel, but living. You look at the people and you read what they are thinking. You see their stories going on. That is what amuses me;—but a play on the stage, what is it? People dressed in clothes that do not belong to them, trying to make themselves look like somebody else—but they never do. One says—that is not I, but the people that know—Bravo, Got! Bravo Regnier! It does not matter what parts they are acting. You do not care for the part. Then why go and look at it?" said Bice with straightforward philosophy.

All this she poured forth upon Jock in a low clear voice, as if there was no one else near. Jock, for his part, was carried away by the flood.

"I don't know about Got and Regnier. But what we are going to see is Shakespeare," he said, with a little awe, "that is not just like a common play."

Mr. Derwentwater had been astonished by Bice's indifference to his own instructive remarks. It was this perhaps more than her beauty which had called his attention to her, and he had listened as well as he could to the low rapid stream of her conversation, not without wonder that she should have chosen Jock as the recipient of her confidence. What she said, though he heard it but imperfectly, interested him still more. He wanted to make her out—it was a new kind of study. While Lucy, by his side, went on tranquilly with some soft talk about the theatre, of which she knew very little, he thought, he made her a civil response, but gave all his attention to what was going on at the other side; and there was suddenly a lull of the general commotion, in which he heard distinctly Bice's next words.

"What is Shakespeare?" she said; then went on with her own reflections. "What I want to see is the world. I have never yet gone into the world; but I must know it, for it is there I have to live. If one could live in Shakespeare," cried the girl, "it would be easy; but I have not been brought up for that; and I want to see the world—just a little corner—because that is what concerns me, not a play. If it is only for the play, I think I shall not go."

"You had much better come," said Jock; "after all it is fun, and some of the fellows will be good. The world is not to be seen at the theatre that I know of," continued the boy. "Rows of people sitting one behind another, most of them as stupid as possible—you don't call that the world? But come—I wish you would come. It is a change—it stirs you up."

"I don't want to be stirred up. I am all living," cried Bice. There seemed to breathe out from her a sort of visible atmosphere of energy and impatient life. Looking across this thrill in the air, which somehow was like the vibration of heat in the atmosphere, Jock's eyes encountered those of his tutor, turned very curiously, and not without bewilderment, to the same point as his own. It gave the boy a curious sensation which he could not define. He had wished to exhibit to Mr. Derwentwater this strange phenomenon in the shape of a girl, with a sense that there was something very unusual in her, something in which he himself had a certain proprietorship. But when MTutor's eyes encountered Jock's with an astonished glance of discovery in them, which seemed to say that he had found out Bice for himself without the interposition of the original discoverer, Jock felt a thrill of displeasure, and almost pain, which he could not explain to himself. What did it mean? It seemed to bring with it a certain defiance of, and opposition to, this king of men.


CHAPTER XXXI

TWO FRIENDS

"Who was that young lady?" Mr. Derwentwater said. "I did not catch the name."

"What young lady?" To suppose for a moment that Jock did not know who was meant would be ridiculous, of course; but, for some reason which he did not explain even to himself, this was the reply he made.

"My dear Jock, there was but one," said MTutor, with much friendliness. "At your age you do not take much notice of the other sex, and that is very well and right; but still it would be wrong to imagine that there is not something interesting in girls occasionally. I did not make her out. She was quite a study to me at the theatre. I am afraid the greater part of the performance, and all the most meritorious portion of it, was thrown away upon her; but still there were gleams of interest. She is not without intelligence, that is clear."

"You mean Bice," said Jock, with a certain dogged air which Mr. Derwentwater had seldom seen in him before, and did not understand. He spoke as if he intended to say as little as was practicable, and as if he resented being made to speak at all.

"Bice—ah! like Dante's Bice," said MTutor. "That makes her more interesting still. Though it is not perhaps under that aspect that one represents to oneself the Bice of Dante—ben son, ben son, Beatrice. No, not exactly under that aspect. Dante's Bice must have been more grand, more imposing, in her dress of crimson or dazzling white."

Jock made no response. It was usual for him to regard MTutor devoutly when he talked in this way, and to feel that no man on earth talked so well. Jock in his omnivorous reading knew perhaps Dante better than his instructor, but he had come to the age when the mind, confused in all its first awakening of emotions, cannot talk of what affects it most. The time had been at which he had discussed everything he read with whosoever would listen, and instructed the world in a child's straightforward way. At that period he had often improved Lucy's mind on the subject of Dante, telling her all the details of that wonderful pilgrimage through earth and heaven, to her great interest and wonder, as something that had happened the other day. Lucy had not in those days been quite able to understand how it was that the gentleman of Florence should have met everybody he knew in the unseen, but she had taken it all in respectfully, as was her wont. Jock, however, had passed beyond this stage, and no longer told Lucy, or any one, stories from his reading; and other sensations had begun to stir in him which he could not put into words. In this way it was a constant admiration to him to hear MTutor, who could always, he thought, say the right thing and never was at a loss. But this evening he was dissatisfied. They were returning from the theatre by a late train, and nothing but Jock's reputation and high character as a boy of boys, high up in everything intellectual, and without reproach in any way, besides the devoted friendship which subsisted between himself and his tutor, could have justified Mr. Derwentwater in permitting him in the middle of the half to go to London to the theatre, and return by the twelve o'clock train. This privilege came to him from the favour of his tutor, and yet for the first time his tutor did not seem the superhuman being he had always previously appeared to Jock. But Mr. Derwentwater was quite unsuspicious of this.

"There is something very much out of the way in the young lady altogether," he said. "That little black dress, fitting her like a glove, and no ornament or finery of any description. It is not so with girls in general. It was very striking—tell me—"

"I didn't think," cried Jock, "that you paid any attention to what women wore."

Mr. Derwentwater yielded to a gentle smile. "Tell me," he said, as if he had not been interrupted, "who this young lady may be. Is she a daughter of the Italian lady, a handsome woman, too, in her way, who was with your people?" The railway carriage in which they were coursing through the blackness of the night was but dimly lighted, and it was not easy to see from one corner to another the expression of Jock's face.

"I don't know," said Jock, in a voice that sounded gruff, "I can't tell who she is—I never asked. It did not seem any business of mine."

"Old fellow," said MTutor, "don't cultivate those bearish ways. Some men do, but it's not good form. I don't like to see it in you."

This silenced Jock, and made his face flame in the darkness. He did not know what excuse to make. He added reluctantly: "Of course I know that she came with the Contessa; but who she is I don't know, and I don't think Lucy knows. She is just—there."

"Well, my boy," said Mr. Derwentwater, "if there is any mystery, all right; I don't want to be prying;" but, as was natural, this only increased his curiosity. After an interval, he broke forth again. "A little mystery," he said, "suits them; a woman ought to be mysterious, with her long robes falling round her, and her mystery of long hair, and all the natural veils and mists that are about her. It is more poetic and in keeping that they should only have a lovely suggestive name, what we call a Christian name, instead of a commonplace patronymic, Miss So-and-so! Yes; I recognise your Bice as by far the most suitable symbol."

It is impossible to say what an amount of unexpressed and inexpressible irritation arose in the mind of Jock with every word. "Your Bice!" The words excited him almost beyond his power of control. The mere fact of having somehow got into opposition to MTutor was in itself an irritation almost more than he could bear. How it was he could not explain to himself; but only felt that from the moment when they had got into their carriage together, Mr. Derwentwater, hitherto his god, had become almost odious to him. The evening altogether had been exciting, but uncomfortable. They had all gone to the theatre, where Jock had been prepared to look on not so much at a fine piece of acting as at a conscientious study, the laboriousness of which was one of its chief qualities. Neither the Contessa nor Bice had been much impressed by that fine view of the performance. Madame di Forno-Populo, indeed, had swept the audience with her opera-glass, and paid very little attention to the stage. She had yawned at the most important moments. When the curtain fell she had woke up, looking with interest for visitors, as it appeared, though very few visitors had come. Bice was put into the corner under shelter of the Contessa, and thence had taken furtive peeps, though without any opera-glass, with her own keen, intelligent young eyes, at the people sitting near, whom Jock had declared not to be in any sense of the word the world. Bice too looked up, when the box door opened, with great interest. She kept well in the shade, but it was evident that she was anxious to see whosoever might come. And very few people came; one or two men who came to pay their respects to Lucy, one or two who appeared with faces of excitement and surprise to ask if it was indeed Madame di Forno-Populo whom they had seen? At these Bice from out her corner gazed with large eyes; they were not persons of an interesting kind. One of them was a Lord Somebody, who was red-faced and had an air which somehow did not suit the place in which Lucy was, and towards whom Sir Tom, though he knew him, maintained an aspect of seriousness not at all usual to his cordial countenance. Bice, it was evident, was struck with a contemptuous amaze at the appearance of these visitors. There was a quick interchange of glances between her and the Contessa with shrugs of the shoulders and much play of fans. Bice's raised eyebrows and curled lips perhaps meant—"Are those your famous friends? Is this all?" Whereas the Contessa answered deprecatingly, with a sort of "wait a little" look. Jock, who generally was pleased to stroll about the lobbies in a sort of mannish way in the intervals between the acts, sat still in his place to watch all this with a wondering sense that here was something going on in which there was a still closer interest, and to notice everything almost without knowing that he noted it, following in this respect, as in most others, the lead of his tutor, who likewise addressed himself to the supervision of everything that went on, discoursing in the meantime to Lucy about the actors' "interpretation" of the part, and how far he, Mr. Derwentwater, agreed with their view. To Lucy, indeed, the action of the play was everything, and the intervals between tedious. She laughed and cried, and followed every movement, and looked round, hushing the others when they whispered, almost with indignation. Lucy was far younger, Jock decided, than Bice or even himself. He, too, had learned already—how had he learned it?—that the play going on upon the stage was less interesting than that which was being performed outside. Even Jock had found this out, though he could not have told how. Shakespeare, indeed, was far greater, nobler; but the excitement of a living story, the progress of events of which nobody could tell what would come next, had an interest transcending even the poetry. That was what people said, Jock was aware, in novels and other productions; but until to-night he never believed it was true.

And then there was the journey from town, with all the curious sensation of parting at the theatre doors, and returning from that shining world of gaslight, and ladies' dresses, into the dimness of the railway, the tedious though not very long journey, the plunging of the carriage through the blackness of the night; and along with these the questions of Mr. Derwentwater, so unlike him, so uncalled-for, as Jock could not help thinking. What had he to do with Bice? What had any one to do with her? So far as she belonged to any one, it was to himself, Jock; her first friend, her companion in her walks, he to whom she had spoken so freely, and who had told her his opinion with such simplicity. When Jock remembered that he had told her she was not pretty his cheeks burned. There had stolen into his mind, he could not tell how, a very different feeling now—not perhaps a different opinion. When he reflected it did not seem to him even now that pretty was the word to use—but the impression of Bice which was in his mind was something that made the boy thrill. He did not understand it, nor could he tell what it was. But it made him quiver with resentment when there was any question about her—anything like this cold-blooded investigation which Mr. Derwentwater had attempted to make. It troubled Jock all the more that it should be MTutor who made it. When our god, our model of excellence, comes down from his high state to anything that is petty, or less than perfect, how sore is the pang with which we acknowledge it. "To be wroth with those we love doth work like madness in the brain." Jock had both these pangs together. He was angry because MTutor had been interfering with matters in which he had no concern, and he was pained because MTutor had condescended to ask questions and invite gossip, like the smaller beings well enough known in the boy-world as in every other, who make gossip the chief object of their existence. Could there be anything in the idol of his youth akin to these? He felt sore and disappointed, without knowing why, with a dim consciousness that there were many other people whom Mr. Derwentwater might have inquired about without awakening any such feelings in him. When the train stopped, and they got out, it was strange to walk down the silent, midnight streets by MTutor's side, without the old sensation of pleasure with which the boy felt himself made into the man's companion. He was awakened out of his maze of dark and painful feelings by the voice of Derwentwater calling upon him to admire the effect of the moonlight upon the river as they crossed the bridge. For long after that scene remained in Jock's mind against a background of mysterious shadows and perplexity. The moon rode in the midst of a wide clearing of blue between two broken banks of clouds. She was almost full, and approaching her setting. She shone full upon the river, sweeping from side to side in one flood of silver, broken only by a few strange little blacknesses, the few boats, like houseless stragglers out by night and without shelter, which lay here and there by a wharf or at the water's edge.

The scene was wonderfully still and solemn, not a motion to be seen either on street or stream. "How is it, do you think," said Mr. Derwentwater, "that we think so little of the sun when it is he that lights up a scene like this, and so much of the moon?"

Jock was taken by surprise by this question, which was of a kind which his tutor was fond of putting, and which brought back their old relations instantaneously. Jock seemed to himself to wake up out of a strange inarticulate dream of displeasure and embarrassment, and to feel himself with sudden remorse, a traitor to his friend. He said, faltering: "I don't know; it is always you that finds out the analogies. I don't think that my mind is poetical at all."

"You do yourself injustice, Jock," said Derwentwater, his arm within that of his pupil in their old familiar way. And then he said: "The moon is the feminine influence which charms us by showing herself clearly as the source of the light she sheds. The sun we rarely think of at all, but only of what he gives us—the light and the heat that are our life. Her," he pointed to the sky, "we could dispense with, save for the beauty of her."

"I wish," said Jock, "I could think of anything so fine. But do you think we could do without women like that?" said the inquiring young spirit, ready to follow with his bosom bare whithersoever this refined philosophy might lead.

"You and I will," said the instructor. "There are grosser and there are tamer spirits to whom it might be different. I would not wrong you by supposing that you, my boy, could ever be tempted in the gross way; and I don't think you are of the butterfly dancing kind."

"I should rather think not!" said Jock, with a short laugh.

"Then, except as a beautiful object, setting herself forth in conscious brightness, like that emblem of woman yonder," said MTutor with a wave of his hand, admiring, familiar, but somewhat contemptuous, towards the moon, "what do we want with that feminine influence? Our lives are set to higher uses, and occupied with other aims."

Jock was perfectly satisfied with this profession of faith. He went along the street with his tutor's arm in his, and a vague elation as of something settled and concluded upon in his mind. Their footsteps rang upon the pavement with a manly tramp as they paced away from the light on the bridge into the shadow of the old houses with their red roofs. They had gone some way before, being above all things loyal, Jock thought it right to put in a proviso. "Not intellectually, perhaps," he said, "but I can't forget how much I owe to my sister. I should have been a most forlorn little wretch when I was a child, and I shouldn't be much now, but for Lucy standing by me. It's not well to forget that, is it, sir? though Lucy is not at all clever," he added in an undertone.

"You are a loyal soul," said MTutor, with a pressure of his arm, "but Woman does not mean our mothers and sisters." Here he permitted himself a little laugh. "It shows me how much inferior is my position to that of your youth, my dear boy," he said, "when you give me such an answer. Believe me it is far finer than anything you suppose me to be able to say."

Jock did not know how to respond to this speech. It half angered, half pleased him, but on the whole he was more ashamed of the supposed youthfulness than satisfied with the approbation. No one, however young, likes the imputation of innocence; and Jock had feelings rising within him of which he scarcely knew the meaning, but which made him still more sensible of the injustice of this view. He was too proud, however, to explain himself even if he had been able to do so, and the little way that remained was trodden in silence. The boy, however, could not help a curious sensation of superiority as he went to his room through the sleeping-house, feeling the stillness of the slumber into which he stole, treading very quietly that he might not disturb any one. He stopped for a moment with a candle in his hand and looked down the long passage with its line of closed doors on each side, holding his breath with a half smile of sympathy, respect for the hush of sleep, yet keen superiority of life and emotion over all the unconscious household. His own brain and heart seemed tingling with the activity and tumult of life in them. It seemed to him impossible to sleep, to still the commotion in his mind, and bring himself into harmony with that hushed atmosphere and childish calm.

CHAPTER XXXII

YOUTHFUL UNREST

Easter was very early that year, about as early as Easter can be, and there was in Jock's mind a disturbing consciousness of the holidays, and the manner in which he was likely to spend them, which no doubt interfered to a certain extent with his work. He ought to have been first in the competition for a certain school prize, and he was not. It was carried off to the disappointment of Jock's house, and, indeed, of the greater part of the school, by a King's scholar, which was the fate of most of the prizes. Mr. Derwentwater was deeply cast down by this disappointment. He expressed himself on the subject indeed with all the fine feeling for which he was distinguished. "The loss of a distinction," he said, "is not in itself a matter to disturb us; but I own I should be sorry to think that you were failing at all in that intellectual energy which has already placed you so often at the head of the lists—that, my dear fellow, I should unfeignedly regret; but not a mere prize, which is nothing." This was a very handsome way of speaking of it; but that MTutor was disappointed there could be no doubt. To Jock himself it gave a keen momentary pang to see his own name only third in that beadroll of honour; but so it was. The holidays had all that to answer for; the holidays, or rather what they were to bring. When he thought of the Hall and the company there, Jock felt a certain high tide in his veins, an awakening of interest and anticipation which he did not understand. He did not say to himself that he was going to be happy. He only looked forward with an eager heart, with a sense of something to come, which was different from the routine of ordinary life. MTutor after many hindrances and hesitations was at last going to accept the invitation of Sir Tom, and accompany his pupil. This Jock had looked forward to as the greatest of pleasures. But somehow he did not feel so happy about it now. He did not seem to himself to want Mr. Derwentwater. In some ways, indeed, he had become impatient of Mr. Derwentwater. Since that visit to the theatre, involuntarily without any cause for it, there had commenced to be moments in which MTutor was tedious. This sacrilege was unconscious, and never yet had been put into words; but still the feeling was there; and the beginning of any such revolution in the soul must be accompanied with many uneasinesses. Jock was on the stroke, so to speak, of seventeen. He was old for his age, yet he had been almost childish too in his devotion to his books, and the subjects of his school life. The last year had introduced many new thoughts to his mind by restoring him to the partial society of his sister and her house; but into these new subjects he had carried the devotion of his studious habits and the enthusiasm of his discipleship, transferring himself bodily with all his traditions into the new atmosphere. But a change somehow had begun in him, he could not tell how. He was stirred beyond the lines of his former being—sentiments, confusions of spirit quite new to him, were vaguely fermenting, he could not tell how; and school work, and prizes, and all the emulations of sixth form had somehow tamed and paled. The colour seemed to have gone out of them. And the library of MTutor, that paradise of thought, that home of conversation, where so many fine things used to be said—that too had palled upon the boy's uneasy soul. He felt as if he should prefer to leave everything behind him,—books and compositions and talk, and even MTutor himself. Such a state of mind is sure to occur some time or other in a boy's experiences; but in this case it was too early, and Mr. Derwentwater, who was very deeply devoted to his pupils, was much exercised on the subject. He had lost Jock's confidence, he thought. How had he lost his confidence? was it that some other less wholesome influence was coming in? Thus there were feelings of discomfort between them, hesitations as to what to say, instinctive avoidance of some subjects, concealed allusions to others. It might even be said that in a very refined and superior way, such as was alone possible to such a man, Mr. Derwentwater occasionally talked at Jock. He talked of the pain and grief of seeing a young heart closed to you which once had been open, and of the poignant disappointment which arises in an elder spirit when its spiritual child—its disciple—gets beyond its leading. Jock, occupied with his own thoughts, only partially understood.

It was in this state of mind that they set out together, amid all the bustle of breaking up, to pay their promised visit. Jock, who up to this moment had hated London, and looked with alarm upon society, had eagerly accepted his tutor's proposal that after the ten days which they were to spend at the Hall they should go to Normandy together for the rest of the holidays, which was an arrangement very pleasant in anticipation. But by this time neither of the two was at all anxious to carry it out. Mr. Derwentwater had begun to talk of the expediency of giving a little attention to one's own country. "We are just as foolish as the ignorant masses," he said, "though we think ourselves so wise. Why not Devonshire instead of Normandy? it is finer in natural scenery. Why not London instead of Paris? there is no spell in mere going, as the ignorant say 'abroad.'" When you come to think of it, in just the same proportion as one is superior to the common round of gaping British tourists, by going on a walking tour in Normandy, one is superior to the walkers in Normandy by choosing Devonshire.

These remarks were preliminary to the intention of giving up the plan altogether, and by the time they set out it was tacitly understood that this was to be the case. It was to be given up—not for Devonshire. The pair of friends had become two—they were to do each what was good in his own eyes. Jock would remain "at home," whether that home meant the Hall or Park Lane, and Mr. Derwentwater, after his week's visit, should go on—where seemed to him good.

There was a considerable party gathered in the inner drawing-room when Jock and his companion presented themselves there. The scene was very different from that to which Jock had been accustomed, when the tea-table was a sort of fireside adjunct to the warmth and brightness centred there. Now the windows were full of a clear yellow sky, shining a little shrilly after rain, and promising in its too-clear and watery brightness more rain to come; and many people were about, some standing up against the light, some lounging in the comfortable chairs, some talking together in groups, some hanging about Lucy and her tea service. Lucy said, "Oh, is it you, Jock?" and kissed him, with a look of pleasure; but she had not run out to meet him as of old. Lucy, indeed, was changed, perhaps more evidently changed than any member of the family. She was far more self-possessed than she had ever been before. She did not now turn to her husband with that pretty look, half-smiling, half-wistful, to know how she had got through her domestic duties. There was a slight air of hurry and embarrassment about her eyes. The season had not begun, and she could not have been overdone by her social duties; but something had aged and changed her. Some old acquaintances came forward and shook hands with Jock; and Sir Tom, when he saw who it was, detached himself from the person he was talking to, and came forward and gave him a sufficiently cordial welcome. The person with whom he was talking was the Contessa. She was in her old place in the room, the comfortable sofa which she had taken from Lady

Randolph, and where Sir Tom, leaning upon the mantelpiece, as an Englishman loves to do, could talk to her in the easiest of attitudes. Jock, though he was not discerning, thought that Sir Tom looked aged and changed too. The people in general had a tired afternoon sort of look about them. They were not like people exulting to get out of town, and out of darkness and winter weather to the fresh air and April skies. Perhaps, however, this effect was produced by the fact that looking for one special person in the assembly Jock had not found her. He had never cared who was there before. Except Lucy, the whole world was much the same to him. To talk to her now and then, but by preference alone, when he could have her to himself and nobody else was by, and then to escape to the library, had been the height of his desire. Now he no longer thought of the library, or even, save in a secondary way, of Lucy. He looked about for some one else. There was the Contessa, sure enough, with one man on the sofa by her side and another seated in front of her, and Sir Tom against the mantelpiece lounging and talking. She was enchanting them all with her rapid talk, with the pretty, swift movements of her hands, her expressive looks and ways. But there was no shadow of Bice about the room. Jock looked at once behind the table, where she had been always visible when the Contessa was present. But Bice was not there. There was not a trace of her among the people whom Jock neither knew nor cared to know. But everything went on cheerfully, notwithstanding this omission, which nobody but Jock seemed to remark. Ladies chattered softly as they sipped their tea, men standing over them telling anecdotes of this person and that, with runs of soft laughter here and there. Lucy at the tea-table was the only one who was at all isolated. She was bending over her cups and saucers, supplying now one and now another, listening to a chance remark here and there, giving an abstracted smile to the person who might chance to be next to her. What was she thinking of? Not of Jock, who had only got a smile a little more animated than the others. Mr. Derwentwater did not know anybody in this company. He stood on the outskirts of it, with that look of mingled conciliation and defiance which is natural to a man who feels himself overlooked. He was more disappointed even than Jock, for he had anticipated a great deal of attention, and not to find himself nobody in a fashionable crowd.

Things did not mend even at dinner. Then the people were more easily identified in their evening clothes, exposing themselves steadily to all observers on either side of the table; but they did not seem more interesting. There were two or three political men, friends of Sir Tom, and some of a very different type who were attached to the Contessa—indeed, the party consisted chiefly of men, with a few ladies thrown in. The ladies were not much more attractive. One of them, a Lady Anastasia something, was one of the most inveterate of gossip collectors, a lady who not only provided piquant tales for home consumption, but served them up to the general public afterwards in a newspaper—the only representatives of ordinary womankind being a mother and two daughters, who had no particular qualities, and who duly occupied a certain amount of space, without giving anything in return. But Bice was not visible. She who had been so little noticed, yet so far from insignificant, where was she? Could it be that the Contessa had left her behind, or that Lucy had objected to her, or that she was ill, or that— Jock did not know what to think. The company was a strange one. Those sedate, political friends of Sir Tom found themselves with a little dismay in the society of the lady who wrote for what she called the Press, and the gentlemen from the clubs. One of the guests was the young Marquis Montjoie, who had quite lately come into his title and the world. He had been at school with Jock a few years before, and he recognised Mr. Derwentwater with a curious mixture of awe and contempt. "Hallo!" he had cried when he perceived him first, and he had whispered something to the Contessa which made her laugh also. All this Jock remarked vaguely in his uneasiness and disappointment. What was the good of coming home, he said to himself, if— What was the use of having so looked forward to the holidays and lost that prize, and disappointed everybody, if— There rose such a ferment in Jock's veins as had never been there before. When the ladies left the room after dinner it was he that opened the door for them, and as Lucy looked up with a smile into her brother's face she met from him a scowl which took away her breath.

Why did he scowl at Lucy? and why think that in all his life he had never seen so dull a company before? Their good things after dinner were odious to his ears; and to think, that even MTutor should be able to laugh at such miserable jokes and take an interest in such small talk! That fellow Montjoie, above all, was intolerable to Jock. He had been quite low down in the school when he left, a being of no account, a creature called by opprobrious names, and not worthy to tie the shoes of a member of Sixth Form. But when he rattled loudly on about nothing at all, even Sir Tom did not refuse to listen. What was Montjoie doing here? When the gentlemen streamed into the drawing-room, a procession of black coats, Jock, who came last, could not help being aware that he was scowling at everybody. He met the eyes of one of those inoffensive little girls in blue, and made her jump, looking at her as if he would eat her. And all the evening through he kept prowling about with his hands in his pockets, now looking at the books in the shelves, now frowning at Lucy, who could not think what was the matter with her brother. Was Jock ill? What had happened to him? The young ladies in blue sang an innocent little duet, and Jock stared at the Contessa, wondering if she was going to sing, and if the door would open and the slim figure in the black frock come in as by a signal and place herself at the piano. But the Contessa only laughed behind her fan, and made a little pretence at applause when the music ceased, having talked all through it, she and the gentlemen about her, of whom Montjoie was one and the loudest. No, she was not going to sing. When the door opened it was only to admit the servants with their trays and the tea which nobody wanted. What was the use of looking forward to the holidays if— Mr. Derwentwater, perhaps, had similar thoughts. He came up to Jock behind the backs of the other people, and put an uneasy question to him.

"I thought you said that Madame di Forno-Populo sang?"

"She used to," said Jock laconically.

"The music here does not seem of a high class," said MTutor. "I hope she will sing. Italians, though their music is sensuous, generally know something about the art."

To this Jock made no reply, but hunched his shoulders a little higher, and dug his hands down deeper into his pockets.

"By the way, is the—young lady who was with Madame di Forno-Populo here no longer?" said MTutor in a sort of accidental manner, as if that had for the first time occurred to him. He raised his eyes to Jock's face, which was foolish, and they both reddened in spite of themselves; Mr. Derwentwater with sudden confusion, and Jock with angry dismay.

"Not that I know of," said the boy. "I haven't heard anything." Then he went on hurriedly: "No more than I know what Montjoie's doing here. What's he been asked here for I wonder? He can't amuse anybody much." These words, however, were contradicted practically as soon as they were said by a peal of laughter which rose from the Contessa's little corner, all caused as it was evident by some pleasantry of Montjoie's.

"It seems that he does, though," said Mr. Derwentwater; and then he added with a smile, "We are novices in society, you and I. We do best in our own class; not to know that Montjoie will be in the very front of society, the admired of all admirers at least for a season or two! Isn't he a favourite of fortune, the best parti, a golden youth in every sense of the word—"

"Why, he was a scug!" cried Jock, with illimitable disdain. This mysterious and terrible monosyllable was applied at school to a youth hopelessly low down and destitute of any personal advantages to counterbalance his inferiority. Jock launched it at the Marquis, evidently now in a very different situation, as if it had been a stone.

"Hush!" said MTutor blandly. "You will meet a great many such in society, and they will think themselves quite as good as you."

Then the mother of the young ladies in blue approached and disturbed this tête-à-tête.

"I think you were talking of Lord Montjoie," she said. "I hear he is so clever; there are some comic songs he sings, which, I am told, are quite irresistible. Mr. Trevor, don't you think you could induce him to sing one?—as you were at school with him, and are a sort of son of the house?"

At this Jock glowered with eyes that were alarming to see under the deep cover of his eyebrows, and MTutor laughed out. "We had not so exalted an opinion of Montjoie," he said; and then, with a politic diversion of which he was proud, "Would not your daughters favour us again? A comic song in the present state of our feelings would be more than we could bear."

"What a clever fellow he is after all!" said Jock to himself admiringly, "how he can manage people and say the right thing at the right moment! I dare say Lucy will tell me if I ask her," he said, quite irrelevantly, as the lady, well pleased to hear her daughters appreciated, sailed away. There was something in the complete sympathy of Mr. Derwentwater's mind, even though it irritated, which touched him. He put the question point blank to Lucy when he found an opportunity of speaking to her. "I say, Lucy, where is Bice? You have got all the old fogeys about the place, and she is not here," the boy said.

"Is that why you are glooming upon everybody so?" said the unfeeling Lucy. "You cannot call your friend Lord Montjoie an old fogey, Jock. He says you were such friends at school."

"I—friends!" cried Jock with disdain. "Why, he was nothing but a scug."

Thus Lucy, too, avoided the question; but it was not because she had any real reluctance to speak of Bice, though this was what Jock could not know.

CHAPTER XXXIII

THE CONTESSA PREPARES THE WAY

"I never sing," said the Contessa, with that serene smile with which she was in the habit of accompanying a statement which her hearers knew to be quite untrue. "Oh never! It is one of my possibilities which are over—one of the things which you remember of me in—other days—"

"So far back as March," said Sir Tom; "but we all recognise that in a lady's calendar that may mean a century."

"Put it in the plural, mon ami—centuries, that is more correct," said the Contessa, with her dazzling smile.

"And might one ask why this sudden acceleration of time?" asked one of the gentlemen who were always in attendance, belonging, so to speak, to the Contessa's side of the party. She opened out her lovely hands and gave a little shrug to her shoulders, and elevation of her eyebrows.

"It is easy to tell: but whether I shall tell you is another question—"

"Oh, do, do, Countess," cried young Montjoie, who was somewhat rough in his attentions, and treated the lady with less ceremony than a less noble youth would have ventured upon. "Come, don't keep us all in suspense. I must hear you, don't you know; all the other fellows have heard you. So, please, get over the preliminaries, and let's come to the music. I'm awfully fond of music, especially singing. I'm a dab at that myself—"

The Contessa let her eyes dwell upon this illustrious young man. "Why," she said, "have I been prevented from making acquaintance with the art in which my Lord Montjoie is—a dab—"

At this there was a laugh, in which the good-natured young nobleman did not refuse to join. "I say, you know! it's too bad to make fun of me like this," he cried; "but I'll tell you what, Countess, I'll make a bargain with you. I'll sing you three of mine if you'll sing me one of yours."

The Contessa smiled with that gracious response which so often answered instead of words. The other ladies had withdrawn, except Lucy, who waited somewhat uneasily till her guest was ready. Though Madame di Forno-Populo had never lost the ascendency which she had acquired over Lady Randolph by throwing herself upon her understanding and sympathy, there were still many things which Lucy could not acquiesce in without uneasiness, in the Contessa's ways. The group of men about her chair, when all the other ladies took their candles and made their way upstairs, wounded Lucy's instinctive sense of what was befitting. She waited, punctilious in her feeling of duty, though the Contessa had not hesitated to make her understand that the precaution was quite unnecessary—and though even Sir Tom had said something of a similar signification. "She is old enough to take care of herself. She doesn't want a chaperon," Sir Tom had said; but nevertheless Lucy would take up a book and sit down at the table and wait: which was the more troublesome that it was precisely at this moment that the Contessa was most amusing and enjoyed herself most. Sir Tom's parliamentary friends had disappeared to the smoking-room when the ladies left the room. It was the other kind of visitors, the gentlemen who had known the Contessa in former days, and were old friends likewise of Sir Tom, who gathered round her now—they and young Lord Montjoie, who was rather out of place in the party, but who admired the Contessa greatly, and thought her better fun than any one he knew.

The Contessa gave the young man one of those speaking smiles which were more eloquent than words. And then she said: "If I were to tell you why, you would not believe me. I am going to retire from the world."

At this there was a little tumult of outcry and laughter. "The world cannot spare you, Contessa." "We can't permit any such sacrifice." And, "Retire! Till to-morrow?" her courtiers said.

"Not till to-morrow. I do more than retire. I abdicate," said the Contessa, waving her beautiful hands as if in farewell.

"This sounds very mysterious; for an abdication is different from a withdrawal; it suggests a successor."

"Which is an impossibility," another said.

The Contessa distributed her smiles with gracious impartiality to all, but she kept a little watch upon young Montjoie, who was eager amid the ring of her worshippers. "Nevertheless, it is more than a successor," she said, playing with them, with a strange pleasure. To be thus surrounded, flattered more openly than men ever venture to flatter a woman whom they respect, addressed with exaggerated admiration, contemplated with bold and unwavering eyes, had come by many descents to be delightful to the Contessa. It reminded her of her old triumphs—of the days when men of a different sort brought homage perhaps not much more real but far more delicate, to her feet. A long career of baths and watering-places, of Baden and Homburg, and every other conceivable resort of temporary gaiety and fashion, had brought her to this. Sir Tom, who was not taking much share in the conversation, stood with his arm on the mantelpiece, and watched her and her little court with compassionate eyes. He had laughed often before; but he did not laugh now. Perhaps the fact that he was himself no longer her first object helped to change the aspect of affairs. He had consented to invite these men as old acquaintances; but it was intolerable to him to see this scene going on in the room in which his wife was; and the Contessa's radiant satisfaction seemed almost horrible to him in Lucy's presence. Lucy was seated at some distance from the group, her face turned away, her head bent, to all appearance very intent upon the book she was reading. He looked at her with a sort of reverential impatience. She was not capable of understanding the degradation which her own pure and simple presence made apparent. He could not endure her to be there sanctioning the indecorum;—and yet the tenacity with which she held her place, and did what she thought her duty to her guest, filled him with a wondering pride. No other scene, perhaps, he thought, in all England, could have presented a contrast so curious.

"The Contessa speaks in riddles," said one of the circle. "We want an OEdipus."

"Oh, come, Countess," said young Montjoie, "don't hang us up like this. We are all of us on pins and needles, don't you know? It all began about you singing. Why don't you sing? All the fellows say it's as good as Grisi. I never heard Grisi, but I know every note Patti's got in her voice; and I want to compare, don't you know?"

The Contessa contemplated the young man with a sort of indulgent smile like a mother who withholds a toy.

"When are you going away?" she said. "You will soon go back to your dear London, to your clubs and all your delights."

"Oh, come, Countess," repeated Montjoie, "that isn't kind. You talk as if you wanted to get rid of a fellow. I'm due at the Duke's on Friday, don't you know?"

"Then it shall be on Thursday," said the Contessa, with a laugh.

"What shall be on Thursday?"

The others all came round her with eager questions.

"I am going on Wednesday," said one. "What is this that is going to happen?"

"And why am I to be excluded?"

"And I? If there is to be anything new, tell us what it is."

"Inquisitors! and they say that curiosity belongs to women," said the Contessa. "Messieurs, if I were to tell you what it was, it would be no longer new."

"Well, but hang it all," cried young Montjoie, who was excited and had forgotten his manners, "do tell us what it is. Don't you see we don't even know what kind of thing you mean? If it's music—"

Madame di Forno-Populo laughed once more. She loved to mystify and raise expectations. "It is not music," she said. "It is my reason for withdrawing. When you see that, you will understand. You will all say the Contessa is wise. She has foreseen exactly the right moment to retire."

And with this she rose from the sofa with a sudden movement which took her attendants by surprise. She was not given to shaking hands. She withdrew quickly from Montjoie's effort to seize her delicate fingers, which she waved to the company in general. "My Lucy," she said, "I have kept you waiting! to this extent does one forget one's self in your delightful house. But, my angel, you should not permit me to do it. You should hold up your finger, and I would obey."

"Bravo," said Montjoie's voice behind their backs in a murmur of delight. "Oh, by Jove, isn't that good? Fancy, a woman like her, and that simple—"

One of the elder men gave Montjoie something like a kick, inappropriate as the scene was for such a demonstration. "You little—think what you are saying," he cried.

But Sir Tom was opening the door for the ladies, and did not hear. Lucy was tired and pale. She looked like a child beside the stately Contessa. She had taken no notice of Madame di Forno-Populo's profession of submission. In her heart she was longing to run to the nursery, to see her boy asleep, and make sure that all was well; and she was not only tired with her vigil, but uneasy, disapproving. She divined what the Contessa meant, though not even Sir Tom had made it out. Perhaps it was feminine instinct that instructed her on this point. Perhaps the strong repugnance she had, and sense of opposition to what was about to be done, quickened her powers of divination. She who had never suspected anybody in all her life fathomed the Contessa's intentions at a glance. "That boy!" she said to herself as she followed up the great staircase. Lucy divined the Contessa, and the Contessa divined that she had divined her. She turned round when they reached the top of the stairs and paused for a moment looking at Lady Randolph's face, lit up with the light of her candle. "My sweetest," said the Contessa, "you do not approve. It breaks my heart to see it. But what can I do! This is my way, it is not yours; but to me it is the only way."

Lucy could do nothing but shake her head as she turned the way of the nursery where her boy was sleeping. The contrast gave her a pang. Bice, too, was no doubt sleeping the deep and dreamless sleep of youth behind one of those closed doors; poor Bice! secluded there to increase the effect of her eventual appearance, and about whom her protectress was draping all those veils of mystery in order to tempt the fancy of a commonplace youth not much more than a schoolboy! And yet the Contessa loved her charge, and persuaded herself that she was acting for Bice's good. Poor Bice, who was so good to little Tom! Was there nothing to be done to save her?

"What's going to happen on Thursday?" the men of the Contessa's train asked of Sir Tom, as they followed him to the smoking-room, where Mr. Derwentwater, in a velvet coat, was already seated smoking a mild cigarette, and conversing with one of the parliamentary gentlemen. Jock hung about in the background, turning over the books (for there were books everywhere in this well-provided house) rather with the intention of making it quite evident that he went to bed when he liked, and could stay up as late as any one, than from any hankering after that cigar which a Sixth Form fellow, so conscientious as Jock was, might not trifle with. "Oh, here are those two duffers; those saps, don't you know," Montjoie said, with a grimace, as he perceived them on entering the room; in which remark he was perhaps justified by the epithets which these two superior persons applied to him. The two parties did not amalgamate in the smoking-room any more than in other places. The new comers surrounded Sir Tom in a noisy little crowd, demanding of him an explanation of the Contessa's meaning. This, however, was subdued presently by a somewhat startling little incident. The gentlemen were discussing the Contessa with the greatest freedom. "It's rather astounding to meet her in a good house, just like any one else," one man forgot himself sufficiently to say, but he came to his recollection very quickly on meeting Sir Tom's eyes. "I beg your pardon, Randolph, of course that's not what I mean. I mean after all those years." "Then I hope you will remember to say exactly what you mean," said Sir Tom, "on other occasions. It will simplify matters."

This momentary incident, though it was quiet enough, and expressed in tones rather less than more loud than the ordinary conversation, made a sensation in the room, and produced first an involuntary stillness, and then an eager access of talk. It had the effect, however, of making everybody aware that the Contessa intended to make, on Thursday, some revelation or other, an intimation which moved Jock and his tutor as much or even more than it moved the others. Mr. Derwentwater even made advances to Montjoie, whom he had steadily ignored, in order to ascertain what it was. "Something's coming off, that's all we can tell," that young patrician said. "She is going to retire, so she says, from the world, don't you know? That's like a tradesman shutting up shop when he's made his fortune, or a prima donna going off the stage. It ain't so easy to make out, is it, how the Forno-Populo can retire from the world? She can't be going to take poison, like the great Sarah, and give us a grand dying seance in Lady Randolph's drawing-room. That would be going a bit too far, don't you know?"

"It is going a bit too far to imagine such a thing," Derwentwater said.

"Oh, come, you know, it isn't school-time," cried Montjoie, with a laugh. And though Mr. Derwentwater was as much superior to the little lordling as could be conceived, he retired disconcerted from this passage of arms. To be reminded that you are a pedagogue is difficult to bear, especially an unsuccessful pedagogue, attempting to exert authority which exists no longer. MTutor prided himself on being a man of the world, but he retired a little with an involuntary sense of offence from this easy setting down. He rose shortly after and took Jock by the arm and led him away. "You are not smoking, which I am glad to see—and shows your sense," he said. "Come out and have a breath of air before we go upstairs. Can you imagine anything more detestable than that little precocious roué, that washed-out little man-about-town," he added with some energy, as they stepped out of the open windows of the library, left open in case the fine night should have seduced the gentlemen on to the terrace to smoke their cigars. It was a lovely spring night, soft and balmy, with a sensation of growth in the air, the sky very clear, with airy white clouds all lit up by the moon. The quiet and freshness gave to those who stepped into it a curious sensation of superiority to the men whom they left in the warm brightly-lit room, with its heavy atmosphere and artificial delights. It felt like a moral atmosphere in contrast with the air all laden with human emanations, smoke, and the careless talk of men. These two were perhaps somewhat inclined to feel a superiority in any circumstances. They did so doubly in these.

"He was always a little cad," said Jock.

"To hear a lady's name from his mouth is revolting," said Derwentwater. "We are all too careless in that respect. I admire Madame di Forno-Populo for keeping her—is it her daughter or niece?—out of the way while that little animal is here."

"Oh, Bice would soon make him know his place," said Jock; "she is not just like one of the girls that are civil, you know. She is not afraid of telling you what she thinks of you. I know exactly how she'd look at Montjoie." Jock permitted himself an abrupt laugh in the pleasure of feeling that he knew her ways far better than any one. "She would soon set him down—the little beast!—in his right place."

As they walked up and down the terrace their steps and voices were very audible in the stillness of the night; and the windows were lighted in the east wing, showing that the inhabitants were still up there and about. While Jock spoke, one of these windows opened quite suddenly, and for a single moment a figure like a shadow appeared in it. The light movement, sudden as a bird's on the wing, would have betrayed her (she felt) to Jock, even if she had not spoken. But she waved her hand and called out "Good-night" in a voice full of laughter. "Don't talk secrets, for we can hear you," she said. "Good-night!" And so vanished again, with a little echo of laughter from within. The young men were both excited and disconcerted by this interruption. It gave them a sensation of shame for the moment as if they had been caught in a discussion of a forbidden subject; and then a tingling ran through their veins. Even MTutor for the moment found no fine speech in which to express his sense of this sudden momentary tantalising appearance of the mystic woman standing half visible out of the background of the unknown. He did think some very fine things on the subject after a time, with a side glance of philosophical reflection that her light laugh of mockery as she momentarily revealed herself, was an outcome of this sceptical century, and that in a previous age her utterance would have been a song or a sigh. But at the moment even Mr. Derwentwater was subjugated by the thrill of sensation and feeling, and found nothing to say.

CHAPTER XXXIV

IN SUSPENSE

It was thus that Bice was engaged while Lucy imagined her asleep in her innocence, unaware of the net that was being spread for her unsuspecting feet. Bice was neither asleep nor unsuspecting. She was innocent in a way inconceivable to the ordinary home-keeping imagination, knowing no evil in the devices to which she was a party; but she was not innocent in the conventional sense. That any high feminine ideal should be affected by the design of the Contessa or by her own participation in it had not occurred to the girl. She had been accustomed to smile at the high virtue of those ladies in the novels who would not receive the addresses of the eldest son of their patroness, and who preferred a humble village and the delights of self-sacrifice to all the grandeurs of an ambitious marriage. That might be well enough in a novel, Bice thought, but it was not so in life. In her own case there was no question about it. The other way it was which seemed to her the virtuous way. Had it been proposed to her to throw herself away upon a poor man whom she might be supposed to love, and so prove herself incapable of being of any use to the Contessa, and make all her previous training and teaching of no effect, Bice's moral indignation would have been as elevated as that of any English heroine at the idea of marrying for interest instead of love. The possibility did not occur to her at all; but it would have been rejected with disdain had it attempted to force its way across the threshold of her mind. She loved nobody—except the Contessa; which was a great defence and preservation to her thoughts. She accepted the suggestion that Montjoie should be the means of raising her to that position she was made for, with composure and without an objection. It was not arranged upon secretly, without her knowledge, but with her full concurrence. "He is not very much to look at. I wish he had been more handsome," the Contessa said; but Bice's indifference on this point was sublime. "What can it matter?" she said loftily. She was not even very deeply interested in his disposition or mental qualities. Everything else being so suitable, it would have been cowardly to shrink from any minor disadvantage. She silenced the Contessa in the attempt to make the best of him. "All these things are so secondary," the girl said. Her devotion to the career chosen for her was above all weakly arguments of this kind. She looked upon them even with a certain scorn. And though there was in her mind some excitement as to her appearance "in the world," as she phrased it, and her skill "to please," which was as yet untried, it was, notwithstanding with the composure of a nature quite unaware of any higher questions involved, that she took her part in all the preparations. Her knowledge of the very doubtful world in which she had lived had been of a philosophical character. She was quite impartial. She had no prejudices. Those of whom she approved were those who had carried out their intentions, whatever they might be, as she should do by marrying an English Milord with a good title and much money. She meant, indeed, to spend his money, but legitimately. She meant to become a great lady by his means, but not to do him any harm. Bice had an almost savage purity of heart, and the thought that any of the stains she knew of should touch her was incredible, impossible; neither was it in her to be unkind, or unjust, or envious, or ungenerous. Nothing of all this was involved in the purely business operation in which she was engaged. According to her code no professions of attachment or pretence of feeling were necessary. She had indeed no theories in her mind about being a good wife; but she would not be a bad one. She would keep her part of the compact; there should be nothing to complain of, nothing to object to. She would do her best to amuse the man she had to live with and make his life agreeable to him, which is a thing not always taken into consideration in marriage-contracts much more ideal in character. He should not be allowed to be dull, that was one thing certain. Regarding the matter in this reasonable point of view, Bice prepared for the great event of Thursday with just excitement enough to make it amusing. It might be that she should fail. Few succeed at the very first effort without difficulty, she said to herself; but if she failed there would be nothing tragical in the failure, and the season was all before her. It could scarcely be hoped that she would bring down her antagonist the first time she set lance in rest.

She was carefully kept out of sight during the intervening days; no one saw her; no one had any acquaintance with the fact of her existence. The precautions taken were such that Bice was never even encountered on the staircase, never seen to flit in or out of a room, and indeed did not exist at all for the party in the house. Notwithstanding these precautions she had the needful exercise to keep her in health and good looks, and still romped with the baby and held conversations with the sympathetic Lucy, who did not know what to say to express her feeling of anxious disapproval and desire to succour, without, at the same time, injuring in Bice's mind her nearest friend and protectress. She might, indeed, have spared herself the trouble of any such anxiety, for Bice neither felt injured by the Contessa's scheme nor degraded by her precautions. It amused the girl highly to be made a secret of, to run all the risks of discovery and baffle the curious. The fun of it was delightful to her. Sometimes she would amuse herself by hanging till the last practicable moment in the gallery at the top of the staircase, on the balcony at the window, or at the door of the Contessa's room which was commanded by various other doors; but always vanished within in time to avoid all inquisitive eyes, with the laughter and delight of a child at the danger escaped, and the fun of the situation. In these cases the Contessa would sometimes take fright, but never, so light was the temper of this scheming woman, this deep plotter and conspirator, refused to join in the laughter when the flight was made and safety secured. They were like a couple of children with a mystification in hand, notwithstanding that they were planning an invasion so serious of all the proprieties, and meant to make so disreputable and revolting a bargain. But this was not in their ideas. Bice went out very early in the morning before any one was astir, to take needful exercise in the park, and gather early primroses and the catkins that hung upon the trees. On one of these occasions she met Mr. Derwentwater, of whom she was not afraid; and at another time, when skirting the shrubberies at a somewhat later hour to keep clear of any stragglers, Jock. Mr. Derwentwater talked to her in a tone which amused the girl. He spoke of Proserpina gathering flowers, herself a—and then altered and grew confused under her eye.

"Herself a— What?" said Bice. "Have you forgotten what you were going to say?"

"I have not forgotten—herself a fairer flower. One does not forget such lovely words as these," he said, injured by the question. "But when one comes face to face with the impersonation of the poet's idea—"

"It was poetry, then?" said Bice. "I know very little of that. It is not in Tauchnitz, perhaps? All I know of English is from the Tauchnitz. I read, chiefly, novels. You do not approve of that? But, yes, I like them; because it is life."

"Is it life?" said Derwentwater, who was somewhat contemptuous of fiction.

"At least it is England," said Bice. "The girls who will not make a good marriage because of some one else, or because it is their parents who arrange it. That is how Lady Randolph speaks. She says that nothing is right but to fall—how do you call it?—in love?—It is not comme il faut even to talk of that."

Derwentwater blushed like a girl. He was more inexperienced in many ways than Bice. "And do you regard it in another point of view?" he said.

Bice laughed out with frank disdain. "Certainly, I regard it different—oh, quite different. That is not what happens in life."

"And do you consider life is chiefly occupied with getting married?" he continued, feeling, along with a good deal of quite unnecessary excitement, a great desire to know what was her way of looking at this great subject. Visions had been flashing recently through his mind, which pointed a little this way too.

"Altogether," said Bice, with great gravity, "how can you begin to live till you have settled that? Till then you do not know what is going to happen to you. When you get up in the morning you know not what may come before the night; when you walk out you know not who may be the next person you meet; perhaps your husband. But then you marry, and that is all settled; henceforward nothing can happen!" said Bice, throwing out her hands. "Then, after all is settled, you can begin to live."

"This is very interesting," said Derwentwater, "I am so glad to get at a real and individual view. But this, perhaps, only applies to—ladies? It is, perhaps, not the same with men?"

Bice gave him a careless, half-contemptuous glance. "I have never known anything," she said, "about men."

There are many girls, much more innocent in outward matters than Bice, who would have said these words with an intention agaçante—the intention of leading to a great deal more badinage. But Bice spoke with a calm, almost scornful, composure. She had no desire to agacer. She looked him in the face as tranquilly as if he had been an old woman. And so far as she was concerned he might have been an old woman; for he had virtually no existence in his capacity of young man. Had she possessed any clue to the thoughts that had taken rise in his mind, the new revelation which she had conveyed to him, Bice's amazement would have been without bounds. But instinct indicated to her that the interview should proceed no further. She waved her hand to him as she came to a cross road which led into the woods. "I am going this way," she cried, darting off round the corner of a great tree. He stood and looked after her bewildered, as her light figure skimmed along into the depths of the shadows. "Then, after all is settled, you can begin to live," he repeated to himself. Was it true? He had got up the morning on which he saw her first without any thought that everything might be changed for him that day. And now it was quite true that there lay before him an interval which must be somehow filled up before he could begin to live. How was it to be filled up? Would she have anything to do with the settling which must precede his recommencement of existence? He went on with his mind altogether absorbed in these thoughts, and with a thrill and tingling through all his veins. And that was the only time he encountered Bice, for whom in fact, though he had not hitherto allowed it even to himself, he had come to the Hall—till the great night.

Jock encountered her the next day not so early, at the hour indeed when the great people were at breakfast. He had been one of the first to come downstairs, and he had not lingered at table as persons do who have letters to read, and the newspapers, and all that is going on to talk about. He met her coming from the park. She put out her hand when she saw him as if to keep him off.

"If you wish to speak to me," she said, "you must turn back and walk with me. I do not want any one to see me, and they will soon be coming out from breakfast."

"Why don't you want any one to see you?" Jock said.

Bice had learned the secret of the Contessa's smile; but this which she cast upon Jock had something mocking in it, and ended in a laugh. "Oh, don't you know?" she said, "it is so silly to be a boy!"

"You are no older than I am," cried Jock, aggrieved; "and why don't you come down to dinner as you used to do? I always liked you to come. It is quite different when you are not there. If I had known I should not have come home at all this Easter," Jock cried.

"Oh!" cried Bice, "that means that you like me, then?—and so does Milady. If I should go away altogether—"

"You are not going away altogether? Why should you? There is no other place you could be so well as here. The Contessa never says a word, but laughs at a fellow, which is scarcely civil; and she has those men about her that are—not—; but you—why should you go away?" cried Jock with angry vehemence. He looked at her with eyes lowering fiercely under his eyebrows; yet in his heart he was not angry but wretched, as if something were rending him. Jock did not understand how he felt.

"Oh, now, you look at me as if you would eat me," said Bice, "as if I were the little girl in the red hood and you the wolf— But it is silly, for how should I stay here when Milady is going away? We are all going to London—and then! it will soon be decided, I suppose," said Bice, herself feeling a little sad for the first time at the idea, "what is going to be done with me."

"What is going to be done with you?" cried Jock hoarsely, for he was angry and grieved, and full of impatient indignation, though he scarcely knew why.

Bice turned upon him with that lingering smile which was like the Contessa's. But, unlike the Contessa's, it ended as usual in a laugh. She kissed her hand to him, and darted round the corner of the shrubbery just as some one appeared from breakfast. "Good-bye," she said, "do not be angry," and so vanished like lightning. This was one of the cases which made her heart beat with fun and exhilaration, when she was, as she told the Contessa, nearly caught. She got into the shelter of the east rooms, panting with the run she had made, her complexion brilliant, her eyes shining. "I thought I should certainly be seen this time," she said.

The Contessa looked at the girl with admiring eyes. "I could almost have wished you had," she said. "You are superb like that." They talked without a shade of embarrassment on this subject, upon which English mothers and children would blush and hesitate.

This was the day, the great day of the revelation which the Contessa had promised. There had been a great deal of discussion and speculation about it in the company. No one, even Sir Tom, knew what it was. Lucy, though she was not clever, had her wits sharpened in this respect, and she had divined; but no one else had any conception of what was coming. Two of the elder men had gone, very sorry to miss the great event, whatever it was. And young Montjoie had talked of nothing else since the promise had been made. The conversation in the drawing-room late in the afternoon chiefly turned on this subject, and the lady visitors too heard of it, and were not less curious. She who had the two daughters addressed herself to Lucy for information. She said: "I hear some novelty is expected to-night, Lady Randolph, something the Contessa has arranged. She is very clever, is she not? and sings delightfully, I know. There is so much more talent of that kind among foreigners than there is among us. Is it tableaux? The girls are so longing to know."

"Oh, yes, we want so much to know," said the young ladies in blue.

"I don't think it is tableaux," Lucy said; "but I have not been told what it is."

This the ladies did not believe, but they asked no further questions. "It is clear that she does not wish us to know; so, girls, you must say nothing," was the conclusion of the mother.

They said a great deal, notwithstanding this warning. The house altogether was excited on the subject, and even Mr. Derwentwater took part in the speculations. He looked upon the Contessa as one of those inscrutable women of the stage, the Sirens who beguile everybody. She had some design upon Montjoie, he felt, and it was only the youth's impertinence which prevented Mr. Derwentwater from interfering. He watched with the natural instinct of his profession and a strong impulse to write to the lad's parents and have him taken away. But Montjoie had no parents. He had attained his majority, and was supposed by the law capable of taking care of himself. What did that woman mean to do with the boy? She had some designs upon him. But there was nobody to whom Mr. Derwentwater could confide his suspicions, or whom he could ask what the Contessa meant. MTutor had not on the whole a pleasant visit. He was disappointed in that which had been his chief object—his favourite pupil was detached from him, he knew not how—and this other boy, whom, though he did not love him, he could not help feeling a sort of responsibility for, was in danger from a designing woman, a woman out of a French play, L'Aventurière, something of that sort. Mr. Derwentwater felt that he could not drag himself away, the attractions were so strong. He wanted to see the dénoûement; still more he wanted to see Bice. No drama in the world had so powerful an interest. But though it was so impossible to go away, it was not pleasant to stay. Jock did not want him. Lucy, though she was always sweet and friendly, had a look of haste and over-occupation; her eyes wandered when she talked to him; her mind was occupied with other things. Most of the men of the party were more than indifferent; were disagreeable to him. He thought they were a danger for Jock. And Bice never was visible; that moment on the balcony—those few minutes in the park—the half dozen words which had been so "suggestive," he thought, which had woke so many echoes in his mind—these were all he had had of her. Had she intended them to awaken echoes? He asked himself this question a thousand times. Had she willingly cast this seed of thought into his mind to germinate—to produce—what result? If it was so, then, indeed, all the little annoyances of his stay would be a cheap price to pay. It did not occur to this judicious person, whose influence over his pupils was so great, and who had studied so deeply the mind of youth, that a girl of sixteen was but little likely to be consciously suggestive—to sow, with any intention in her mind, seeds of meaning to develop in his. To do him justice, he was as unconscious of the limits of sixteen in Bice's case as we all are in the case of Juliet. She was of no age. She was the ideal woman capable of comprehensions and intentions as far above anything possible to the genus boy as heaven was above earth. It would have been a profanation, a sacrilege too dreadful to be thought of, to compare that ethereal creature with the other things of her age with which he was so familiar. Of her age! Her age was the age of romance, of love, of poetry, of all ineffable things.

"I say, Countess," said Montjoie, "I hope you're not forgetting. This is the night, don't you know. And here we are all ready for dinner and nothing has happened. When is it coming? You are so awfully mysterious; it ain't fair upon a fellow."

"Is every one in the room?" said the Contessa, with an indulgent smile at the young man's eagerness. They all looked round, for everybody was curious. And all were there—the lady who wrote for the Press, and the lady with the two daughters, the girls in blue; and Sir Tom's parliamentary friends standing up against the mantelpiece, and Mr. Derwentwater by himself, more curious than any one, keeping one eye on Montjoie, as if he would have liked to send him to the pupil-room to do a poena; and Jock indifferent, with his back to the door. All the rest were expectant except Jock, who took no notice. The Contessa's special friends were about her chair, rubbing their hands, and ready to back the Forno-Populo for a new sensation. The Contessa looked round, her eye dwelling for a moment upon Lucy, who looked a little fluttered and uncomfortable, and upon Sir Tom, who evidently knew nothing, and was looking on with a smile.

"Now you shall see," she said, "why I abdicate," and made a sign, clapping softly her beautiful hands.

There was a momentary pause. Montjoie, who was standing out in the clear space in the centre of the room, turned round at the Contessa's call. He turned towards the open door, which was less lighted than the inner room. It was he who saw first what was coming. "Oh, by Jove!" the young Marquis said.

CHAPTER XXXV

## THE DÉBUT

The door was open. The long drawing-room afforded a sort of processional path for the newcomer. Her dress was not white like that of the ordinary débutante. It had a yellow golden glow of colour, warm yet soft. She walked not with the confused air of a novice perceiving herself observed, but with a slow and serene gait like a young queen. She was not alarmed by the consciousness that everybody was looking at her. Not to have been looked at would have been more likely to embarrass Bice. Her beautiful throat and shoulders were uncovered, her hair dressed more elaborately than that of English girls in general. English girls—the two innocents in blue, who were nice girls enough, and stood with their mouths and eyes open in speechless wonder and admiration—seemed of an entirely different species from this dazzling creature. She made a momentary pause on the threshold, while all the beholders held their breath. Montjoie, for one, was struck dumb. His commonplace countenance changed altogether. He looked at her with his face growing longer, his jaw dropping. It was more than a sensation, it was such a climax of excitement and surprise as does not happen above once or twice in a lifetime. The whole company were moved by similar feelings, all except the Contessa, lying back in her chair, and Lucy, who stood rather troubled, moving from one foot to another, clasping and unclasping her hands. Jock, roused by the murmur, turned round with a start, and eyed her too with looks of wild astonishment. She stood for a moment looking at them all—with a smile which was half mischievous, half appealing—on the threshold, as Bice felt it, not only of Lady Randolph's drawing-room, but of the world.

Sir Tom had started at the sight of her as much as any one. He had not been in the secret. He cried out, "By Jove!" like Montjoie. But he had those instincts which are, perhaps, rather old-fashioned, of protection and service to women. He belonged to the school which thinks a girl should not walk across a room without some man's arm to sustain her, or open a door for herself. He started forward with a little sense of being to blame, and offered her his arm. "Why didn't you send for me to bring you in if you were late?" he cried, with a tone in which there was some tremor and vexation. The effectiveness of her appearance was terrible to Sir Tom. She looked up at him with a look of pleasure and kindness, and said, "I was not late," with a smile. She looked taller, more developed in a single day. But for that little pucker of vexation on Sir Tom's forehead they would have looked like a father and daughter, the father proudly bringing his young princess into the circle of her adorers. Bice swept him towards Lucy, and made a low obeisance to Lady Randolph, and took her hand and kissed it. "I must come to you first," she said.

"Well?" said the Contessa, turning round to her retainers with a quick movement. They were all gazing at the débutante so intently that they had no eyes for her. One of them at length replied, with something like solemnity: "Oh, I understand what you mean, Contessa; anybody but you would have to abdicate." "But not you," said another, who had some kindness in his heart. The Contessa rose up with an air of triumph. "I do not want to be compelled," she said, "I told you. I give up. I will take your arm Mr. St. John, as a private person, having relinquished my claims, and leave milord to the new régime."

This was how it came about, in the slight scuffle caused by the sudden change of programme, that Bice, in all her splendour, found herself going in to the dining-room on Lord Montjoie's arm. Notwithstanding that he had been struck dumb by her beauty, little Montjoie was by no means happy when this wonderful good fortune fell upon him. He would have preferred to gaze at her from the other side of the table: on the whole, he would have been a great deal more at his ease with the Contessa. He would have asked her a hundred questions about this wonderful beauty; but the beauty herself rather frightened the young man. Presently, however, he regained his courage, and as lack of boldness was not his weak point, soon began to lose the sense of awe which had been so strong upon him. She smiled;

she was as ready to talk as he was, as the overwhelming impression she had made upon him began to be modified by familiarity. "I suppose," he said, when he had reached this point, "that you arrived to-day?" And then, after a pause, "You speak English?" he added, in a hesitating tone. She received this question with so merry a laugh that he was quite encouraged.

"Always," she said, "since I was a child. Was that why you were afraid of me?"

"Afraid?" he said; and then he looked at her almost with a recurrence of his first fright, till her laugh reassured him. "Yes I was frightened," Lord Montjoie said; "you looked so—so—don't you know? I was struck all of a heap. I suppose you came to-day? We were all on the outlook from something the Contessa said. You must be clever to get in without anybody seeing you."

"I was far more clever than that," said Bice; "you don't know how clever I am."

"I dare say," said Lord Montjoie, admiringly, "because you don't want it. That's always the way."

"I am so clever that I have been here all the time," said Bice, with another laugh so joyous,—"so jolly," Montjoie said, that his terrors died away. But his surprise took another development at this extraordinary information.

"By Jove!" he cried, "you don't mean that, Miss—Mademoiselle—I am so awfully stupid I never heard— that is to say I ain't at all clever at foreign names."

"Oh, never mind," cried Bice; "neither am I. But yours is delightful; it is so easy, Milord. Ought I to say Milord?"

"Oh," cried Montjoie, a little confused. "No; I don't think so—people don't as a rule."

"Lord Montjoie, that is right? I like always to know—"

"So do I," said Montjoie; "it's always best to ask, ain't it, and then there can be no mistakes? But you don't mean to say that? You here yesterday and all the time? I shouldn't think you could have been hid. Not the kind of person, don't you know."

"I can't tell about being the kind of person. It has been fun," said Bice; "sometimes I have seen you all coming, and waited till there was just time to fly. I like leaving it till the last moment, and then there is the excitement, don't you know."

"By Jove, what fun!" said Montjoie. He was not clever enough, few people are, to perceive that she had mimicked himself in tone and expression. "And I might have caught you any day," he cried. "What a muff I have been."

"If I had allowed myself to be caught I should have been a greater—what do you call it? You wear beautiful things to do your smoking in, Lord Montjoie; what is it? Velvet? And why don't you wear them to dinner?—you would look so much more handsome. I am very fond myself of beautiful clothes."

"Oh, by Jove!" cried Montjoie again, with something like a blush. "You've seen me in those things! I only wear them when I think nobody sees. They're something from the East," he added, with a tone of careless complacency; for, as a matter of fact, he piqued himself very much upon this smoking-suit which had not, at the Hall, received the applause it deserved.

"You go and smoke like that among other men? Yes, I perceive," said Bice, "you are just like women, there is no difference. We put on our pretty things for other ladies, because you cannot understand them; and you do the same."

"Oh, come now, Miss— Forno-Populo! you don't mean to tell me that you got yourself up like that for the sake of the ladies?" cried the young man.

"For whom, then?" said Bice, throwing up her head; but afterwards, with the instinct of a young actress, she remembered her rôle, which it was fun to carry out thoroughly. She laughed. "You are the most clever," she said. "I see you are one that women cannot deceive."

Montjoie laughed, too, with gratified vanity and superior knowledge. "You are about right there," he said. "I am not to be taken in, don't you know. It's no good trying it on with me. I see through ladies' little pretences. If there were no men you would not care what guys you were; and no more do we."

Bice made no reply. She turned upon him that dazzling smile of which she had learned the secret from the Contessa, which was unfathomable to the observer but quite simple to the simple-minded; and then she said: "Do you amuse yourself very much in the evening? I used to hear the voices and think how pleasant it would have been to be there."

"Not so pleasant as you think," said the young man. "The only fun was the Contessa's, don't you know. She's a fine woman for her age, but she's— Goodness! I forgot. She's your—"

"She is passée," said the girl calmly. "You make me afraid, Lord Montjoie. How much of a critic you are, and see through women, through and through." At this the noble Marquis laughed with true enjoyment of his own gifts.

"But you ain't offended?" he said. "There was no harm meant. Even a lady can't, don't you know, be always the same age."

"Don't you think so?" said Bice. "Oh, I think you are wrong. The Contessa is of no age. She is the age she pleases—she has all the secrets. I see nobody more beautiful."

"That may be," said Montjoie; "but you can't see everybody, don't you know. She's very handsome and all that—and when the real thing isn't there—but when it is, don't you know—"

"English is very perplexing," said Bice, shaking her head, but with a smile in her eyes which somewhat belied her air of simplicity. "What may that be—the real thing? Shall I find it in the dictionary?" she asked; and then their eyes met and there was another burst of laughter, somewhat boisterous on his part, but on hers with a ring of lightheartedness which quenched the malice. She was so young that she had a pleasure in playing her rôle, and did not feel any immorality involved.

While this conversation was going on, which was much observed and commented on by all the company, Jock from one end of the table and Mr. Derwentwater from the other, looked on with an eager observation and breathless desire to make out what was being said which gave an expression of anxiety to the features of MTutor, and one of almost ferocity to the lowering countenance of Jock. Both of these gentlemen were eagerly questioned by the ladies next them as to who this young lady might be.

"Terribly theatrical, don't you think, to come into a room like that?" said the mother of the girls in blue. "If my Minnie or Edith had been asked to do it they would have died of shame."

"I do not deny," said Mr. Derwentwater, "the advantage of conventional restraints. I like the little airs of seclusion, of retirement, that surround young ladies. But the—" he paused a little for a name, and then with that acquaintance with foreign ways on which Mr. Derwentwater prided himself, added, "the Signorina was at home."

"The Signorina! Is that what you call her—just like a person that is going on the stage. She will be the—niece, I suppose?"

Jock's next neighbour was the lady who was engaged in literature. She said to Jock: "I must get you to tell me her name. She is lovely. She will make a great sensation. I must make a few notes of her dress after dinner—would you call that yellow or white? Whoever dressed her knew what they were about. Mademoiselle, I imagine, one ought to call her. I know that's French, and she's Italian, but still— The new beauty! that's what she will be called. I am so glad to be the first to see her; but I must get you to tell me her name."

Among the gentlemen there was no other subject of conversation, and but one opinion. A little hum of curiosity ran round the table. It was far more exciting than tableaux, which was what some of the guests had expected to be arranged by the Contessa. Tableaux! nothing could have been equal to the effect of that dramatic entry and sudden revelation. "As for Montjoie, all was up with him, but the Contessa knew what she was about. She was not going to throw away her effects," they said. "There could be no doubt for whose benefit it all was." The Contessa graciously baffled with her charming smile all the questions that were poured upon her. She received the compliments addressed to her with gracious bows, but she gave no reply to any one. As she swept out of the room after dinner she tapped Montjoie lightly on the arm with her fan. "I will sing for you to-night," she said.

In the drawing-room the elements were a little heterogeneous without the gentlemen. The two girls in blue gazed at this wonderful new competitor with a curiosity which was almost alarm. They would have liked to make acquaintance, to draw her into their little party of youth outside the phalanx of the elders. But Bice took no more note of them than if they had been cabbages. She was in great excitement, all smiles and glory. "Do I please you like this?" she said, going up to Lucy, spreading out all her finery with the delight of a child. Lucy shrank a little. She had a troubled anxious look, which did not look like pleasure; but Lady Anastasia, who wrote for the newspapers, walked round and round the débutante and took notes frankly. "Of course I shall describe her dress. I never saw anything so lovely," the lady said. Bice, in the glow of her golden yellow, and of her smiles and delight, with the noble correspondent of the newspapers examining her, found the acutest interest in the position. The Contessa from her sofa smiled upon the scene, looking on with the air of a gratified exhibitor whose show had succeeded beyond her hopes. Lady Randolph, with an air of anxiety in her fair and simple countenance, stood behind, looking at Bice with protecting yet disturbed and troubled looks. The mother and daughters at the other side looked on, she all solid and speechless with disapproval, they in a flutter of interest and wonder and gentle envy and offence. More than a tableau; it was like an act out of a play. And when the gentlemen came in what a sudden quickening of the interest! Bice rose to the action like a heroine when the great scene has come, and the others all gathered round with a spectatorship that was almost breathless. The worst feature of the whole to those who were interested in Bice was her own evident enjoyment. She talked, she distributed her smiles right and left, she mimicked yet flattered Montjoie with a dazzling youthful assurance which confounded Mr. Derwentwater, and made Jock furious, and brought looks of pain not only to the face of Lucy but also to that of Sir Tom, who was less easily shocked. She was like a young actress in her first triumph, filling her rôle with a sort of enthusiasm, enjoying it with all her heart. And when the Contessa rose to sing, Bice followed her to the piano with an air as different as possible from the swift, noiseless self-effacement of her performance on previous occasions. She looked round upon the company with a sort of malicious triumph, a laugh on her lips as of some delightful mystification, some surprise of which she was in the secret. "Come and listen," she said to Jock, lightly touching him on the shoulder as she passed him. The Contessa's singing was already known. It was considered by some with a certain contempt, by others with admiration, as almost as good as professional. But when instead of one of her usual performances there arose in splendid fulness the harmony of two voices, that of Bice suddenly breaking forth in all the freshness of youth, unexpected, unprepared for, the climax of wonder and enthusiasm was reached. Lady Anastasia, after the first start and thrill of wonder, rushed to the usual writing-table and dashed off a hurried note, which she fastened to her fan in her excitement. "Everybody must know of this!" she cried. One of the young ladies in the background wept with admiration, crying, "Mamma, she is heavenly," while even the virtuous mother was moved. "They must intend her for the stage," that lady said, wondering, withdrawing from her rôle of disapproval. As for the gentlemen, those of them who were not speechless with enthusiasm were almost noisy in their excitement. Montjoie pressed into the first rank, almost touching Bice's dress, which she drew away between two bars, turning half round with a slight shake of her head and a smile in her eyes, even while the loveliest notes were flowing forth from her melodious throat. The listeners could hear the noble lord's "by Jove," in the midst of the music, and even detect the slight quaver of laughter which followed in Bice's wonderful voice.

The commotion of applause, enthusiasm, and wonder afterwards was indescribable. The gentlemen crowded round the singers—even the parliamentary gentlemen had lost their self-control, while the young lady who had wept forgot her timidity to make an eager approach to the débutante.

"It was heavenly: it was a rapture: oh, sing again!" cried Miss Edith, which was much prettier than Lord Montjoie's broken exclamations, "Oh, by Jove! don't you know," to which Bice was listening with delighted mockery.

Bice had been trained to pay very little attention to the opinions of other girls, but she gave the young lady in blue a friendly look, and launched over her shoulder an appeal to Jock. "Didn't you like it, you?" she cried, with a slight clap together of her hands to call his attention.

Jock glared at her over Miss Edith's shoulder. "I don't understand music," he said, in his most surly voice. These were the distinct utterances which enchanted Bice amid the murmurs of more ordinary applause. She was delighted with them. She clapped her hands once more with a delight which was contagious. "Ah, I know now, this is what it is to have succès," she cried.

"Now," said the Contessa, "it is the turn of Lord Montjoie, who is a dab—that is the word—at singing, and who promised me three for one."

At this there rose a hubbub of laughter, in the midst of which, though with many protestations and remonstrances, "don't you know," that young nobleman was driven to the fulfilment of his promise. In the midst of this commotion, a sign as swift as lightning, but, unlike lightning, imperceptible, a lifting of the eyebrows, a movement of a finger, was given and noted. In such a musical assembly the performance of a young marquis, with nobody knows how many thousands a year and entirely his own master, is rarely without interest. Mr. Derwentwater turned his back with marked indifference, and Jock with a sort of snort went away altogether. But of the others, the majority, though some with laughter and some with sneers, were civil, and listened to the performance. Jock marched off with a disdain beyond expression; but he had scarcely issued forth into the hall before he heard a rustle behind him, and, looking back, to his amazement saw Bice in all the glory of her golden robes.

"Hush!" she cried, smothering a laugh, and with a quick gesture of repression, "don't say anything. It must not be discovered that I have run away!"

"Why have you run away? I thought you thought no end of that little scug," cried savage Jock.

Bice turned upon him that smile that said everything and nothing, and then flew like a bird upstairs.

## CHAPTER XXXVI

### THE EVENING AFTER

The outcry that rose when, after Montjoie's comic song, a performance of the broadest and silliest description, was over, it was discovered that Bice had disappeared, and especially the blank look of the performer himself when turning round from the piano he surveyed the company in vain for her, gratified the Contessa beyond measure. She smiled radiantly upon the assembly in answer to all their indignant questions. "It has been for once an indulgence," she said; "but little girls must keep early hours." Montjoie was wounded and disappointed beyond measure that it should have been at the moment of his performance that she was spirited away. His reproaches were vehement, and there was something of the pettishness of a boy in their indignant tones. "I shouldn't have sung a note if I'd thought what was going on," he cried. "Contessa, I would not have believed you could have been so mean—and I singing only to please you."

"But think how you have pleased me—and all these ladies!" cried the Contessa. "Does not that recompense you?" Montjoie guessed that she was laughing at him, but he did not, in fact, see anything to laugh about. It was natural enough that the other ladies should be pleased; still he did not care whether they were pleased or not, and he did care much that the object of his admiration had not waited to hear him. The Contessa found the greatest amusement in his boyish sulk and resentment, and the rest of the evening was passed in baffling the questions with which, now that Bice was gone, her friends overpowered her. She gave the smallest possible dole of reply to their interrogations, but smiled upon the questioners with sunshiny smiles. "You must come and see me in town," she said to Montjoie. It was the only satisfaction she would give him. And she perceived at a much earlier hour than usual that Lucy was waiting for her to go to bed. She gave a little cry of distress when this seemed to flash upon her.

"Sweet Lucy! it is for me you wait!" she cried. "How could I keep you so late, my dear one?"

Montjoie was the foremost of those who attended her to the door, and got her candle for her, that indispensable but unnecessary formula.

"Of course I shall look you up in town; but we'll talk of that to-morrow. I don't go till three—to-morrow," the young fellow said.

The Contessa gave him her hand with a smile, but without a word, in that inimitable way she had, leaving Montjoie a prey to such uncertainty as poisoned his night's rest. He was not humble-minded, and he knew that he was a prize which no lady he had met with as yet had disregarded; but for the first time his bosom was torn by disquietude. Of course he must see her to-morrow. Should he see her to-morrow? The Contessa's smile, so radiant, so inexplainable, tormented him with a thousand doubts.

Lucy had looked on at all this with an uneasiness indescribable. She felt like an accomplice, watching this course of intrigue, of which she indeed disapproved entirely, but could not clear herself from a certain guilty knowledge of. That it should all be going on under her roof was terrible to her, though it was not for Montjoie but for Bice that her anxieties were awakened. She followed the Contessa upstairs, bearing her candle as if they formed part of a procession, with a countenance absolutely opposed in expression to the smiles of Madame di Forno-Populo. When they reached the Contessa's door, Lucy, by a sudden impulse, followed her in. It was not the first time that she had been allowed to cross the threshold of that little enchanted world which had filled her with wonder on her first entrance, but which by this time she regarded with composure, no longer bewildered to find it in her own house. Bice sprang up from a sofa on which she was lying on their entrance. She had taken off her beautiful dress, and her hair was streaming over her shoulders, her countenance radiant with delight. She threw herself upon the Contessa, without perceiving the presence of Lady Randolph.

"But it is enchanting; it is ravishing. I have never been so happy," she cried.

"My child," said the Contessa, "here is our dear lady who is of a different opinion."

"Of what opinion?" Bice cried. She was startled by the sudden appearance, when she had no thought of such an apparition, of Lucy's face so grave and uneasy. It gave a contradiction which was painful to the girl's excitement and delight.

"Indeed, I did not mean to find fault," said Lucy. "I was only sorry—" and here she paused, feeling herself incapable of expressing her real meaning, and convicted of interference and unnecessary severity by the girl's astonished eyes.

"My dear one," said the Contessa, "it is only that we look from two different points of view. You will not object to little Bice that she finds society intoxicating when she first goes into it. The child has made what you call a sensation. She has had her little succès. That is nothing to object to. An English girl is perhaps more reticent. She is brought up to believe that she does not care for succès. But Bice is otherwise. She has been trained for that, and to please makes her happy."

"To please—whom?" cried Lady Randolph. "Oh, don't think I am finding fault. We are brought up to please our parents and people who—care for us—in England."

Here Bice and the Contessa mutually looked at each other, and the girl laughed, putting her hands together. "She is pleased most of all," she cried; "she is all my parents. I please her first of all."

"What you say is sweet," said the Contessa, smiling upon Lucy; "and she is right too. She pleases me most of all. To see her have her little triumph, looking really her very best, and her dress so successful, is to me a delight. I am nearly as much excited as the child herself!"

Lucy looked from one to another, and felt that it was impossible for her to say what she wished to say. The girl's pleasure seemed so innocent, and that of her protectress and guardian so generous, so tender. All that had offended Lucy's instincts, the dramatic effort of the Contessa, the careful preparation of all the effects, the singling out of young Montjoie as the object, all seemed to melt away in the girlish delight of Bice, and the sympathetic triumph of her guardian. She did not know what to say to them. It was she who was the culprit, putting thoughts of harm which had not found any entrance there into the girl's mind. She flushed with shame and an uneasy sense that the tables were thus turned upon her; and yet how could she depart without some warning? It was not only her own troubled uncomfortable feeling; but had she not read the same, still more serious and decided, in her husband's eyes?

"I don't know what to say," said Lucy. "But Sir Tom thinks so too. He will tell you better, he knows better. Lord Montjoie is—I do not know why he was asked. I did not wish it. He is—dear Madame di Forno-Populo, you have seen so much more than I—he is vulgar—a little. And Bice is so young; she may be deceived."

For a moment a cloud, more dark than had ever been seen there before, overshadowed the Contessa's face. But Bice burst forth into a peal of laughter, clapping her hands. "Is that vulgar?" the girl cried. "I am glad. Now I know how he is different. It is what you call fun, don't you know?" she cried with sudden mimicry, at which Lucy herself could not refuse to laugh.

"I waited outside to hear a little of the song. It was so wonderful that I could not laugh; and to utter all that before you, Madama, after he had heard you—oh, what courage! what braveness!" cried Bice. "I did not think any one could be so brave!"

"You mean so simple, dear child," said the Contessa, whose brow had cleared; "that is really what is so wonderful in these English men. They are so simple, they never see how it is different. It is brave if you please, but still more simple-minded. Little Montjoie is so. He knows no better; not to me only, but even to you, Bice, with that voice of yours, so pure, so fresh, he listens, then performs as you heard. It is wonderful, as you say. But you have not told me, Lucy, my sweetest, what you think of the little one's voice."

"I think," said Lucy, with that disapproval which she could not altogether restrain, "that it is very wonderful, when it is so fine, that we never heard it before—"

"Ah, Bice," cried the Contessa, "our dear lady is determined that she will not be pleased to-night. We had prepared a little surprise, and it is a failure. She will not understand that we love to please. She will have us to be superior, as if we were English."

"Indeed, indeed," cried Lucy, full of compunction, "I know you are always kind. And I know your ways are different—but—" with a sort of regretful reflectiveness, shaking her head.

"All England is in that but," said the Contessa. "It is what has always been said to me. In our country we love to arrange these little effects, to have surprises, impromptus, events that are unexpected. Bice, go, my child, go to bed, after this excitement you must rest. You did well, and pleased me at least. My sweet Lucy," she said, when the girl with instant obedience had disappeared into the next room, "I know how you see it all from your point of view. But we are not as you, rich, secure. We must make while we can our coup. To succeed by one coup, that is my desire. And you will not interfere?"

"Oh, Contessa," cried Lucy, "will you not spare the child? It is like selling her. She is too good for such a man. He is scarcely a man; he is a boy. I am ashamed to think that you should care to please—him, or any one like him. Oh, let it come naturally! Do not plan like this, and scheme and take trouble for—"

"For an establishment that will make her at once safe and sure; that will give her so many of the things that people care for—beautiful houses, a good name, money— I have schemed, as you say, for little things much of my life," said the Contessa, shaking her head with a mournful smile; "I have told you my history: for very, very little things—for a box at the opera, for a carriage, things which are nothing, sweetest Lucy. You have plenty; such things are nothing to you. You cannot understand it. But that is me, my dear one. I have not a higher mind like you; and shall I not scheme," cried the Contessa, with sudden energy, "for the child, to make her safe that she may never require scheming? Ah, my Lucy! I have the heart of a mother to her, and you know what a mother will do."

Lucy was silent, partly touched, partly resisting. If it ever could be right to do evil that good might come, perhaps this motive might justify it. And then came the question how much, in the Contessa's code, was evil, of these proceedings? She was silenced, if not satisfied. There is a certain casuistry involved in the most Christian charity: "thinketh no evil," sometimes even implies an effort to think that there is no harm in evil according to the intention in it. Lucy's intellect was confused, though not that unobtrusive faculty of judgment in her which was infallible, yet could be kept dumb.

"My love," said the Contessa, suddenly kissing her as a sort of dismissal, "think that you are rich and we poor. If Bice had a provision, if she had even as much as you give away to your poor friends and never think of again, how different would all things be for her! But she has nothing; and therefore I prepare my little tableaux, and study all the effects I can think of, and produce her as in a theatre, and shut her up to agacer the audience, and keep her silent and make her sing, all for effect; yes, all for effect. But what can I do? She has not a penny, not a penny, not even like your poor friends."

The sudden energy with which this was said was indescribable. The Contessa's countenance, usually so ivory-pale, shone with a sort of reflection as if of light within, her eyes blazed, her smile gave place to a seriousness which was almost indignation. She looked like a heroine maintaining her right to do all that human strength could do for the forlorn and oppressed; and there was, in fact, a certain abandon of feeling in her which made her half unconsciously open the door, and do what was tantamount to turning her visitor out, though her visitor was mistress of the house. Her feelings had, indeed, for the moment, got the better of the Contessa. She had worked herself up to the point of indignation, that Lucy who could, if she would, deliver Bice from all the snares of poverty, had not done so, and was not, so far as appeared, intending to do so. To find fault with the devices of the poor, and yet not to help them—is not that one of the things least easily supportable of all the spurns of patient merit? The Contessa was doing what she could, all she could in her own fashion, strenuously, anxiously. But Lucy was doing nothing, though she could have done it so easily: and yet she found fault and criticised. Madame di Forno-Populo was swept by a great flood of instinctive resentment. She put her hostess to the door in the strength of it, tenderly with a kiss but not less hotly, and with full meaning. Such impulses had stood her instead of virtue on other occasions; she felt a certain virtue as of superior generosity and self-sacrifice in her proceedings now.

As for Lucy, still much confused and scarcely recognising the full meaning of the Contessa's warmth, she made her way to her own room in a haze of disturbed and uneasy feeling. Somehow—she could not tell how—she felt herself in the wrong. What was it she had done? What was it she had left undone? To further the scheme by which young Montjoie was to be caught and trapped and made the means of fortune and endowment to Bice was not possible. In such cases it is usually of the possible victim, the man against whom such plots are formed, that the bystander thinks; but Lucy thought of young Montjoie only with an instinctive dislike, which would have been contempt in a less calm and tolerant mind. That Bice, with all her gifts, a creature so full of life and sweetness and strength, should be handed over to this trifling commonplace lad, was in itself terrible to think of. Lucy did not think of the girl's beauty, or of that newly-developed gift of song which had taken her by surprise, but only and simply of herself, the warm-hearted and smiling girl, the creature full of fun and frolic whom she had learned to be fond of, first, for the sake of little Tom, and then for her own. Little Tom's friend, his playmate, who had found him out in his infant weakness and made his life so much brighter! And then Lucy asked herself what the Contessa could mean, what it was that made her own interference a sort of impertinence, why her protests had been received with so little of the usual caressing deference? Thoughts go fast, and Lucy had not yet reached the door of her own room, when it flashed upon her what it was. She put down her candle on a table in the corridor, and stood still to realise it. This gallery at the head of the great staircase was dimly lighted, and the hall below threw up a glimmer, reflected in the oaken balusters and doors of the closed rooms, and dying away in the half-lit gloom above. There were sounds below far off that betrayed the assembly still undispersed in the smoking-room, and some fainter still, above, of the ladies who had retired to their rooms, but were still discussing the strange events of the evening. In the centre of this partial darkness stood Lucy, with her candle, the only visible representative of all the hidden life around, suddenly pausing, asking herself—

Was this what it meant? Undoubtedly, this was what it meant. She had the power, and she had not used it. With a word she could make all their schemes unnecessary, and relieve the burden on the soul of the woman who had the heart of a mother for Bice. Tears sprang up into Lucy's eyes unawares as this recollection suddenly seized her. The Contessa was not perfect—there were many things in her which Lady Randolph could with difficulty excuse to herself: but she had the heart of a mother for Bice. Oh, yes, it was true, quite true. The heart of a mother! and how was it possible that another mother could look on at this and not sympathise; and how was it that the idea had never occurred to her before—that she had never thought how changed in a moment might be Bice's position, if only— Here she picked up her candle again, and went away hastily to her room. She said to herself that she was keeping Fletcher up, and that this was unkind. But, as a matter of fact, she was not thinking about Fletcher. There had sprung up in her soul a fear which was twofold and contradictory. If one of those alarms was justified, then the other would be fallacious; and yet the existence of the one doubled the force of the other. One of these elements of fear—the contradiction, the new terror—was wholly unthought of, and had never troubled her peace before. She thought—and this was her old burden, the anxiety which had already restrained her action and made her forego what she had never failed to feel as her duty, the carrying out of her father's will—of her husband's objection, of his opposition, of the terrible interview she had once had with him, when she had refused to acquiesce in his command. And then, with a sort of stealthy horror, she thought of his departure from that opposition, and asked herself, would he, for Bice's sake, consent to that which he had so much objected to in other cases? This it was that made her shrink from herself and her own thoughts, and hurry into her room for the solace of Fletcher's companionship, and to put off as long as she could the discussion of the question. Would Sir Tom agree to everything? Would he make no objections—for Bice's sake?

## CHAPTER XXXVII

## THE CONTESSA'S TACTICS

That morning the whole party came down to breakfast expectant, for, notwithstanding the Contessa's habit of not appearing, it was supposed that the young lady whom most people supposed to have arrived very recently must be present at the morning meal. Young Montjoie, who was generally very late, appeared among the first; and there was a look of curiosity and anxiety in his face as he turned towards the door every time it was opened, which betrayed his motive. But this expectation was not destined to be repaid. Bice did not appear at breakfast. She did not even come downstairs, though the Contessa did, for luncheon. When Madame di Forno-Populo came in to this meal there was a general elevation of all heads and eager look towards her, to which she replied with her usual smile but no explanation of any kind; nor would she make any reply, even to direct questions. She did nothing but smile when Montjoie demanded to know if Miss Forno-Populo was not coming downstairs, if she had gone away, if she were ill, if she would appear before three o'clock—with which questions he assailed her in downright fashion. When the Contessa did not smile she put on a look of injured sweetness. "What!" she said, "Am I then so little thought of? You have no more pleasure, ficklest of young men, in seeing me?" "Oh, I assure you, Countess," he cried, "that's all right, don't you know; but a fellow may ask. And then it was your own doing to make us so excited."

"Yes, a fellow may ask," said the Contessa, smiling; but this was all the response she would give, nothing that could really throw the least light upon the subject of his curiosity. The other men of her following looked on with undisguised admiration at this skilled and accomplished woman. To see how she held in hand the youth whom they all considered as her victim was beautiful they thought; and bets even were going amongst them as to the certainty that she would land her big fish. Sir Tom, at the head of the table, did not regard the matter so lightly. There was a curve of annoyance in his forehead. He did not understand what game she was playing. It was, without doubt, a game of some sort, and its object was transparent enough; and Sir Tom could not easily forgive the dramatic efforts of the previous night, or endure the thought that his house was the scene of tactics so little creditable. He was vexed with the Contessa, with Bice, even with Lucy, who, he could not keep from saying to himself, should have found some means of baulking such an intention. He was somewhat mollified by the absence of Bice now, which seemed to him, perhaps, a tribute to his own evident disapproval; but still he was uneasy. It was not a fit thing to take place in his house. He saw far more clearly than he had done before that a stop should have been put ere now to the Contessa's operations, and in the light of last night's proceedings perceived his own errors in judgment—those errors which he had, indeed, been sensible of, yet condoned in himself with that wonderful charity which we show towards our own mistakes and follies. He ought not to have asked her to the Hall; he ought not to have permitted himself to be flattered and amused by her society, or to have encouraged her to remain, or to have been so weak as to ask the people she wished, which was the crowning error of all. He had invited Montjoie, a trifling boy in whom he felt little or no interest, to please her, without any definite idea as to what she meant, but only with an amused sense that she had designs on the lad which Montjoie was quite knowing enough to deliver himself from. But the turn things had taken displeased Sir Tom. It was too barefaced, he said to himself. He, too, felt like his more innocent wife, as if he were an accomplice in a social crime.

"I've been swindled, don't you know," Montjoie said; "I've been taken a mean advantage of. None of these other beggars are going away like me. They will get all the good of the music to-night, and I shall be far away. I could cry to think of it, I could, don't you know; but you don't care a bit, Countess."

The Contessa, as usual, smiled. "Enfant!" she said.

"I am not an infant. I am just the same age as everybody, old enough to look after myself, don't you know, and pay for myself, and all that sort of thing. Besides, I haven't got any parents and guardians. Is that why you take such a base advantage of me?" cried the young man.

"It is, perhaps, why—" The Contessa was not much in the way of answering questions; and when she had said this she broke off with a laugh. Was she going to say that this was why she had taken any trouble about him, with a frankness which it is sometimes part of the astutest policy to employ.

"Why what? why what? Oh, come, you must tell me now," the young man said.

"Why one takes so much interest in you," said the Contessa sweetly. "You shall come and see me, cher petit Marquis, in my little house that is to be, in Mayfair; for you have found me, n'est ce pas, a little house in Mayfair?" she said, turning to another of her train.

"Hung with rose-coloured curtains and pink glass in the windows, according to your orders, Contessa," said the gentleman appealed to.

"How good it is to have a friend! but those curtains will be terrible," said the Contessa, with a shiver, "if it were not that I carry with me a few little things in a great box."

"Oh, my dear Contessa, how many things you must have picked up!" cried Lady Anastasia. "That peep into your boudoir made me sick with envy; those Eastern embroideries, those Persian rugs! They have furnished me with a lovely paragraph for my paper, and it is such a delightful original idea to carry about one's pet furniture like one's dresses. It will become quite the fashion when it is known. And how I shall long to see that little house in Mayfair!"

The Contessa smiled upon Lady Anastasia as she smiled upon the male friends that surrounded her. Her paper and her paragraphs were not to be despised, and those little mysterious intimations about the new beauty which it delighted her to make. Madame di Forno-Populo turned to Montjoie afterwards with a little wave of the hand. "You are going?" she said; "how sad for us! we shall have no song to make us gay to-night. But come and you shall sing to us in Mayfair."

"Countess, you are only laughing at me. But I shall come, don't you know," said Montjoie, "whether you mean it or not."

The company, who were so much interested in this conversation, did not observe the preoccupied looks of the master and mistress of the house, although to some of the gentlemen the gravity of Sir Tom was apparent enough. And not much wonder that he should be grave. Even the men who were most easy in their own code looked with a certain severity and astonishment upon him who had opened his door to the adventuress-Contessa, of whom they all judged the worst, without even the charitable acknowledgment which her enemy the Dowager had made, that there was nothing in her past history bad enough to procure her absolute expulsion from society. The men who crowded round her when she appeared, who flattered and paid their court to her, and even took a little credit to themselves as intimates of the siren, were one and all of opinion that to bring her into his house was discreditable to Sir Tom. They were even a little less respectful to Lucy for not knowing or finding out the quality of her guest. If Tom Randolph was beginning to find out that he had been a fool it was wonderful he had not made the discovery sooner. For he had been a fool, and no mistake! To bring that woman to England, to keep her in his house, to associate her in men's minds with his wife—the worst of his present guests found it most difficult to forgive him. But they were all the more interested in the situation from the fact that Sir Tom was beginning to feel the effects of his folly. He said very little during that meal. He took no notice of the badinage going on between the Contessa and her train. When he spoke at all it was to that virtuous mother at his other hand, who was not at all amusing, and talked of nothing but Edith and Minnie, and her successful treatment of them through all the nursery troubles of their life.

Lucy, at the other end of the table, was scarcely more expansive. She had been relieved by the absence of Bice, which, in her innocence, she believed to be a concession to her own anxiety, feeling a certain gratitude to the Contessa for thus foregoing the chance of another interview with Montjoie. It could never have occurred to Lucy to suppose that this was policy on the Contessa's part, and that her refusal to satisfy Montjoie was in reality planned to strengthen her hold on him, and to increase the curiosity she pretended to baffle. Lucy had no such artificial idea in her mind. She accepted the girl's withdrawal as a tribute to her own powers of persuasion, and a proof that though the Contessa had been led astray by her foreign notions, she was yet ready to perceive and adopt the more excellent way. This touched Lucy's heart and made her feel that she was herself bound to reciprocate the generosity. They had done it without knowing anything about the intention in her mind, and it should be hers to carry out that intention liberally, generously, not like an unwilling giver. She cast many a glance at her husband while this was going through her mind. Would he object as before? or would he, because it was the Contessa who was to be benefited, make no objection? Lucy did not know which of the two it would be most painful to her to bear. She had read carefully the paragraph in her father's will about foreigners, and had found there was no distinct objection to foreigners, only a preference the other way. She knew indeed, but would not permit herself to think, that these were not persons who would have commended themselves to Mr. Trevor as objects of his bounty. Mr. Churchill, with his large family, was very different. But to endow two frivolous and expensive women with a portion of his fortune was a thing to which he never would have consented. With a certain shiver she recognised this; and then she made a rush past the objection and turned her back upon it. It was quite a common form of beneficence in old times to provide a dower for a girl that she might marry. What could there be wrong in providing a poor girl with something to live upon that she might not be forced into a mercenary marriage? While all the talk was going on at the other end of the table she was turning this over in her mind—the manner of it, the amount of it, all the details. She did not hear the talk, it was immaterial to her, she cared not for it. Now and then she gave an anxious look at Sir Tom at the other end. He was serious. He did not laugh as usual. What was he thinking of? Would his objections be forgotten because it was the Contessa or would he oppose her and struggle against her? Her heart beat at the thought of the conflict which might be before her; or perhaps if there was no conflict, if he were too willing, might not that be the worst of all!

Thus the background against which the Contessa wove her web of smiles and humorous schemes was both dark and serious. There were many shadows behind that frivolous central light. Herself the chief actor, the plotter, she to whom only it could be a matter of personal advantage, was perhaps the least serious of all the agents in it. The others thought of possibilities dark enough, of perhaps the destruction of family peace in this house which had been so hospitable to her, which had received her when no other house would; and some, of the success of a plan which did not deserve to succeed, and some of the danger of a youth to whom at present all the world was bright. All these things seemed to be involved in the present crisis. What more likely than that Lucy, at last enlightened, should turn upon her husband, who no doubt had forced this uncongenial companion upon her, should turn from Sir Tom altogether, and put her trust in him no longer! And the men who most admired the Contessa were those who looked with the greatest horror upon a marriage made by her, and called young Montjoie poor little beggar and poor devil, wondering much whether he ought not to be "spoken to." The men were not sorry for Bice, nor thought of her at all in the matter, save to conclude her a true pupil of the guardian whom most of them believed to be her mother. But in this point where the others were wanting Lucy came in, whose simple heart bled for the girl about to be sacrificed to a man whom she could not love. Thus tragical surmises floated in the air about Madame di Forno-Populo, that arch plotter whose heart was throbbing indeed with her success, and the hope of successes to come, but who had no tragical alarms in her breast. She was perfectly easy in her mind about Sir Tom and Lucy. Even if a matrimonial quarrel should be the result, what was that to an experienced woman of the world, who knew that such things are only for the minute? and neither Bice nor Montjoie caused her any alarm. Bice was perfectly pleased with the little Marquis. He amused her. She had not the slightest objection to him; and as for Montjoie, he was perfectly well able to take care of himself. So that while everybody else was more or less anxious, the Contessa in the centre of all her webs was perfectly tranquil. She was not aware that she wished harm to any man, or woman either. Her light heart and easy conscience carried her quite triumphantly through all.

When Montjoie had gone away, carrying in his pocket-book the address of the little house in Mayfair, and when the party had dispersed to walk or ride or drive, as each thought fit, Lucy, who was doing neither, met her husband coming out of his den. Sir Tom was full of a remorseful sense that he had wronged Lucy. He took her by both hands, and drew her into his room. It was a long time since he had met her with the same effusion. "You are looking very serious," he said, "you are vexed, and I don't wonder; but I see land, Lucy. It will be over directly—only a week more—"

"I thought you were looking serious, Tom," she said.

"So I was, my love. All that business last night was more than I could stand. You may think me callous enough, but I could not stand that."

"Tom!" said Lucy, faltering. It seemed an opportunity she could not let slip—but how she trembled between her two terrors! "There is something that I want to say to you."

"Say whatever you like, Lucy," he cried; "but for God's sake don't tremble, my little woman, when you speak to me. I've done nothing to deserve that."

"I am not trembling," said Lucy, with the most innocent and transparent of falsehoods. "But oh, Tom, I am so sorry, so unhappy."

"For what?" he said. He did not know what accusation she might be going to bring against him; and how could he defend himself? Whatever she might say he was sure to be half guilty; and if she thought him wholly guilty, how could he prevent it? A hot colour came up upon his middle-aged face. To have to blush when you are past the age of blushing is a more terrible necessity than the young can conceive.

"Oh, Tom!" cried Lucy again, "for Bice! Can we stand by and let her be sacrificed? She is not much more than a child; and she is always so good to little Tom."

"For Bice!" he cried. In the relief of his mind he was ready to have done anything for Bice. He laughed with a somewhat nervous tremulous outburst. "Why, what is the matter with her?" he said. "She did her part last night with assurance enough. She is young indeed, but she ought to have known better than that."

"She is very young, and it is the way she has been brought up—how should she know any better? But, Tom, if she had any fortune she would not be compelled to marry. How can we stand by and see her sacrificed to that odious young man?"

"What odious young man?" said Sir Tom, astonished, and then with another burst of his old laughter such as had not been heard for weeks, he cried out: "Montjoie! Why, Lucy, are you crazy? Half the girls in England are in competition for him. Sacrificed to—! She will be in the greatest luck if she ever has such a chance."

Lucy gave him a reproachful look.

"How can you say so? A little vulgar boy—a creature not worthy to—"

"My dear, you are prejudiced. You are taking Jock's view. That worthy's opinion of a fellow who never rose above Lower Fourth is to be received with reservation. A fellow may be a scug, and yet not a bad fellow—that is what Jock has yet to learn."

"Oh, Tom, I cannot laugh," said Lucy. "What can she do, the Contessa says? She must marry the first that offers, and in the meantime she attracts notice like that. It is dreadful to think of it. I think that some one—that we—I—ought to interfere."

"My innocent Lucy," said Sir Tom, "how can you interfere? You know nothing about the tactics of such people. I am very penitent for my share in the matter. I ought not to have brought so much upon you."

"Oh, Tom," cried Lucy again, drawing closer to him, eager to anticipate with her pardon any blame to which he might be liable. And then she added, returning to her own subject: "She is of English parentage—on one side."

Why this fact, so simply stated, should have startled her husband so much, Lucy could not imagine. He almost gasped as he met her eyes, as if he had received or feared a sudden blow, and underneath the brownness of his complexion grew suddenly pale, all the ruddy colour forsaking his face. "Of English parentage!" he said, faltering, "do you mean?—what do you mean? Why—do you tell this to me?"

Lucy was surprised, but saw no significance in his agitation. And her mind was full of her own purpose. "Because of the will which is against foreigners," she said simply. "But in that case she would not be a foreigner, Tom. I think a great deal of this. I want to do it. Oh, don't oppose me! It makes it so much harder when you go against me."

He gazed at her with a sort of awe. He did not seem able to speak. What she had said, though she was unconscious of any special meaning in it, seemed to have acted upon him like a spell. There was something tragic in his look which frightened Lucy. She came closer still and put her hand upon his arm.

"Oh, it is not to trouble you, Tom; it is not that I want to go against you! But give me your consent this once. Baby is so fond of her, and she is so good to him. I want to give something to Bice. Let me make a provision for her?" she said, pleading. "Do not take all the pleasure out of it and oppose me. Oh, dear Tom, give me your free consent!" Lucy cried.

He kept gazing at her with that look of awe. "Oppose you!" he said. What was the shock he had received which made him so unlike himself? His very lips quivered as he spoke. "God forgive me; what have I been doing?" he cried. "Lucy, I think I will never oppose you more."


## CHAPTER XXXVIII

## DISCOVERIES

This interview had an agitating and painful effect upon Lucy, though she could not tell why. It was not what she expected or feared—neither in one sense nor the other. He had neither distressed her by opposing her proceedings, nor accepted her beneficence towards the Contessa with levity and satisfaction, both of which dangers she had been prepared for. Instead, however, of agitating her by the reception he gave to her proposal, it was he who was agitated by something which in entire unconsciousness she had said. But what that could be Lucy could not divine. She had said nothing that could affect him personally so far as she knew. She went over every word of the conversation without being able to discover what could have had this effect. But she could find nothing, there was no clue anywhere that her unconscious mind could discover. She concluded finally with much compunction that it was the implied reproach that he had taken away all pleasure in what she did by opposing her, that had so disturbed her husband. He was so kind. He had not been able to bear even the possibility that his opposition had been a source of pain. "I think I will never oppose you any more." In an answering burst of generosity Lucy said to herself that she did not desire this; that she preferred that he should find fault and object when he disapproved, not consent to everything. But the reflection of the disturbance she had seen in her husband's countenance was in her mind all day; she could not shake it off; and he was so grave that every look she cast at him strengthened the impression. He did not approach the circle in which the Contessa sat all the evening, but stood apart, silent, taking little notice of anybody until Mr. Derwentwater secured his ear, when Sir Tom, instead of his usual genial laugh at MTutor's solemnities, discharged little caustic criticisms which astonished his companion. Mr. Derwentwater was going away next day, and he, too, was preoccupied. After that conversation with Sir Tom, he betook himself to Lucy, who was very silent too, and doing little for the entertainment of her guests. He made her sundry pretty speeches, such as are appropriate from a departing guest.

"Jock has made up his mind to stay behind," he said. "I am sorry, but I am not surprised. I shall lose a most agreeable travelling companion; but, perhaps, home influences are best for the young."

"I don't know why Jock has changed his mind, Mr. Derwentwater. He wanted very much to go."

"He would say that here's metal more attractive," said the tutor with an offended smile; and then he paused, and, clearing his throat, asked in a still more evident tone of offence—"Does not your young friend the Signorina appear again? I thought from her appearance last night that she was making her début."

"Yes, it was like it," said Lucy. "The Contessa is not like one of us," she added after a moment. "She has her own ways—and, perhaps, I don't know—that may be the Italian fashion."

"Not at all," Mr. Derwentwater said promptly. He was an authority upon national usages. "But I am afraid it was very transparent what the Contessa meant," he said, after a pause.

To this Lucy made no reply, and the tutor, who was sensitive, especially as to bad taste, reddened at his inappropriate observation. He went on hastily; "The Signorina—or should I say Mademoiselle di Forno-Populo?—has a great deal of charm. I do not know if she is so beautiful as her mother—"

"Oh, not her mother," cried Lucy quickly, with a smile at the mistake.

"Is she not her mother? The young lady's face indeed is different. It is of a higher order—it is full of thought. It is noble in repose. She does not seem made for these scenes of festivity, if you will pardon me, Lady Randolph, but for the higher retirements—"

"Oh, she is very fond of seeing people," said Lucy. "You must not suppose she is too serious for her age. She enjoyed herself last night."

"There is no age," said Mr. Derwentwater, "at which one can be too serious—and especially in youth, when all the world is before one, when one cannot tell what effect a careless step may have one way or another. It is just that sweet gravity that charms me. I think she was quite out of her element, excuse me for saying so, Lady Randolph, last night."

"Do you think so? Oh, I am afraid not. I am afraid she liked it," said Lucy. "Jock, don't you think Bice liked it. I should much rather think not, but I am afraid—I am afraid—"

"She couldn't like that little cad," said Jock, who had drawn near with an instinctive sense that something was going on which concerned him. "But she's never solemn either," added the boy.

"Is that for me, Jock?" said MTutor, with a pensive gentleness of reproach. "Well, never mind. We must all put up with little misunderstandings from the younger generation. Some time or other you will judge differently. I should like to have had an opportunity again of such music as we heard last night; but I suppose I must not hope for it."

"Oh, do you mean Lord Montjoie's song?" cried one of the young ladies in blue, who had drawn near. "Wasn't it fun? Of course I know it wasn't to be compared to the Contessa; but I've no musical taste. I always confess it—that's Edith's line. But Lord Montjoie was fun. Don't you think so, dear Lady Randolph," Miss Minnie said.

Mr. Derwentwater gave her one glance, and retired, Jock following. "Perhaps that's your opinion too," he said, "that Lord Montjoie's was fun?"

"He's a scug," said Jock, laconically, "that's all I think about him."

Mr. Derwentwater took the lad's arm. "And yet," he said, "Jock, though you and I consider ourselves his superiors, that is the fellow that will carry off the prize. Beauty and genius are for him. He must have the best that humanity can produce. You ought to be too young to have any feeling on the subject; but it is a humiliating thought."

"Bice will have nothing to say to him," said Jock, with straightforward application of the abstract description; but MTutor shook his head.

"How can we tell the persecutions to which Woman is subject?" he said. "You and I, Jock, are in a very different position. But we should try to realise, though it is difficult, those dangers to which she is subject. Kept indoors," said MTutor, with pathos in his voice, "debarred from all knowledge of the world, with all the authorities about her leading one way. How can we tell what is said to her? with a host of petty maxims preaching down a daughter's heart—strange!" cried Mr. Derwentwater, with a closer pressure of the boy's arm, "that the most lovely existence should thus continually be led to link itself with the basest. We must not blame Woman; we must keep her idea sacred, whatever happens in our own experience."

"It always sets one right to talk to you," cried Jock, full of emotion. "I was a beast to say that."

"My boy, don't you think I understand the disturbance in your mind?" with a sigh, MTutor said.

They had left the drawing-room during the course of this conversation, and were crossing the hall on the way to the library, when some one suddenly drew back with a startled movement from the passage which led to Sir Tom's den. Then there followed a laugh, and "Oh, is it only you!" after which there came forth a slim shadow, as unlike as possible to the siren of the previous night. "We have met before, and I don't mind. Is there any one else coming?" Bice said.

"Why do you hide and skulk in corners?" cried Jock. "Why shouldn't you meet any one? Have you done something wrong?"

This made Bice laugh still more. "You don't understand," she said.

"Signorina," said Mr. Derwentwater (who was somewhat proud of having remembered this good abstract title to give to the mysterious girl), "I am going away to-morrow, and perhaps I shall never hear you again. Your voice seemed to open the heavenly gates. Why, since you are so good as to consider us different from the others, won't you sing to us once more?"

"Sing?" said Bice, with a little surprise; "but by myself my voice is not much—"

"It is like a voice out of heaven," Mr. Derwentwater said fervently.

"Do you really, really think so?" she said with a wondering look. She was surprised, but pleased too. "I don't think you would care for it without the Contessa's; but, perhaps—" Then she looked round her with a reflective look. "What can I do? There is no piano, and then these people would hear." After this a sudden idea struck her. She laughed aloud like a child with sudden glee. "I don't suppose it would be any harm! You belong to the house—and then there is Marietta. Yes! Come!" she cried suddenly, rushing up the great staircase and waving her hand impatiently, beckoning them to follow. "Come quick, quick," she cried; "I hear some one coming," and flew upstairs. They followed her, Mr. Derwentwater passing Jock, who hung back a little, and did not know what to think of this adventure. "Come quick," she cried, darting along the dimly-lighted corridor with a laugh that rang lightly along like the music to which her steps were set. "Oh, come in, come in. They will hear, but they will not know where it comes from." The young men stupefied, hesitating, followed her. They found themselves among all the curiosities and luxuries of the Contessa's boudoir. And in a moment Bice had placed herself at the little piano which was placed across one of the corners, its back covered with a wonderful piece of Eastern embroidery which would have invited Derwentwater's attention had he been able to fix that upon anything but Bice. As it was, he gave a half regard to these treasures. He would have examined them all with the devotion of a connoisseur but for her presence, which exercised a spell still more subtle than that of art.

The sound of the singing penetrated vaguely even into the drawing-room, where the Contessa, startled, rose from her seat much earlier than usual. Lucy, who attended her dutifully upstairs according to her usual custom, was dismayed beyond measure by seeing Jock and his tutor issue from that door. Bice came with them, with an air of excitement and triumphant satisfaction. She had been singing, and the inspiration and applause had gone to her head. She met the ladies not with the air of a culprit, but in all the boldness of innocence. "They like to hear me, even by myself," she cried; "they have listened, as if I had been an angel." And she clapped her hands with almost childish pleasure.

"Perhaps they think you are," said the Contessa, who shook her head, yet smiled with sympathy. "You must not say to these messieurs below that you have been in my room. Oh, I know the confidences of a smoking-room! You must not brag, mes amis. For Bice does not understand the convenances, nor remember that this is England, where people meet only in the drawing-room."

"Divine forgetfulness!" murmured Derwentwater. Jock, for his part, turned his back with a certain sense of shame. He had liked it, but he had not thought it right. The room altogether, with its draperies and mysteries, had conveyed to him a certain intoxication as of wrong-doing. Something that was dangerous was in the air of it. It was seductive, it was fascinating; he had felt like a man banished when Bice had started from the piano and bidden them "Go away; go away!" in the same laughing tone in which she had bidden them come. But the moment he was outside the threshold his impulse was to escape—to rush out of sight—and obliterate even from his own mind the sense that he had been there. To meet the Contessa, and still more his sister, full in the face, was a shock to all his susceptibilities. He turned his back upon them, and but that his fellow-culprit made a momentary stand, would have fled away. Lucy partook of Jock's feeling. It wounded her to see him at that door. She gave him a glance of mingled reproach and pity; a vague sense that these were siren-women dangerous to all mankind stole into her heart.

But Lucy was destined to a still greater shock. The party from the smoking-room was late in breaking up. The sound of their steps and voices as they came upstairs roused Lady Randolph, not from sleep—for she had been unable to sleep—but from the confused maze of recollections and efforts to think which distracted her placid soul. She was not made for these agitations. The constitution of her mind was overset altogether. The moment that suspicion and distrust came in there was no further strength in her. She was lying not thinking so much as remembering stray words and looks which drifted across her memory as across a dim mirror, with a meaning in them which she did not grasp. She was not clever. She could not put this and that together with the dolorous skill which some women possess. It is a skill which does not promote the happiness of the possessor, but perhaps it is scarcely more happy to stand in the midst of a vague mass of suggestions without being able to make out what they mean, which was Lucy's case. She did not understand her husband's sudden excitement; what it had to do with Bice, with the Contessa, with her own resolution and plans she could not tell, but felt vaguely that many things deeply concerning her were in the air, and was unhappy in the confusion of her thoughts. For a long time after the sounds of various persons coming upstairs had died away, Lucy lay silent waiting for her husband's appearance—but at last unable to bear the vague wretchedness of her thoughts any longer, got up and put on a dressing-gown and stole out into the dark gallery to go to the nursery to look at her boy asleep, which was her best anodyne. The lights were all extinguished except the faint ray that came from the nursery door, and Lucy went softly towards that, anxious to disturb little Tom by no sound. As she did so a door suddenly opened, sending a glare of light into the dark corridor. It was the door of the Contessa's room, and with the light came Sir Tom, the Contessa herself appearing after him on the threshold. She was still in her dinner dress, and her appearance remained long impressed upon Lucy's imagination like a photograph without colour, in shadow and light. She gave Sir Tom a little packet apparently of letters, and then she held out both hands to him, which he took in his. Something seemed to flash through Lucy's heart like a knife, quivering like the "pale death" of the poet, in sight and sense. The sudden surprise and pang of it was such for a moment that she seemed turned into stone, and stood gazing like a spectre in her white flowing dress, her face more white, her eyes and mouth open in the misery and trouble of the moment. Then she stole back softly into her room—her head throbbing, her heart beating—and buried her face in her pillow and closed her eyes. Even baby could not soothe her in this unlooked-for pang. And then she heard his step come slowly along the gallery. How was she to look at him? how listen to him in the shock of such an extraordinary discovery? She took refuge in a semblance of sleep.

CHAPTER XXXIX

LUCY'S DISCOVERY

When it happens to an innocent and simple soul to find out suddenly at a stroke the falsehood of some one upon whose truth the whole universe depends, the effect is such as perhaps has never been put forth by any attempt at psychological investigation. When it happens to a great mind, we have Hamlet with all the world in ruins round him—all other thoughts as of revenge or ambition are but secondary and spasmodic, since neither revenge nor advancement can put together again the works of life or make man delight him, or woman either. But Lady Randolph was not a Hamlet. She had no genius, nor even a great intellect to be unhinged—scarcely mind enough to understand how it was that the glory had paled out of earth and sky, and all the world seemed different when she rose from her uneasy bed next morning, pale, after a night without sleep, in which she had not been able to have even the relief of restlessness, but had lain motionless, without even a sigh or tear, so crushed by the unexpected blow that she could neither fathom nor understand what had happened to her. She was too pure herself to jump at any thought of gross infidelity. She felt she knew not what—that the world had gone to pieces— that she did not know how to shape it again into anything—that she could not look into her husband's face, or command her voice to speak to him, for shame of the thought that he had failed in truth. Lucy felt somehow as if she were the culprit. She was ashamed to look him in the face. She made an early visit to the nursery, and stayed there pretending various little occupations until she heard Sir Tom go down stairs. He had returned so much to the old ways, and now that the house was full, and there were other people to occupy the Contessa, had shown so clearly (as Lucy had thought) that he was pleased to be liberated from his attendance upon her, that the cloud that had risen between them had melted away; and indeed, for some time back, it had been Lucy who was the Contessa's stay and support, a change at which Sir Tom had sometimes laughed. All had been well between the husband and wife during the early part of the season parliamentary, the beginning of their life in London. Sir Tom had been much engrossed with the cares of public life, but he had been delightful to Lucy, whose faith in him and his new occupations was great. And it was exhilarating to think that the Contessa had secured that little house in Mayfair for her own campaign, and that something like a new honeymoon was about to begin for the pair, whose happiness had seemed for a moment to tremble in the balance. Lucy had been looking forward to the return to London with a more bright and conscious anticipation of well-being than she had ever experienced. In the first outset of life happiness seems a necessary of existence. It is calculated upon without misgiving; it is simple nature, beyond question. But when the natural "of course" has once been broken, it is with a warmer glow of content that we see the prospect once more stretching before us bright as at first and more assured. This is how Lucy had been regarding her life. It was not so simple, so easy as it once had been, but the happiness to which she was looking forward, and which she had already partially entered into possession of, was all the more sweet and dear, that she had known, or fancied herself about to know, the loss and absence of it. Now, in a moment, all that fair prospect, that blessed certainty, was gone. The earth was cut away from under her feet; she felt everything to be tottering, falling round her, and nothing in all the universe to lay hold of to prop herself up; for when the pillars of the world are thus unrooted the heaving of the earthquake and the falling of the ruins impart a certain vertigo and giddy instability even to heaven.

Fletcher, Lucy's maid, who was usually discreet enough, waited upon her mistress that morning with a certain air of importance, and of knowing something which she was bursting with eagerness to tell, such as must have attracted Lady Randolph's attention in any other circumstances. But Lucy was far too much occupied with what was in her own mind to observe the perturbation of the maid, who consequently had no resource, since her mistress would not question her, than to introduce herself the subject on which she was so anxious to utter her mind. She began by inquiring if her ladyship had heard the music last night. "The music?" Lucy said.

"Oh, my lady, haven't you heard what a singer Miss Beachy has turned out?" Fletcher cried.

Lucy, to whom all this seemed dim and far away as if it had happened years ago, answered with a faint smile—"Yes, she has a lovely voice."

"It is not my place," said Fletcher, "being only a servant, to make remarks; but, my lady, if I might make so bold, it do seem to the like of us an 'orrible thing to take advantage of a young lady like your ladyship that thinks no harm."

"You should not make such remarks," said Lucy, roused a little.

"No, my lady; but still a woman is a woman, even though but a servant. I said to Mrs. Freshwater I was sure your ladyship would never sanction it. I never thought that of Miss Beachy, I will allow. I always said she was a nice young lady; but evil communications, my lady—we all know what the Bible says. Gentlemen upstairs in her room and her singing to them, and laughing and talking like as no housemaid in the house as valued her character would do—"

"Fletcher," said Lucy, "you must say no more about this. It was Mr. Jock and Mr. Derwentwater only who were with Miss Bice—and with my permission," she added after a moment, "as he is going away to-morrow." Such deceits are so easy to learn.

"Oh-oh!" Miss Fletcher cried, with a quaver in her voice. "I beg your pardon, my lady; I'm sure—I thought—there must be something underneath, and that Miss Beachy would never— And when she was down with Sir Thomas in the study it would be the same, my lady?" the woman said.

"With Sir Thomas in the study!" The words went vaguely into Lucy's mind. It had not seemed possible to increase the confusion and misery in her brain, but this produced a heightening of it, a sort of wave of bewilderment and pain greater than before, a sense of additional giddiness and failing. She gave a wave of her hand and said something, she scarcely knew what, which silenced Fletcher; and then she went down stairs to the new world. She did not go to the nursery even, as was her wont; her heart turned from little Tom. She felt that to look at him would be more than she could bear. There was no deceit in him, no falsehood—as yet; but perhaps when he grew up he would cheat her too. He would pretend to love her and betray her trust; he would kiss her, and then go away and scoff at her; he would smile, and smile, and be a villain. Such words were not in Lucy's mind, and it was altogether out of nature that she should even receive the thought: which made it all the more terrible when it was poured into her soul. And it cannot be told what discoveries she seemed to make even in the course of that morning in this strange condition of her mind. There was a haze over everything, but yet there was an enlightenment even in the haze. She saw in her little way, as Hamlet saw the falsehood of his courtiers, his gallant young companions, and the schemes of Polonius, and even Ophelia in the plot to trap him. She saw how false all these people were in their civilities, in their extravagant thanks and compliments to her as they went away; for the Easter recess was just over, and everybody was going. The mother and her daughters said to her, "Such a delightful visit, dear Lady Randolph!" with kisses of farewell and wreathed smiles; and she perceived, somehow by a sort of second sight, that they added to each other, "Oh, what a bore it has been; nobody worth meeting," and "how thankful I am it's over!" which was indeed what Miss Minnie and Miss Edith said. If Lucy had seen a little deeper she would have known that this too was a sort of conventional falsity which the young ladies said to each other, according to the fashion of the day, without any meaning to speak of; but one must have learned a great many lessons before one comes to that.

Then Jock, who had been woke up in quite a different way, took leave of MTutor, that god of his old idolatry, without being able to refrain from some semblance of the old absorbing affection.

"I am so sorry you are not coming with me, old fellow," Mr. Derwentwater said.

Jock replied, "So am I," with an effort, as if firing a parting volley in honour of his friend: but then turned gloomily with an expression of relief. "I'm glad he's gone, Lucy."

"Then you did not want to go with him, Jock?"

"I wouldn't have gone for anything. I've just got to that—that I can't bear him," cried Jock.

And Lucy, in the midst of the ruins, felt her head go round: though here too it was the falsehood that was fictitious, had she but known. It is not, however, in the nature of such a shock that any of those alleviating circumstances which modify the character of human sentiment can be taken into account. Lucy had taken everything for gospel in the first chapter of existence; she had believed what everybody said; and like every other human soul, after such a discovery as she had made, she went to the opposite extremity now—not wittingly, not voluntarily—but the pillars of the earth were shaken, and nothing stood fast.

They went up to town next day. In the meantime she had little or no intercourse with the Contessa, who was preparing for the journey and absorbed in letter-writing, making known to everybody whom she could think of, the existence of the little house in Mayfair. It is doubtful whether she so much as observed any difference in the demeanour of her hostess, having in fact the most unbounded confidence in Lucy, whom she did not believe capable of any such revulsion of feeling. Bice was more clear-sighted, but she thought Milady was displeased with her own proceedings, and sought no further for a cause. And the only thing the girl could do was to endeavour by all the little devices she could think of to show the warm affection she really felt for Lucy—a method which made the heart of Lucy more and more sick with that sense of falsehood which sometimes rose in her, almost to the height of passion. A woman who had ever learned to use harsh words, or to whose mind it had ever been possible to do or say anything to hurt another, would no doubt have burst forth upon the girl with some reproach or intimation of doubt which might have cleared the matter so far as Bice went. But Lucy had no such words at her command. She could not say anything unkind. It was not in her. She could be silent, indeed, but not even that, so far as to "hurt the feelings" of her companion. The effect, therefore, was only that Lucy laboured to maintain a little artificial conversation, which in its turn reacted upon her mind, showing that even in herself there was the same disposition to insincerity which she had begun to discover in the world. She could say nothing to Bice about the matters which a little while before, when all was well, she had grieved over and objected to. Now she had nothing to say on such subjects. That the girl should be set up to auction, that she should put forth all those arts in which she had been trained, to attract and secure young Montjoie, or any like him, were things which had passed beyond her sphere. To think of them rendered her heart more sick, her head more giddy. But if Bice married some one whom she did not love, that was not so bad as to think that perhaps she herself all this time had been living with, and loving, in sacred trust and faith, a man who even by her side was full of thoughts unknown to her, given to another. Sometimes Lucy closed her eyes in a sort of sick despair, feeling everything about her go round and round. But she said nothing to throw any light upon the state of her being. Sir Tom felt a little gravity—a little distance in his wife; but he himself was much occupied with a new and painful subject of thought. And Jock observed nothing at all, being at a stage when man (or boy) is wholly possessed with affairs of his own. He had his troubles, too. He was not easy about that breach with his master now that they were separated. When Bice was kind to him a gleam of triumph, mingled with pity, made him remorseful towards that earlier friend; and when she was unkind a bitter sense of fellowship turned Jock's thoughts towards that sublime ideal of masculine friendship which is above the lighter loves of women. How can a boy think of his sister when absorbed in such a mystery of his own?—even if he considered his sister at all as a person whom it was needful to think about—which he did not, Lucy being herself one of the pillars of the earth to his unopened eyes.

All this, however, made no difference in Lucy's determination. She wrote to Mr. Rushton that very morning, after this revolution in her soul, to instruct him as to her intentions in respect to Bice, and to her other trustee in London to request him to see her immediately on her arrival in Park Lane. Nothing should be changed in that matter, for why, she said to herself, should Bice suffer because Sir Tom was untrue? It seemed to her that there was more reason than ever why she should rouse herself and throw off her inaction. No doubt there were many people whom she could make, if not happy, yet comfortable. It was comfortable (everybody said) to have enough of money—to be well off. Lucy had no experience of what it was to be without it. She thought to herself she would like to try, to have only what she actually wanted, to cook the food for her little family, to nurse little Tom all by herself, to live as the cottagers lived. There was in her mind no repugnance to any of the details of poverty. Her wealth was an accident; it was the habit of her race to be poor, and it seemed to Lucy that she would be happier could she shake off now all those external circumstances which had grown, like everything else, into falsehoods, giving an appearance of well-being which did not exist. But other people thought it well to have money, and it was her duty to give it. A kind of contempt rose within her for all that withheld her previously. To avoid her duty because it would displease Sir Tom—what was that but falsehood too? All was falsehood, only she had never seen it before.

They reached town in the afternoon of a sweet April day, the sky aglow with a golden sunset, against which the trees in the park stood out with their half-developed buds: and all the freshness of the spring was in the long stretches of green, and the softened jubilee of sound to which somehow, as the air warms towards summer, the voices of the world outside tune themselves. The Contessa and Bice in great spirits and happiness, like two children home from school, had left the Randolph party at the railway, to take possession of the little house in Mayfair. They had both waved their hands from the carriage window and called out, "Be sure you come and see us," as they drove away. "You will come to-night," they had stipulated with Sir Tom and Jock. It was like a new toy which filled them with glee. Could it be possible that those two adventurers going off to their little temporary home with smiles so genuine, with so simple a delight in their new beginning, were not, in their strange way, innocent, full of guile and shifts as one was, and the other so apt a scholar? Lucy would have joined in all this pleasure two days ago, but she could not now. She went home to her luxurious house, where all was ready, as if she had not been absent an hour. How wonderfully wealth smooths away the inconveniences of change! and how little it has to do, Lucy thought, with the comfort of the soul! No need for any exertion on her part, any scuffling for the first arrival, any trouble of novelty. She came from the Hall to London without any sense of change. Had she been compelled to superintend the arrangement of her house, to make it habitable, to make it pretty, that would have done her good. But the only thing for her to do was to see Mr. Chervil, her trustee, who waited upon her according to her request, and who, after the usual remonstrances, took her instructions about the gift to Bice very unwillingly, but still with a forced submission. "If I cannot make you see the folly of it, Lady Randolph, and if Sir Thomas does not object, I don't know what more is to be said." "There is nothing more to be said," Lucy said, with a smile; but there was this difficulty in the proceeding which she had not thought of, that Bice's name all this time was unknown to her—Beatrice di Forno-Populo, she supposed, but the Contessa had never called her so, and it was necessary to be exact, Mr. Chervil said. He hailed this as an occasion of delay. He was not so violent as he had been on previous occasions when Lucy was young; and he did not, like Mr. Rushton, assume the necessity of speaking to Sir Tom. Mr. Chervil was a London solicitor, and knew very little about Sir Tom. But he was glad to seize upon anything that was good for a little delay.

After this interview was over it was a mingled vexation and relief to Lucy to see the Dowager drive up to the door. Lady Randolph the elder was always in London from the first moment possible. She preferred the first bursting of the spring in the squares and parks. She liked to see her friends arrive by degrees, and to feel that she had so far the better of them. She came in, full as she always was of matter, with a thousand things to say. "I have come to stay to dinner, if you will have me," she said, "for of course Tom will be going out in the evening. They are always so glad to get back to their life." And it was, perhaps, a relief to have Lady Randolph to dinner, to be saved from the purely domestic party, to which Jock scarcely added any new element; but it was hard for Lucy to encounter even the brief questionings which were addressed to her in the short interval before dinner. "So you have got rid of that woman at last," Lady Randolph said; "I hear she has got a house in Mayfair."

"Yes, Aunt Randolph, if you mean the Contessa," said Lucy.

"And that she intends to make a bold coup to get the girl off her hands. These sort of people so often succeed: I shouldn't wonder if she were to succeed. I always said the girl would be handsome, but I think she might have waited another year."

To this Lucy made no reply, and it was necessary for the Dowager to carry on the conversation, so to speak, at her own cost.

"I hope most earnestly, Lucy," she said, "that now you have got clear of them you will not mix yourself up with them again. You were placed in an uneasy position, very difficult to get out of, I will allow; but now that you have shaken them off, and they have proved they can get on without you, don't, I entreat you, mix yourself up with them again."

Lucy could not keep the blood from mounting, and colouring her face. She had always spoken of the Contessa calmly before. She tried to keep her composure now. "Dear Aunt Randolph, I have not shaken them off. They have gone away of themselves, and how can I refuse to see them? There is to be a party here for them on the 26th."

"Oh, my dear, my dear, that was very imprudent! I had hoped you would keep clear of them in London. It is one thing showing kindness to an old friend in the country, and it is quite another—"

Here Lucy made an imperative gesture, almost commanding silence. Sir Tom was coming into the room. She was seated in the great bay window against the early twilight, the soft radiance of which dazzled the eyes of the elder lady, and prevented her from perceiving her nephew's approach. But Lady Randolph, before she rose to meet him, gave a startled look at Lucy. "Have you found it out, then?" she said involuntarily, in her great surprise.

## CHAPTER XL

### THE DOWAGER'S EXPLANATION

The Dowager was a woman far more clever than Lucy, who knew the world. And she was apt perhaps, instead of missing the meaning of the facts around her, to put too much significance in them. Now, when the little party met at dinner, Lady Randolph saw in the faces of both husband and wife more than was there, though much was there. Sir Tom was more grave than became a man who had returned into life, as his aunt said, and was looking forward to resuming the better part of existence—the House, the clubs, the quick throb of living which is in London. His countenance was full of thought, and there was both trouble and perplexity in it, but not the excitement which the Dowager supposed she found there, and those signs of having yielded to an evil influence which eyes accustomed to the world are so ready to discover. Lucy for her part was pale and silent. She had little to say, and scarcely addressed her husband at all. Lady Randolph, and that was very natural, took those signs of heart sickness for tokens of complete enlightenment, for the passion of a woman who had entered upon that struggle with another woman for a man's love which, even when the man is her husband, has something degrading in it. There had been a disclosure, a terrible scene, no doubt, a stirring up of all the passions, Lady Randolph thought. No doubt that was the reason why the Contessa had loosed her clutches, and left the house free of her presence; but Lucy was still trembling after the tempest, and had not learned to take any pleasure in her victory. This was the conclusion of the woman of the world.

The dinner was not a lengthy one, and the ladies went upstairs again, with a suppressed constraint, each anxious to know what the other was on her guard not to tell. They sat alone expectant for some time, making conversation, taking their coffee, listening, and watching each how the other listened, for the coming of the gentlemen, or rather for Sir Tom; for Jock, in his boyish insignificance, counted for little. The trivial little words that passed between them during this interval were charged with a sort of moral electricity, and stung and tingled in the too conscious silence. At length, after some time had elapsed: "I am glad I came," said Lady Randolph, "to sit with you, Lucy, this first evening; for of course Tom cannot resist, the first evening in town, the charms of his club."

"His club! Oh, I think he has gone to see the house," Lucy said. "He promised—; it is not very far off."

"The house? You mean that woman's house. Lucy, I have no patience with you any more than I have with Tom. Why don't you put a stop to it? why don't you—for I suppose you have found out what sort of a woman she is by this time, and why she came here?"

"She came—to introduce Bice and establish her in the world," Lucy said, in a faint tone. "Oh! Aunt Randolph, please do not let us discuss it! It is not what I like to think of. Bice will be sacrificed to the first rich man who asks her; or at least that is what the Contessa means."

"My dear Lucy," said the Dowager, calmly, "that is reasonable enough. I wish the Contessa meant no worse than that. Most girls are persuaded to marry a rich man if he asks them. I don't think so much of that. But it will not be so easy as she thinks," the Dowager added. "It is true that beauty does much—but not everything; and a girl in that position, with no connections, or, at least, none that she would not be better without—"

Lucy's attention strayed from this question, which once had been so important, and which now seemed so secondary; but the conversation must be maintained. She said at random: "She has a beautiful voice."

"Has she? And the Contessa herself sings very well. That will no doubt be another attraction," said Lady Randolph, in her impartial way. "But the end of it all is, who will she get to go, and who will invite them? It is vain to lay snares if there is nothing to be caught."

"They will be invited—here," said Lucy, faltering a little. "I told you I am to have a great gathering on the 26th."

"I could not believe my ears. You!—and she is to appear here for the first time to make her début. Good heavens, Lucy! What can I say to you—that girl!"

"Why not, Aunt Randolph?" said Lucy (oh, what does it matter—what does it matter, that she should make so much fuss about it? she was saying in herself); "I have always liked Bice, and she has been very good to little Tom."

"Well," cried the angry lady, forgetting herself, and smiling the fierce smile of wrath, "there is no doubt that it is perfectly appropriate—the very thing that ought to happen if we lived according to the rules of nature, without thought of conventionalities and decorums, and so forth—oh, perfectly appropriate! If you don't object I know no one who has any right to say a word."

Even now Lucy was scarcely roused enough to be surprised by the vehemence of these words. "Why should I object?" she said; "or why should any one say a word?" Her calm, which was almost indifference, excited Lady Randolph more and more.

"You are either superhuman," she said, with exasperation, "or you are— Lucy, I don't know what words to use. You put one out of every reckoning. You are like nobody I ever knew before. Why should you object? Why, good heavens! you are the only person that has any right— Who should object if not you?"

"Aunt Randolph," said Lucy, rousing herself with an effort, "would you please tell me plainly what you mean? I am not clever. I can't make things out. I have always liked Bice. To save her from being made a victim I am going to give her some of the money under my father's will—and if I could give her— What is the matter?" she cried, stopping short suddenly, and in spite of herself growing pale.

Lady Randolph flung up her hands in dismay. She gave something like a shriek as she exclaimed: "And Tom is letting you do this?" with horror in her tone.

"He has promised that he will not oppose," Lucy said; "but why do you speak so, and look so? Bice—has done no harm."

"Oh, no; Bice has done no harm," cried Lady Randolph bitterly; "nothing, except being born, which is harm enough, I think. But do you mean to tell me, Lucy, that Tom—a man of honour, notwithstanding all his vagaries—Tom—lets you do this and never says a word? Oh, it is too much. I have always stood by him. I have been his support when every one else failed. But this is too much, that he should put the burden upon you—that he should make you responsible for this girl of his—"

"Aunt Randolph!" cried Lucy, rising up quickly and confronting the angry woman. She put up her hand with a serious dignity that was doubly impressive from her usual simpleness. "What is it you mean? This girl of his! I do not understand. She is not much more than a child. You cannot, cannot suppose that Bice—that it is she—that she is—" Here she suddenly covered her face with her hands. "Oh, you put things in my mind that I am ashamed to think of," Lucy cried.

"I mean," said Lady Randolph, who in the heat of this discussion had got beyond her own power of self-restraint, "what everybody but yourself must have seen long ago. That woman is a shameless woman, but even she would not have had the effrontery to bring any other girl to your house. It was more shameless, I think, to bring that one than any other; but she would not think so. Oh, cannot you see it even now? Why, the likeness might have told you; that was enough. The girl is Tom's girl. She is your husband's—"

Lucy uncovered her face, which was perfectly colourless, with eyes dilated and wide open. "What?" she whispered, looking intently into Lady Randolph's face.

"His own child—his—daughter—though I am bitterly ashamed to say it," the Dowager said.

For a moment everything seemed to waver and turn round in Lucy's eyes, as if the walls were making a circuit with her in giddy space. Then she came to her feet with the sensation of a shock, and found herself standing erect, with the most amazing incomprehensible sense of relief. Why should she have felt relieved by this communication which filled her companion with horror? A softer air seemed to breathe about Lucy, she felt solid ground under her feet. For the first moment there seemed nothing but ease and sweet soothing and refreshment in what she heard.

"His—daughter?" she said. Her mind went back with a sudden flash upon the past, gathering up instantaneously pieces of corroborative evidence, things which she had not noted at the moment, which she had forgotten, yet which came back nevertheless when they were needed: the Contessa's mysterious words about Bice's parentage, her intimation that Lucy would one day be glad to have befriended her: Sir Tom's sudden agitation when she had told him of Bice's English descent: finally, and most conclusive of all, touching Lucy with a most unreasonable conviction and bringing a rush of warm feeling to her heart, Baby's adoption of the girl and recommendation of her to his mother. Was it not the voice of nature, the voice of God? Lucy had no instinctive sense of recoil, no horror of the discovery. She did not realise the guilt involved, nor was she painfully struck, as some women might have been, by this evidence of her husband's previous life "If it is so," she said quietly, "there is more reason than ever, Aunt Randolph, that I should do everything I can for Bice. It never came into my mind before. I see now—various things: but I do not see why it should—make me unhappy," she added with a faint smile which brought the water to her eyes; "it must have been—long before I knew him. Will you tell me who was her mother? Was she a foreigner? Did she die long ago?"

"Oh, Lucy, Lucy," cried Lady Randolph, "is it possible you don't see? Who would take all that trouble about her? Who would burden themselves with another woman's girl that was no concern of theirs? Who would—can't you see? can't you see?"

There came over Lucy's face a hot and feverish flush. She grew red to her hair, agitation and shame took possession of her; something seemed to throb and swell as if it would burst in her forehead. She could not speak. She could not look at her informant for shame of the revelation that had been made. All the bewildered sensations which for the moment had been stilled in her breast sprang up again with a feverish whirl and tumult. She tottered back to the chair on which she had been sitting and dropped down upon it, holding by it as if that were the only thing in the world secure and steadfast. It was only now that Lady Randolph seemed to awake to the risks and dangers of this bold step she had taken. She had roused the placid soul at last. To what strange agony, to what revenge might she have roused it? She had looked for tears and misery, and fleeting rage and mad jealousy. But Lucy's look of utter giddiness and overthrow alarmed her more than she could say.

"Lucy! Oh, my love, you must recollect, as you say, that it was all long before he knew you—that there was no injury to you!"

Lucy made a movement with her hand to bar further discussion, but she could not say anything. She pointed Lady Randolph to her chair, and made that mute prayer for silence, for no more. But in such a moment of excitement there is nothing that is more difficult to grant than this.

"Oh, Lucy," the Dowager cried, "forgive me! Perhaps I ought not to have said anything. Oh, my dear, if you will but think what a painful position it was for me. To see you so unsuspicious, ready to do anything, and even Tom taking advantage of you. It is not more than a week since I found it all out, and how could I keep silence? Think what a painful position it was for me."

Lucy made no reply. There seemed nothing but darkness round her. She put out her hand imploring that no more might be said; and though there was a great deal more said, she scarcely made out what it was. Her brain refused to take in any more. She suffered herself to be kissed and blessed, and said good-night to, almost mechanically. And when the elder lady at last went away, Lucy sat where Lady Randolph had left her, she did not know how long, gazing woefully at the ruins of that crumbled world which had all fallen to pieces about her. All was to pieces now. What was she and what was the other? Why should she be here and not the other? Two, were there?—two with an equal claim upon him? Was everything false, even the law, even the external facts which made her Tom's wife. He had another wife and a child. He was two, he was not one true man; one for baby and her, another for Bice and the Contessa. When she heard her husband coming in Lucy fled upstairs like a hunted thing, and took refuge in the nursery where little Tom was sleeping. Even her bourgeoise horror of betraying herself, of letting the servants suspect that anything was wrong, had no effect upon her to-night.

## CHAPTER XLI

SEVERED

Sir Tom came home later, so much later than he intended that he entered the house with such a sense of compunction as had not visited him since the days when the alarm of being caught was a part of the pleasure. He had no fear of a lecture from Lucy, whose gifts were not of that kind; but he was partially conscious of having neglected her on her first night in town, as well as having sinned against her in matters more serious. And he did not know how to explain his detention at the Contessa's new house, or the matters which he had been discussing there. It was a sensible relief to him not to find her in any of the sitting-rooms, all dark and closed up, except his own room, in which there was no trace of her. She had gone to bed, which was so sensible, like Lucy's unexaggerated natural good sense: he smiled to himself—though, at the same time, a wondering question within himself, whether she felt at all, passed through his mind—a reflection full of mingled disappointment and satisfaction. But when, a full hour after his return, after a tranquil period of reflection, he went leisurely upstairs, expecting to find her peacefully asleep, and found her not, nor any evidence that she had ever been there, a great wave of alarm passed over the mind of Sir Tom. He paused confounded, looking at her vacant place, startled beyond expression. "Lucy!" he cried, looking in his dismay into every corner, into his own dressing-room, and even into the large wardrobe where her dresses hung, like shells and husks, which she had laid aside. And then he made an agitated pause, standing in the middle of the room, not knowing what to think. It was by this time about two in the morning; the middle of the night, according to Lucy. Where could she have gone? Then he bethought himself with an immediate relief, which was soon replaced by poignant anxiety, of the only possible reason for her absence—a reason which would explain everything—little Tom. When this thought occurred to him all the excitement that had been in Sir Tom's mind disappeared in a moment, and he thought of nothing but that baby lying, perhaps tossing uneasily, upon his little bed, his mother watching over him; most sacred group on earth to him, who, whatever his faults might be, loved them both dearly. He took a candle in his hand and, stepping lightly, went up the stairs to the nursery door. There was no sound of wailing within, no pitiful little cry to tell the tale; all was still and dark. He tried the door softly, but it would not open. Then another terror awoke, and for the moment took his breath from him. What had happened to the child? Sir Tom suffered enough at this moment to have expiated many sins. There came upon him a vision of the child extended motionless upon his bed, and his mother by him refusing to be comforted. What could it mean? The door looked as if hope had departed. He knocked softly, yet imperatively, divided between the horror of these thoughts and the gentle every-day sentiment which forbade any noise at little Tom's door. It was some time before he got any reply—a time which seemed to him interminable. Then he suddenly heard Lucy's voice close to the door whispering. There had been no sound of any footsteps. Had she been there all the time listening to all his appeals and taking no notice?

"Open the door," he said anxiously. "Speak to me. What is the matter? Is he ill? Have you sent for the doctor? Let me in."

"We are all shut up and settled for the night," said Lucy, through the door.

"Shut up for the night? Has he been very ill?" Sir Tom cried.

"Oh, hush, you will wake him; no, not very ill: but I am going to stay with him," said the voice inside with a quiver in it.

"Lucy, what does this mean? You are concealing something from me. Have you had the doctor? Good God, tell me. What is the matter? Can't I see my boy?"

"There is nothing—nothing to be alarmed about," said Lucy from within. "He is asleep—he is—doing well. Oh! go to bed and don't mind us. I am going to stay with him."

"Don't mind you? that is so easy," he cried, with a broken laugh; then the silence stealing to his heart, he cried out, "Is the child—?" But Sir Tom could not say the word. He shivered, standing outside the closed door. The mystery seemed incomprehensible, save on the score of some great calamity. The bitterness of death went over him; but then he asked himself what reason there could be to conceal from him any terrible sudden blow. Lucy would have wanted him in such a case, not kept him from her. In this dread moment of sudden panic he thought of everything but the real cause, which made a more effectual barrier between them than that closed door.

"He is well enough now," said Lucy's voice, coming faintly out of the darkness. "Oh, indeed, there is nothing the matter. Please go away; go to bed. It is so late. I am going to stay with him."

"Lucy," said Sir Tom, "I have never been shut out before. There is something you are concealing from me. Let me see him and then you shall do as you please."

There was a little pause, and then slowly, reluctantly, Lucy opened the door. She was still fully dressed as she had been for dinner. There was not a particle of colour in her face. Her eyes had a scared look and were surrounded by wide circles, as if the orbit had been hollowed out. She stood aside to let him pass without a word. The room in which little Tom slept was an inner room. There was scarcely any light in either, nothing but the faint glimmer of the night-lamp. The sleeping-room was hushed and full of the most tranquil quiet, the regular soft breathing of the sleeping child in his little bed, and of his nurse by him, who was as completely unaware as he of any intrusion. Sir Tom stole in and looked at his boy, in the pretty baby attitude of perfect repose, his little arms thrown up over his head. The anxiety vanished from his heart, but not the troubled sense of something wrong, a mystery which altogether baffled him. Mystery had no place here in this little sanctuary of innocence. But what did it mean? He stole out again to where Lucy stood, scared and silent in her white dress, with a jewelled pendant at her neck which gleamed strangely in the half light.

"He seems quite well now. What was it, and why are you so anxious?" he asked. "Did the doctor—"

"There was no need for a doctor. It is only—myself. I must stay with him, he might want me—" And nobody else does, Lucy was about to say, but pride and modesty restrained her. Her husband looked at her earnestly. He perceived with a curious pang of astonishment that she drew away from him, standing as far off as the limited space permitted and avoiding his eye.

"I don't understand it," he said; "there is something underneath; either he has been more ill than you will let me know, or—there is something else—"

She gave him no answering look, made no wondering exclamation what could there be else? as he had hoped; but replied hurriedly, as she had done before, "I want to stay with him. I must stay with him for to-night—"

It was with the most extraordinary sense of some change, which he could not fathom or divine, that Sir Tom consented at last to leave his wife in the child's room and go to his own. What did it mean? What had happened to him, or was about to happen? He could not explain to himself the aspect of the slight little youthful figure in her airy white dress, with the diamonds still at her throat, careless of the hour and time, standing there in the middle of the night, shrinking away from him, forlorn and wakeful with her scared eyes. At this hour on ordinary occasions Lucy was fast asleep. When she came to see her boy, if society had kept her up late, it was in the ease of a dressing-gown, not with any cold glitter of ornaments. And to see her shrink and draw herself away in that strange repugnance from his touch and shadow confounded him. He was not angry, as he might have been in another case, but pitiful to the bottom of his heart. What could have come to Lucy? Half a dozen times he turned back on his way to his room. What meaning could she have in it? What could have happened to her? Her manifest shrinking from him had terrified him, and filled his mind with confusion. But controversy of any kind in the child's room at the risk of waking him in the middle of the night was impossible, and no doubt, he tried to say to himself, it must be some panic she had taken, some sudden alarm for the child, justified by reasons which she did not like to explain to him till the morning light restored her confidence. Women were so, he had often heard: and the women he had known in his youth had certainly been so—unreasoning creatures, subject to their imagination, taking fright when no occasion for fright was, incapable of explaining. Lucy had never been like this; but yet Lucy, though sensible, was a woman too, and if it is not permitted to a woman to take an unreasoning panic about her only child, she must be hardly judged indeed. Sir Tom was not a hard judge. When he got over the painful sense that there must be something more in this than met the eye, he was half glad to find that Lucy was like other women—a dear little fool, not always sensible. He thought almost the better of her for it, he said to himself. She would laugh herself at her panic, whatever it was, when little Tom woke up fresh and fair in the morning light.

With this idea he did what he could to satisfy himself. The situation was strange, unprecedented in his experience; but he had many subjects of thought on his own part which returned to his mind as the surprise of the moment calmed down. He had a great deal to think about. Old difficulties which seemed to have passed away for long years were now coming back again to embarrass and confuse him. "Our pleasant vices are made the whips to scourge us," he said to himself. The past had come back to him like the opening of a book, no longer merely frivolous and amusing, as in the Contessa's talk, touched with all manner of light emotions, but bitter, with tragedy in it, and death and desolation. Death and life: he had heard enough of the dead to make them seem alive again, and of the living to confuse their identity altogether; but he had not yet succeeded in clearing up the doubt which had been thrown into his mind. That question about Bice's parentage, "English on one side," tormented him still. He had made again an attempt to discover the truth, and he had been foiled. The probabilities seemed all in favour of the solution which at the first word had presented itself to him; but still there was a chance that it might not be so.

His mind had been full and troubled enough, when he returned to the still house, and thought with compunction how many thoughts which he could not share with her he was bringing back to Lucy's side. He could not trust them to her, or confide in her, and secure her help, as in many other circumstances he would have done without hesitation. But he could not do that in this case,—not so much because she was his wife, as because she was so young, so innocent, so unaware of the complications of existence. How could she understand the temptations that assail a young man in the heyday of life, to whom many indulgences appear permissible or venial, which to her limited and innocent soul would seem unpardonable sins? To live even for a few years with a stainless nature like that of Lucy, in whom there was not even so much knowledge as would make the approaches of vice comprehensible, is a new kind of education to the most experienced of men. He had not believed it to be possible to be so altogether ignorant of evil as he had found her; and how could he explain to her and gain her indulgent consideration of the circumstances which had led him into what in her vocabulary would be branded with the name of vice? Sir Tom even now did not feel it to be vice. It was unfortunate that it had so happened. He had been a fool. It was almost inconceivable to him now how for the indulgence of a momentary passion he could have placed himself in a position that might one day be so embarrassing and disagreeable. He had not behaved ill at the moment; it was the woman who had behaved ill. But how in the name of wonder to explain all this to Lucy? Lucy, who was not conscious of any reason why a man's code of morals should be different from that of a woman! When Sir Tom returned to this painful and difficult subject, the immediate question as to Lucy's strange conduct died from his mind. It became more easy, by dint of repeating it, to believe that a mere unreasonable panic about little Tom was the cause of her withdrawal. It was foolish, but a loving and lovely foolishness which a man might do more than forgive, which he might adore and smile at, as men love to do, feeling that for a woman to be thus silly is desirable, a counterpoise to the selfishness and want of feeling which are so common in the world. But how to make this spotless creature understand that a man might slip aside and yet not be a dissolute man, that he might be betrayed into certain proceedings which would not perhaps bear the inspection of severe judges, and yet be neither vicious nor heartless. This problem, after he had considered it in every possible way, Sir Tom finally gave up with a sort of despair. He must keep his secret within his own bosom. He must contrive some means of doing what, in case his hypothesis was right, would now be clearly a duty, without exciting any suspicion on Lucy's part. That, he thought with a compunction, would be easy enough. There was no one whom it would cost less trouble to deceive. With these thoughts he went to sleep in the room which seemed strangely lonely without her presence. Perhaps, however, it was not ungrateful to him to be alone to think all those thoughts without the additional sense of treachery which must have ensued had he thought them in her presence. There was no treachery. He had been all along, he thought to himself, a man somewhat sinned against in the matter. To be sure it was wrong—according to all rules of morals, it was necessary to admit this; but not more wrong, not so much wrong, as most other men had been. And, granting the impropriety of that first step, he had nothing to reproach himself with afterwards. In that respect he knew he had behaved both liberally and honourably, though he had been deceived. But how—how—good heavens!—explain this to Lucy? In the silence of her room, where she was not, he actually laughed out to himself at the thought; laughed with a sense of all impossibility beyond all laws or power of reasoning. What miracle would make her understand? It would be easier to move the solid earth than to make her understand.

But it was altogether a very strange night—such a night as never had been passed in that house before; and fearful things were about in the darkness, ill dreams, strange shadows of trouble. When Sir Tom woke in the morning and found no sign that his wife had been in the room or any trace of her, there arose once more a painful apprehension in his mind. He hurried half-dressed to the nursery to ask for news of the child, but was met by the nurse with the most cheerful countenance, with little Tom holding by her skirts, in high spirits, and fun of babble and glee.

"He has had a good night, then?" the father said aloud, lifting the little fellow to his shoulder.

"An excellent night, Sir Thomas," the woman said, "and not a bit tired with his journey, and so pleased to see all the carriages and the folks passing."

Sir Tom put the boy down with a cloud upon his face.

"What was the cause, then, of Lady Randolph's anxiety last night?"

"Anxiety, Sir Thomas! Oh no; her ladyship was quite pleased. She do always say he is a regular little town-bird, and always better in London. And so she said when I was putting him to sleep. And he never stirred, not from the moment he went off till six o'clock this morning, the darling. I do think now, Sir Thomas, as we may hope he's taken hold of his strength."

Sir Tom turned away with a blank countenance. What did it mean, then? He went back to his dressing-room, and completed his toilette without seeing anything of Lucy. The nurse seemed quite unconscious of her mistress's vigil by the baby's side. Where, then, had Lucy passed the night, and why taken refuge in that nursery? Sir Tom grew pale, and saw his own countenance white and full of trouble, as if it had been a stranger's, in the glass. He hurried downstairs to the breakfast-room, into which the sun was shining. There could not have been a more cheerful sight. Some of the flowers brought up from the Hall were on the table; there was a merry little fire burning; the usual pile of newspapers were arranged for him by Williams's care, who felt himself a political character too, and understood the necessity of seeing what the country was thinking. Jock stood at the window with a book, reading and watching the changeful movements outside. But the chair at the head of the table was vacant. "Have you seen Lucy?" he said to Jock, with an anxiety which he could scarcely disguise. At this moment she came in, very guilty, very pale, like a ghost. She gave him no greeting, save a sort of attempt at a smile and warning look, calling his attention to Williams, who had followed her into the room with that one special dish which the butler always condescended to place on the table. Sir Tom sat down to his newspapers confounded, not knowing what to think or to say.

CHAPTER XLII

LADY RANDOLPH WINDS UP HER AFFAIRS

Lucy contrived somehow to elude all private intercourse with her husband that morning. She was not alone with him for a moment. To his question about little Tom and her anxiety of last night she made as slight an answer as possible. "Nurse tells me he is all right." "He is quite well this morning," Lucy replied with quiet dignity, as if she did not limit herself to nurse's observations. She talked a little to Jock about his school and how long the holidays lasted, while Sir Tom retired behind the shield of his newspapers. He did not get much benefit from them that morning, or instruction as to what the country was thinking. He was so much more curious to know what his wife was thinking, that simple little girl who knew no evil. The most astute of men could not have perplexed Sir Tom so much. It seemed to him that something must have happened, but what? What was there that any one could betray to her? not the discovery that he himself thought he had made. That was impossible. If any one else had known it he surely must have known it. It could not be anything so unlikely as that.

But Lucy gave him no opportunity of inquiring. She went away to see the housekeeper, to look after her domestic affairs; and then Sir Tom made sure he should find her in the nursery, whither he took his way, when he thought he had left sufficient time for her other occupations. But Lady Randolph was not there. He heard from Fletcher, whose disturbed countenance seemed to reflect his own, that her mistress had gone out. She was the only one of the household who shared his certainty that something had happened out of the ordinary routine. Fletcher knew that her mistress had not undressed in the usual way; that she had not gone to bed. Her own services had not been required either in the morning or evening, and she had a strong suspicion that Lady Randolph had passed the night on a sofa in the little morning-room upstairs. To Fletcher's mind it was not very difficult to account for this. Quarrels between husband and wife are common enough. But her consciousness and sympathetic significance of look struck Sir Tom with a troubled sense of the humour of the situation which broke the spell of his increasing agitation, if but for a moment. It was droll to think that Fletcher should be in a manner his confidant, the only participator in his woes.

Lucy had gone out half to avoid her husband, half with a determination to expedite the business which she had begun, with very different feelings the day before. The streets were very gay and bright on that April morning, with all the quickening of life which many arrivals and the approach of the season, with all its excitements, brings. Houses were opening up, carriages coming out, even the groups of children and nurse-maids in the Park making a sensible difference on the other side of the great railing. It was very unusual for her to find herself in the streets alone, and this increased the curious dazed sensation with which she went out among all these real people, so lively and energetic, while she was still little more than a dream-woman, possessed by one thought, moving along, she knew not how, with a sense of helplessness and unprotectedness, which made the novelty all the more sensible to her. She went on for what seemed to be a long time, following mechanically the line of the pavement, without knowing what she was doing, along the long course of Park Lane, and then into the cheerful bustle of Piccadilly, where, with a sense of morning ease and leisure, not like the artificiality of the afternoon, so many people were coming and going, all occupied in business of their own, though so different from the bustle of more absorbing business, the haste and obstruction of the city. Lucy was not beautiful enough or splendid enough to attract much attention from the passers-by in the streets, though one or two sympathetic and observant wayfarers were caught by the look of trouble in her face. She had never walked about London, and she did not know where she was going. But she did not think of this. She thought only on one subject,—about her husband and that other life which he had, of which she knew nothing, which might, for anything she could tell, have been going on side by side with the life she knew and shared. This was the point upon which Lucy's mind had given way. The revelation as to Bice had startled and shaken her soul to its foundations; but after the shock things had fallen into their place again, and she had felt no anger, though much pain and pity. Her mind had thrown itself back into the unknown past almost tenderly towards the mother who had died long ago, to whom perhaps Bice had been what little Tom was now to herself. But when the further statement reached her ears all that softening which seemed to have swept over her disappeared in a moment. A horrible bewilderment had seized her. Was he two men, with two wives, two lives, two children dear to him?

It is usual to talk of women as being the most severe judges of each other's failures in one particular at least, an accusation which no doubt is true of both sexes, though generally applied, like so many universal truths, to one. And an injured wife is a raging fury in those primitive characterisations which are so common in the world. But the ideas which circled like the flakes in a snowstorm through the mind of Lucy were of a kind incomprehensible to the vulgar critic who judges humanity in the general. Her ways of thinking, her modes of judging were as different as possible from those of minds accustomed to generalisation and lightly acquainted with the vices of the world. Lucy knew no general; she knew three persons involved in an imbroglio so terrible that she saw no way out of it. Herself, her husband, another woman. Her mind was the mind almost of a child. It had resisted all that dismal information which the chatter of society conveys. She knew that married people were "not happy" sometimes. She knew that there were wretched stories of which she held that they could not be true. She was of Desdemona's mind, and did not believe that there was any such woman. And when she was suddenly strangely brought face to face with a tragedy of her own, that was not enough to turn this innocent and modest girl into a raging Eleanor. She was profoundly reasonable in her simple way, unapt to blame; thinking no evil, and full of those prepossessions and fixed canons of innocence which the world-instructed are incapable not only of understanding, but of believing in the existence of. A connection between a man and a woman was to her, in one way or other, a marriage. Into the reasons, whatever they might have been, that could have brought about any such connection without the rites that made it sacred, she could not penetrate or inquire. It was a subject too terrible, from which her mind retreated with awe and incomprehension. Never could it, she felt, have been intended so, at least on the woman's side. The mock marriage of romance, the deceits practised on the stage and in novels upon the innocent, she believed in without hesitation, everything in the world being more comprehensible than impurity. There might be villainous men, betrayers, seducers, Lucy could not tell; there might be monsters, griffins, fiery dragons, for anything she knew; but a woman abandoned by all her natural guard of modesties and reluctances, moved by passion, capable of being seduced, she could not understand. And still more impossible was it to imagine such sins as the outcome of mere levity, without any tragic circumstances; or to conceive of the mysteries of life as outraged and intruded upon by folly, or for the darker bait of interest. Her heart sickened at such suggestions. She knew there were poor women in the streets, victims of want and vice, poor degraded creatures for whom her heart bled, whom she could not think of for the intolerable pang of pity and shame. But all these questions had nothing to do with the sudden revelation in which she herself had so painful a part. These broken reflections were in her mind like the falling of snow. They whirled through the vague world of her troubled soul without consequence or coherence; all that had nothing to do with her. Her husband was no villain, and the woman—the beautiful, smiling woman, so much fairer, greater, more important than Lucy, she was no wretched, degraded creature. What was she then? His wife—his true wife? And if so, what was Lucy? Her brain reeled and the world went round her in a sickening whirl. The circumstances were too terrible for resentment. What could anger do, or any other quick-springing short-lived emotion? What did it matter even what Lucy felt, what any one felt? It was far beyond that. Here was fact which no emotion could undo. A wife and a child on either side, and what was to come of it; and how could life go on with this to think of, never to be forgotten, not to be put aside for a moment? It brought existence to a stand-still. She did not know what was the next step she must take, or how she could go back, or what she must say to the man who, perhaps, was not her husband, or how she could continue under that roof, or arrange the commonest details of life. There was but one thing clear before her, the business which she was bent on hurrying to a conclusion now.

She found herself in the bustle of the streets that converge upon the circus at the end of Piccadilly as she thus went on thinking, and there Lucy looked about her in some dismay, finding that she had reached the limit of the little world she knew. She was afraid of plunging alone into those bustling ways, and almost afraid of the only other alternative, which, however, she adopted, of calling a cab and giving the driver the address of Mr. Chervil in the city. To do this, and to mount into the uneasy jingling cab, gave her a little shock of the unaccustomed, which was like a breach of morals to Lucy. It seemed, though she had been independent enough in more important matters, the most daring step she had ever taken on her own responsibility. But the matter of the cab, and the aspect of this unknown world into which it conveyed her, occupied her mind a little, and stopped the tumult of her thoughts. She seemed scarcely to know what she had come about when she found herself set down at the door of Mr. Chervil's office, and ascending the grimy staircase, meeting people who stared at her, and wondered what a lady could be doing there. Mr. Chervil himself was scarcely less surprised. He said, "Lady Randolph!" with a cry of astonishment when she was shown in. And she found some difficulty, which she had not thought of, in explaining her business. He reminded her that she had given him the same instructions yesterday when he had the honour of waiting upon her in Park Lane. He was far more respectful to Lady Randolph than he had been to Lucy Trevor in her first attempts to carry out her father's will.

"I assure you," he said, "I have not neglected your wishes. I have written to Rushton on the subject. We both know by this time, Lady Randolph, that when you have made up your mind—and you have the most perfect right to do so—though we may not like it, nor think it anything but a squandering of money, still we are aware we have no right to oppose—"

"It is not that," said Lucy faintly. "It is that the circumstances have changed since yesterday. I want to—I should like to—"

"Give up your intention? I am delighted to hear it. For you must allow me to say, as a man of business—"

"It is not that," Lucy repeated. "I want to increase the sum. I find the young lady has a claim—and I want it to be done immediately, without the loss of a day. Oh, I am more, much more in earnest about it than I was yesterday. I want it settled at once. If it is not settled at once difficulties might arise. I want to double the amount. Could you not telegraph to Mr. Rushton instead of writing? I have heard that people telegraph about business."

"Double the amount! Have you thought over this? Have you had Sir Thomas's advice? It is a very important matter to decide so suddenly. Pardon me, Lady Randolph, but you must know that if you bestow at this rate you will soon not have very much left to you."

"Ah, that would be a comfort!" cried Lucy; and then there came over her the miserable thought that all the circumstances were changed, and to have a subject of disagreement between her husband and herself removed would not matter now. Once it had been the only subject, now— The suddenness of this realisation of the change filled her eyes with tears. But she restrained herself with a great effort. "Yes," she said, "I should be glad, very glad, to have done all my father wished—for many things might happen. I might die—and then who would do it?"

"We need not discuss that very unlikely contingency," said Mr. Chervil. (He said to himself: Sir Tom wouldn't, that is certain.) "But even under Mr. Trevor's will," he added, "this will be a very large sum to give—larger, don't you think, than he intended; unless there is some very special claim?"

"It is a special claim," cried Lucy, "and papa made no conditions. I was to be free in doing it. He left me quite free."

"Without doubt," the lawyer said. "I need not repeat my opinion on the subject, but you are certainly quite free. And you have brought me the young lady's name, no doubt, Lady Randolph? Yesterday, you recollect you were uncertain about her name. It is important to be quite accurate in an affair of so much importance. She is a lucky young lady. A great many would like to learn the secret of pleasing you to this extent."

Lucy looked at him with a gasp. She did not understand the rest of his speech or care to hear it. Her name? What was her name? If she had not known it before, still less did she know it now.

"Oh," she cried, "what does it matter about a name? People, girls, change their names. She is Beatrice. You might leave a blank and it could be filled up after. She is going to—marry. She is—must everything be delayed for that?—and yet it is of no importance—no importance that I can see," Lucy said, wringing her hands.

"My dear Lady Randolph! Let me say that to give a very large sum of money to a person with whose very name you are unacquainted—forgive me, but in your own interests I must speak. Let me consult with Sir Thomas."

"I do not wish my husband to be consulted. He has promised me not to interfere, and it is my business, not his," Lucy said, with a flush of excitement. And though there was much further conversation, and the lawyer did all he could to move her, it need not be said that Lucy was immovable. He went down to the door with her to put her into her carriage, as he supposed, not unwilling even in that centre of practical life to have the surrounding population see on what confidential terms he was with this fine young lady. But when he perceived that no carriage was there, and Lucy, not without a tremor, as of a very strange request, and one which might shock the nerves of her companion, asked him to get a cab for her, Mr. Chervil's astonishment knew no bounds.

"I never thought how far it was," Lucy said, faltering and apologetic. "I thought I might perhaps have been able to walk."

"Walk!" he cried, "from Park Lane?" with consternation. He stood looking after her as she drove away, saying to himself that the old man had undoubtedly been mad, and that this poor young thing was evidently cracked too. He thought it would be best to write to Sir Thomas, who was not Sir Tom to Mr. Chervil; but if it was going to happen that the poor young lady should show what he had no doubt was the hereditary weakness, Mr. Chervil could not restrain a devout wish that it might show itself decisively before half her fortune was alienated. No Sir Thomas in existence would carry out a father-in-law's will of such an insane character as that.

In the meanwhile Lucy jingled home in her cab, feeling more giddy, more heartsick than ever. There now came upon her with more potency than ever, since now it was the matter immediately before her, the question what was she to do? What was she to do? She had eluded Sir Tom on the night before, and obliged him to accept, without any demand for explanation, her strange retirement. But now what was she to do? Little Tom would not answer for a pretext again. She must either resume the former habits of her life, subdue herself entirely, meet him with a cheerful face, ignore the sudden chasm that had been made between them—or— She looked with terrified eyes at this blank wall of impossibility, and could see no way through it. Live with him as of old, in a pretence of union where no union could be, or explain how it was that she could not do so. Both these things were impossible—impossible!—and what, then, was she to do?

## CHAPTER XLIII

### THE LITTLE HOUSE IN MAYFAIR

The little house in Mayfair was very bright and gay. What conventional words are those! It was nothing of the kind. It was dim and poetical. No light that could be kept out of it was permitted to come in. The quality of light in London, even in April, is not exquisite, and perhaps the Contessa's long curtains and all the delicate draperies which she loved to hang about her were more desirable to see than that very poor thing in the way of daylight which exists in Mayfair. Bice, who was a child of light, objected a little to this shutting out, and she would have objected strongly, being young enough to love the sunshine for itself, but for the exquisite reason which the Contessa gave for the interdict she had put upon it. "Cara," she said, "if you were all white and red like those English girls (it is tant soit peu vulgar between ourselves, and not half so effective as your blanc mat), then you might have as much light as you pleased; but to put yourself in competition with them on their own ground—no, Bice mia. But in this light there is nothing to desire."

"Don't you think, then, Madama," said Bice, piqued, "that no light at all would be better still, and not to be seen the best—"

"Darling!" said the Contessa, with that smile which embodied so many things. It answered for encouragement and applause and gentle reproof, and many other matters which words could but indifferently say, and it was one of her favourite ways of turning aside a question to which she did not think fit to give any reply. And Bice swallowed her pique and asked no more. The lamps were all shaded like the windows in this bower of beauty. There was scarcely a corner that was not draped with some softly-falling, richly-tinted tissue. A delicate perfume breathed through this half-lighted world. Thus, though neither gay nor bright, it realised the effect which in our day, in the time when everything was different, was meant by these words. It was a place for pleasure, for intimate society, and conversation, and laughter, and wit; for music and soft words; and, above all, for the setting off of beauty, and the expression of admiration. The chairs were soft, the carpets like moss; there were flowers everywhere betraying themselves by their odour, even when you could not see them. The Contessa had spared no expense in making the little place—which she laughed at softly, calling it her doll's house—as perfect as it could be made.

And here the two ladies began to live a life very different from that of the Randolphs' simple dwelling. Bice, it need scarcely be said, had fulfilled all the hopes of her patroness, else had she never been produced with such bewildering mystery, yet deftness, to dazzle the eyes of young Montjoie at the Hall. She had realised all the Contessa's expectations, and justified the bills which Madame di Forno-Populo looked upon with a certain complacency as they came in, as something creditable to her, as proof of her magnificence of mind and devotion to the best interests of her protégée. And now they had entered upon their campaign. It had annoyed her in this new beginning, amid all its excitements and hopes, to be called upon by Sir Tom for explanations which it was not to her interest to give; which she had, indeed, when she deliberately sowed the seed of mystery, resolved not to give. To allow herself to be brought to book was not in her mind at all, and she was clever enough to mystify even Sir Tom, and keep his mind in a suspense and uncertainty very painful to him. But she had managed to elude his inquiries, and though it had changed the demeanour of Sir Tom, and entirely done away with the careless good humour which had been so pleasant, still she felt herself now independent of the Randolphs, and had begun her life very cheerfully and with every promise of great enjoyment. The Contessa "received" every day and all day long, from the time when she was visible, which was not, however, at a very early hour. About four the day of the ladies began. Sometimes, indeed, before that hour two favoured persons, not always the same, who had accompanied them home from the Park, would be admitted to share a dainty little luncheon. Bice now rode at the hour when everybody rides, with the Contessa, who was a graceful horsewoman, and never looked to greater advantage than in the saddle. The two beautiful Italians, as they were called, had in this way, within a week of their arrival, caused a sensation in the Row, and already their days overflowed with amusement and society. Few ladies visited the little house in Mayfair, but then they were not much wanted there. The Contessa was not one of those vulgar practitioners who profess in words their preference for men's society. But she said, so sweetly that it was barbarous to laugh (though many of her friends did so), that, having one close companion of her own sex, her dearest Bice, who was everything to her, she was independent of the feminine element. "And then they are so busy, these ladies of fashion; they have no leisure; they have so many things to do. It is a thraldom, a heavy thraldom, though the chains are gilded." "Shall we see you at Lady Blank Blank's to-night? You must be going to the Duchess's? Of course we shall meet at the Highton Grandmodes!" "Ah!" cried the Contessa, spreading out her white hands, "it is fatiguing even only to hear of it. We love our ease, Bice and I; we go nowhere where we are expected to go."

The gentlemen to whom this speech was made laughed "consumedly." They even made little signs to each other behind back, and exploded again. When she looked round at them they said the Contessa was a perfect mimic, better than anything on the stage, and that she had perfectly caught the tone of that old Lady Barbe Montfichet, who went everywhere (whom, indeed, the Contessa did not know), and laughed again. But it was not at the Contessa's power of mimicry that they laughed. It was at the delicious falsehood of her pretensions, and the thought that if she pleased she might appear at the Highton Grandmodes, or meet the best society at Lady Blank Blank's. These gentlemen knew better; and it was a joke of which they never tired. They were not, perhaps, the most desirable class of people in society who had the entrée in the Contessa's little house; they were old acquaintances who had known her in her progress through the world, mingled with a few young men whom they brought with them, partly because the boys admired these two lovely foreign women; partly because, with a certain easy benevolence that cost them nothing, they wanted the Contessa's little girl, whoever she was, to have her chance. But few, if any, of these astute gentlemen, young or old, was in any doubt as to the position she held.

Nor was she altogether without female visitors. Lady Anastasia, that authority of the press, who made the public acquainted with the movements of distinguished strangers and was not afraid of compromising herself, sometimes made one at the little parties and enjoyed them much. The Dowager Lady Randolph's card was left at the Contessa's door, as was that of the Duchess, who had looked upon her with such consternation at Lucy's party in the country. What these ladies meant it would be curious to know. Perhaps it was a lingering touch of kindness, perhaps a wish to save their credit in case it should happen by some bewildering turn of fortune that La Forno-Populo might come uppermost again. Would she dare to have herself put forward at the Drawing-room was what these ladies asked each other with bated breath. It was possible, nay, quite likely, that she might succeed in doing so, for there were plenty of good-natured people who would not refuse if she asked them, and of course so close a scrutiny was not kept upon foreigners as upon native subjects; while, as a matter of fact, the Dowager Lady Randolph was right in her assertion that, so far as could be proved, there was nothing absolutely fatal to a woman's reputation in the history of the Contessa. Would she have the courage to dare that ordeal, or would she set up a standard of revolt, and declare herself superior to that hall-mark of fashion? She was clever enough, all the people who knew her allowed, for either rôle; either to persuade some good woman, innocent and ignorant enough, to be responsible for her, and elude the researches of the Lord Chamberlain, or else to retreat bravely in gay rebellion and declare that she was not rich enough, nor her diamonds good enough, for that noonday display. For either part the Contessa was clever enough.

Meanwhile Bice had all the enjoyment, without any of the drawbacks of this new life. It was far more luxurious, splendid, and even amusing, than the old existence of the watering-places. To ride in the Park and feel herself one of that brilliant crowd, to be surrounded by a succession of lively companions, to have always "something going on," that delight of youth, and a continual incense of admiration rising around her enough to have turned a less steady head, filled Bice's cup with happiness. But perhaps the most penetrating pleasure of all was that of having carried out the Contessa's expectations and fulfilled her hopes. Had not Madame di Forno-Populo been satisfied with the beauty of her charge, none of these expenses would have been incurred, and this life of many delights would never have been; so that the soothing and exhilarating consciousness of having indeed deserved and earned her present well-being was in Bice's mind. The future, too, opened before her a horizon of boundless hope. To have everything she now had and more, along with that one element of happiness which had always been wanting, the certainty that it would last, was the happy prospect within her grasp. Her head was so steady, and the practical sense of the advantage so great, that the excitement and pleasure did not intoxicate her; but everything was delightful, novel, breathing confidence and hope. The guests at the table, where she now took her place, equal in importance to the Contessa herself, all flattered and did their best to please her. They amused her, either because they were clever or because they were ridiculous—Bice, with youthful cynicism, did not much mind which it was. When they went to the opera, a similar crowd would flutter in and out of the box, and appear afterwards to share the gay little supper and declare that no prime-donne on the stage could equal the two lovely blending voices of the Contessa and her ward. To sit late talking, laughing, singing, surrounded by all this worship, and to wake up again to a dozen plans and the same routine of pleasure next day, what heart of seventeen (and she was not quite seventeen) could resist it? One thing, however, Bice missed amid all this. It was the long gallery at the Hall, the nursery in Park Lane, little Tom crowing upon her shoulder, digging his hands into her hair, and Lucy looking on—many things, yet one. She missed this, and laughed at herself, and said she was a fool—but missed it all the same. Lucy had come, as in duty bound, and paid her call. She had been very grave—not like herself. And Sir Tom was very grave; looking at her she could not tell how; no longer with his old easy good humour, with a look of criticism and anxiety—an uneasy look, as if he had something to say to her and could not. Bice felt instinctively that if he ever said that something it would be disagreeable, and avoided his presence. But it troubled her to lose this side of her landscape, so to speak. The new was entrancing, but the old was a loss. She missed it, and thought herself a fool for missing it, and laughed, but felt it the more.

The only member of the household with whom she remained on the same easy terms as before was Jock, who came to the house in Mayfair at hours when nobody else was admitted, though he was quite unaware of the privilege he possessed. He came in the morning when Bice, too young to want the renewal which the Contessa sought in bed and in the mysteries of the toilette, sometimes fretted a little indoors at the impossibility of getting the air into her lungs, and feeling the warmth of the morning light. She was so glad to see him that Jock was deeply flattered, and sweet thoughts of the most boundless foolishness got in to his head. Bice ran to her room, and found one of her old hats which she had worn in the country, and tied a veil over her face, and came flying downstairs like a bird.

"We may go out and run in the Park so long as no one sees us," she cried. "Oh, come; nobody can see me through this veil."

"And what good will the air do you through that veil?" said Jock contemptuously. "You can't see the sun through it; it makes the whole world black. I would not go out if I were you with that thing over my face, the only chance I had for a walk. I'd rather stay at home; but perhaps you like it. Girls are such—"

"What? You are going to swear, and if you swear I will simply turn my back. Well, perhaps you didn't mean it. But I mean it. Boys are such— What? little prudes, like the old duennas in the books, and that is what you are. You think things are wrong that are not wrong. But it is to an Englishman the right thing to grumble," Bice said, with a smile of reconciliation as they stepped into the street. On that sweet morning even the street was delightful. It restored them to perfect satisfaction with each other as they made their way to the Park, which stretched its long lines of waving grass almost within sight.

"And I suppose," said Jock, after a pause, "that you like being here?"

Bice gave him a look half friendly, half disdainful. "I like living," she said. "In the country in what you call the quiet, it is only to be half alive: we are always living here. But you never come to see us ride, to be among the crowd. You are never at the opera. You don't talk as those others do—"

"Montjoie, for instance," said Jock, with a strange sense of jealousy and pain.

"Very well, Montjoie. He is what you call fun; he has always something to say, bêtises perhaps, but what does that matter? He makes me laugh."

"Makes you laugh! at his wit perhaps?" cried Jock. "Oh, what things girls are! Laugh at what a duffer like that, an ass, a fellow that has not two ideas, says."

"You have a great many ideas," said Bice; "you are clever—you know a number of things; but you are not so amusing, and you are not so good-natured. You scold me; and you say another, a friend, is an ass—"

"He was never any friend of mine," said Jock, with a hot flush of anger. "That fellow! I never had anything to say to him."

"No," said Bice, with a smiling disdain which cut poor Jock like a knife. "I made a mistake, that was not possible, for he is a man and you are only a boy."

To describe Jock's feelings under this blow would be beyond the power of words. He inferior to Montjoie! he only a boy while the other was a man! Rage was nothing in such an emergency. He looked at her with eyes that were almost pathetic in their sense of unappreciated merit, and, deeper sting still, of folly preferred. In spite of himself, Locksley Hall and those musings which have become, by no fault of the poet's, the expression of a despair which is half ridiculous, came into his mind. He did not see the ridicule. "Having known me to decline"—his eyes became moist with a dew of pain—"If you think that," he said slowly, "Bice—"

Bice answered only with a laugh. "Let us make haste; let us run," she cried. "It is so early, no one will see us. Why don't you ride, it is like flying? And to run is next best." She stopped after a flight, swift as a bird, along an unfrequented path which lay still in the April sunshine, the lilac bushes standing up on each side all athrill and rustling with the spring, with eyes that shone like stars, and that unusual colour which made her radiant. Jock, though he could have gone on much faster, was behind her for the moment, and came up after her, more occupied by the shame of being outrun and laughed at than by admiration of the girl and her beauty. She was more conscious of her own splendour of bloom than he was: though Bice was not vain, and he was more occupied by the thought of her than by any other thought.

"Girls never think of being able to stay," he said, "you do only what can be done with a rush; but that's not running. If you had ever seen the School Mile—"

"Oh no, I want to see no miles," cried Bice; "this is what I like, to have all my fingers tingle." Then she suddenly calmed down in a moment, and walked along demurely as the paths widened out to a more frequented thoroughfare. "What I want," she said, "is little Tom upon my shoulder, and to hear him scream and hold by my hair. Milady does not look as if I pleased her now. She has come once only and looked—not as she once looked. But she is still kind. She has made this ball for me—for me only. Did you know? do you dance then, if nothing else? Oh, you shall dance since the ball is for me. I love dancing—to distraction; but not once have I had a single turn, not once, since we came to England," Bice said with a sigh, which rose into a laugh in another moment, as she added, "It will be for me to come out, as you say, to be introduced into society, and after that we shall go everywhere, the Contessa says."

CHAPTER XLIV

THE SIEGE OF LONDON

The Contessa, but perhaps not more than half, believed what she said. Everything was on the cards in this capricious society of England, which is not governed by the same absolute laws as in other places. It seemed to be quite possible that she and her charge might be asked everywhere after their appearance at the ball which, she should take care to tell everybody, Lucy was giving for Bice. It was always possible in England that some great leader of fashion, some great lady whose nod gave distinction, might take pity upon Bice's youth and think it hard that she should suffer, even if without any relentings towards the Contessa. And Madame di Forno-Populo was very strong on the point, already mentioned, that there was nothing against her which could give any one a right to shut her out. The mere suggestion that the doors of society might or could be closed in her face would have driven another woman into frantic indignation, but the Contessa had passed that stage. She took the matter quite reasonably, philosophically. There was no reason. She had been poor and put to many shifts. Sometimes she had been compelled to permit herself to be indebted to a man in a way no woman should allow herself to be. She was quite aware of this, and was not, therefore, angry with society for its reluctance to receive her; but she said to herself, with great energy, that there was no cause. She was not hopeless even of the drawing-room, nor of getting the Duchess herself, a model of all the virtues, to present her, if the ball went off well at Park Lane. She said to herself that there was nothing on her mind which would make her shrink from seeking admission to the presence of the Queen. She was not afraid even of that royal lady's penetrating eye. Shiftiness, poverty, debts, modes of getting money that were, perhaps, equivocal, help too lightly accepted, all these are bad enough; but they are not in a woman the unpardonable sin. And a caprice in English society was always possible. The young beauty of Bice might attract the eye of some one whose notice would throw down all obstacles; or it might touch the heart of some woman who was so high placed as to be able to defy prejudice. And after that, of course, they would go everywhere, and every prognostication of success and triumph would come true.

Nevertheless, if things did not go on so well as this, the Contessa had furnished herself with what to say. She would tell Bice that the women were jealous, that she had been pursued by their hostility wherever she went, that a woman who secured the homage of men was always an object of their spite and malice, that it was a sort of persecution which the lovely had to bear from the unlovely in all regions. Knowing that it was fully more likely that she should fail than succeed, the Contessa had carefully provided herself with this ancient plea and would not hesitate to use it if necessary; but these were grands moyens, not to be resorted to save in case of necessity. She would herself have been willing enough to dispense with recognition and live as she was doing now, among the old and new admirers who had never failed her, enjoying everything except those dull drawing-rooms and heavy parties for which her soul longed, yet which she despised heartily, which she would have undergone any humiliation to get admission to, and turned to ridicule afterwards with the best grace in the world. She despised them, but there was nothing that could make up for absence from them; they alone had in their power the cachet, the symbol of universal acceptance. All these things depended upon the ball at Park Lane. Something had been going on there since she separated herself from that household which the Contessa did not understand. Sir Tom, indeed, was comprehensible. The discovery which he thought he had made, the things which she had allowed him to divine, and even permitted him to prove for himself without making a single assertion on her own part, were quite sufficient to account for his changed looks. But Lucy, what had she found out? It was not likely that Sir Tom had communicated his discovery to her. Lucy's demeanour confused the Contessa more than words can say. The simple creature had grown into a strange dignity, which nothing could explain. Instead of the sweet compliance and almost obedience of former days, the deference of the younger to the older woman, Lucy looked at her with grave composure, as of an equal or superior. What had happened to the girl? And it was so important that she should be friendly now and kept in good humour! Madame di Forno-Populo put forth all her attractions, gave her dear Lucy her sweetest looks and words, but made very little impression. This gave her a little tremor when she thought of it; for all her plans for the future were connected with the ball on the 26th at Park Lane.

This ball appeared to Lucy, too, the most important crisis in her life. She had made a sacrifice which was heroic that nothing might go wrong upon that day. Somehow or other, she could not tell how, for the struggle had been desperate within her, she had subdued the emotion in her own heart and schooled herself to an acceptance of the old routine of her life until that event should be over. All her calculations went to that date, but not beyond. Life seemed to stop short there. It had been arranged and settled with a light heart in the pleasure of knowing that the Contessa had taken a house for herself, and that, consequently, Lucy was henceforward to be once more mistress of her own. She had been so ashamed of her own pleasure in this prospect, so full of compunctions in respect to her guest, whose departure made her happy, that she had thrown herself with enthusiasm into this expedient for making it up to them. She had said it was to be Bice's ball. When the Dowager's revelation came upon her like a thunderbolt, as soon as she was able to think at all, she had thought of this ball with a depth of emotion which was strange to be excited by so frivolous a matter. It was a pledge of the warmest friendship, but those for whom it was to be, had turned out the enemies of her peace, the destroyers of her happiness: and it was high festival and gaiety, but her heart was breaking. Lady Randolph, afraid of what she had done, yet virulent against the Contessa, had suggested that it should be given up. It was easy to do such a thing—a few notes, a paragraph in the newspaper, a report of a cousin dead, or a sudden illness; any excuse would do. But Lucy was not to be so moved. There was in her soft bosom a sense of justice which was almost stern, and through all her troubles she remembered that Bice, at least, had a claim upon all Sir Thomas Randolph could do for her, such as nobody else could have. Under what roof but his should she make her first appearance in the world? Lucy held sternly with a mixture of bitterness and tenderness to Bice's rights. In all this misery Bice was without blame, the only innocent person, the one most wronged, more wronged even than was Lucy herself. She it was who would have to bear the deepest stigma, without any fault of hers. Whatever could be done to advance her (as she counted advancement), to make her happy (as she reckoned happiness) it was right she should have it done. Lucy suppressed her own wretchedness heroically for this cause. She bore the confusion that had come into her life without saying a word for the sake of the other young creature who was her fellow-sufferer. How hard it was to do she could not have told, nor did any one suspect, except, vaguely, Sir Tom himself, who perceived some tragic mischief that was at work without knowing how it had come there or what it was. He tried to come to some explanation, but Lucy would have no explanation. She avoided him as much as it was possible to do. She had nothing to say when he questioned her. Till the 26th! Nothing, she was resolved, should interfere with that. And then—but not the baby in the nursery knew less than Lucy what was to happen then.

They had come to London on the 2d, so that this day of fate was three weeks off, and during that time the Contessa had made no small progress in her affairs. Three weeks is a long time in a house which is open to visitors, even if only from four o'clock in the afternoon, every day, and without intermission; and indeed that was not the whole, for the ladies were accessible elsewhere than in the house in Mayfair. It had pleased the Contessa not to be visible when Lord Montjoie called at a somewhat early hour on the very earliest day. He was a young man who knew the world, and not one to have things made too easy for him. He was all aflame accordingly to gain the entrée thus withheld, and when the Contessa appeared for the first time in the Park, with her lovely companion, Montjoie was eagerly on the watch, and lost no time in claiming acquaintance, and joining himself to her train. He was one of the two who were received to luncheon two or three days afterwards. When the ladies went to the opera he was on thorns till he could join them. He was allowed to go home with them for one song, and to come in next afternoon for a little music. And from that time forward there was no more question of shutting him out. He came and went almost when he pleased, as a young man may be permitted to do when he has become one of the intimates in an easy-going, pleasure-loving household, where there is always "something going on." He was so little flattered that never during all these days and nights had he once been allowed to repeat the performance upon which he prided himself, and with which he had followed up the singing of the Contessa and Bice at the Hall. The admirable lady whom they had met there, with her two daughters, had been eager that Lord Montjoie should display this accomplishment of his, and the girls had been enchanted by his singing; but the Contessa, though not so irreproachable, would have none of it. And Bice laughed freely at the young nobleman who had so much to bestow, and they both threw at him delicate little shafts of wit, which never pierced his stolid complacency, though he was quite quick withal to see the fun when other gentlemen looked at each other over the Contessa's shoulder, and burst into little peals of laughter at her little speeches about the Highton Grandmodes and other such exclusive houses. Montjoie knew all about La Forno-Populo. "But yet that little Bice," he said, "don't you know?" No one like her had come within Montjoie's ken. He knew all about the girls in blue or in pink or in white, who asked him to sing. But Bice, who laughed at his accomplishment and at himself, and was so saucy to him, and made fun of him, he allowed, to his face, that was very different. He described her in terms that were not chivalrous, and his own emotions in words still less ornate; but before the fortnight was over the best judges declared among themselves that, by Jove, the Forno-Populo had done it this time, that the little one knew how to play her cards, that it was all up with Montjoie, poor little beggar, with other elegances of a similar kind. The man who had taken the Contessa's house for her, and a great deal of trouble about all her arrangements, whom she described as a very old friend, and whose rueful sense that house-agents and livery stables might eventually look to him if she had no success in her enterprise did not impair his fidelity, went so far as to speak seriously to Montjoie on the subject. "Look here, Mont," he said, "don't you think you are going it rather too strong? There is not a thing against the girl, who is as nice as a girl can be, but then the aunt, you know—"

"I'm glad she is the aunt," said Montjoie. "I thought she was the mother: and I always heard you were devoted to her."

"We are very old friends," said this disinterested adviser. "There's nothing I would not do for her. She is the best soul out, and was the loveliest woman I can tell you—the girl is nothing to what she was. Aunt or cousin, I am not sure what is the relationship; but that's not the question. Don't you think you are coming it rather strong?"

"Oh, I've got my wits about me," said Montjoie; and then he added, rather reluctantly—for it is the fashion of his kind to be vulgar and to keep what generosity or nobleness there is in them carefully out of sight—"and I've no relations, don't you know? I've got nobody to please but myself—"

"Well, that is a piece of luck anyhow," the Mentor said; and he told the Contessa the gist of the conversation next morning, who was highly pleased by the news.

The curious point in all this was that Bice had not the least objection to Montjoie. She was a clever girl and he was a stupid young man, but whether it was that her entirely unawakened heart had no share at all in the matter, or that her clear practical view of affairs influenced her sentiments as well as her mind, it is certain that she was quite pleased with her fate, and ready to embrace it without the least sense that it was a sacrifice or anything but the happiest thing possible. He amused her, as she had said to Jock. He made her laugh, most frequently at himself; but what did that matter? He had a kind of good looks, and that good nature which is the product of prosperity and well-being, and a sense of general superiority to the world. Perhaps the girl saw no man of a superior order to compare him with; but, as a matter of fact, she was perfectly satisfied with Montjoie. Mr. Derwentwater and Jock were more ridiculous to her than he was, and were less in harmony with everything she had previously known. Their work, their intellectual occupations, their cleverness and aspirations were out of her world altogether. The young man-about-town who had nothing to do but amuse himself, who was always "knocking about," as he said, whose business was pleasure, was the kind of being with whom she was acquainted. She had no understanding of the other kind. He who had been her comrade in the country, whose society had amused her there, and for whom she had a sort of half-condescending affection, was droll to her beyond measure, with his ambitions and great ideas as to what he was to do. He, too, made her laugh; but not as Montjoie did. She laughed, though this would have immeasurably surprised Jock, with much less sympathy than she had with the other, upon whom he looked with so much contempt. They were both silly to Bice,—silly as, in her strange experience, she thought it usual and natural for men to be,—but Montjoie's manner of being silly was more congenial to her than the other. He was more in tune with the life she had known. Hamburg, Baden, Wiesbaden, and all the other Bads, even Monaco, would have suited Montjoie well enough. The trade of pleasure-making has its affinities like every other, and a tramp on his way from fair to fair is more en rapport with a duke than the world dreams of. Thus Bice found that the young English marquis, with more money than he knew how to spend, was far more like the elegant adventurer living on his wits, than all those intervening classes of society, to whom life is a more serious, and certainly a much less festive and costly affair. She understood him far better. And instead of being, as Lucy thought, a sacrifice, an unfortunate victim sold to a loveless marriage for the money and the advantages it would bring, Bice went on very gaily, her heart as unmoved as possible, to what she felt to be a most congenial fate.

And they all waited for the 26th and the ball with growing excitement. It would decide many matters. It would settle what was to be the character of the Contessa's campaign. It might reintroduce her into society under better auspices than ever, or it might—but there was no need to foretell anything unpleasant. And very likely it would conclude at the same source as it began, Bice's triumph—a débutante who was already the affianced bride of the young Marquis of Montjoie, the greatest parti in the kingdom. The idea was like wine, and went to the Contessa's head.

She had in this interval of excitement a brief little note from Lucy, which startled her beyond measure for the moment. It was to ask the exact names of Bice. "You shall know in a few days why I ask, but it is necessary they should be written down in full and exactly," Lucy said. The Contessa had half forgotten, in the new flood of life about her, what was in Lucy's power, and the further advantage that might come of their relations, and she did not think of this even now, but felt with momentary tremor as if some snare lay concealed under these simple words. After a moment's consideration, however, she wrote with a bold and flowing hand:

"SWEET LUCY—The child's name is Beatrice Ersilia. You cannot, I am sure, mean her anything but good by such a question. She has not been properly introduced, I know—I am fantastic, I loved the Bice, and no more.

"DARLING, A TE."

This was signed with a cipher, which it was not very easy to make out—a little mystery which pleased the Contessa. She thus involved in a pleasant little uncertainty her own name, which nobody knew.

CHAPTER XLV

THE BALL

Lady Randolph's ball was one of the first of the season, and as it was the first ball she had ever given, and both Lucy and her husband were favourites in society, it was looked forward to as the forerunner of much excitement and pleasure, and with a freshness of interest and anticipation which, unless in April, is scarcely to be expected in town. The rooms in Park Lane, though there was nothing specially exquisite or remarkable in their equipment, were handsome and convenient. They formed a good background for the people assembled under their many lights without withdrawing the attention of any one from the looks, the dresses, the bright eyes, and jewels collected within, which, perhaps, after all, is an advantage in its way. And everybody who was in town was there, from the Duchess, upon whom the Contessa had designs of so momentous a character, down to those wandering young men-about-town who form the rank and file of the great world and fill up all the corners. There was, it is true, not much room to dance, but a bewildering amount of people, great names, fine toilettes, and beautiful persons.

The Contessa timed her arrival at the most effective moment, when the rooms were almost full, but not yet crowded, and most of the more important guests had already arrived. It was just after the first greetings of people seeing each other for the first time were over, and an event of some kind was wanted. At such a moment princes and princesses are timed to arrive and bring the glory of the assembly to a climax. Lucy had no princess to honour her. But when out of the crowd round the doorway there were seen to emerge two beautiful and stately women unknown, the sensation was almost as great. One of them, who had the air of a Queen-Mother, was in dark dress studiously arranged to be a little older, a little more massive and magnificent than a woman of the Contessa's age required to wear (and which, accordingly, threw up all the more, though this, to do her justice, was a coquetry more or less unintentional, her unfaded beauty); and the other, an impersonation of youth, contemplated the world by her side with that open-eyed and sovereign gaze, proud and modest, but without any of the shyness or timidity of a débutante which becomes a young princess in her own right. There was a general thrill of wonder and admiration wherever they were seen. Who were they, everybody asked? Though the name of the Forno-Populo was too familiarly known to a section of society, that is not to say that the ladies of Lucy's party, or even all the men had heard it bandied from mouth to mouth, or were aware that it had ever been received with less than respect: and the universal interest was spoiled only here and there in a corner by the laugh of the male gossips, who made little signs to each other, in token of knowing more than their neighbours. It was said among the more innocent that this was an Italian lady of distinction with her daughter or niece, and her appearance, if a little more marked and effective than an English lady's might have been, was thus fully explained and accounted for by the difference in manners and that inalienable dramatic gift, which it is common to believe in England, foreigners possess. No doubt their entrance was very dramatic. The way in which they contrasted and harmonised with each other was too studied for English traditions, which, in all circumstances, cling to something of the impromptu, an air of accidentalism. They were a spectacle in themselves as they advanced through the open central space, from which the ordinary guests instinctively withdrew to leave room for them. "Is it the Princess?" people asked, and craned their necks to see. It must at least be a German Serenity—the Margravine of Pimpernikel, the Hereditary Princess of Weissnichtwo—but more beautiful and graceful than English prejudice expects German ladies to be. Ah, Italian! that explained everything—their height, their grace, their dark beauty, their effective pose. The Latin races alone know how to arrange a spectacle in that easy way, how to produce themselves so that nobody could be unimpressed. There was a dramatic pause before them, a hum of excitement after they had passed. Who were they? Evidently the most distinguished persons present—the guests of the evening. Sir Tom, uneasy enough, and looking grave and preoccupied, which was so far from being his usual aspect, led them into the great drawing-room, where the Duchess, who had daughters who danced, had taken her place. He did not look as if he liked it, but the Contessa, for her part, looked round her with a radiant smile, and bowed very much as the Queen does in a state ceremonial to the people she knew. She performed a magnificent curtsey, half irony, half defiance, before the Dowager Lady Randolph, who looked on at this progress speechless. How Lucy could permit it; how Tom could have the assurance to do it; occupied the Dowager's thoughts. She had scarcely self-command to make a stiff sweep of recognition as the procession passed.

The Duchess was at the upper end of the room, with all her daughters about her. Besides the younger ones who danced, there were two countesses supporting their mother. She was the greatest lady present, and she felt the dignity. But when she perceived the little opening that took place among the groups about, and, looking up, perceived the Contessa sweeping along in that regal separation, you might have blown her Grace away with a breath. Not only was the Duchess the most important person in the room, but her reception of the newcomer would be final, a sort of social life or death for the Contessa. But the supplicant approached with the air of a queen, while the arbiter of fate grew pale and trembled at the sight. If there was a tremor in her Grace's breast there was no less a tremor under the Contessa's velvet. But Madame di Forno-Populo had this great advantage, that she knew precisely what to do, and the Duchess did not know: she was fully prepared, and the Duchess taken by surprise: and still more that her Grace was a shy woman, whose intellect, such as it was, moved slowly, while the Contessa was very clever, and as prompt as lightning. She perceived at a glance that the less time the great lady had to think the better, and hastened forward for a step or two, hurrying her stately pace, "Ah, Duchess!" she said, "how glad I am to meet so old an acquaintance. And I want, above all things, to have your patronage for my little one. Bice—the Duchess, an old friend of my prosperous days, permits me to present you to her." She drew her young companion forward as she spoke, while the Duchess faltered and stammered a "How d'ye do?" and looked in vain for succour to her daughters, who were looking on. Then Bice showed her blood. It had not been set down in the Contessa's programme what she was to do, so that the action took her patroness by surprise, as well as the great lady whom it was so important to captivate. While the Duchess stood stiff and awkward, making a conventional curtsey against her will, and with a conventional smile on her mouth, Bice, with the air of a young princess, innocently, yet consciously superior to all her surroundings, suddenly stepped forward, and taking the Duchess's hand, bent her stately young head to kiss it. There was in the sudden movement that air of accident, of impulse, which we all love. It overcame all the tremors of the great lady. She said, "My dear!" in the excitement of the moment, and bent forward to kiss the cheek of this beautiful young creature, who was so deferential, so reverent in her young pride. And the Duchess's daughters did not disapprove! Still more wonderful than the effect on the Duchess was the effect upon these ladies, of whose criticisms their mother stood in dread. They drew close about the lovely stranger, and it immediately became apparent to the less important guests that the Italian ladies, the heroines of the evening, had amalgamated with the ducal party—as it was natural they should.

Never had there been a more complete triumph. The Contessa stepped in and made hay while the sun shone. She waved off with a scarcely perceptible movement of her hand several of her intimates who would have gathered round her, and vouchsafed only a careless word to Montjoie, who had hastened to present himself. The work to which she devoted herself was the amusement of the Duchess, who was not, to tell the truth, very easily amused. But Madame di Forno-Populo had infinite resources, and she succeeded. She selected the Dowager Lady Randolph for her butt, and made fun of her so completely that her Grace almost exceeded the bounds of decorum in her laughter.

"You must not, really; you must not—she is a great friend of mine," the Duchess said. But perhaps there was not much love between the two ladies. And thus by degrees the conversation was brought round to the Populina palace and the gay scenes so long ago.

"You must have heard of our ruin," the Contessa said, looking full into the Duchess's face; "everybody has heard of that. I have been too poor to live in my own house. We have wandered everywhere, Bice and I. When one is proud it is more easy to be poor away from home. But we are in very high spirits to-day, the child and I," she added. "All can be put right again. My little niece has come into a fortune. She has made an inheritance. We received the news to-night only. That is how I have recovered my spirits— and to see you, Duchess, and renew the beautiful old times."

"Oh, indeed!" the Duchess said, which was not much; but then she was a woman of few words.

"Yes, we came to London very poor," said the Contessa. "What could I do? It was the moment to produce the little one. We have no Court. Could I seek for her the favour of the Piedmontese? Oh no! that was impossible. I said to myself she shall come to that generous England, and my old friends there will not refuse to take my Bice by the hand."

"Oh no; I am sure not," said the Duchess.

As for Bice she had long ere now set off with Montjoie, who had hung round her from the moment of her entrance into the room, and whose admiration had grown to such a height by the cumulative force of everybody else's admiration swelling into it, that he could scarcely keep within those bounds of compliment which are permitted to an adorer who has not yet acquired the right to be hyperbolical.

"Oh yes, it's pretty enough: but you don't see half how pretty it is, for you can't see yourself, don't you know?" said this not altogether maladroit young practitioner. Bice gave him a smile like one of the Contessa's smiles, which said everything that was needful without giving her any trouble. But now that the effect of her entrance was attained, and all that dramatic business done with, the girl's soul was set upon enjoyment. She loved dancing as she loved every other form of rapid movement. The only drawback was that there was so little room. "Why do they make the rooms so small?" she said pathetically; a speech which was repeated from mouth to mouth like a witticism, as something so characteristic of the young Italian, w hose marble halls would never be overcrowded: though, as a matter of fact, Bice knew very little of marble halls.

"Were you ever in the gallery at the Hall?" she asked. "To go from one end to the other, that was worth the while. It was as if one flew."

"I never knew they danced down there," said Montjoie. "I thought it very dull, don't you know, till you appeared. If I had known you had dances, and fun going on, and other fellows cutting one out—"

"There was but one other fellow," said Bice gravely. "I have seen in this country no one like him. Ah, why is he not here? He is more fun than any one, but better than fun. He is—"

Montjoie's countenance was like a thunder-cloud big with fire and flame.

"Trevor, I suppose you mean. I never thought that duffer could dance. He was a great sap at school, and a hideous little prig, giving himself such airs! But if you think all that of him—"

"It was not Mr. Trevor," said Bice. Then catching sight of Lady Randolph at a little distance, she made a dart towards her on her partner's arm.

"I am telling Lord Montjoie of my partner at the Hall," she said. "Ah, Milady, let him come and look! How he would clap his hands to see the lights and the flowers. But we could not have our gymnastique with all the people here."

Lucy was very pale; standing alone, abstracted amid the gay crowd, as if she did not very well know where she was.

"Baby? Oh, he is quite well, he is fast asleep," she said, looking up with dim eyes. And then there broke forth a little faint smile on her face. "You were always good to him," she said.

"So it was the baby," said Montjoie, delighted. "What a one you are to frighten a fellow. If it had been Trevor I think I'd have killed him. How jolly of you to do gymnastics with that little beggar; he's dreadfully delicate, ain't he, not likely to live? But you're awfully cruel to me. You think no more of giving a wring to my heart than if it was a bit of rag. I think you'd like to see the blood come."

"Let us dance," said Bice with great composure. She was bent upon enjoyment. She had not calculated upon any conversation. Indeed she objected to conversation on this point even when it did not interfere with the waltz. All could be settled much more easily by the Contessa, and if marriage was to be the end, that was a matter of business not adapted for a ballroom. She would not allow herself to be led away to the conservatory or any other retired nook such as Montjoie felt he must find for this affecting purpose. Bice did not want to be proposed to. She wanted to dance. She abandoned him for other partners without the slightest evidence of regret. She even accepted, when he was just about to seize upon her at the end of a dance, Mr. Derwentwater, preferring to dance the Lancers with him to the bliss of sitting out with Lord Montjoie. That forsaken one gazed at her with a consternation beyond words. To leave him and the proposal that was on his very lips for a square dance with a tutor! The young Marquis gazed after her as she disappeared with a certain awe. It could not be that she preferred Derwentwater. It must be her cleverness which he could not fathom, and some wonderful new system of Italian subtlety to draw a fellow on.

"I like it better than standing still—I like it—enough," said Bice. "To dance, that is always something." Mr. Derwentwater also felt, like Lord Montjoie, that the young lady gave but little importance to her partner.

"You like the rhythm, the measure, the woven paces and the waving hands," her companion said.

Bice stared at him a little, not comprehending. "But you prefer," he continued, "like most ladies, the modern Bacchic dance, the whirl, the round, though what the old Puritans call promiscuous dancing of men and women together was not, I fear, Greek—"

"I know nothing of the Greeks," said Bice. "Vienna is the best place for the valse, but Greek—no, we never were there."

"I am thinking of classic terms," said MTutor with a smile, but he liked her all the better for not knowing. "We have in vases and in sculpture the most exquisite examples. You have never perhaps given your attention to ancient art? I cannot quite agree with Mr. Alma Tadema on that point. He is a great artist, but I don't think the wild leap of his dances is sanctioned by anything we possess."

"Do not take wild leaps," said Bice, "but keep time. That is all you require in a quadrille. Why does every one laugh and go wrong. But it is a shame! One should not dance if one will not take the trouble. And why does he not do anything?" she said, in the pause between two figures, suddenly coming in sight of Jock, who stood against the wall in their sight, following her about with eyes over which his brows were curved heavily; "he does not dance nor ride; he only looks on."

"He reads," said Mr. Derwentwater. "The boy will be a great scholar if he keeps it up."

"One cannot read in society," said Bice. "Now, you must remember, you go that way; you do not come after me."

"I should prefer to come after you. That is the heavenly way when one can follow such a leader. You remember what your own Dante—"

"Oh!" murmured Bice, with a long sigh of impatience, "I have no Dante. I have a partner who will not give himself the pains—Now," she said, with an emphatic little pat of her foot and movement of her hands. Her soul was in the dance, though it was only the Lancers. With a slight line of annoyance upon her forehead she watched his performance, taking upon herself the responsibility, pushing him by his elbow when he went wrong, or leading him in the right way. Mr. Derwentwater had thought to carry off his mistakes with a laugh, but this was not Bice's way of thinking. She made him a little speech when the dance was over.

"I think you are a great scholar too," she said; "but it will be well that you should not come forward again with a lady to dance the Lancers, for you cannot do it. And that will sometimes make a girl to have the air of being also awkward, which is not just."

Mr. Derwentwater grew very red while this speech was making to him. He was a man of great and varied attainments, and had any one told him that he would blush about so trivial a matter as a Lancers—! But he grew very red and almost stammered as he said with humility, "I am afraid I am very deficient, but with you to guide me—Signorina, there is one divine hour which I never forget—when you sang that evening. May I call? May I see you for half an hour to-morrow?"

"Oh," said Bice, with a deep-drawn breath, "here is some one else coming who does not dance very well! Talk to him about the Greek, and Lord Montjoie will take me. To-morrow! oh yes, with pleasure," she said as she took Montjoie's arm and darted away into the crowd. Montjoie was all glowing and radiant with pride and joy.

"I thought I'd hang off and on and take my chance, don't you know? I thought you'd soon get sick of that sort. You and I go together like two birds. I have been watching you all this time, you and old Derwentwater. What was that he said about to-morrow? I want to talk about to-morrow too—unless, indeed to-night—"

"Oh, Lord Montjoie," cried Bice, "dance! It was not to talk you came here, and you can dance better than you talk," she added, with that candour which distinguished her. And Montjoie flew away with her rushing and whirling. He could dance. It was almost his only accomplishment.

CHAPTER XLVI

THE BALL CONTINUED

Other eyes than those of her lovers followed Bice through this brilliant scene. Sir Tom had been living a strange stagnant life since that day before he left the Hall, when Lucy, innocently talking of Bice's English parentage, had suddenly roused him to the question—Who was Bice, and who her parents, English or otherwise? The suggestion was very sudden and very simple, conveying in it no intended hint or innuendo. But it came upon Sir Tom like a sudden thunderbolt, or rather like the firing of some train that had been laid and prepared for explosion. The tenor of his fears and suspicions has already been indicated. Nor has it ever been concealed from the reader of this history that there were incidents in Sir Tom's life upon which he did not look back with satisfaction, and which it would have grieved him much to have revealed to his wife in her simplicity and unsuspecting trust in him. One of these was a chapter of existence so long past as to be almost forgotten, yet unforgettable, which gave, when he thought of it, an instant meaning to the fact that a half-Italian girl of English parentage on one side should have been brought mysteriously, without warning or formal introduction, to his house by the Contessa. From that time, as has been already said, the disturbance in his mind was great. He could get no satisfaction one way or another. But to-night his uneasiness had taken a new and unexpected form. Should it so happen that Bice's identity with a certain poor baby, born in Tuscany seventeen years before, might some day be proved, what new cares, what new charge might it not place upon his shoulders? At such a thought Sir Tom held his very breath.

The first result of such a possibility was, that he might find himself to stand in a relationship to the girl for whom he had hitherto had a careless liking and no more, which would change both his life and hers; and already he watched her with uneasy eyes and with a desire to interfere which bewildered him like a new light upon his own character. He could scarcely understand how he had taken it all so lightly before and interested himself so little in the fate of a young creature for whom it would not be well to be brought up according to the Contessa's canons, and follow her example in the world. He remembered, in the light of this new possibility, the levity with which he had received his wife's distress about Bice, and how lightly he had laughed at Lucy's horror as to the Contessa's ideas of marriage, and of what her protégée was to do. He had said if they could catch any decent fellow with money enough it was the best thing that could happen to the girl, and that Bice would be no worse off than others, and that she herself, after the training she had gone through, was very little likely to have any delicacy on the subject. But when it had once occurred to him that the girl of whom he spoke so lightly might be his own child, an extraordinary change came over Sir Tom's views. He laughed no longer—he became so uneasy lest something should be done or said to affect Bice's good name, or throw her into evil hands, that his thoughts had circled unquietly round the house in Mayfair, and he had spent far more of his time there on the watch than he himself thought right. He knew very well the explanation that would be given of those visits of his, and he did not feel sure that some good-natured friends might not have already suggested suspicion to Lucy, who had certainly been very strange since their arrival in town. But he would not give up his watch, which was in a way, he said to himself, his duty, if— He followed the girl's movements with disturbed attention, and would hurry into the Park to ride by her, to shut out an unsuitable cavalier, and make little lectures to her as to her behaviour with an embarrassed anxiety which Bice could not understand but which amused more than it benefited the Contessa, to whom this result of her mystification was the best fun in the world. But it was not amusing to Sir Tom. He regarded the society of men who gathered about the ladies with disgust. Montjoie was about the best—he was not old enough to be much more than silly—but even Montjoie was not a person whom he would himself choose to be closely connected with. Then came the question: If it should turn out that she was that child, was it expedient that any one should know of it? Would it be better for her to be known as Sir Thomas Randolph's daughter, even illegitimate, or as the relative and dependent of the Forno-Populo? In the one case, her interests would have no guardian at all; in the other, what a shock it would give to his now-established respectability and the confidence all men had in him, to make such a connection known. Turning over everything in his thoughts, it even occurred to Sir Tom that it would be better for him to confess an early secret marriage, and thus save his own reputation and give to Bice a lawful standing ground. The poor young mother was dead long ago; there could be no harm in such an invention. Lucy could not be wounded by anything which happened so long before he ever saw her. And Bice would be saved from all stigma; if only it was Bice! if only he could be sure!

But Sir Tom, whose countenance had not the habit of expressing anything but a large and humorous content, the careless philosophy of a happy temper and easy mind, was changed beyond description by the surging up of such thoughts. He became jealous and suspicious, watching Bice with a constant impulse to interfere, and even—while disregarding all the safeguards of his own domestic happiness for this reason—in his heart condemned the girl because she was not like Lucy, and followed her movements with a criticism which was as severe as that of the harshest moralist.

Nobody in that lighthearted house could understand what had come over the good Sir Tom, not even the Contessa, who after a manner knew the reason, yet never imagined that the idea, which gave her a sort of malicious pleasure, would have led to such a result. Sir Tom had always been the most genial of hosts, but in his present state of mind even in this respect he was not himself. He kept his eye on Bice with a sternness of regard quite out of keeping with his character. If she should flirt unduly, if she began to show any of those arts which made the Contessa so fascinating, he felt, with a mingling of self-ridicule which tickled him in spite of his seriousness, that nothing could keep him from interposing. He had been charmed in spite of himself, even while he saw through and laughed at the Contessa's cunning ways; but to see them in a girl who might, for all he knew, have his own blood in her veins was a very different matter. He felt it was in him to interpose roughly, imperiously—and if he did so, would Bice care? She would turn upon him with smiling defiance, or perhaps ask what right had he to meddle in her affairs. Thus Sir Tom was so preoccupied that the change in Lucy, the effort she made to go through her necessary duties, the blotting out of all her simple kindness and brightness, affected him only dully as an element of the general confusion, and nothing more.

But the Contessa, for her part, was radiant. She was victorious all along the line. She had received Lucy's note informing her of the provision she meant to make for Bice only that afternoon, and her heart was dancing with the sense of wealth, of money to spend and endless capability of pleasure. Whatever happened this was secure, and she had already in the first hour planned new outlays which would make Lucy's beneficence very little of a permanent advantage. But she said nothing of it to Bice, who might (who could tell, girls being at all times capricious) take into her little head that it was no longer necessary to encourage Montjoie, on whom at present she looked complacently enough as the probable giver of all that was best in life. This was almost enough for one day; but the Contessa fully believed in the proverb that there is nothing that succeeds like success, and had faith in her own fortunate star for the other events of the evening. And she had been splendidly successful. She had altogether vanquished the timid spirit of the Duchess, that model of propriety. Her entry upon the London world had been triumphant, and she had all but achieved the honours of the drawing-room. Unless the Lord Chamberlain should interfere, and why should he interfere? her appearance in the larger world of society would be as triumphant as in Park Lane. Her beautiful eyes were swimming in light, the glow of satisfaction and triumph. It fatigued her a little indeed to play the part of a virtuous chaperon, and stand or sit in one place all the evening, awaiting her débutante between the dances, talking with the other virtuous ladies in the same exercise of patience, and smilingly keeping aloof from all participation at first hand in the scene which would have helped to amuse her indeed, but interfered with the fulfilment of her rôle. But she had internal happiness enough to make up to her for her self-denial. She would order that set of pearls for Bice and the emerald pendant for herself which had tempted her so much, to-morrow. And the Duchess was to present her, and probably this evening Montjoie would propose. Was it possible to expect in this world a more perfect combination of successes?

Mr. Derwentwater went off somewhat discomfited to make a tour of the rooms after the remorseless address of Bice. He tried to smile at the mock severity of her judgment. He, no more than Montjoie, would believe that she meant only what she said. This accomplished man of letters and parts agreed, if in nothing else, in this, with the young fool of quality, that such extreme candour and plain speaking was some subtle Italian way of drawing an admirer on. He put it into finer words than Montjoie could command, and said to himself that it was that mysterious adorable feminine instinct which attracted by seeming to repel. And even on a more simple explanation it was comprehensible enough. A girl who attached so much importance to the accomplishments of society would naturally be annoyed by the failure in these of one to whom she looked up. A regret even moved his mind that he had not given more attention to them in earlier days. It was perhaps foolish to neglect our acquirements, which after all would not take very much trouble, and need only be brought forward, as Dogberry says, when there was no need for such vanities. He determined with a little blush at himself to note closely how other men did, and so be able another time to acquit himself to her satisfaction. And even her severity was sweet; it implied that he was not to her what other men were, that even in the more trifling accessories of knowledge she would have him to excel. If he had been quite indifferent to her, why should she have taken this trouble? And then that "To-morrow; with pleasure." What did it mean? That though she would not give him her attention to-night, being devoted to her dancing (which is what girls are brought up to in this strangely imperfect system), she would do so on the earliest possible occasion. He went about the room like a man in a dream, following everywhere with his eyes that vision of beauty, and looking forward to the next step in his life-drama with an intoxication of hope which he did not attempt to subdue. He was indeed pleased to experience a grande passion. It was a thing which completed the mental equipment of a man. Love—not humdrum household affection, such as is all that is looked for when the exigencies of life make a wife expedient, and with full calculation of all he requires the man sets out to look for her and marry her. This was very different, an all-mastering passion, disdainful of every obstacle. To-morrow! He felt an internal conviction that, though Montjoie might dance and answer for the amusement of an evening, that bright and peerless creature would not hesitate as to who should be her guide for life.

It was while he was thus roaming about in a state of great excitement and a subdued ecstasy of anticipation, that he encountered Jock, who had not been enjoying himself at all. At this great entertainment Jock had been considered a boy, and no more. Even as a boy, had he danced there might have been some notice taken of him, but he was incapable in this way, and in no other could he secure any attention. At a party of a graver kind there were often people who were well enough pleased to talk to Jock, and from men who owed allegiance to his school a boy who had distinguished himself and done credit to the old place was always sure of notice. But then, though high up in Sixth Form, and capable of any eminence in Greek verse, he was nobody; while a fellow like Montjoie, who had never got beyond the rank of lower boy, was in the front of affairs, the admired of all admirers, Bice's chosen partner and companion. The mind develops with a bound when it has gone through such an experience. Jock stood with his back against the wall, and watched everything from under his eyebrows. Sometimes there was a glimmer as of moisture in those eyes, half veiled under eyelids heavily curved and puckered with wrath and pain, for he was very young, not much more than a child, notwithstanding his manhood. But what with a keenness of natural sight, and what with the bitter enlightening medium of that moisture, Jock saw the reality of the scene more clearly than Mr. Derwentwater, roaming about in his dream of anticipation, self-deceived, was capable of doing. He caught sight of Jock in his progress, and, though it was this sentiment which had separated them, its natural effect was also to throw them together. MTutor paused and took up a position by his pupil's side. "What a foolish scene considered philosophically," he said; "and yet how many human interests in solution, and floating adumbrations of human fate! I have been dancing," Mr. Derwentwater continued, with some solemnity and a full sense of the superior position involved, "with, I verily believe, the most beautiful creature in the world."

Jock looked up, fixing him with a critical, slightly cynical regard. He had been well aware of Mr. Derwentwater's very ineffective performance, and divined too clearly the sentiments of Bice not to feel all a spectator's derision for this uncalled-for self-complacency; but he made no remark.

"There is nothing trivial in the exercise in such a combination. I incline to think that beauty is almost the greatest of all the spectacles that Nature sets before us. The effect she has upon us is greater than that produced by any other influence. You are perhaps too young to have your mind awakened on such a subject—"

To hear this foolish wisdom pouring forth, while the listener felt at every breath how his own bosom thrilled with an emotion too deep to be put into words, with a passion, hopeless, ridiculous, to which no one would accord any sympathy or comment but a laugh! Heaven and earth! and all because a fellow was some dozen years older, thinking himself a man, and you only a boy!

"—but you have a fine intelligence, and it can never be amiss for you to approach a great subject on its most elevated side. She is not much older than you are, Jock."

"She is not so old as I am. She is three months younger than I am," cried Jock, in his gruffest voice.

"And yet she is a revelation," said Mr. Derwentwater. "I feel that I am on the eve of a great crisis in my being. You have always been my favourite, my friend, though you are so much younger; and in this I feel we are more than ever sympathetic. Jock, to-morrow—to-morrow I am to see her, to tell her— Come out on the balcony, there is no one there, and the moonlight and the pure air of night are more fit for such heart opening than this crowded scene."

"What are you going to tell her?" said Jock, with his eyebrows meeting over his eyes and his back against the wall. "If you think she'll listen to what you tell her! She likes Montjoie. It is not that he's rich and that, but she likes him, don't you know, better than any of us. Oh, talk about mysteries," cried Jock, turning his head away, conscious of that moisture which half-blinded him, but which he could not get rid of, "how can you account for that? She likes him, that fellow, better than either you or me!"

Better than Jock; far better than this man, his impersonation of noble manhood, whom the most levelling of all emotions, the more than Red Republican Love, had suddenly brought down to, nay, below, Jock's level—for not only was he a fool like Jock, but a hopeful fool, while Jock had penetrated the fulness of despair, and dismissed all illusion from his youthful bosom. The boy turned his head away, and the voice which he had made so gruff quavered at the end. He felt in himself at that moment all the depths of profound and visionary passion, something more than any man ever was conscious of who had an object and a hope. The boy had neither; he neither hoped to marry her nor to get a hearing, nor even to be taken seriously. Not even the remorse of a serious passion rejected, the pain of self-reproach, the afterthought of pity and tenderness would be his. He would get a laugh, nothing more. That schoolboy, that brother of Lady Randolph's, who does not leave school for a year! He knew what everybody would say. And yet he loved her better than any one of them! MTutor startled, touched, went after him as Jock turned away, and linking his arm in his, said something of the kind which one would naturally say to a boy. "My dear fellow, you don't mean to tell me—? Come, Jock! This is but your imagination that beguiles you. The heart has not learned to speak so soon," MTutor said, leaning upon Jock's shoulder. The boy turned upon him with a fiery glow in his eyes.

"What were you saying about dancing?" he said. "They seem to be making up that Lancers business again."

CHAPTER XLVII

NEXT MORNING

"You have news to tell me, Bice mia?"

There was a faint daylight in the streets, a blueness of dawn as the ladies drove home.

"Have I? I have amused myself very much. I am not fatigued, no. I could continue as long—as long as you please," Bice answered, who was sitting up in her corner with more bloom than at the beginning of the evening, her eyes shining, a creature incapable of fatigue. The Contessa lay back in hers, with a languor which was rather adapted to her rôle as a chaperon than rendered necessary by the fatigue she felt. If she had not been amused, she was triumphant, and this supplied a still more intoxicating exhilaration than that of mere pleasure.

"Darling!" she said, in her most expressive tone. She added a few moments after, "But Lord Montjoie! He has spoken? I read it in his face—"

"Spoken? He said a great deal—some things that made me laugh, some things that were not amusing. After all he is perhaps a little stupid, but to dance there is no one like him!"

"And you go together—to perfection—"

"Ah!" said Bice, with a long breath of pleasure, "when the people began to go away, when there was room! Certainly we deserted our other partners, both he and I. Does that matter in London? He says No."

"Not, my angel, if you are to marry."

"That was what he said," said Bice, with superb calm. "Now, I remember that was what he said; but I answered that I knew nothing of affairs—that it was to dance I wanted, not to talk; and that it was you, Madama, who disposed of me. It seemed to amuse him," the girl said reflectively. "Is it for that reason you kiss me? But it was he that spoke, as you call it, not I."

"You are like a little savage," cried the Contessa. "Don't you care then to make the greatest marriage, to win the prize, to settle everything with no trouble, before you are presented or anything has been done at all?"

"Is it settled then?" said Bice. She shrugged her shoulders a little within her white cloak. "Is that all?—no more excitement, nothing to look forward to, no tr-rouble? But it would have been more amusing if there had been a great deal of tr-rouble," the girl said.

This was in the blue dawn, when the better portion of the world which does not go to balls was fast asleep, the first pioneers of day only beginning to stir about the silent streets, through which now and then the carriage of late revellers like themselves darted abrupt with a clang that had in it something of almost guilt. Twelve hours after, the Contessa in her boudoir—with not much more than light enough to see the flushed and happy countenance of young Montjoie, who had been on thorns all the night and morning with a horrible doubt in his mind lest, after all, Bice's careless reply might mean nothing more than that fine system of drawing a fellow on—settled everything in the most delightful way.

"Nor is she without a sou, as perhaps you think. She has something that will not bear comparison with your wealth, yet something—which has been settled upon her by a relation. The Forno-Populi are not rich—but neither are they without friends."

Montjoie listened to this with a little surprise and impatience. He scarcely believed it, for one thing; and when he was assured that all was right as to Bice herself, he cared but little for the Forno-Populi. "I don't know anything about the sous. I have plenty for both," he said, "that had a great deal better go to you, don't you know. She is all I want. Bice! oh that's too foreign. I shall call her Bee, for she must be English, don't you know, Countess, none of your Bohem—Oh, I don't mean that; none of your foreign ways. They draw a fellow on, but when it's all settled and we're married and that sort of thing, she'll have to be out and out English, don't you know?"

"But that is reasonable," said the Contessa, who could when it was necessary reply very distinctly. "When one has a great English name and a position to keep up, one must be English. You shall call her what you please."

"There's one thing more," Montjoie said with a little redness and hesitation, but a certain dogged air, with which the Contessa had not as yet made acquaintance. "It's best to understand each other, don't you know; it's sort of hard-hearted to take her right away. But, Countess, you're a woman of the world, and you know a fellow must start fair. You keep all those sous you were talking of, and just let us knock along our own way. I don't want the money, and I dare say you'll find a use for it. And let's start fair; it'll be better for all parties, don't you know," the young man said. He reddened, but he met the Contessa's eye unflinchingly, though the effort to respond to this distinct statement in the spirit in which it was made cost her a struggle. She stared at him for a moment across the dainty little table laden with knick-knacks. It was strange in the moment of victory to receive such a sudden decisive defeat. There was just a possibility for a moment that this brave spirit should own itself mere woman, and break down and cry. For one second there was a quiver on her lip; then she smiled, which for every purpose was the better way.

"You would like," she said, "to see Bice. She is in the little drawing-room. The lawyers will settle the rest; but I understand your suggestion, Lord Montjoie." She rose with all her natural stately grace, which made the ordinary young fellow feel very small in spite of himself. The smile she gave him had something in it that made his knees knock together.

"I hope," he said, faltering, "you don't mind, Countess. My people, though I've not got any people to speak of, might make themselves disagreeable about—don't you know? you—you're a woman of the world."

The Contessa smiled upon him once more with dazzling sweetness. "She is in the little drawing-room," she said.

And so it was concluded, the excitement, the tr-rouble, as Bice said; it would have been far more amusing if there had been a great deal more tr-rouble. The Contessa dropped down in the corner of the sofa from which she had risen. She closed her eyes for the moment, and swallowed the affront that had been put upon her, and what was worse than the affront, the blow at her heart which this trifling little lord had delivered without flinching. This was to be the end of her schemes, that she was to be separated summarily and remorselessly from the child she had brought up. The Contessa knew, being of the same order of being, that, already somewhat disappointed to find the ardour of the chase over and all the excitement of bringing down the quarry, Bice, who cared little more about Montjoie than about any other likely person, would be as ready as not to throw him off if she were to communicate rashly the conditions on which he insisted. But, though she was of the same order of being, the Contessa was older and wiser. She had gone through a great many experiences. She knew that rich young English peers, marquises, uncontrolled by any parent or guardians, were fruit that did not grow on every bush, and that if this tide of fortune was not taken at its flood there was no telling when another might come. Now, though Bice was so dear, the Contessa had still a great many resources of her own, and was neither old nor tired of life. She would make herself a new career even without Bice, in which there might still be much interest—especially with the aid of a settled income. The careless speech about the sous was not without an eloquence of its own. Sous make everything that is disagreeable less disagreeable, and everything that is pleasant more pleasant. And she had got her triumph. She had secured for her Bice a splendid lot. She had accomplished what she had vowed to do, which many scoffers had thought she would never do. She was about to be presented at the English Court, and all her soils and spots from the world cleared from her, and herself rehabilitated wherever she might go. Was it reasonable then to break her heart over Montjoie and his miserable conditions? He could not separate Bice's love from her, though he might separate their lives—and that about the sous was generous. She was not one who would have sold her affections or given up anybody whom she loved for money. But still there were many things to be said, and for Bice's advantage what would she not do? The Contessa ended by a resolution which many a better woman would not have had the courage to make. She buried Montjoie's condition in her own heart—never to hint its existence—to ignore it as if it had not been. Many a more satisfactory person would have flinched at this. Most of us would at least have allowed the object of our sacrifice to be aware what we were doing for them. The Contessa did not even, so far as this, yield to the temptation of fate.

In the meantime Bice had gone through her own little episode. Mr. Derwentwater came about noon, before the Contessa was up; but he did not know the Contessa's habits, and he was admitted, which neither Montjoie nor any of the Contessa's friends would have been. He was overjoyed to find the lady of his affections alone. This made everything, he thought, simple and easy for him, and filled him with a delightful confidence that she was prepared for the object of his visit and had contrived to keep the Contessa out of the way. His heart was beating high, his mind full of excitement. He took the chair she pointed him to, and then got up again, poising his hat between his hands.

"Signorina," he said, "they say that a woman always knows the impression she has made."

"Why do you call me Signorina?" said Bice. "Yes, it is quite right. But then it is so long that I have not heard it, and it is only you that call me so."

"Perhaps," said Mr. Derwentwater, with a little natural complacency, "others are not so well acquainted with your beautiful country and language. What should I call you? Ah, I know what I should like to call you. Beatrice, loda di deo vera. You are like the supreme and sovran lady whom every one must think of who hears your name."

Bice looked at him with a half-comic attention. "You are a very learned man," she said, "one can see that. You always say something that is pretty, that one does not understand."

This piqued the suitor a little and brought the colour to his cheek. "Teach me," he said, "to make you understand me. If I could show you my heart, you would see that from the first moment I saw you the name of Bice has been written—"

"Oh, I know it already," cried Bice, "that you have a great devotion for poetry. Unhappily I have no education. I know it so very little. But I have found out what you mean about Bice. It is more soft than you say it. There is no sound of tch in it at all. Beeshè, like that. Your Italian is very good," she added, "but it is Tuscan, and the bocca romana is the best."

Mr. Derwentwater was more put out than it became a philosopher to be. "I came," he cried, with a kind of asperity, "for a very different purpose, not to be corrected in my Italian. I came—" but here his feelings were too strong for him, "to lay my life and my heart at your feet. Do you understand me now?

To tell you that I love you—no, that is not enough, it is not love, it is adoration," he said. "I have never known what it meant before. However fair women might be, I have passed them by; my heart has never spoken. But now! Since the first moment I saw you, Bice—"

The girl rose up; she became a little alarmed. Emotion was strange to her, and she shrank from it. "I have given," she said, "to nobody permission to call me by my name."

"But you will give it to me! to your true lover," he cried. "No one can admire and adore you as much as I do. It was from the first moment. Bice, oh, listen! I have nothing to offer you but love, the devotion of a life. What could a king give more? A true man cannot think of anything else when he is speaking to the woman he loves. Nothing else is worthy to offer you. Bice, I love you! I love you! Have you nothing, nothing in return to say to me?"

All his self-importance and intellectual superiority had abandoned him. He was so much agitated that he saw her but dimly through the mists of excitement and passion. He stretched out his hands appealing to her. He might have been on his knees for anything he knew. It seemed incredible to him that his strong passion should have no return.

"Have you nothing, nothing to say to me?" he cried.

Bice had been frightened, but she had regained her composure. She looked on at this strange exhibition of feeling with the wondering calm of extreme youth. She was touched a little, but more surprised than anything else. She said, with a slight tremor, "I think it must be all a mistake. One is never so serious— oh, never so serious! It is not something of—gravity like that. Did not you know? I am intended to make a marriage—to marry well, very well—what you call a great marriage. It is for that I am brought here. The Contessa would never listen—Oh, it is a mistake altogether—a mistake! You do not know what is my career. It has all been thought of since I was born. Pray, pray, go away, and do not say any more."

"Bice," he cried, more earnestly than ever, "I know. I heard that you were to be sacrificed. Who is the lady who is going to sacrifice you to Mammon? she is not your mother; you owe her no obedience. It is your happiness, not hers, that is at stake. And I will preserve you from her. I will guard you like my own soul; the winds of heaven shall not visit your cheek roughly. I will cherish you; I will adore you. Come, only come to me."

His voice was husky with emotion; his last words were scarcely audible, said within his breath in a high strain of passion which had got beyond his control. The contrast between this tremendous force of feeling and her absolute youthful calm was beyond description. It was more wonderful than anything ever represented on the tragic stage. Only in the depth and mystery of human experience could such a wonderful juxtaposition be.

"Mr. Derwentwater," she said, trembling a little, "I cannot understand you. Go away, oh, go away!"

"Bice!"

"Go away, oh, go away! I am not able to bear it; no one is ever so serious. I am not great enough, nor old enough. Don't you know," cried Bice, with a little stamp of her foot, "I like the other way best? Oh, go away, go away!"

He stood quiet, silently gazing at her till he had regained his power of speech, which was not for a moment or two. Then he said hoarsely, "You like—the other way best?"

She clasped her hands together with a mingling of impatience and wonder and rising anger. "I am made like that," she cried. "I don't know how to be so serious. Oh, go away from me. You tr-rouble me. I like the other best."

He never knew how he got out of the strange, unnatural atmosphere of the house in which he seemed to leave his heart behind him. The perfumes, the curtains, the half lights, the blending draperies, were round him one moment; the next he found himself in the greenness of the Park, with the breeze blowing in his face, and his dream ended and done with.

He had a kind of vision of having touched the girl's reluctant hand, and even of having seen a frightened look in her eyes as if he had awakened some echo or touched some string whose sound was new to her. But if that were so, it was not he, but only some discovery of unknown feeling that moved her. When he came to himself, he felt that all the innocent morning people in the Park, the children with their maids, the sick ladies and old men sunning themselves on the benches, the people going about their honest business, cast wondering looks at his pale face and the agitation of his aspect. He took a long walk, he did not know how long, with that strange sense that something capital had happened to him, something never to be got over or altered, which follows such an incident in life. He was even conscious by and by, habit coming to his aid, of a curious question in his mind if this was how people usually felt after such a wonderful incident—a thing that had happened quite without demonstration, which nobody could ever know of, yet which made as much change in him as if he had been sentenced to death. Sentenced to death! that was what it felt like more or less. It had happened, and could never be undone, and he walked away and away, but never got beyond it, with the chain always round his neck. When he got into the streets where nobody took any notice of him, it struck him with surprise, almost offence. Was it possible that they did not see that something had happened—a mystery, something that would never be shaken off but with life?

He met Jock as he walked, and without stopping gave him a sort of ghastly smile, and said, "You were right; she likes that best," and went on again, with a sense that he might go on for ever like the wandering Jew, and never get beyond the wonder and the pain.

And there is no doubt that Bice was glad to hear Montjoie's laugh, and the nonsense he talked, and to throw off that sudden impression which had frightened her. What was it? Something which was in life, but which she had not met with before. "We are to have it all our own way, don't you know?" Montjoie said. "I have no people, to call people, and she is not going to interfere. We shall have it all our own way, and have a good time, as the Yankees say. And I am not going to call you Bice, which is a silly sort of name, and spells quite different from its pronunciation. What are you holding back for? You have no call to be shy with me now. Bee, you belong to me now, don't you know?" the young fellow said, with demonstrations from which Bice shrunk a little. She liked, yes, his way; but, but yet—she was perhaps a little savage, as the Contessa said.

CHAPTER XLVIII

THE LAST BLOW

Lucy stood out stoutly to the last gasp. She did not betray herself, except by the paleness, the seriousness which she could not banish from her countenance. Her guests thought that Lady Randolph must be ill, that she was disguising a bad headache, or even something more serious, under the smile with which she received them. "I am sure you ought to be in bed," the older ladies said, and when they took their leave of her, after their congratulations as to the success of the evening, they all repeated this in various tones. "I am sure you are quite worn out; I shall send in the morning to ask how you are," the Duchess said. Lucy listened to everything with a smile which was somewhat set and painful. She was so worn out with emotion and pain that at last neither words nor looks made much impression upon her. She saw the Contessa and Bice stream by to their carriage with a circle of attendants, still in all the dazzle and flash of their triumph; and after that the less important crowd, the insignificant people who lingered to the last, the girls who would not give up a last waltz, and the men who returned for a final supper, swam in her dazed eyes. She stood at the door mechanically shaking hands and saying "Good-night." The Dowager, moved by curiosity, anxiety, perhaps by pity, kept by her till a late hour, though Lucy was scarcely aware of it. When she went away at last, she repeated with earnestness and a certain compunction the advice of the other ladies. "You don't look fit to stand," she said. "If you will go to bed I will wait till all these tiresome people are gone. You have been doing too much, far too much." "It does not matter," Lucy said, in her semi-consciousness hearing her own voice like something in a dream. "Oh, my dear, I am quite unhappy about you!" Lady Randolph cried. "If you are thinking of what I told you, Lucy, perhaps it may not be true." There was a bevy of people going away at that moment, and she had to shake hands with them. She waited till they were gone and then turned, with a laugh that frightened the old lady, towards her.

"You should have thought of that before," she said. Perhaps it might not be true! Can heaven be veiled and the pillars of the earth pulled down by a perhaps? The laugh sounded even to herself unnatural, and the elder Lady Randolph was frightened by it, and stole away almost without another word. When everybody was gone Sir Tom stood by her in the deserted rooms, with all the lights blazing and the blue day coming in through the curtains, as grave and as pale as she was. They did not look like the exhausted yet happy entertainers of the (as yet) most successful party of the season. Lucy could scarcely stand and could not speak at all, and he seemed little more fit for those mutual congratulations, even the "Thank heaven it is well over," with which the master and the mistress of the house usually salute each other in such circumstances. They stood at different ends of the room, and made no remark. At last, "I suppose you are going to bed," Sir Tom said. He came up to her in a preoccupied way. "I shall go and smoke a cigar first, and it does not seem much good lighting a candle for you." They both looked somewhat drearily at the daylight, now no longer blue, but rosy. Then he laid his hand upon her shoulder. "You are dreadfully tired, Lucy, and I think there has been something the matter with you these few days. I'd ask you what it was, but I'm dead beat, and you are dreadfully tired too." He stopped and kissed her forehead, and took her hand in his in a sort of languid way. "Good-night; go to bed my poor little woman," he said.

It is terrible to be wroth with those we love. Anger against them is deadly to ourselves. It "works like madness in the brain;" it involves heaven and earth in a gloom that nothing can lighten. But when that anger being just, and such as we must not depart from, is crossed by those unspeakable relentings, those quick revivals of love, those sudden touches of tenderness that carry all before them, what anguish is equal to those bitter sweetnesses? Lucy felt this as she stood there with her husband's hand upon her shoulder, in utter fatigue, and broken down in all her faculties. Through all those dark and bitter mists which rose about her, his voice broke like a ray of light: her timid heart sprang up in her bosom and went out to him with an abandon which, but for the extreme physical fatigue which produces a sort of apathy, must have broken down everything. For a moment she swayed towards him as if she would have thrown herself upon his breast.

When this movement comes to both the estranged persons, there follows a clearing away of difficulties, a revolution of the heart, a reconciliation when that is possible, and sometimes when it is not possible. But it very seldom happens that this comes to both at the same time. Sir Tom remained unmoved while his wife had that sudden access of reawakened tenderness. He was scarcely aware even how far she had been from him, and now was quite unaware how near. His mind was full of cares and doubts, and an embarrassing situation which he could not see how to manage. He was not even aware that she was moved beyond the common. He took his hand from her shoulder, and without another word let her go away.

Oh, those other words that are never spoken! They are counterbalanced in the record of human misfortune by the many other words which are too much, which should never have been spoken at all. Thus all explanation, all ending of the desperate situation, was staved off for another night.

Lucy woke next morning in a kind of desperation. No new event had happened, but she could not rest. She felt that she must do something or die, and what could she do? She spent the early morning in the nursery, and then went out. This time she was reasonable, not like that former time when she went out to the city. She knew very well now that nothing was to be gained by walking or by jolting in a disagreeable cab. On the former occasion that had been something of a relief to her; but not now. It is scarcely so bad when some out-of-the-way proceeding like this, some strange thing to be done, gives the hurt and wounded spirit a little relief. She had come to the further stage now when she knew that nothing of the sort could give any relief; nothing but mere dull endurance, going on, and no more. She drove to Mr. Chervil's office quietly, as she might have gone anywhere, and thus, though it seems strange to say so, betrayed a deeper despair than before. She took with her a list of names with sums written opposite. There was enough there put down to make away with a large fortune. This one so much, that one so much. This too was an impulse of the despair in her mind. She was carrying out her father's will in a lump. It meant no exercise of discrimination, no careful choice of persons to be benefited, such as he had intended, but only a hurried rush at a duty which she had neglected, a desire to be done with it. Lucy was on the eve, she felt, of some great change in her life. She could not tell what she might be able to do after; whether she should live through it or bring her mind and memory unimpaired through it, or think any longer of anything that had once been her duty. She would get it done while she could. She was very sensible that the money she had given to Bice was not in accordance with what her father would have wished: neither were these perhaps. She could not tell, she did not care. At least it would be done with, and could not be done over again.

"Lady Randolph," said Mr. Chervil, in dismay, "have you any idea of the sum you are—throwing away?"

"I have no idea of any sum," said Lucy, gently, "except just the money I spend, so much in my purse. But you have taught me how to calculate, and that so much would—make people comfortable. Is not that what you said? Well, if it was not you, it was—I do not remember. When I first got the charge of this into my hands—"

"Lady Randolph, you cannot surely think what you are doing. At the worst," said the distressed trustee, "this was meant to be a fund for—beneficence all your life: not to be squandered away, thousands and thousands in a day—"

"Is it squandered when it gives comfort—perhaps even happiness? And how do you know how long my life may last? It may be over—in a day—"

"You are ill," said the lawyer. "I thought so the moment I saw you. I felt sure you were not up to business to-day."

"I don't think I am ill," said Lucy; "a little tired, for I was late last night—did not you know we had a ball, a very pretty ball?" she added, with a curious smile, half of gratification, half of mockery. "It was a strange thing to have, perhaps, just—at this moment."

"A very natural thing," said Mr. Chervil. "I am glad to know it; you are so young, Lady Randolph, pardon me for saying so."

"It was not for me," said Lucy; "it was for a young lady—my husband's—"

Was she going out of her senses? What was she about to say?

"A relation?" said Mr. Chervil. "Perhaps the young lady for whom you interested yourself so much in a more important way? They are fortunate, Lady Randolph, who have you for a friend."

"Do you think so? I don't know that any one thinks so." She recovered herself a little and pointed to the papers. "You will carry that out, please. I may be going away. I am not quite sure of my movements. As soon as you can you will carry this out."

"Going away—at the beginning of the season!"

"Oh, there is nothing settled; and besides you know life—life is very insecure."

"At your age it is very seldom one thinks so," said the lawyer, at which she smiled only, then rose up, and without any further remark went away. He saw her to her carriage, not now with any recollection of the pleasant show and the exhibition of so fine a client to the admiration of his neighbours. He had a heart after all, and daughters of his own; and he was troubled more than he could say. He stood bare-headed and saw her drive away, with a look of anxiety upon his face. Was it the same bee in her bonnet which old Trevor had shown so conspicuously? was it eccentricity verging upon madness? He went back to his office and wrote to Sir Tom, enclosing a copy of Lucy's list. "I must ask your advice in the matter instead of offering you mine," he wrote. "Lady Randolph has a right, of course, if she chooses to press matters to an extremity, but I can't fancy that this is right."

Lucy went home still in the same strange excitement of mind. All had been executed that was in her programme. She had gone through it without flinching. The ball—that strange, frivolous-tragic effort of despair—it was over, thank heaven! and Bice had got full justice in her—was it in her—father's house? She could not have been introduced to greater advantage, Lucy thought, with a certain forlorn, simple pride, had she been Sir Tom's acknowledged daughter. Oh, not to so much advantage! for the Contessa, her guardian, her—was far more skilful than Lucy ever could have been. Bice had got her triumph; nothing had been neglected. And the other business was in train—the disposing of the money. She had made her wishes fully known, and even taken great trouble, calculating and transcribing to prevent any possibility of a mistake. And now, now the moment had come, the crisis of life when she must tell her husband what she had heard, and say to him that this existence could not go on any longer. A man could not have two lives. She did not mean to upbraid him. What good would it do to upbraid? none, none at all; that would not make things as they were again, or return to her him whom she had lost. She had not a word to say to him, except that it was impossible—that it could not go on any more.

To think that she should have this to say to him made everything dark about her as Lucy went home. She felt as if the world must come to an end to-night. All was straightforward, now that the need of self-restraint was over. She contemplated no delay or withdrawal from her position. She went in to accomplish this dark and miserable necessity like a martyr going to the cross. She would go and see baby first, who was his boy as well as hers. Sir Tom no doubt would be in his library, and would come out for luncheon after a while, but not until she had spoken. But first she would go, just for a little needful strength, and kiss her boy.

Fletcher met her at the head of the stairs.

"Oh, if you please, my lady—not to hurry you or frighten you—but nurse says please would you step in and look at baby."

Suddenly, in a moment, Lucy's whole being changed. She forgot everything. Her languor disappeared and her fatigue. She sprang up to where the woman was standing. "What is it? is he ill? Is it the old—" She hurried along towards the nursery as she spoke.

"No, my lady, nothing he has had before; but nurse thinks he looks—oh, my lady, there will be nothing to be frightened about—we have sent for the doctor."

Lucy was in the room where little Tom was, before Fletcher had finished what she was saying. The child was seated on his nurse's knee. His eyes were heavy, yet blazing with fever. He was plucking with his little hot hands at the woman's dress, flinging himself about her, from one arm, from one side to the other. When he saw his mother he stretched out towards her. Just eighteen months old; not able to express a thought; not much, you will say, perhaps, to change to a woman the aspect of heaven and earth. She took him into her arms without a word, and laid her cheek—which was so cool, fresh with the morning air, though her heart was so fevered and sick—against the little cheek, which burned and glowed. "What is it? Can you tell what it is?" she said in a whisper of awe. Was it God Himself who had stepped in—who had come to interfere?

Then the baby began to wail with that cry of inarticulate suffering which is the most pitiful of all the utterances of humanity. He could not tell what ailed him. He looked with his great dazed eyes pitifully from one to another as if asking them to help him.

"It is the fever, my lady," said the nurse. "We have sent for the doctor. It may not be a bad attack."

Lucy sat down, her limbs failing her, her heart failing her still more, her bonnet and out-door dress cumbering her movements, the child tossing and restless in her arms. This was not the form his ailments had ever taken before. "Do you know what is to be done? Tell me what to do for him," she said.

There was a kind of hush over all the house. The servants would not admit that anything was wrong until their mistress should come home. As soon as she was in the nursery and fully aware of the state of affairs, they left off their precautions. The maids appeared on the staircases clandestinely as they ought not to have done. Mrs. Freshwater herself abandoned her cosy closet, and declared in an impressive voice that no bell must be rung for luncheon—nor anything done that could possibly disturb the blessed baby, she said as she gave the order. And Williams desired to know what was preparing for Mr. Randolph's dinner, and announced his intention of taking it up himself. The other meal, the lunch, in the dining-room, was of no importance to any one. If he could take his beef-tea it would do him good, they all said.

It seemed as if a long time passed before the doctor came; from Sir Tom to the youngest kitchen-wench, the scullery-maid, all were in suspense. There was but one breath, long drawn and stifled, when he came into the house. He was a long time in the nursery, and when he came out he went on talking to those who accompanied him. "You had better shut off this part of the house altogether," he was saying, "hang a sheet over this doorway, and let it be always kept wet. I will send in a person I can rely upon to take the night. You must not let Lady Randolph sit up." He repeated the same caution to Sir Tom, who came out with a bewildered air to hear what he had said. Sir Tom was the only one who had taken no fright. "Highly infectious," the Doctor said. "I advise you to send away every one who is not wanted. If Lady Randolph could be kept out of the room so much the better, but I don't suppose that is possible; anyhow, don't let her sit up. She is just in the condition to take it. It would be better if you did not go near the child yourself; but, of course, I understand how difficult that is. Parents are a nuisance in such cases," the Doctor said, with a smile which Sir Tom thought heartless, though it was intended to cheer him. "It is far better to give the little patient over to scientific unemotional care."

"But you don't mean to say that there is danger, Doctor," cried Sir Tom. "Why, the little beggar was as jolly as possible only this morning."

"Oh, we'll pull him through, we'll pull him through," the good-natured Doctor said. He preferred to talk all the time, not to be asked questions, for what could he say? Nurse looked very awful as she went upstairs, charged with private information almost too important for any woman to contain. She stopped at the head of the stairs to whisper to Fletcher, shaking her head the while, and Fletcher, too, shook her head and whispered to Mrs. Freshwater that the doctor had a very bad opinion of the case. Poor little Tom had got to be "the case" all in a moment. And "no constitution" they said to each other under their breath.

Thus the door closed upon Lucy and all her trouble. She forgot it clean, as if it never had existed. Everything in the world in one moment became utterly unimportant to her, except the fever in those heavy eyes. She reflected dimly, with an awful sense of having forestalled fate, that she had made a pretence that he was ill to shield herself that night, the first night after their arrival. She had said he was ill when all was well. And lo! sudden punishment scathing and terrible had come to her out of the angry skies.


CHAPTER XLIX

THE EXPERIENCES OF BICE

Sir Tom was concerned and anxious, but not alarmed like the women. After all it was a complaint of which children recovered every day. It had nothing to do with the child's lungs, which had been enfeebled by his former illness. He had as good a chance as any other in the present malady. Sir Tom was much depressed for an hour or two, but when everything was done that could be done, and an experienced woman arrived to whom the "case," though "anxious," as she said, did not appear immediately alarming, he forced his mind to check that depression, and to return to the cares which, if less grave, harassed and worried him more. Lucy was invisible all day. She spoke to him through the closed door from behind the curtain, but in a voice which he could scarcely hear and which had no tone of individuality in it, but only a faint human sound of distress. "He is no better. They say we cannot expect him to be better," she said. "Come down, dear, and have some dinner," said the round and large voice of Sir Tom, which even into that stillness brought a certain cheer. But as it sounded into the shut-up room, where nobody ventured to speak above their breath, it was like a bell pealing or a discharge of artillery, something that broke up the quiet, and made, or so the poor mother thought, the little patient start in his uneasy bed. Dinner! oh how could he ask it, how could he think of it? Sir Tom went away with a sigh of mingled uneasiness and impatience. He had always thought Lucy a happy exception to the caprices and vagaries of womankind. He had hoped that she was without nerves, as she had certainly been without those whims that amuse a man in other people's wives, but disgust him in his own. Was she going to turn out just like the rest, with extravagant terrors, humours, fancies—like all of them? Why should not she come to dinner, and why speak to him only from behind the closed door? He was annoyed and almost angry with Lucy. There had been something the matter, he reflected, for some time. She had taken offence at something; but surely the appearance of a real trouble might, at least, have made an end of that. He felt vexed and impatient as he sat down with Jock alone. "You will have to get out of this, my boy," he said, "or they won't let you go back to school; don't you know it's catching?" To have infection in one's house, and to be considered dangerous by one's friends, is always irritating. Sir Tom spoke with a laugh, but it was a laugh of offence. "I ought to have thought of it sooner," he said; "you can't go straight to school, you know, from a house with fever in it. You must pack up and get off at once."

"I am not afraid," cried Jock. "Do you think I am such a cad as to leave Lucy when she's in trouble? or—or—the little one either?" Jock added, in a husky voice.

"We are all cads in that respect nowadays," said Sir Tom. "It is the right thing. It is high principle. Men will elbow off and keep me at a distance, and not a soul will come near Lucy. Well, I suppose, it's all right. But there is some reason in it, so far as you are concerned. Come, you must be off to-night. Get hold of MTutor, he's still in town, and ask him what you must do."

After dinner Sir Tom strolled forth. He did not mean to go out, but the house was intolerable, and he was very uneasy on the subject of Bice. It felt, indeed, something like a treason to Lucy, shut up in the child's sick-room, to go to the house which somehow or other was felt to be in opposition, and dimly suspected as the occasion of her changed looks and ways. He did not even say to himself that he meant to go there. And it was not any charm in the Contessa that drew him. It was that uneasy sense of a possibility which involved responsibility, and which, probably, he would never either make sure of or get rid of. The little house in Mayfair was lighted from garret to basement. If the lights were dim inside they looked bright without. It had the air of a house overflowing with life, every room with its sign of occupation. When he got in, the first sight he saw was Montjoie striding across the doorway of the small dining-room. Montjoie was very much at home, puffing his cigarette at the new comer. "Hallo, St. John!" he cried, then added with a tone of disappointment, "Oh! it's you."

"It is I, I'm sorry to say, as you don't seem to like it," said Sir Tom.

The young fellow looked a little abashed. "I expected another fellow. That's not to say I ain't glad to see you. Come in and have a glass of wine."

"Thank you," said Sir Tom. "I suppose as you are smoking the ladies are upstairs."

"Oh, they don't mind," said Montjoie; "at least the Contessa, don't you know? She's up to a cigarette herself. I shouldn't stand it," he added, after a moment, "in—Mademoiselle. Oh, perhaps you haven't heard. She and I—have fixed it all up, don't you know?"

"Fixed it all up?"

"Engaged, and that sort of thing. I'm a kind of boss in this house now. I thought, perhaps, that was why you were coming, to hear all about it, don't you know?"

"Engaged!" cried Sir Tom, with a surprise in which there was no qualification. He felt disposed to catch the young fellow by the throat and pitch him out of doors.

"You don't seem over and above pleased," said Montjoie, throwing away his cigarette, and confronting Sir Tom with a flush of defiance. They stood looking at each other for a moment, while Antonio, in the background, watched at the foot of the stairs, not without hopes of a disturbance.

"I don't suppose that my pleasure or displeasure matters much: but you will pardon me if I pass, for my visit was to the Contessa," Sir Tom said, going on quickly. He was in an irritable state of mind to begin with. He thought he ought to have been consulted, even as an old friend, much more as— And the young ass was offensive. If it turned out that Sir Tom had anything to do with it Montjoie should find that to be the best parti of the season was not a thing that would infallibly recommend him to a father at least. The Contessa had risen from her chair at the sound of the voices. She came forward to Sir Tom with both her hands extended as he entered the drawing-room. "Dear old friend! congratulate me. I have accomplished all I wished," she said.

"That was Montjoie," said Sir Tom. He laughed, but not with his usual laugh. "No great ambition, I am afraid. But," he said, pressing those delicate hands not as they were used to be pressed, with a hard seriousness and imperativeness, "you must tell me! I must have an explanation. There can be no delay or quibbling longer."

"You hurt me, sir," she said with a little cry, and looked at her hands, "body and mind," she added, with one of her smiles. "Quibbling—that is one of your English words a woman cannot be expected to understand. Come then with me, barbarian, into my boudoir."

Bice sat alone somewhat pensively with one of those favourite Tauchnitz volumes from which she had obtained her knowledge of English life in her hand. It was contraband, which made it all the dearer to her. She was not reading, but leaning her chin against it lost in thought. She was not pining for the presence of Montjoie, but rather glad after a long afternoon of him that he should prefer a cigarette to her company. She felt that this was precisely her own case, the cigarette being represented by the book or any other expedient that answered to cover the process of thought.

Bice was not used to these processes. Keen observation of the ways of mankind in all the strange exhibitions of them which she had seen in her life had been the chief exercise of her lively intelligence. To Mr. Derwentwater, perhaps, may be given the credit of having roused the girl's mind, not indeed to sympathy with himself, but into a kind of perturbation and general commotion of spirit. Events were crowding quickly upon her. She had accepted one suitor and refused another within the course of a few hours. Such incidents develop the being; not, perhaps, the first in any great degree—but the second was not in the programme, and it had perplexed and roused her. There had come into her mind glimmerings, reflections, she could not tell what. Montjoie was occupied in something of the same manner downstairs, thinking it all over with his cigarette, wondering what Society and what his uncle would say, for whom he had a certain respect. He said to himself on the whole that he did not care that for Society! She suited him down to the ground. She was the jolliest girl he had ever met, besides being so awfully handsome. It was worth while going out riding with her just to see how the fellows stared and the women grew green with envy; or coming into a room with her, Jove! what a sensation she would make, and how everybody would open their eyes when she appeared blazing in the Montjoie diamonds! His satisfaction went a little deeper than this, to do him justice. He was, in his way, very much in love with the beautiful creature whom he had made up his mind to secure from the first moment he saw her. But, perhaps, if it had not been for the triumph of her appearance at Park Lane, and the hum of admiration and wonder that rose around her, he would not have so early fixed his fate; and the shadow of the uncle now and then came like a cloud over his glee. After the sudden gravity with which he remembered this, there suddenly gleamed upon him a vision of all his plain cousins gathering round his bride to scowl her down, and blast her with criticism and disapproval, which made him burst into a fit of laughter. Bice would hold her own; she would give as good as she got. She was not one to be cowed or put down, wasn't Bee! He felt himself clapping his hands and urging her on to the combat, and celebrated in advance with a shout of laughter the discomfiture of all those young ladies. But she should have nothing more to do with the Forno-Populo. No; his wife should have none of that sort about her. What did old Randolph mean always hanging about that old woman, and all the rest of the old fogeys? It was fun enough so long as you had nothing to do with them, but, by Jove, not for Lady Montjoie. Then he rushed upstairs to shower a few rough caresses upon Bice and take his leave of her, for he had an evening engagement formed before he was aware of the change which was coming in his life. He had been about her all the afternoon, and Bice, disturbed in her musings by this onslaught and somewhat impatient of the caresses, beheld his departure with satisfaction. It was the first evening since their arrival in town, which the ladies had planned to spend alone.

And then she recommenced these thinkings which were not so easy as those of her lover: but she was soon subject to another inroad of a very different kind. Jock, who had never before come in the evening, appeared suddenly unannounced at the door of the room with a pale and heavy countenance. Though Bice had objected to be disturbed by her lover, she did not object to Jock; he harmonised with the state of her mind, which Montjoie did not. It seemed even to relieve her of the necessity of thinking when he appeared—he who did thinking enough, she felt, with half-conscious humour, for any number of people. He came in with a sort of eagerness, yet weariness, and explained that he had come to say good-bye, for he was going off—at once.

"Going off! but it is not time yet," Bice said.

"Because of the fever. But that is not altogether why I have come either," he said, looking at her from under his curved eyebrows. "I have got something to say."

"What fever?" she said, sitting upright in her chair.

Jock took no notice of the question; his mind was full of his own purpose. "Look here," he said huskily, "I know you'll never speak to me again. But there's something I want to say. We've been friends—"

"Oh yes," she said, raising her head with a gleam of frank and cordial pleasure, "good friends—camarades—and I shall always, always speak to you. You were my first friend."

"That is" said Jock, taking no notice, "you were—friends. I can't tell what I was. I don't know. It's something very droll. You would laugh, I suppose. But that's not to the purpose either. You wouldn't have Derwentwater to-day."

Bice looked up with a half laugh. She began to consider him closely with her clear-sighted penetrating eyes, and the agitation under which Jock was labouring impressed the girl's quick mind. She watched every change of his face with a surprised interest, but she did not make any reply.

"I never expected you would. I could have told him so. I did tell him you liked the other best. They say that's common with women," Jock said with a little awe, "when they have the choice offered, that it is always the worst they take."

But still Bice did not reply. It was a sort of carrying out without any responsibility of hers, the vague wonder and questionings of her own mind. She had no responsibility in what Jock said. She could even question and combat it cheerfully now that it was presented to her from outside, but for the moment she said nothing to help him on, and he did not seem to require it, though he paused from time to time.

"This is what I've got to say," Jock went on almost fiercely. "If you take Montjoie it's a mistake. He looks good-natured and all that; he looks easy to get on with. You hear me out, and then I'll go away and never trouble you again. He is not—a nice fellow. If you were to go and do such a thing as—marry him, and then find it out! I want you to know. Perhaps you think it's mean of me to say so, like sneaking, and perhaps it is. But, look here, I can't help it. Of course you would laugh at me—any one would. I'm a boy at school. I know that as well as you do—" Something got into Jock's voice so that he paused, and made a gulp before he could go on. "But, Bice, don't have that fellow. There are such lots; don't have him. I don't think I could stand it," Jock cried. "And look here, if it's because the Contessa wants money, I have some myself. What do I want with money? When I am older I shall work. There it is for you, if you like. But don't—have that fellow. Have a good fellow, there are plenty—there are fellows like Sir Tom. He is a good man. I should not," said Jock, with a sort of sob, which came in spite of himself, and which he did not remark even, so strong was the passion in him. "I should not—mind. I could put up with it then. So would Derwentwater. But, Bice—"

She had risen up, and so had he. They were neither of them aware of it. Jock had lost consciousness, perception, all thought of anything but her and this that he was urging upon her. While as for Bice the tide had gone too high over her head. She felt giddy in the presence of something so much more powerful than any feeling she had ever known, and yet gazed at him half alarmed, half troubled as she was, with a perception that could not be anything but humorous of the boy's voice sounding so bass and deep, sometimes bursting into childish, womanish treble, and the boy's aspect which contrasted so strongly with the passion in which he spoke. When Sir Tom's voice made itself audible, coming from the boudoir in conversation with the Contessa, the effect upon the two thus standing in a sort of mortal encounter was extraordinary. Bice straining up to the mark which he was setting before her, bewildered with the flood on which she was rising, sank into ease again and a mastery of the situation, while Jock, worn out and with a sense that all was over, sat down abruptly, and left, as it were, the stage clear.

"The poor little man is rather bad, I fear," said Sir Tom, coming through the dim room. There was something in his voice, an easier tone, a sound of relief. How had the Contessa succeeded in cheering him? "And what is worse (for he will do well I hope) is the scattering of all her friends from about Lucy. I am kept out of it, and it does not matter, you see; but she, poor little woman,"—his voice softened as he named her with a tone of tenderness—"nobody will go near her," he said.

The Contessa gave a little shiver, and drew about her the loose shawl she wore. "What can we say in such a case? It is not for us, it is for those around us. It is a risk for so many—"

"My aunt," said Sir Tom, "would be her natural ally; but I know Lady Randolph too well to think of that. And there is Jock, whom we are compelled to send away. We shall be like two crows all alone in the house."

"Is it this you told me of, fever?" cried Bice, turning to Jock. "But it is I that will go—oh, this moment! It is no tr-rouble. I can sit up. I never am sleepy. I am so strong nothing hurts me. I will go directly, now."

"You!" they all cried, but the Contessa's tones were most high. She made a protest full of indignant virtue.

"Do you think," she said, "if I had but myself to think of that I would not fly to her? But, child in your position! fiancée only to-day—with all to do, all to think of, how could I leave you? Oh, it is impossible; my good Lucy, who is never unreasonable, she will know it, she will understand. Besides, to what use, my Bice? She has nurses for day and night. She has her dear husband, her good husband, to be with her. What does a woman want more? You would be de trop. You would be out of place. It would be a trouble to them. It would be a blame to me. And you would take it, and bring it back and spread it, Bice—and perhaps Lord Montjoie—"

Bice looked round her bewildered from one to another.

"Should I be de trop?" she said, turning to Sir Tom with anxious eyes.

Sir Tom looked at her with an air of singular emotion. He laid his hand caressingly on her shoulder: "De trop? no; never in my house. But that is not the question. Lucy will be cheered when she knows that you wanted to come. But what the Contessa says is true; there are plenty of nurses—and my wife—has me, if I am any good; and we would not have you run any risk—"

"In her position!" cried the Contessa; "fiancée only to-day. She owes herself already to Lord Montjoie, who would never consent, never; it is against every rule. Speak to her, mon ami, speak to her; she is a girl who is capable of all. Tell her that now it is thought criminal, that one does not risk one's self and others. She might bring it here, if not to herself, to me, Montjoie, the domestics." The Contessa sank into a chair and began fanning herself; then got up again and went towards the girl clasping her hands. "My sweetest," she cried, "you will not be entétée, and risk everything. We shall have news, good news, every morning, three, four times a day."

"And Milady," said Bice, "who has done everything, will be alone and in tr-rouble. Sir Tom, he must leave her, he must attend to his affairs. He is a man; he must take the air; he must go out in the world. And she—she will be alone: when we have lived with her, when she has been more good, more good than any one could deserve. Risk! The doctor does not take it, who is everywhere, who will, perhaps, come to you next, Madama; and the nurses do not take it. It is a shame," cried the girl, throwing up her fine head, "if Love is not as good as the servants, if to have gratitude in your heart is nothing! And the risk, what is it? An illness, a fever. I have had a fever—"

"Bice, you might bring—what is dreadful to think of," cried the Contessa, with a shiver. "You might die."

"Die!" the girl cried, in a voice like a silver trumpet with a keen sweetness of scorn and tenderness combined. "Après?" she said, throwing back her head. She was not capable of those questions which Mr. Derwentwater and his pupil had set before her. But here she was upon different ground.

"Oh, she is capable of all! she is a girl that is capable of all," cried the Contessa, sinking once more into a chair.

CHAPTER L

THE EVE OF SORROW

Sir Tom stepped out into the night some time after, holding Jock by the arm. The boy had a sort of thrill and tremble in him as if he had been reading poetry or witnessing some great tragic scene, which the elder man partially understood without being at all aware that Jock had himself been an actor in this drama. He himself had been dismissed out of it, so to speak. His mind was relieved, and yet he was not so satisfied as he expected to be. It had been proved to him that he had no responsibility for Bice, and his anxiety relieved on that subject; relieved, oh yes: and yet was he a little disappointed too. It would have been endless embarrassment, and Lucy would not have liked it. Still he had been accustoming himself to the idea, and, now that it was broken clean off, he was not so much pleased as he had expected. Poor little Bice! her little burst of generous gratitude and affection had gone to his heart. If that little thing who (it appeared) had died in Florence so many years ago had survived and grown a woman, as an hour ago he had believed her to have done, that is how he should have liked her to feel and to express herself. Such a sense of approval and admiration was in him that he felt the disappointment the more. Yes, he supposed it was a disappointment. He had begun to get used to the idea, and he had always liked the girl; but of course it was a relief—the greatest relief—to have no explanation to make to Lucy, instead of the painful one which perhaps she would only partially believe. He had felt that it would be most difficult to make her understand that, though this was so, he had not been in any plot, and had not known of it any more than she did when Bice was brought to his house. This would have been the difficult point in the matter, and now, heaven be praised! all that was over, and there was no mystery, nothing to explain. But so strange is human sentiment that the world felt quite impoverished to Sir Tom, though he was much relieved. Life became for the moment a more commonplace affair altogether. He was free from the annoyance. It mattered nothing to him now who she married—the best parti in society, or Jock's tutor, or anybody the girl pleased. If it had not been for that exhibition of feeling Sir Tom would probably have said to himself, satirically, that there could be little doubt which the Contessa's ward and pupil would choose. But after that little scene he came out very much shaken, touched to the heart, thinking that perhaps life would have been more full and sweet had his apprehensions been true. She had been overcome by the united pressure of himself and the Contessa, and for the moment subdued, though the fire in her eye and swelling of her young bosom seemed to say that the victory was very incomplete. He would have liked the little one that died to have looked like that, and felt like that, had she lived to grow a woman like Bice. Great heaven, the little one that died! The words as they went through his mind sent a chill to Sir Tom's breast. Might it be that they would be said again—once more—and that far-back sin bring thus a punishment all the more bitter for being so long delayed. Human nature will never get to believe that God is not lying in wait somewhere to exact payment of every account.

"She understands that," said Jock suddenly. "She don't know the meaning of other things."

"What may be the other things?" said Sir Tom, feeling a half jealousy of anything that could be said to Bice's disadvantage. "I don't think she is wanting in understanding. Ah, I see. You don't know how any one could resist the influence of MTutor, Jock."

Through the darkness under the feeble lamp Jock shot a glance at his elder of that immeasurable contempt which youth feels for the absence of all penetration shown by its seniors, and their limited powers of observation. But he said nothing. Perhaps he could not trust himself to speak.

"Don't think I'm a scoffer, my boy," said Sir Tom. "MTutor's a very decent fellow. Let us go and look him up. He would be better, to my thinking, if he were not quite so fine, you know. But that's a trifle, and I'm an old fogey. You are not going back to Park Lane to-night."

"After what you heard her say? Do you think I've got no heart either? If I could have it instead of him!"

"But you can't, my boy," Sir Tom said with a pressure of Jock's arm. "And you must not make Lucy more wretched by hanging about. There's the mystery," he broke out suddenly. "You can't—none of us can. What might be nothing to you or me may be death to that little thing, but it is he that has to go through with it; life is a horrible sort of pleasure, Jock."

"Is it a pleasure?" the boy said under his breath. Life in him at that moment was one big heavy throbbing through all his being, full of mysterious powers unknown, of which Death was the least—yet, coming as he did a great shadow upon the feeblest, a terrible and awe-striking power beyond the strength of man to understand.

After this night, so full of emotion, there came certain days which passed without sign or mark in the dim great house looking out upon all the lively sights and sounds of the great park. The sun rose and reddened the windows, the noon blazed, the gray twilight touched everything into colour. In the chamber which was the centre of all interest no one knew or cared how the hours went, and whether it was morning or noon or night. Instead of these common ways of reckoning, they counted by the hours when the doctor came, when the child must have his medicine, when it was time to refresh the little cot with cool clean linen, or sponge the little hot hands. The other attendants took their turns and rested, but Lucy was capable of no rest. She dozed sometimes with her eyes half opened, hearing every movement and little cry. Perhaps as the time went on and the watch continued her faculties were a little blunted by this, so that she was scarcely full awake at any time, since she never slept. She moved mechanically about, and was conscious of nothing but a dazed and confused misery, without anticipation or recollection. Something there was in her mind besides, which perhaps made it worse; she could not tell. Could anything make it worse? The heart, like any other vessel, can hold but what it is capable of, and no more.

It is not easy to estimate what is the greatest sorrow of human life. It is that which has us in its grip, whatever it may be. Bereavement is terrible until there comes to you a pang more bitter from living than from dying: and one grief is supreme until another tops it, and the sea comes on and on in mountain waves. But perhaps of all the endurances of nature there is none which the general consent would agree upon as the greatest, like that of a mother watching death approach, with noiseless, awful step, to the bed of her only child. If humanity can approach more near the infinite in capacity of suffering, it is hard to know how. We must all bow down before this extremity of anguish, humbly begging the pardon of that sufferer, that in our lesser griefs, we dare to bemoan ourselves in her presence. And whether it is the dear companion—man or woman grown—or the infant out of her clasping arms, would seem to matter very little. According as it happens, so is the blow the most terrible. To Lucy, enveloped by that woe, there could have been no change that would not have lightened something (or so she felt) of her intolerable burden. Could he have breathed his fever and pain into words, could he have told what ailed him, could he have said to her only one little phrase of love, to be laid up in her heart! But the pitiful looks of those baby eyes, now bright with fever, now dull as dead violets, the little inarticulate murmurings, the appeals that could not be comprehended, added such a misery as was almost too much for flesh and blood to bear. This terrible ordeal was what Lucy had to go through. The child, though he had, as the maids said, no constitution, and though he had been enfeebled by illness for half his little lifetime, fought on hour after hour and day after day. Sometimes there was a look in his little face as of a conscious intelligence fighting a brave battle for life. His young mother beside him rose and fell with his breath, lived only in him, knew nothing but the vicissitudes of the sick room, taking her momentary broken rest when he slept, only to start up when, with a louder breath, a little cry, the struggle was resumed. The nurses could not, it would be unreasonable to expect it, be as entirely absorbed in their charge as was his mother. They got to talk at last, not minding her presence, quite freely in half whispers about other "cases," of patients and circumstances they had known. Stories of children who had died, and of some who had been miraculously raised from the brink of the grave, and of families swept away and houses desolated, seemed to get into the air of the room and float about Lucy, catching her confused ear, which was always on the watch for other sounds. Three or four times a day Sir Tom came to the door for news, but was not admitted, as the doctor's orders were stringent. There was no one admitted except the doctor; no cheer or comfort from without came into the sick room. Sir Tom did his best to speak a cheerful word, and would fain have persuaded Lucy to come out into the corridor, or to breathe the fresh air from a balcony. But Lucy, had she been capable of leaving the child, had a dim recollection in her mind that there was something, she could not tell what, interposing between her and her husband, and turned away from him with a sinking at her heart. She remembered vaguely that she had something else—some other possessions to comfort him—not this child alone as she had. He had something that he could perhaps love as well—but she had nothing; and she turned away from him with an instinctive sense of the difference, feeling it to be a wrong to her boy. But for this they might have comforted each other, and consulted each other over the fever and its symptoms. And she might have stolen a few moments from her child's bed and thrown herself on her husband's bosom and been consoled. But after all what did it matter? Could anything have made it more easy to bear? When sorrow and pain occupy the whole being, what room is there for consolation, what importance in the lessening by an infinitesimal shred of sorrow!

This had gone on for—Lucy could not tell how many days (though not in reality for very many), when there came one afternoon in which everything seemed to draw towards the close. It is the time when the heart fails most easily and the tide of being runs most low. The light was beginning to wane in those dim rooms, though a great golden sunset was being enacted in purple and flame on the other side of the house. The child's eyes were dull and glazed; they seemed to turn inward with that awful blank which is like the soul's withdrawal; its little powers seemed all exhausted. The little moan, the struggle, had fallen into quiet. The little lips were parched and dry. Those pathetic looks that seemed to plead for help and understanding came no more. The baby was too much worn out for such painful indications of life. The women had drawn aside, all their talk hushed, only a faint whisper now and then of directions from the most experienced of the two to the subordinates aiding the solemn watch. Lucy sat by the side of the little bed on the floor, sometimes raising herself on her knees to see better. She had fallen into the chill and apathy of despair.

At this time a door opened, not loudly or with any breach of the decorum of such a crisis, but with a distinct soft sound, which denoted some one not bound by the habits of a sick room. A step equally distinct, though soft, not the noiseless step of a watcher, came in through the outer room and to the bed. The women, who were standing a little apart, gave a low, involuntary cry. It looked like health and youthful vigour embodied which came sweeping into the dim room to the bedside of the dying child. It was Bice, who had asked no leave, who fell on her knees beside Lucy and stooped down her beautiful head, and kissed the hand which lay on the baby's coverlet. "Oh, pardon me," she said, "I could not keep away any longer. They kept me by force, or I would have come long, long since. I have come to stay, that you may have some rest, for I can nurse him—oh, with all my heart!"

She had said all this hurriedly in a breath before she looked at the child. Now she turned her head to the little bed. Her countenance underwent a sudden change. The colour forsook her cheeks, her lips dropped apart. She turned round to the nurse with a low cry, with a terrified question in her eyes.

"You see," said Lucy, speaking with a gasp as if in answer to some previous argument, "she thinks so, too—" Then there was a terrible pause. There seemed to come another "change," as the women said, over the little face, out of which life ebbed at every breath. Lucy started to her feet; she seized Bice's arm and raised her, which would have been impossible in a less terrible crisis. "Go," she said; "Go, Bice, to your father, and tell him to come, for my boy is dying Go—go!"


CHAPTER LI

THE LAST CRISIS

"Go to your father." Bice did not know what Lucy meant. The words bewildered her beyond description, but she did not hesitate what to do. She went downstairs to Sir Tom, who sat with his door opened and his heart sinking in his bosom waiting to hear. There was no need for any words. He followed her at once, almost as softly and as noiselessly as she had come. And when they entered the dim room, where by this time there was scarcely light enough for unaccustomed eyes to see, he went up to Lucy and put his arms round her as she stood leaning on the little bed. "My love," he said, "my love; we must be all in all to each other now." His voice was choked and broken, but it did not reach Lucy's heart. She put him away from her with an almost imperceptible movement. "You have others," she said hoarsely; "I have nothing, nothing but him." Just then the child stirred faintly in his bed, and first extending her arms to put them all away from her, Lucy bent over him and lifted him to her bosom. The nurse made a step forward to interfere, but then stepped back again wringing her hands. The mother had risen into a sort of sublimity, irresponsible in her great woe—if she had killed him to forestall her agony a little, as is the instinct of desperation, they could not have interfered. She sat down, and gathered the child close, close in her embrace, his head upon her breast, holding him as if to communicate life to him with the contact of hers. Her breath, her arms, her whole being enveloped the little dying creature with a fulness of passionate existence expanded to its highest. It was like taking back the half-extinguished germ into the very bosom and core of life. They stood round her with an awe of her, which would permit no intrusion either of word or act. Even the experienced nurse who believed that the little spark of life would be shaken out by this movement, only wrung her hands and said nothing. The rest were but as spectators, gathering round to see the tragedy accomplished and the woman's heart shattered before their eyes.

Which was unjust too—for the husband who stood behind was as great a sufferer. He was struck in everything a man can feel most, the instincts of paternal love awakened late, the pride a man has in his heir, all were crushed in him by a blow that seemed to wring his very heart out of his breast; but neither did any one think of him, nor did he think of himself. The mother that bare him!—that mysterious tie that goes beyond and before all, was acknowledged by them all without a word. It was hers to do as she pleased. The moments are long at such a time. They seemed to stand still on that strange scene. The light remained the same; the darkness seemed arrested, perhaps because it had come on too early on account of clouds overhead; perhaps because time was standing still to witness the easy parting of a soul not yet accustomed to this earth; the far more terrible rending of the woman's heart.

Presently a sensation of great calm fell, no one could tell how, into the room. The terror seemed to leave the hearts of the watchers. Was it the angel who had arrived and shed a soothing from his very presence though he had come to accomplish the end?

Another little change, almost imperceptible, Lucy beginning to rock her child softly, as if lulling him to sleep. No one moved, or even breathed, it seemed, for how long? some minutes, half a lifetime. Then another sound. Oh, God in heaven! had she gone distracted, the innocent creature, the young mother, in her anguish? She began to sing—a few low notes, a little lullaby, in a voice ineffable, indescribable, not like any mortal voice. One of the women burst out into a wail—it was the child's nurse—and tried to take him from the mother's arms. The other took her by the shoulders and turned her away. "What does it matter, a few minutes more or less; she'll come to herself soon enough, poor dear," said the attendant with a sob. Thus the group was diminished. Sir Tom stood with one hand on his wife's chair, his face covered with the other, and in his heart the bitterness of death; Bice had dropped down on her knees by the side of that pathetic group; and in the midst sat the mother bent over, almost enfolding the child, cradling him in her own life. Bice was herself not much more than a child; to her all things were possible—miracles, restorations from the dead. Her eyes were full of tears, but there was a smile upon her quivering mouth. It was at her Lucy looked, with eyes full of something like that "awful rose of dawn" of which the poet speaks. They were dilated to twice their natural size. She made a slight movement, opening to Bice the little face upon her bosom, bidding her look as at a breathless secret to be kept from all else. Was it a reflection or a faint glow of warmth upon the little worn cheek? The eyes were no longer open, showing the white, but closed, with the eyelashes shadowing against the cheek. There came into Lucy's eyes a sort of warning look to keep the secret, and the wonderful spectacle was, as it were, closed again, hidden with her arms and bending head. And the soft coo of the lullaby went on.

Presently the women stole back, awed and silenced, but full of a reviving thrill of curiosity. The elder one, who was from the hospital and prepared for everything, drew nearer, and regarded with a scientific, but not unsympathetic eye, the mother and the child. She withdrew a little the shawl in which the infant was wrapped, and put her too-experienced, instructed hands upon his little limbs, without taking any notice of Lucy, who remained passive through this examination. "He's beautiful and warm," said the woman, in a wondering tone. Then Bice rose to her feet with a quick sudden movement, and went to Sir Tom and drew his hand from his face. "He is not dying, he is sleeping," she said. "And I think, miss, you're right. He has taken a turn for the better," said the experienced woman from the hospital. "Don't move, my lady, don't move; we'll prop you with cushions—we'll pull him through still, please God," the nurse said, with a few genuine tears.

When the doctor came some time after, instead of watching the child's last moments, he had only to confirm their certainty of this favourable change, and give his sanction to it; and the cloud that had seemed to hang over it all day lifted from the house. The servants began to move about again and bustle. The lamps were lighted. The household resumed their occupations, and Williams himself in token of sympathy carried up Mr. Randolph's beef-tea. When Lucy, after a long interval, was liberated from her confined attitude and the child restored to his bed, the improvement was so evident that she allowed herself to be persuaded to lie down and rest. "Milady," said Bice, "I am not good for anything, but I love him. I will not interfere, but neither will I ever take away my eyes from him till you are again here." There was no use in this, but it was something to the young mother. She lay down and slept, for the first time since the illness began; slept not in broken, painful dozings, but a real sleep. She was not in a condition to think; but there was a vague feeling in her mind that here was some one, not as others were, to whom little Tom was something more than to the rest. Consciously she ought to have shrunk from Bice's presence; unconsciously it soothed her and warmed her heart.

Sir Tom went back to his room, shaken as with a long illness, but feeling that the world had begun again, and life was once more liveable. He sat down and thought over every incident, and thanked God with such tears as men too, like women, are often fain to indulge in, though they do it chiefly in private. Then, as the effect of this great crisis began to go off a little, and the common round to come back, there recurred to his mind Lucy's strange speech, "You have others—" What others was he supposed to have? She had drawn herself away from him. She had made no appeal to his sympathy. "You have—others. I have nothing but him." What did Lucy mean? And then he remembered how little intercourse there had been of late between them, how she had kept aloof from him. They might have been separated and living in different houses for all the union there had been between them. "You have others—" What did Lucy mean?

He got up, moved by the uneasiness of this question, and began to pace about the floor. He had no others; never had a man been more devoted to his own house. She had not been exacting, nor he uxorious. He had lived a man's life in the world, and had not neglected his duties for his wife; but he reminded himself, with a sort of indignant satisfaction, that he had found Lucy far more interesting than he expected, and that her fresh curiosity, her interest in everything, and the just enough of receptive intelligence, which is more agreeable than cleverness, had made her the most pleasant companion he had ever known. It was not an exercise of self-denial, of virtue on his part, as the Dowager and indeed many other of his friends had attempted to make out, but a real pleasure in her society. He had liked to talk to her, to tell her his own past history (selections from it), to like, yet laugh at her simple comments. He never despised anything she said, though he had laughed at some of it with a genial and placid amusement. And that little beggar! about whom Sir Tom could not even think to-day without a rush of water to his eyes—could any man have considered the little fellow more, or been more proud of him or fond? He could not live in the nursery, it was true, like Lucy, but short of that—"Others." What could she mean? There were no others. He was content to live and die, if but they might be spared to him, with her and the boy. A sort of chill doubt that somebody might have breathed into her ear that suggestion about Bice's parentage did indeed cross his mind; but ever since he had ascertained that this fear was a delusion, it had seemed to him the most ridiculous idea in the world. It had not seemed so before; it had appeared probable enough, nay, with many coincidences in its favour. And he had even been conscious of something like disappointment to find that it was not true. But now it seemed to him too absurd for credence; and what creature in the world, except himself, could have known the circumstances that made it possible? No one but Williams, and Williams was true.

It was not till next morning that the ordinary habits of the household could be said to be in any measure resumed. On that day Bice came down to breakfast with Sir Tom with a smiling brightness which cheered his solitary heart. She had gone back out of all her finery to the simple black frock, which she told him had been the easiest thing to carry. This was in answer to his question, "How had she come? Had the Contessa sent her?" Bice clapped her hands with pleasure, and recounted how she had run away.

"The news were always bad, more bad; and Milady all alone. At length the time came when I could bear it no longer. I love him, my little Tom; and Milady has always been kind, so kind, more kind than any one. Nobody has been kind to me like her, and also you, Sir Tom; and baby that was my darling," the girl said.

"God bless you, my dear," said Sir Tom; "but," he added, "you should not have done it. You should have remembered the infection."

Bice made a little face of merry disdain and laughed aloud. "Do I care for infection? Love is more strong than a fever. And then," she added, "I had a purpose too."

Sir Tom was delighted with her girlish confidences about her frock and her purpose. "Something very grave, I should imagine, from those looks."

"Oh, it is very grave," said Bice, her countenance changing. "You know I am fiancée. There has been a good deal said to me of Lord Montjoie; sometimes that he was not wise, what you call silly, not clever, not good to have to do with. That he is not clever one can see; but what then? The clever they do not always please. Others say that he is a great parti, and all that is desirable. Myself," she added with an air of judicial impartiality, "I like him well enough; even when he does not please me, he amuses. The clever they are not always amusing. I am willing to marry him since it is wished, otherwise I do not care much. For there is, you know, plenty of time, and to marry so soon—it is a disappointment, it is no longer exciting. So it is not easy to know distinctly what to do. That is what you call a dilemma," Bice said.

"It is a serious dilemma," said Sir Tom, much amused and flattered too. "You want me then to give you my advice—"

"No," said Bice, which made his countenance suddenly blank, "not advice. I have thought of a way. All say that it is almost wicked, at least very wrong to come here (in the Tauchnitz it would be miserable to be afraid, and so I think), and that the fever is more than everything. Now for me it is not so. If Lord Montjoie is of my opinion, and if he thinks I am right to come, then I shall know that, though he is not clever— Yes; that is my purpose. Do you think I shall be right?"

"I see," said Sir Tom, though he looked somewhat crestfallen. "You have come not so much for us, though you are kindly disposed towards us, but to put your future husband to the test. There is only this drawback, that he might be an excellent fellow and yet object to the step you have taken. Also that these sort of tests are very risky, and that it is scarcely worth while for this, to run the risk of a bad illness, perhaps of your life."

"That is unjust," said Bice with tears in her eyes. "I should have come to Milady had there been no Montjoie at all. It is first and above all for her sake. I will have a fever for her, oh willingly!" cried the girl.

Then she added after a little pause: "Why did she bid me 'go to your father and tell him—?' What does that mean, go to my father? I have never had any father."

"Did she say that?" Sir Tom cried. "When? and why?"

"It was when all seemed without hope. She was kneeling by the bed, and he, my little boy, my little darling! Ah," cried Bice, with a shiver. "To think it should have been so near! when God put that into her mind to save him. She said 'Go to your father, and tell him my boy is dying.' What did she mean? I came to you; but you are not my father."

He had risen up in great agitation and was walking about the room. When she said these words he came up to her and laid his hand for a moment on her head. "No," he said, with a sense of loss which was painful; "No, the more's the pity, Bice. God bless you, my dear."

His voice was tremulous, his hand shook a little. The girl took it in her pretty way and kissed it. "You have been as good to me as if it were so. But tell me what Milady means? for at that moment she would say nothing but what was at the bottom of her heart."

"I cannot tell you, Bice," said Sir Tom, almost with tears. "If I have made her unhappy, my Lucy, who is better than any of us, what do I deserve? what should be done to me? And she has been unhappy, she has lost her faith in me. I see it all now."

Bice sat and looked at him with her eyes full of thought. She was not a novice in life though she was so young. She had heard many a tale not adapted for youthful ears. That a child might have a father whose name she did not bear and who had never been disclosed to her was not incomprehensible, as it would have been to an English girl. She looked him severely in the face, like a young Daniel come to judgment. Had she been indeed his child to what a terrible ordeal would Sir Tom have been exposed under the light of those steady eyes. "Is it true that you have made her unhappy?" she said, as if she had the power of death in her hands.

"No!" he said, with a sudden outburst of feeling. "No! there are things in my life that I would not have raked up; but since I have known her, nothing; there is no offence to her in any record of my life—"

Bice looked at him still unfaltering. "You forget us—the Contessa and me. You brought us, though she did not know. We are not like her, but you brought us to her house. Nevertheless," said the young judge gravely, "that might be unthoughtful, but not a wrong to her. Is it perhaps a mistake?"

"A mistake or a slander, or—some evil tongue," he cried.

Bice rose up from the chair which had been her bench of justice, and walked to the door with a stately step, befitting her office, full of thought. Then she paused again for a moment and looked back and waved her hand. "I think it is a pity," she said with great gravity. She recognised the visionary fitness as he had done. They would have suited each other, when it was thus suggested to them, for father and daughter; and that it was not so, by some spite of fate, was a pity. She found Lucy dressed and refreshed sitting by the bed of the child, who had already begun to smile faintly. "Milady," said Bice, "will you go downstairs? There is a long time that you have not spoken to Sir Tom. Is he afraid of your fever? No more than me! But his heart is breaking for you. Go to him, Milady, and I will stay with the boy."

It was not for some time that Lucy could be persuaded to go. He had—others. What was she to him but a portion of his life? and the child was all of hers: a small portion of his life only a few years, while the others had a far older and stronger claim. There was no anger in her mind, all hushed in the exhaustion of great suffering past, but a great reluctance to enter upon the question once more. Lucy wished only to be left in quiet. She went slowly, reluctantly, downstairs. Unhappy? No. He had not made her unhappy. Nothing could make her unhappy now that her child was saved. It seemed to Lucy that it was she who had been ill and was getting better, and she longed to be left alone. Sir Tom was standing against the window with his head upon his hand. He did not hear her light step till she was close to him. Then he turned round, but not with the eagerness for her which Bice had represented. He took her hand gently and drew it within his arm.

"All is going well?" he said, "and you have had a little rest, my dear? Bice has told me—"

She withdrew a little the hand which lay on his arm. "He is much better," she said; "more than one would have thought possible."

"Thank God!" Sir Tom cried; and they were silent for a moment, united in thanksgiving, yet so divided, with a sickening gulf between them. Lucy felt her heart begin to stir and ache that had been so quiet. "And you," he said, "have had a little rest? Thank God for that too. Anything that had happened to him would have been bad enough; but to you, Lucy—"

"Oh, hush, hush," she cried, "that is over; let us not speak of anything happening to him."

"But all is not over," he said. "Something has happened—to us. What did you mean when you spoke to me of others? 'You have others.' I scarcely noticed it at that dreadful moment; but now— Who are those others, Lucy? Whom have I but him and you?"

She did not say anything, but withdrew her hand altogether from his arm, and looked at him. A look scarcely reproachful, wistful, sorrowful, saying, but not in words, in its steady gaze—You know.

He answered as if it had been speech.

"But I don't know. What is it, Lucy? Bice too has something she asked me to explain, and I cannot explain it. You said to her, 'Go to your father.' What is this? You must tell what you mean."

"Bice?" she said, faltering; "it was at a moment when I did not think what I was saying."

"No, when you spoke out that perilous stuff you have got in your heart. Oh, my Lucy, what is it, and who has put it there?"

"Tom," she said, trembling very much. "It is not Bice; she—that—is long ago—if her mother had been dead. But a man cannot have two lives. There cannot be two in the same place. It is not jealousy. I am not finding fault. It has been perhaps without intention; but it is not befitting—oh, not befitting. It cannot—oh, it is impossible! it must not be."

"What must not be? Of what in the name of heaven are you speaking?" he cried.

Once more she fixed on him that look, more reproachful this time, full of meaning and grieved surprise. She drew away a little from his side. "I did not want to speak," she said. "I was so thankful; I want to say nothing. You thought you had left that other life behind; perhaps you forgot altogether. They say that people do. And now it is here at your side, and on the other side my little boy and me. Ah! no, no, it is not befitting, it cannot be—"

"I understand dimly," he said; "they have told you Bice was my child. I wish it were so. I had a child, Lucy, it is true, who is dead in Florence long ago. The mother is dead too, long ago. It is so long past that, if you can believe it, I had—forgotten."

"Dead!" she said. And there came into her mild eyes a scared and frightened look. "And—the Contessa?"

"The Contessa!" he cried.

They were standing apart gazing at each other with something more like the heat of a passionate debate than had ever arisen between them, or indeed seemed possible to Lucy's tranquil nature, when the door was suddenly opened and the voice of Williams saying, "Sir Thomas is here, my lady," reduced them both in an instant to silence. Then there was a bustle and a movement, and of all wonderful sights to meet their eyes, the Contessa herself came with hesitation into the room. She had her handkerchief pressed against the lower part of her face, from above which her eyes looked out watchfully. She gave a little shriek at the sight of Lucy. "I thought," she said, "Sir Tom was alone. Lucy, my angel, my sweetest, do not come near me!" She recoiled to the door which Williams had just closed. "I will say what I have to say here. Dearest people, I love you, but you are charged with pestilence. My Lucy, how glad I am for your little boy—but every moment they tell me increases the danger. Where is Bice? Bice! I have come to bring her away."

"Contessa," said Sir Tom, "you have come at a fortunate moment. Tell Lady Randolph who Bice is. I think she has a right to know."

"Who Bice is? But what has that to do with it? She is fiancée, she belongs to more than herself. And there is the drawing-room in a week—imagine, only in a week!—and how can she go into the presence of the Queen full of infection? I acknowledge, I acknowledge," cried the Contessa, through her handkerchief, "you have been very kind—oh, more than kind. But why then now will you spoil all? It might make a revolution—it might convey to Majesty herself— Ah! it might spoil all the child's prospects. Who is she? Why should you reproach me with my little mystery now? She is all that is most natural; Guido's child, whom you remember well enough, Sir Tom, who married my poor little sister, my little girl who followed me, who would do as I did. You know all this, for I have told you. They are all dead, all dead—how can you make me talk of them? And Bice perhaps with the fever in her veins, ready to communicate it—to Majesty herself, to me, to every one!"

The Contessa sank down on a chair by the door. She drew forth her fan, which hung by her side, and fanned away from her this air of pestilence. "The child must come back at once," she said, with little cries and sobs—an accès de nerfs, if these simple people had known—through her handkerchief. "Let her come at once, and we may conceal it still. She shall have baths. She shall be fumigated. I will not see her or let her be seen. She shall have a succession of headaches. This is what I have said to Montjoie. Imagine me out in the air, that is so bad for the complexion, at this hour! But I think of nothing in comparison with the interests of Bice. Send for her. Lucy, sweet one, you would not spoil her prospects.

Send for her—before it is known." Then she laughed with a hysterical vehemence. "I see; some one has been telling her it was the poor little child whom you left with me, whom I watched over—yes, I was good to the little one. I am not a hard-hearted woman. Lucy: it was I who put this thought into your mind. I said—of English parentage. I meant you to believe so—that you might give something, when you were giving so much, to my poor Bice. What was wrong? I said you would be glad one day that you had helped her:—yes—and I allowed also my enemy the Dowager, to believe it."

"To believe that." Lucy stood out alone in the middle of the room, notwithstanding the shrinking back to the wall of the visitor, whose alarm was far more visible than any other emotion. "To believe that—that she was your child, and—"

Something stopped Lucy's mouth. She drew back, her pale face dyed with crimson, her whole form quivering with remorse and pain as of one who has given a cowardly and cruel blow.

The Contessa rose. She stood up against the wall. It did not seem to occur to her what kind of terrible accusation this was, but only that it was something strange, incomprehensible. She withdrew for a moment the handkerchief from her mouth. "My child? But I have never had a child!" she said.

"Lucy," cried Sir Tom in a terrible voice.

And then Lucy stood aghast between them, looking from one to another. The scales seemed to fall from her eyes. The perfectly innocent when they fall under the power of suspicion go farthest in that bitter way. They take no limit of possibility into their doubts and fears. They do not think of character or nature. Now, in a moment the scales fell from Lucy's eyes. Was her husband a man to treat her with such unimaginable insult? Was the Contessa, with all her triumphant designs, her mendacities, her mendicities, her thirst for pleasure, such a woman? Whoever said it, could this be true?

The Contessa perceived with a start that her hand had dropped from her mouth. She put back the handkerchief again with tremulous eagerness. "If I take it, all will go wrong—all will fall to pieces," she said pathetically. "Lucy, dear one, do not come near me, but send me Bice, if you love me," the Contessa cried. She smiled with her eyes, though her mouth was covered. She had not so much as understood, she, so experienced, so acquainted with the wicked world, so connaisseuse in evil tales—she had not even so much as divined what innocent Lucy meant to say.


CHAPTER LII

THE END

Bice was taken away in the cab, there being no reason why she should remain in a house where Lucy was no longer lonely or heartbroken—but not by her patroness, who was doubly her aunt, but did not love that old-fashioned title, and did love a mystery. The Contessa would not trust herself in the same vehicle with the girl who had come out of little Tom's nursery, and was no doubt charged with pestilence. She walked, marvel of marvels, with a thick veil over her face, and Sir Tom, in amused attendance, looking with some curiosity through the gauze at this wonder of a spring morning which she had not seen for years. Bice, for her part, was conveyed by the old woman who waited in the cab, the mother of one of the servants in the Mayfair house, to her humble home, where the girl was fumigated and disinfected to the Contessa's desire. She was presented a week after, the strictest secrecy being kept about these proceedings; and mercifully, as a matter of fact, did not convey infection either to the Contessa or to the still more distinguished ladies with whom she came in contact. What a day for Madame di Forno-Populo! There was nothing against her. The Duchess had spent an anxious week, inquiring everywhere. She had pledged herself in a weak hour; but though the men laughed, that was all. Not even in the clubs was there any story to be got hold of. The Duchess had a son-in-law who was clever in gossip. He said there was nothing, and the Lord Chamberlain made no objection. The Contessa di Forno-Populo had not indeed, she said loftily, ever desired to make her appearance before the Piedmontese; but she had the stamp upon her, though partially worn out, of the old Grand Ducal Court of Tuscany—which many people think more of—and these two stately Italian ladies made as great a sensation by their beauty and their stately air as had been made at any drawing-room in the present reign. The most august and discriminating of critics remarked them above all others. And a Lady, whose knowledge of family history is unrivalled, like her place in the world, condescended to remember that the Conte di Forno-Populo had married an English lady. Their dresses were specially described by Lady Anastasia in her favourite paper; and their portraits were almost recognisable in the Graphic, which gave a special (fancy) picture of the drawing-room in question. Triumph could not farther go.

It was not till after this event that Bice revealed the purpose which was one of her inducements for that visit to little Tom's sick bed. On the evening of that great day, just before going out in all her splendour to the Duchess's reception held on that occasion, she took her lover aside, whose pride in her magnificence and all the applause that had been lavished on her knew no bounds.

"Listen," she said, "I have something to tell you. Perhaps, when you hear it, all will be over. I have not allowed you to come near me nor touch me—"

"No, by Jove! It has been stand off, indeed! I don't know what you mean by it," cried Montjoie ruefully; "that wasn't what I bargained for, don't you know?"

"I am going to explain," said Bice. "You shall know, then, that when I had those headaches—you remember—and you could not see me, I had no headaches, mon ami. I was with Milady Randolph in Park Lane, in the middle of the fever, nursing the boy."

Montjoie gazed at her with round eyes. He recoiled a step, then rushing at his betrothed, notwithstanding her Court plumes and flounces, got Bice in his arms. "By Jove!" he cried, "and that was why! You thought I was frightened of the fever; that is the best joke I have heard for ages, don't you know? What a pluck you've got, Bee! And what a beauty you are, my pretty dear! I am going to pay myself all the arrears."

"Don't," said Bice, plaintively; the caresses were not much to her mind, but she endured them to a certain limit. "I wondered," she said with a faint sigh, "what you would say."

"It was awfully silly," said Montjoie. "I couldn't have believed you were so soft, Bee, with your training, don't you know? And how did you come over her to let you go? She was in a dead funk all the time. It was awfully silly; you might have caught it, or given it to me, or a hundred things, and lost all your fun; but it was awfully plucky," cried Montjoie, "by Jove! I knew you were a plucky one;" and he added, after a moment's reflection, in a softened tone, "a good little girl too."

It was thus that Bice's fate was sealed.

That afternoon Lucy received a note from Lady Randolph in the following words:—

"DEAREST LUCY—I am more glad than I can tell you to hear the good news of the dear boy. Probably he will be stronger now than he has ever been, having got over this so well.

"I want to tell you not to think any more of what I said that day. I hope it has not vexed you. I find that my informant was entirely mistaken, and acted upon a misconception all the time. I can't tell how sorry I am ever to have mentioned such a thing; but it seemed to be on the very best authority. I do hope it has not made any coolness between Tom and you.

"Don't take the trouble to answer this. There is nothing that carries infection like letters, and I inquire after the boy every day.—Your loving
M. RANDOLPH."

"It was not her fault," said Lucy, sobbing upon her husband's shoulder. "I should have known you better, Tom."

"I think so, my dear," he said quietly, "though I have been more foolish than a man of my age ought to be; but there is no harm in the Contessa, Lucy."

"No," Lucy said, yet with a grave face. "But Bice will be made a sacrifice: Bice, and—" she added with a guilty look, "I shall have thrown away that money, for it has not saved her."

"Here is a great deal of money," said Sir Tom, drawing a letter from his pocket, "which seems also in a fair way of being thrown away."

He took out the list which Lucy had given to her trustee, which Mr. Chervil had returned to her husband, and held it out before her. It was a very curious document, an experiment in the way of making poor people rich. The names were of people of whom Lucy knew very little personally; and yet it had not been done without thought. There was nobody there to whom such a gift might not mean deliverance from many cares. In the abstract it was not throwing anything away. Perhaps, had there been some public commission to reward with good incomes the struggling and honourable, these might not have been the chosen names; but yet it was all legitimate, honest, in the light of Lucy's exceptional position. The husband and wife stood and looked at it together in this moment of their reunion, when both had escaped from the deadliest perils that could threaten life—the loss of their child, the loss of their union. It was hard to tell which would have been the most mortal blow.

"He says I must prevent you; that you cannot have thought what you were doing; that it is madness, Lucy."

"I think I was nearly mad," said Lucy simply. "I thought to get rid of it whatever might happen to me—that was best."

"Let us look at it now in our full senses," said Sir Tom.

Lucy grasped his arm with both her hands. "Tom," she said in a hurried tone, "this is the only thing in which I ever set myself against you. It was the beginning of all our trouble; and I might have to do that again. What does it matter if perhaps we might do it more wisely now? All these people are poor, and there is the money to make them well off; that is what my father meant. He meant it to be scattered again, like seed given back to the reaper. He used to say so. Shall not we let it go as it is, and be done with it and avoid trouble any more?"

He stood holding her in his arms, looking over the paper. It was a great deal of money. To sacrifice a great deal of money does not affect a young woman who has never known any need of it in her life, but a man in middle age who knows all about it, that makes a great difference. Many thoughts passed through the mind of Sir Tom. It was a moment in which Lucy's heart was very soft. She was ready to do anything for the husband to whom, she thought, she had been unjust. And it was hard upon him to diminish his own importance and cut off at a stroke by such a sacrifice half the power and importance of the wealth which was his, though Lucy might be the source of it. Was he to consent to this loss, not even wisely, carefully arranged, but which might do little good to any one, and to him harm unquestionable? He stood silent for some time thinking, almost disposed to tear up the paper and throw it away. But then he began to reflect of other things more important than money; of unbroken peace and happiness; of Lucy's faithful, loyal spirit that would never be satisfied with less than the entire discharge of her trust, of the full accord, never so entirely comprehensive and understanding as now, that had been restored between them; and of the boy given back from the gates of hell, from the jaws of death. It was no small struggle. He had to conquer a hundred hesitations, the disapproval, the resistance of his own mind. It was with a hand that shook a little that he put it back. "That little beggar," he said, with his old laugh—though not his old laugh, for in this one there was a sound of tears—"will be a hundred thousand or so the poorer. Do you think he'd mind, if we were to ask him? Come, here is a kiss upon the bargain. The money shall go, and a good riddance, Lucy. There is now nothing between you and me."

Bice was married at the end of the season, in the most fashionable church, in the most correct way. Montjoie's plain cousins had asked—asked! without a sign of enmity!—to be bridesmaids, "as she had no sisters of her own, poor thing!" Montjoie declared that he was "ready to split" at their cheek in asking, and in calling Bice "poor thing," she who was the most fortunate girl in the world. The Contessa took the good the gods provided her, without grumbling at the fate which transferred to her the little fortune which had been given to Bice to keep her from a mercenary marriage. It was not a mercenary marriage, in the ordinary sense of the word. To Bice's mind it was simply fulfilling her natural career; and she had no dislike to Montjoie. She liked him well enough. He had answered well to her test. He was not clever, to be sure; but what then? She was well enough content, if not rapturous, when she walked out of the church Marchioness of Montjoie on her husband's arm. There was a large and fashionable assembly, it need not be said. Lucy, in a first place, looking very wistful, wondering if the girl was happy, and Sir Tom saying to himself it was very well that he had no more to do with it than as a friend. There were two other spectators who looked upon the ceremony with still more serious countenances, a man and a boy, restored to each other as dearest friends. They watched all the details of the service with unfailing interest, but when the beautiful bride came down the aisle on her husband's arm, they turned with one accord and looked at each other. They had been quite still until that point, making no remark. She passed them by, walking as if on air, as she always walked, though ballasted now for ever by that duller being at her side. She was not subdued under her falling veil, like so many brides, but saw everything, them among the rest, as she passed, and showed by a half smile her recognition of their presence. There was no mystic veil of sentiment about her; no consciousness of any mystery. She walked forth bravely, smiling, to meet life and the world. What was there in that beautiful, beaming creature to suggest a thought of future necessity, trouble, or the most distant occasion for help or succour? Perhaps it is a kind of revenge we take upon too great prosperity to say to ourselves: "There may come a time!"

These two spectators made their way out slowly among the crowd. They walked a long way towards their after destination without a word. Then Mr. Derwentwater spoke:

"If there should ever come a time when we can help her, or be of use to her, you and I—for the time must come when she will find out she has chosen evil instead of good—"

"Oh, humbug!" cried Jock roughly, with a sharpness in his tone which was its apology. "She has done what she always meant to do—and that is what she likes best."

"Nevertheless—" said MTutor with a sigh.


Margaret Oliphant – A Concise Bibliography

A canon of more than 120 works, including novels, travel books, histories, and volumes of literary criticism.

Novels

Margaret Maitland (1849)
Merkland (1850)
Caleb Field (1851)
John Drayton (1851)
Adam Graeme (1852)
The Melvilles (1852)
Katie Stewart (1852)
Harry Muir (1853)
Ailieford (1853)
The Quiet Heart (1854)
Magdalen Hepburn (1854)
Zaidee (1855)
Lilliesleaf (1855)
Christian Melville (1855)
The Athelings (1857)
The Days of My Life (1857)
Orphans (1858)
The Laird of Norlaw (1858)
Agnes Hopetoun's Schools and Holidays (1859)
Lucy Crofton (1860)
The House on the Moor (1861)
The Last of the Mortimers (1862)
Heart and Cross (1863)
Salem Chapel (1863)
The Rector (1863)
Doctor's Family (1863)
The Perpetual Curate (1864)

Miss Marjoribanks (1866)
Phoebe Junior (1876)
A Son of the Soil (1865)
Agnes (1866)
Madonna Mary (1867)
Brownlows (1868)
The Minister's Wife (1869)
The Three Brothers (1870)
John: A Love Story (1870)
Squire Arden (1871)
At his Gates (1872)
Ombra (1872
May (1873)
Innocent (1873)
The Story of Valentine and his Brother (1875)
A Rose in June (1874)
For Love and Life (1874)
Whiteladies (1875)
An Odd Couple (1875)
The Curate in Charge (1876)
Carità (1877)
Young Musgrave (1877)
Mrs. Arthur (1877)
The Primrose Path (1878)
Within the Precincts (1879)
The Fugitives (1879)
A Beleaguered City (1879)
The Greatest Heiress in England (1880)
He That Will Not When He May (1880)
In Trust (1881)
Harry Joscelyn (1881)
Lady Jane (1882)
A Little Pilgrim in the Unseen (1882)
The Lady Lindores (1883)
Sir Tom (1883)
Hester (1883)
It Was a Lover and his Lass (1883)
The Lady's Walk (1883)
The Wizard's Son (1884)
Madam (1884)
The Prodigals and their Inheritance (1885)
Oliver's Bride (1885)
A Country Gentleman and his Family (1886)
A House Divided Against Itself (1886)
Effie Ogilvie (1886)
A Poor Gentleman (1886)
The Son of his Father (1886)
Joyce (1888)

Cousin Mary (1888)
The Land of Darkness (1888)
Lady Car (1889)
Kirsteen (1890)
The Mystery of Mrs. Biencarrow (1890)
Sons and Daughters (1890)
The Railway Man and his Children (1891)
The Heir Presumptive and the Heir Apparent (1891)
The Marriage of Elinor (1891)
Janet (1891)
The Cuckoo in the Nest (1892)
Diana Trelawny (1892)
The Sorceress (1893)
A House in Bloomsbury (1894)
Sir Robert's Fortune (1894)
Who Was Lost and is Found (1894)
Lady William (1894)
Two Strangers (1895)
Old Mr. Tredgold (1895)
The Unjust Steward (1896)
The Ways of Life (1897)


Short stories
Neighbours on the Green (1889)
A Widow's Tale and Other Stories (1898)
That Little Cutty (1898)
The Open Door (1918)


Selected Articles

Mary Russel Mitford (Blackwood's Magazine, Vol. 75, 1854)
Evelin and Pepys (Blackwood's Magazine, Vol. 76, 1854)
The Holy Land (Blackwood's Magazine, Vol. 76, 1854)
Mr. Thackeray and his Novels (Blackwood's Magazine, Vol. 77, 1855)
Bulwer (Blackwood's Magazine, Vol. 77, 1855)
Charles Dickens (Blackwood's Magazine, Vol. 77, 1855)
Modern Novelists—Great and Small (Blackwood's Magazine, Vol. 77, 1855)
Modern Light Literature: Poetry (Blackwood's Magazine, Vol. 79, 1856)
Religion in Common Life (Blackwood's Magazine, Vol. 79, 1856)
Sydney Smith (Blackwood's Magazine, Vol. 79, 1856)
The Laws Concerning Women (Blackwood's Magazine, Vol. 79, 1856)
The Art of Caviling (Blackwood's Magazine, Vol. 80, 1856)
Béranger (Blackwood's Magazine, Vol. 83, 1858)
The Condition of Women (Blackwood's Magazine, Vol. 83, 1858)
The Missionary Explorer (Blackwood's Magazine, Vol. 83, 1858)
Religious Memoirs (Blackwood's Magazine, Vol. 83, 1858)

Social Science (Blackwood's Magazine, Vol. 88, 1860)
Scotland and her Accusers (Blackwood's Magazine, Vol. 90, 1861)
The Chronicles of Carlingford (Blackwood's Magazine 1862–1865)
Girolamo Savonarola (Blackwood's Magazine, Vol. 93, 1863)
The Life of Jesus (Blackwood's Magazine, Vol. 96, 1864)
Giacomo Leopardi (Blackwood's Magazine, Vol. 98, 1865)
The Great Unrepresented (Blackwood's Magazine, Vol. 100, 1866)
Mill on the Subjection of Women (The Edinburgh Review, Vol. 130, 1869)
The Opium-Eater (Blackwood's Magazine, Vol. 122, 1877)
Russian and Nihilism in the Novels of I. Tourgeniéf (Blackwood's Magazine, Vol. 127, 1880)
School and College (Blackwood's Magazine, Vol. 128, 1880)
The Grievances of Women (Fraser's Magazine, New Series, Vol. 21, 1880)
Mrs. Carlyle (The Contemporary Review, Vol. 43, May 1883)
The Ethics of Biography (The Contemporary Review, July 1883)
Victor Hugo (The Contemporary Review, Vol. 48, July/December 1885)
A Venetian Dynasty (The Contemporary Review, Vol. 50, August 1886)
Laurence Oliphant (Blackwood's Magazine, Vol. 145, 1889)
Tennyson (Blackwood's Magazine, Vol. 152, 1892)
Addison, the Humorist (Century Magazine, Vol. 48, 1894)
The Anti-Marriage League (Blackwood's Magazine, Vol. 159, 1896)


Biographies

Edward Irving (1862)
Francis of Assisi (1871)
Count de Montalembert (1872)
Dante (1877)
Cervantes (1880)
Life of Sheridan in the English Men of Letters series (1883)
John Tulloch (1888)
Laurence Oliphant (1892)


Historical & Critical Works

Historical Sketches of the Reign of George II (1869)
The Makers of Florence (1876)
A Literary History of England from 1760 to 1825 (1882)
The Makers of Venice (1887)
Royal Edinburgh (1890)
Jerusalem (1891)
The Makers of Modern Rome (1895)
William Blackwood and his Sons (1897)
The Sisters Brontë. In: Women Novelists of Queen Victoria's Reign (1897)